High Bright Buggy Wheels

LUELLA CREIGHTON

With a New Introduction by **CYNTHIA FLOOD**

OXFORD
UNIVERSITY PRESS

OXFORD
UNIVERSITY PRESS

Oxford University Press is a department of the University of Oxford.
It furthers the University's objective of excellence in research, scholarship,
and education by publishing worldwide. Oxford is a registered trade mark of
Oxford University Press in the UK and in certain other countries.

Published in Canada by
Oxford University Press
8 Sampson Mews, Suite 204,
Don Mills, Ontario M3C 0H5 Canada

www.oupcanada.com

Library and Archives Canada Cataloguing in Publication

Creighton, Luella, 1901–
High bright buggy wheels / Luella Creighton.

(The Wynford Project)
Originally published: McClelland and Stewart, 1951.
ISBN 978-0-19-900920-6

I. Title. II. Series: Wynford Project

PS8505.R45H5 2013   C813'.54   C2013-902032-2

Cover image: Brad Lackey / Lookout Mountain Photography

Printed and bound in the United States of America

1 2 3 4 — 16 15 14 13

Introduction to the Wynford Edition
Cynthia Flood

In autumn 1951, a horse-drawn buggy with costumed actors on board clip-clopped through downtown Toronto. Jack McClelland of McClelland & Stewart sat up front, shouting to pedestrians and drivers while waving copies of my mother's first novel, *High Bright Buggy Wheels*. He sold many books right there on the street. What promotion! The novel, well reviewed, soon went into a second printing. An American edition appeared, the CBC aired a radio drama based on the story, and the People's Choice book club picked it as the book of the month.

Luella Creighton was then living in England while her husband, historian Donald Creighton, researched his biography of Sir John A. Macdonald. Her publishers forwarded her many letters from readers; such letters kept coming her entire life. Some Mennonite readers wrote angrily; others painfully recognized their own lives. Most general readers, though, simply loved the tale of a young woman born into a mode of life too small to contain her. Admiring Tillie's spirit, her honesty, her desire for experience, and her response to beauty, readers championed the heroine through much distress to a happy ending.

Tillie Shantz's creator, Luella Sanders Browning Bruce, was born on August 25, 1901, in the then tiny village of Stouffville, Ontario. Her father, James Walter Bruce, was a wheelwright whose two previous wives had died, one taking twin newborn daughters with her. Days after Luella's birth, puerperal fever killed her mother, Sarah Luella Sanders Bruce, at age twenty-six. Shortly thereafter, James moved his business to Winnipeg, leaving his baby to the loving care of her grieving maternal grandparents and uncles. The little girl heard repeatedly from her family how at Sarah Luella's funeral, with the whole village in tears, the congregation sang "God moves in a mysterious way / His wonders to perform."

Luella was five when James Bruce came back and married yet again, this time to Mary Ann Stouffer, a woman past her childbearing years. Returning to Winnipeg with his family, James charged his new wife with raising Luella. Mary Ann, unlike the Methodist Bruces and Sanderses, stood at the harsh end of the Mennonite spectrum. She viewed her stepdaughter as spoiled rotten and risking hellfire, and aimed to make her behave. The child fought back. Of this period my mother spoke rarely and reluctantly. Even in her nineties, she couldn't say her stepmother's name without tears.

In 1915 the Bruces returned permanently to Stouffville. Teenage Luella, accustomed to greater freedom in the western city, found village life difficult. She felt peculiar, excluded. Troubles at home sharpened when she was denied permission to continue her education beyond the Stouffville Continuation School, with the aim of becoming a teacher. In response, she began running away. The last time she found a job at a shirt factory in Toronto. The family then gave in. Luella entered Normal School in 1919 and successfully completed her training, once overhearing a supervisor say, "That Miss Bruce! An exceptional teacher." After two years in a one-room school near Uxbridge, Luella achieved her great wish and enrolled at Victoria College.

She graduated in 1926, after four happy years in which she made lasting friendships and relished the university's intellectual and social life. Her scrapbooks bulge with dance cards; ribbons; photos of skating parties; and programs from concerts, lectures, plays—and debates. One proposed, "This house is of the opinion that they would rather be Agnes Macphail than Mary Pickford." Miss Luella Bruce spoke for the opposition, undoubtedly with wit and charm.

While at the University of Toronto, Luella also acquired a fiancé, Donald Grant Creighton. The younger son of W.B. Creighton, a Methodist minister and editor of the *Christian Guardian*, Donald was an aspiring historian. Graduating in 1925, he left for Balliol College; in June 1926 Luella sailed for England, and they married at Wesley's Chapel in London. Some joyous weeks of exploring Brittany followed. Then Donald had to return to Oxford, where a married undergraduate was an unrecognized category. The couple therefore found rooms for Luella in Paris, where she became fluent in French (partly through arguments with the landlady) and studied art history at the Sorbonne.

Later, back in Canada, came children (my brother Philip was born in 1929, and I followed in 1940), some years in real estate, and writing. In the early 1930s Luella published children's stories in *The New Outlook*. Turning to adult short fiction, she published "The Cornfield" (a prizewinner) in 1936 and "Miss Kidd" in 1937, and then the novels *High Bright Buggy Wheels* (1951) and *Turn East Turn West* (1954). Creative non-fiction came next with *Tecumseh* (1965) and *The Elegant Canadians* (1967), and also two children's books, *Miss Multipenny and Miss Crumb* (1966) and *The Hitching Post* (1969).

Yes, this young woman went far from Stouffville.

Like her creator, Tillie Shantz also travels. As the novel begins, she seeks a deeper union with her faith, yet plans to leave home temporarily to learn dressmaking in the nearby village of Kinsail (based on Stouffville). After being saved at the camp meeting, she steps out of the tent into cool darkness to recover her poise. An unknown young man, not of her religion, asks directions to his tethered horse, and on impulse Tillie takes a buggy ride with him. Soon she sees this as "a wild and unbridled act," but cannot forget its pleasure. So the struggle begins. Repeatedly Tillie leaves the closed Mennonite circle, and repeatedly she goes back, contrite and self-blaming. She learns, each time, more of the delights of reading, music, dancing, food, colour, shape, clothes, conversation, and decor, and every time finds more skills and capacities within herself.

The novel's incidents develop this basic pattern, the conflicts intensifying. My brother, Philip Creighton, speaking to Toronto's Heliconian Club in 2009, described how our mother designed the book:

[She] had real trouble with the order of *HBBW*. She wrote at an oval dining room table, in a turret on the second floor of our Victorian house. . . . She hung [a] clothesline across her turret and pinned up her novel. There was considerable pinning, unpinning, and re-pinning before she was satisfied. There was some interest in "clotheslining" as an organizational tool in management circles in the early 1960s, but in 1949–50 mother was simply ahead of the curve.

Clotheslining—such an image for a mid-twentieth-century woman writer!

The novel's title has always made readers curious. "Buggy Wheels," fine—but why "High," why "Bright"? When asked, Luella only smiled a small private smile. Perhaps in Stouffville, long ago, a lively pretty girl took a buggy ride with a young man whom she found handsome, and went a little further than intended. One kiss, another. . . .

Some figures in the novel—Keturah, Betsey, and Simon, sinner-hating sectarians all—take their life from Luella's youth. (The women meet a measure of the writer's sympathy, but Simon's extremism wins a brutal punishment.) Other characters feel more invented. Dressmaker Loretta's spontaneity, independence, and friendship model a new kind of single woman's life; she teaches colour and design, helping Tillie see "strong colour now showing through the grey" of her own existence. The music-loving pharmacist George, though amiable and appreciative, and clearly destined to be Tillie's love, has his own rigidities and limited vision. Only through the generosity of Tillie's father Levi—who embodies the best of the Mennonite ways, and who has always generated the most fan mail—can George accept that part of his wife will forever belong to the ways of her childhood. That blending is the story's business.

Moments after meeting George, Tillie calls his horse Maida a "lovely little thing" going at a "beautiful tilting pace." Learning that he will race her, Tillie's shocked. The devil's work! But she

can't sustain her reaction. She already trusts George, is instinctively ready to love him and to be cut off from family and faith to
be with him. At the novel's end, Tillie rejoices when another of
his horses wins the Dominion Day race.

Minor characters enrich the theme of connections. The
Shantzes' maid Bertha is first to realize that Tillie "has a fella
in Kinsail." Later, in spite of the girl's disowned status, Bertha
offers to come and help out, thus linking the old and new
homes. After Tillie's baby dies, she attends church (a last failing
attempt to re-enter), accompanied by Bertha. The Shantzes'
neighbour Jake, bringing news of the stillbirth to their farm,
tells Levi how to find the road to his grieving daughter's house.
Reconciled with her, in the novel's final scene Levi concedes
that George and Tillie's car (that alien machine) will make
their trips to the Shantzes' home quick and easy.

George's work embodies a new medical model based on
classroom study, not skills inherited through households. His
drugstore offers perfume, too, and supplies for the cottagers
whose unproductive lands Levi and his horses pass by. For
the Shantzes, such frivolity and waste typify the world. When
George visits Tillie's parents, he feels small, raw, before their
farm's weathered beauty and the abundance of "the grossmut-
ter's garden." Yet he too is committed to the country. A city boy,
he's chosen Kinsail; he aims to prosper, and to help the village
prosper too. As for Tillie, she selects Mennonite colours for
their home, directs Bertha in cooking traditional foods, plants
fruit trees—*and* prepares ground for a croquet lawn. For fun.

Luella's close observations of southern Ontario—its trees,
crops, skies, landforms, roads, and flowers—reveal her own
and her heroine's love for that countryside, yet the writer
lived for decades in Toronto, quite disconnected from her
rural birthplace. Links with James Bruce's family had never
been more than few and thin. He died when Luella was at
university, her maternal grandparents and stepmother not
long after. Her "dashing uncles," as my brother terms them,
who had so indulged the little girl, still lived in Stouffville,

but contact was rare. (I didn't get to know any of our mother's relatives until I was in my thirties.) In 1963, however, in anticipation of my father's retirement from the University of Toronto, our parents bought a house in Brooklin, Ontario. There Luella achieved both the garden she'd always wanted and also a return to village life. She died at Brooklin in 1996, after seventeen years of widowhood.

The writer and her heroine share many qualities. Like Tillie, Luella loved gardens and reading and cooking, enjoyed entertaining and home decor, maintained high standards of personal behaviour, acted on impulse, lived with energy, and didn't suffer fools gladly. Tillie, however, lacks Luella's curiosity about people and her particular spontaneity; my mother's gift was to make special occasions out of a day's small events. Above all, she found stories everywhere—a cat on a windowsill, a remark overheard on the streetcar, a frowning neighbour. She never came home without a tale to tell, and with her the familiar drive to Muskoka flowered into an epic journey. For a child, she made a wonderful companion.

A crucial difference between the two women: the heroine has a mother, albeit chilly and disapproving, while the writer was motherless. To family and friends, Luella spoke openly of her wish that her own mother had lived. This awareness of absence, this longing, endured all her life. In 1968, after a visit to a childhood friend in Stouffville, she walked through the cemetery where Sarah Luella Sanders Bruce is buried. At her mother's grave, Luella cried so hard she fell to the ground.

Absent mother, cold mother, lost mother, dead mother: these figures recur in Luella Bruce Creighton's fiction, from early short stories to her two published novels, to later novels not completed (*Music in the Park* and *Prelude*) and her second children's book (*The Hitching Post*). These unmothered or badly-mothered women and girls never find a Levi Shantz. Tillie's father seems the ideal parent for whom the writer longed: warm, honest, generous, utterly reliable, fierce in conviction, yet deeply loving and forgiving.

*D*OWN THE EIGHTH concession of Benjamin, beyond
the Ransom Mills crossroad, there lay a lovely
wood. The trees were mostly hardwood, the under-
brush long pastured out by generations of cattle to leave
compact avenues with hard-packed black roadbeds. Overhead, heavy boughs of beech and maple threw stocky
buttresses in support of low arched ceilings.

In the last week of September of the year nineteen hundred and eight, the air of these broad aisles was tremulous
thick gold from leaves fallen and still to fall. Dryness
showed in the rock-ribbed browning beech leaves; the
birches were thin yellow, and the maples were flames of pure
gold and red. A few very tall, very old jack pines stood at
the entrance to the wood, contemptuous of this concession
to the seasons, and flaunted their ragged heads a hundred
feet above the pointed hub of a large marquee pitched
in a clearing towards the southern boundary of the bush.

All summer long, people from the neighbouring village
of Kinsail had come to picnic there, but for this week the

wood became the possession of the brethren of the Mennonite faith, to use as the site of their camp-meeting. For seven days now the woods had been full of the sounds of worship and exhortation rising in the morning, and in the afternoon, and in the evening, from the big round grey-walled Gospel tent. Preachers, local preachers, and elders of the faith had brought their families and pitched their tents in a cluster about the meeting place. A bishop or two had come from a distant city to spend a few days in Christian fellowship with the brethren from Ransom Mills, and Lemonville, and the rich rolling farming country within a radius of thirty miles of Kinsail.

A score of families had been on the grounds all week, acting as hosts to visitors and picking up the threads of acquaintance and friendship. The thin-faced young woman with the bundle of sleeping baby in her rocking arms was one of the youngsters, last year. Two of the old men who had testified, last camp meeting, to the fulness of the Lord's mercy for over four score years had gone to their reward. To see Him, face to face. And Sister Brubacher, gone to be with Jesus, though so young yet, and with all the little children left. God moves in a mysterious way, His wonders to perform. The shell-like black bonnets of the women nodded in wonder, under the glowing trees. Under the trees, and in the tents, and rarely, giggling at their originality, walking in little groups out on the road, like girls again, the women talked and were pleased to hear of each others' fortunes, and how they managed in their kitchens. "A teaspoonful, jah, in the top of the jar, yet."

The afternoon meeting of the last day being over, the men and children of the gathering were set free to stroll about among the tables and tents. Outside the circle of the campers' tents the horses of the visitors were tethered, and their whickering punctuated the gentle bustle of camp life. The young men gathered at the gate to the pasture field as at a kind of club. They stood about in sombre groups; well brushed, brown-knuckled young farmers, casting an occasional glance at the horses, and waiting until it should be time to give them oats, and there would be something for them to do, of the familiar. These muscle-mounted young men hung their hands in unaccustomed emptiness, swaying forward as if to accept a burden they seemed to need, to make them physically complete. They were men of little conversation, and in their faces was a common evidence of purity of spirit and vacuity of mind. They were waiting for their supper.

The young girls set four immensely long narrow trestles with plates and cups for the evening meal. They ran back to the tents for bread and sugar, affecting not to notice the return of the young men. An occasional girl, like a sport among the lilies, carried such an unusual beauty of face or luxuriance of hair, that a hush would fall on the groups of young men as she passed.

Tillie, Elder Shantz's daughter, had this arresting beauty. She was seventeen, tall and lightly built, and carried herself like a young queen. Her hair was very thick and black, with a crisp wave in it which shone red at the crest, in the sun. Her white linen house-cap looked as small as a new baby's bonnet, in the luxuriance of her hair. Neither the silence nor the comments of the group of young men caused her to run or blush, as her companions did. She went swiftly and competently about her business, pausing now and again to bend her head to a wandering child or to pass a pleasant remark to one of the old sisters who moved slowly about the aisles, past being of help, and loath to realize it. She seemed a little impatient with the slower-moving plump girls who showed more zeal than efficiency in the arrangement of platters and gallon-capacity coffee pots on the tables.

Now perhaps it was all ready. She looked over the tables and nodded to a companion. "You can bring the potatoes, Sarah."

"Lambert!" A young, big-eared boy came bashfully out

3

from behind a tent. "Tell Papa he can ring the bell now!" The child ran headlong towards the high-walled tent.

A tall broad-shouldered man with a heavy long beard came singing out from it, holding the boy by one hand, a heavy clappered bell in the other. He walked through the trees with dignity and assurance.

"All ready, now, Tillie? You got lots of help, eh?"

Tillie smiled and glanced over to the cook stoves where a troop of young girls stood waiting with platters. Big motherly women in long full black skirts and double aprons, grey on top and billowing white underneath, stepped from tents to stoves and bent soberly over wash boilers of coffee and iron pots of boiled potatoes.

"Yes. We've got everything ready, I think, now."

Levi Shantz walked a little away from the tables and commandingly rang his bell. In a few minutes the tables were surrounded. The bishop from Kinsail, an old man now, bowed his head and commended the company to the Lord's keeping, and offered thanks for His gifts to the unworthy sons of men. The men and women sat down like the big family they might have been, so closely in feature and expression did they resemble each other. They were big-faced people with fresh high colour and wavy hair. A broad aquiline nose was a dominant characteristic, which gave an impression of strength to both men and women. The men grew old on a tough thin last, but a majority of the women became very stout. The bland sweetness of expression common to young and old contributed most to their resemblance. Since there is no desire for wealth in the brotherhood, no acquisitive line was traced on any face. The real need is to serve and love Him better Who is more lovely than any earthly being. Even after a lifetime of hard physical labour and the inevitable griefs and anxieties of even the most blessed of the Lord's children, there was evident little difference in the expressions of the old women from the smooth unquestioning faces of the young girls.

4

When a son or brother left the community of faith, as sometimes happened, and went the way of the transgressor, there was great grief. And when a little one died, before his parents could feel that his appointed time should have come, then there was deep sorrow. But with the Lord so close at hand, to comfort the sorrowing, and with the certain knowledge, beyond every doubt, that all that happens is done according to His will, and His divine plan, the grief was never unlit by hope. The child is there, safe in the keeping of the Lord, waiting, just as he was, to welcome his mother when she too will be carried to that place where her Father has built a mansion for her. It is only the waiting, perhaps, will be hard. But He knows best. His will be done. Blessed be the name of the Lord. And the erring boy, perhaps he too has his special work to do. Pray that his feet may be guided back to the fold of the ever-loving Saviour who died for him. For God so loved the world that He gave His only begotten Son, that whosoever believed in Him should not perish, but have everlasting life. His only begotten Son! Think of that!

The elder's wife, Betsey, a woman whose febrile temperament had saved her from any accumulation of flesh, watched Tillie and her helpers pass pressed meat and johnny cake and maple syrup up and down the long tables. Tillie was seventeen, nearly eighteen, now. It would not be long until she would marry. Perhaps it would be the right thing, too. Too many ideas she had, already. She wanted to play the piano, better, and learn dressmaking, away from home. Safer if she were settled. The camp-meeting was often a mating place, too. Mrs. Shantz reviewed in her mind the children of other elders, some only distantly known to her, who had sons about twenty, now. Brother Ebb's boy. The one who was so quiet, but such a good way with his orchard; and such a tidy careful boy. And Simon Goudie, who had watched her, last camp meeting, and at the meeting last night had worked with her. All her life she had known Simon. Just child-

5

ren, of course; but now, it might be different. Jake Reesor's boy: that would be near home.

When the long tables were cleared, and the lights cleaned for the evening meeting, she spoke of this matter to her husband.

"Another camp-meeting, Levi, and perhaps Tillie will not be with us, yet."

The elder smiled, brushing the crumbs from his thick grey-black beard, and wiping his mouth with a yard square of gleaming linen.

"Why should she not be with us, then, another camp-meeting? It is the women who are all alike, thinking of marrying, and grandchildren, and putting their minds on those things of this world instead, maybe, of the world our Heavenly Father has promised us. He has gone, you know, Mother, to prepare us a place. He has said that. It is wonderful, wonderful!"

He rose and walked up and down the long aisle the tables made, his hands clasped behind his broad black back, singing softly to himself, a glow of peace and satisfaction radiating from his big face. His wife watched him. It was always this way; always this way. She had all the cares of the house and the children, and Levi lived as a child of the Lord, whom the Lord would look after. It was true, though, praise His name. They were indeed the Lord's children, and He would look after them. But it would not hurt, either, to look about a little and see that Tillie's feet were put in the right path, maybe. She was not just so easy as the other girls of the faith, in every way. And she was not yet saved. Now it was the last night, too, for this camp-meeting. Maybe tonight, the Lord would speak to her, before the meeting was over. Mrs. Shantz went into the sleeping-tent, and dropped to her knees. Here, where there was prayer and singing and worship all about her it was easier for her to pray, like that, than it was at home, where there was always so much on her mind to look after. The elder paused, in his stride, to see her

6

there. He came over beside her, and knelt too, and began to pray, in a loud and fervent tone.

"Oh God, Thou who seest all, and knowest all, and who in the fulness of Thy grace hast seen fit to accept us, sinners, as Thy children, we commit to Thee now the care of our daughter. She is young, O Lord, and she has perhaps, in her youth and carelessness, not sought Thee as she should. There is still something of the world in her. Tonight, let Thy spirit move in her, if it be Thy will."

His voice dropped now to a whisper, and then silence fell upon the praying man and wife, as the communication between them and their God became so clear and pure that the words need not be spoken, between them. For a long time they knelt there, praying in this murmuring, sighing way, for Tillie, and for their young sons, and for themselves, that the way might be made clear to them, and the blessed blood of the Lamb be brought to wash away their sins.

When they rose, the aisles between the tents were empty, and the big swinging lamp had been lit in the preaching-tent. The chairs were nearly all filled. Tillie and her cousins sat near the front, and in the back seats sat the curious people from Kinsail. Most of these were young men, some of them with their girls, who had come to see an entertainment, rather than to be refreshed with the word of God. The new druggist, George Bingham, a slim young man in a dashing grey suit and scarlet tie, carrying a crisp new straw hat with a dazzling diagonal striped ribbon, sat on the aisle seat at the back. From where he sat he could see the left side of Tillie's beautiful face. He thought it was the loveliest thing that he had ever seen in his life.

The singing filled the tent, and spread out like light through the trees surrounding it.

> "Come, Thou Fount of every blessing!
> Tune my heart to sing Thy grace;
> Streams of mercy never ceasing
> Call for songs of loudest praise."

7

George watched her as the elder exhorted and pleaded and preached. One by one a girl, or a boy, a young woman, a young man, would rise and go softly down to the mourner's bench at the front. A tall thin young man with the ravaged face of an El Greco crept up the aisle where Tillie sat. He bent over her, a single question in his mouth. "Sister, are you saved? Sister, are you saved?"

George could see that Tillie's face whitened under the strain. Her hands were clasped into tight fists. Her head was bowed, and she slowly shook it, in reluctant denial.

The triumphant singing changed tone now. Joy and hope vanished, and they sang the old fateful heart-breaking hymn.

> "Almost persuaded, now to believe,
> Almost persuaded, Christ to receive . . .
> Hear now that bitter wail,
> Almost—but lost."

Over the mourners, the penitents at the front, the elders and the bishops worked, feeling for the moment when the spirit would take possession of the seeker. A tall fair girl with tears raining over her pale cheeks rose with a shriek:

"I'm saved! It's true! *Oh,* it's really true!"

With transfigured face she turned to the meeting and, flinging her arms wide, began to sing, in an abandonment of triumph:

> "Jesus is all the world to me,
> My life, my joy, my all."

The congregation entered into her joy with her, and a great swell of triumphal song filled the tent and the woods and the hearts of the people. They rejoiced and the music grew loud and exultant. Tillie stirred in her chair. The song fell, and little drifting singing praises came from the dark corners of the tent, while the crusade

8

for the souls of the sinners went on. The fair girl joined her family. They kissed her, and brought her into their arms. All the people sang again, softly, persuasively, now.

> "Softly and tenderly Jesus is calling,
> Calling for thee, calling for thee."

The thin preacher with the sad, intense face came again to where Tillie sat, lightly shuddering, eyes closed, waiting for the voice which would call her. The townspeople, tired of the show, began to leave; but George stayed on. He had to see what she would do, and nodded absently to his friends, as they left. One by one the buggies rattled off down the hill and out of the gates.

Another man found salvation, and turned to grope his way to a seat, crying and sobbing piteously, the joy not yet come. Tillie could feel the light pressure of the preacher's hand on her shoulder. His persuasive voice reached her. Moved by a sudden lightening of the burden on her heart, she arose, displaying a dignity and independence foreign to that gathering. She stood perfectly still for a moment, looking steadfastly towards the radiant expression on her father's face. Then she gently disengaged herself from the preacher's hand, and went down the aisle alone, towards the bearded elder. He held out his hands to her, his face suffused with joy, and they knelt together. When they rose it was as if the man had seen a light too blinding to be borne. He kissed her lovingly on the forehead. Tillie went swiftly out of the tent alone, stopping for a minute just outside the door, to recover herself. The triumphant booming of her father's voice, raised in exultant song, followed her out. One more sinner brought to repentance.

The thin young preacher watched her go; and as she passed his chair George Bingham picked up his flashy straw hat and was drawn after her. He paused outside the tent, to accustom himself to the darkness. In a moment he

9

could see the white patch of her neck, and her still hands, under the lantern hung from a tree. He knew himself to be unaccountably and unutterably moved. All the singing and the exhortation had meant nothing to him. It was vulgar and foreign and undignified. But the strange, sure beauty of this girl enchanted him.

Tillie turned, at the sound of a cracking branch, and saw him, a black silhouette in the tent doorway, striding towards her. She turned again to the darkness, and walked on. Indistinct groups of men and women in the background turned to hear as he called to her.

"I'm sorry to bother you," he said, "But I've got turned around, sitting in there. I must have gone in another door, or something. I can't seem to find the gate." Tillie stopped and waited for him to go. "I've got my horse tied inside the gate. If you could just put me on the track I'd be all right."

"The short cut to the road is through here. I'll show you."

She turned without any embarrassment, and led him through the line of sleeping-tents, up a little path to a stile over the rail fence. "There they are." She pointed to where the row of tethered horses stood, stamping an occasional impatient foot into the deep dust of the tethering places.

"Why, so they are! But I didn't come in this way?"

"No, you would have come round by the driveway. It's rather confusing."

They stood for a moment in silence there. Sounds from the big tent were only far-away whispers, now, and the light through the trees lay misty and remote. The shadows moving under the trees were cut off from them by the deep band of dark and quiet.

"Which is your horse?"

"The little one there at the end. See, you can see the little white blaze on her forehead. Come on down and look at her. She's a darb."

George vaulted the stile and waited for Tillie. He reached for her hand as she stepped down, and found it cold and strong and light, in his.

"Coming, Maida! Oh, you're a lovely girl, aren't you?"

The little mare raised her head and whinnied. "Bringing a friend, girl. Could you shake hands? Steady now, don't knock the lady down."

Maida pawed the air with her right front foot. She was a lovely little thing, light and narrow and nervous, with big blown nostrils and wild full eyes.

"All right darling, softly now, softly."

Tillie rubbed the mare up behind her ears, and patted the curving neck.

"She's a beautiful animal. How old is she?"

"Five, and practically no sense to show for it."

The mare turned full face about to Tillie, with that anxious inquiry which horses show at any delay they do not understand.

"Jump in and have a little ride, won't you? Come on!" George laid his hand hesitatingly on Tillie's arm, and let it rest there, feeling through it the strength and wholeness of her structure. "Just down to the corner and back, if you're in a hurry?"

He smiled at her, and she felt herself smiling back. She looked back up the little path. Beyond it the lights from the camp and the voices of the people were distantly evident to her. Tonight she had taken her place irrevocably, wholly and finally, as one of God's gloriously accepted children. She must go back at once, and be among them. She should never have left, like this, at all. What was she doing, wandering about away from her family? Down here a strange young man in a strange light suit, with a gay and insistent voice, asked her to go down the road with him. Such a road and such an action lay outside the confines of her life. Suddenly she heard her name. They were calling for her, now. Her name lifted into the air like a frail balloon, and drifted down again, lost. On

11

the brow of the little hill by the stile a man appeared. It was from him that another "Tillie" balloon was thrown into the air.

"They're calling me," she whispered tensely.

George put his hands on her shoulders and turned her towards the step of the buggy. "Get in."

Losing all sense, she climbed in over the wheel, and settled herself with dignity into the shadow of the top.

"Tillie!"

George untied the halter, Maida executed a few backwards dance steps, and they whirled down the road in a dusty clatter just as the moon forced her way out from the pine trees over the tent. George pulled lightly on the reins. The little mare leapt out like a fear-stricken deer.

"Watch her!"

For a few rods Maida kept up her hell-for-leather trot, head high and ears plastered back. Then suddenly she broke it and slid into a beautiful tilting pace. Her ears relaxed and her slight frame seemed hinged longitudinally through her back. Her flying feet described parallel circles in the air as her thin-skinned body rocked diagonally back and forth.

"Why, she's a pacer! Does she always go like that?"

"Just when she's happy. She must like you, or she wouldn't. Always knows who's behind her, don't you, Maidie?"

The mare cocked a nervous ear and increased her stride, until the road seemed to flow past, beneath her rocking body.

"Take it easy, pet, we're not in any hurry."

George loosed his hold on the reins, the wheels quieted and the blur of spokes broke into bright bars of red again. Maida took up a fretful walk. "Whoa, Maida."

He threw the lines over the dashboard, and smiled down at Tillie as the buggy stopped.

"We'll just stay here a minute."

"I must go back." Even to her own ears her voice

12

sounded far away, and unreal. The light from the moon behind them polished Maida's slim flanks, and the brass on her blinkers shone like little gold coins.

A grey fleeced cloud blew over the moon and the shape of the world was gone. In the soft ensuing darkness, remote and intimate within the small refuge of the buggy, there sprang into being an utterly new and delicate state of existence, infinite, absolute, and ephemeral as the dawn. Tillie's hands lay like pale cups on the dark cloth of her skirt, without motion. Above the high black collar the long pure oval of her face, for its serenity and sweetness, might have been Greek marble. George felt his own hands tremble, as if the fringes of destiny lightly brushed by. The two were silent there perhaps for only a minute, but it was unmeasured time. George was conscious of taking note of the scene, as if he might be expected to make a drawing of it later, and must remember the dark mass of the hill up there; and the sound of the creek running under the culvert, and the far-away lanterns of the campers springing up like a handful of giant fireflies released among the trees. When the moon came through again he found that she was smiling at him.

"I must go back, now."

George looked at her wonderingly, as if memorizing her face for future reference. "It's maybe the quiet, partly," he said. "Where I came from there was never any time that didn't have some jackass raising a disturbance next door. Listen, there's no sound at all."

"The creek, under the bridge."

"There's no sense to this. I don't even know your name. I never saw you until tonight. I don't suppose I'll ever see you again." He spoke softly, looking intently at Tillie; but more to himself than to her. "Maybe it's the moonlight. Maybe I'm touched. But this is the stuff you read about. You know it isn't true. Look at me, do I look crazy?"

Tillie looked at him, sharply, startled and moved. Exulta-

13

tion from prolonged emotion had supported her, until now, but she began swiftly to tire. Still, she must laugh a little, too. This strange young man, with the odd way of talking and the wild horse, was in these few minutes more real to her, a greater friend, in some curious way, than even Simon, whom she had known for years, and whose words had brought her to the front tonight. A happy sigh escaped her as she remembered that. Now she was really saved. At last! She smiled in radiant happiness. It was so easy, in the end.

But there was such a gaiety about the young man, and he smiled at her so kindly, and was so funny about his horse! And now he was talking soberly to her. She reached out her hand and touched his, as she would have touched the hand of a child in need, to comfort him.

"I don't think you do. I don't think you look crazy."

She let her hand lie on his for a moment. Something infinitely precious and perfect trembled between them. George closed his other hand over hers. A faintly sick feeling stirred in Tillie's being. She shut her eyes and lifted her shoulder like a woman who has suffered just the premonition of physical pain, and cannot ward it off. She gently replaced her hand on her lap. George picked up the reins. "I can turn around, here."

They drove without words to the open gate of the wood. Tillie jumped out almost before the wheels stopped.

"Good-bye," she said, in a clear, cool, untroubled tone, and was gone. Again from the brow of the little hill a tall thin figure tossed out the wind-lost name, "Tillie!"

14

2

IN THE early morning of the next day, when the tents were down, and the space under the trees all swept and empty, Elder Shantz and his wife climbed into the front seat of the democrat. Tillie and the two little boys filled the back, and the chunky black horses started off on the thirty-mile trip home.

George Bingham, in a fresh white shirt, with his broom in his hand, stood outside his shop, doing a brisk job of sweeping the sidewalk as the green-fringed vehicle passed. He waved a startled hand to Tillie, who turned shyly to smile at him. The elder and his wife did not see the interchange, but the little boys nudged each other and submerged themselves in knowing giggles. They looked back as long as they could see the store, speculating as to what kind of medicine it was, in those big red and blue bottles.

George followed the rig with his eyes until it crawled out of sight like some serious-minded square-backed beetle, up the Gravel Hill. In the bright morning sun the bearded elder and his thin, bonneted wife looked foreign and strange. They came through the village like people returning to a strange country. It was as if he had sat in a theatre, and watched a play. It all took place back there, on the stage, and had no connection with the real people out in the audience. And above all, although that dream-like sequence last night had seemed so real, there could of course never be any transaction between himself and these odd-looking people. It was unlikely, inappropriate and inevitably ridiculous. In the morning, Tillie's face was as beautiful as before. There was no mistake there. But her street bonnet looked stiff and unattractively quaint. There was a separation in that costume as real as the separation of a foreign language.

And yet, last night, he would have thought very differently. He had come home from the camping-grounds in an ecstasy of longing, moved beyond bearing by the girl. He closed his eyes, to see if he could find again that sure and clear sensation which had held him willing captive, last night, and kept him from sleep. The sudden booming of the mail boat in the river locks startled him out of his dream. He shook his head like a dog just out of the water, to scatter the dream from his eyes. There was a Mennonite girl, and last night there had certainly been something; but now the wheels of the democrat had taken her out of the town, and out of his life. There were things for him to do. This was not the way to do them. George gave his sidewalk a last fierce swish and fastened the door back, open for business.

The green-fringed democrat rattled along up the narrowing steep sand-hills to the north of Kinsail. By noon the elder's short black horses had passed through nearly fifteen miles of the sand belt and now turned west towards the broad level lands which the Mennonites had been cultivating for more than a hundred years. The farms here grew fat and prosperous. Fields of dusty golden stubble and black ploughed land, the tender green of the fall wheat and the strong deep green of the still uncut cabbages spread like patchwork over the plain. Apple orchards well tilled and rich with promise fulfilled and yet to be fulfilled stood in farmsteads where the barns were big and red, the houses stone or whitewashed roughcast, big and square and comfortable. It was easy to believe in the goodness of the Lord, as the elder drew in his horses for a breather at the top of a long swinging hill which would lead them down into this fruitful country.

"We could go into Brother Wideman's for our dinner, Betsey? The horses need their rest now." Levi turned to look at his little family, and smiled to see them so brown and healthy looking.

"Wellt Ihr jetzt essen, Kinder?" he asked, for the warm German words still came more easily than English into his mouth.

Mrs. Shantz broke a worried silence. "The horses are not so tired, yet. I think we could eat at Brother Goudie's. It is only a mile and a quarter from the Lemonville schoolhouse corner, over there."

"Jah? You would like to see Sister Goudie? Well, well, it is the women who decide these things."

Elder Shantz lifted the lines and the horses started down the long hill. As they turned into the maple-shaded lane he leaned over to his wife, whispering in her ear as he glanced furtively over his shoulder at the children. She flushed, stirred, and said nothing. The elder straightened his broad black back and drove on, smiling to himself. His good humour had broken into song by the time they reached the driving shed, and he jumped down from the carriage to greet his host like a gay young man, waving his arms and laughing.

The women greeted each other with a gentle dignity. The two Goudie daughters and Tillie set the long table out on the veranda within the angle formed by the summer kitchen and the main house. The little Shantz boys disappeared towards the barns with the little Goudie boys. When the meal was ready, Abraham Goudie came smiling in, his face red from washing at the pump and severe rubbing with a coarse towel. He held out his hands to them all and greeted them warmly, and with love.

The spirit of the camp-meeting seemed still upon the fourteen who stood at their chairs by the table waiting for grace to be said.

> *"Jesu segne diese Speise,*
> *Uns zur Kraft und Dir zum Preise."*

They raised their heads again, all but Levi Shantz, who in complete forgetfulness of the others went on for long minutes more, communing with his God in the fulness of gratitude for His great goodness to the sons of men. The little boys, longing for him to finish, stole peeks at his broad tanned face to see when at last he would bring forth his mighty "Amen" and they might dip into the steaming bowls and be filled. Sister Goudie sighed; Levi was over long in his petitions, and the potatoes grew cold. The hired girl shuffled, causing her chair to squeak harshly. The children of both families were reduced to silent helpless giggling, fat red cheeks blown out with unexploded mirth. But the big voice boomed on, unheeding earthly interruption: "And for these dear ones whose table Thou hast furnished, dear Lord, we ask Thy blessing. On these, and on their dear son whom Thou hast chosen as more particularly Thine own, to go out into Thy far fields and bring Thy little ones in. Bless him, O Lord, and make Thy name to be ever a light and a guide to his path. May he find and gather many precious souls to Christ."

Mrs. Shantz stirred self-consciously at the reference to Simon. She was annoyed that he should not be here, and that no one had said where he was. It was no secret that he had sought Tillie, both this camp-meeting and last; and now, maybe it was time that words could be said, and he was not even here.

"And for these little ones here, at this table, these tenderest of the lambs of Thy flock, we ask, O Lord, a special blessing. Take them and guide them in the path which is called straight."

He paused, and the small boys, sobered by this mention of themselves, hoped again. But it was a swelling in his throat that had caused Levi to falter. He began again in a low, pleading, earnest tone.

"And among us, O God, is one of Thy ewe lambs, only yesterday come to Thee. On her, O Lord, on her we ask Thy special blessing."

18

His lips moved for a while in silence, and then he cleared his throat with a roar and ended his prayer with a reverberating "Amen." His yard-square linen handkerchief flourished in surrender; he wiped tears from his eyes, sweat from his face, and sat down. Up and down the long table, "Amen, amen, Brother, amen," the grave voices responded.

At last the brown bowls moved out from the middle of the table and were emptied into white plates. Crusty cakes of sausage-meat, thick smooth slabs of beefsteak tomatoes, bowls of cabbage shredded with bacon in sour cream, tall loaves of home-made bread, circulated under the dappling shade of black walnut trees. The children spoke little during the meal, answering the kindly questions that came their way but offering no comments to the company in general. The Goudie girls and the hired girl carried off the empty bowls and platter to make room for the pies that waited, cooling, on the scrubbed pine table in the summer kitchen across the square of grass.

They came back carrying twelve-inch granite plates on which staunch squash pies lay buried under a two-inch smother of whipped cream. The girls came laughing along, straight and plump and tall, their little white bonnet-strings lifted back in the light breeze. Against the grey siding of the summer kitchen, the spangled grass in the foreground, the black tree-trunks beyond them on the right, they made a satisfying picture, solid and strong and sombre, accented lightly by the laughing faces.

At this moment Simon Goudie, still in the scanty blacks of the camp-meeting, crossed the winter kitchen and appeared at the door. His mother looked up and welcomed him with the gentle smile that gave her simple face its peculiar charm. She rose from her chair and bustled off across the grass.

"You're nearly too late," she said, picking a big white plate from the pile on the warming-oven. "But sit down there, there's hot meat yet, in the stove."

Simon held up his hand in imperious protest. "Don't get anything for me; I had dinner at Brother Brubacher's."

Mrs. Goudie's fat hand fell disconsolately to the folds of her black skirt.

"You've had dinner already?"

Simon nodded and turned abruptly back into the house. He had caught a glimpse of Tillie, and embarrassment sent him away from the company as awkwardly as if he had been a self-conscious spinster faced with a congregation of whistling young men. He ran up the back stairs to the boys' room, pursued by this new and turbulent emotion. Seated at the bountiful Brubacher table he had seen the Shantz democrat go by, and felt this swelling and rushing within him. His face he knew to be flushed and the beating of his heart had blurred Brother Brubacher's droning voice. An urgent impulse to run after the rig would have pulled him from the table, and set him on the road; but there was still the pie to be had, and more coffee, and then the reading of the Word. And in any case, what could he say to the Brubachers? That Tillie Shantz might be in the rig, that he must find her, must not lose her, must leap like a wild thing and go at once to her? He could not. The prayer and the reading stilled the wild impetus, and he became calm within and without.

But when they rose from their knees and the faint sound of wheels came again to his ears, his heart leapt anew. Scarcely waiting to say "God be with you" he backed out and drove swiftly off home, urging his rangy black driver to a shambling run in his impatience. As he turned into the lane, and saw the Shantz carriage standing there, his throat contracted and he jerked the horse to a resentful walk. Shame overwhelmed him. It seemed to him that everyone in the house would know of his wild ride. The children would snicker meaningfully, when he came in. He was humiliated by his lack of self-control. Why should he tear himself roughly from a brother in the Lord to run after a woman who only yesterday, when in the ecstasy of his emotion he had cried out to her, had not turned her head, even, but had walked out into the night? But he had run. He had been blown like a crisp leaf by the winds of his desire to this place, whirled like a leaf against the insentient wall. And now here, he seemed dry and numb, and without volition. He knelt a few minutes by his low wooden bedstead and then, drawn irresistibly, descended to the company.

Tillie rested a calm gaze upon him, for an unsmiling moment. Levi broke the odd constraint, calling out heartily through a mouthful of the pie.

"Here's the preacher! Here's the preacher! Come and be with us!" He jumped from his chair, waving a big hand towards the table, signalling him to approach. Simon reddened and came towards the group. He pulled out a chair and sat down, his long legs diagonally out from the table, nodding to Levi, and faintly smiling. The little boys moved slowly off. The women rose from the table, and for a few minutes Simon and the other men sat there, waiting for Levi to finish. Simon was acutely conscious of Tillie behind him, carrying off dishes. She bent over his shoulder to pick up a heavy white coffee pot and a loaf of bread. His muscles stiffened at her closeness. He whirled about and caught her arm, forgetting the faces of his family about him. "Why did you not answer me, when I called you?"

She was bent awkwardly towards him, her body arrested in movement, and both welcoming and resenting the restraint.

"Come out with me now, I want to talk to you."

The serenity of Tillie's face did not alter, but a trace of sternness appeared about her mouth. She shook her head and pulled her hand away, straightening herself again, and carrying her burden free. But for a faint slow flush creeping up her neck and face there might have been no encounter. There was nothing in her demeanour to show the tumult within.

21

Tillie went about her business of clearing the table, carrying before her piles of plates across the square of grass, with Simon following behind. It did not occur to him to offer to relieve her of her load. He shambled behind her like a dumb stupid creature obeying an instinct that was beyond his understanding. The little boys in the elderberry thicket behind the smoke-house peered out and laughed to see the great elder brother at such a disadvantage. Simon found himself in the clatter of the summer kitchen, Tillie gone again on her zealous mission while he was left to talk, evidently, with the hired girl. A stir of pride told him that he was acting in a bewildered and undignified way, but it seemed impossible for him to extricate himself. His mother, coming in to wrap a jar of pickles as a present for the visitors, found him leaning limply against the long table, without purpose. She opened her mouth to speak, glanced at Tillie who came in again, and went out in silence. Rage joined with pride in Simon's heart. What did the girl think she was doing, to act in this way? She was making a fool of him. He plunged out of the door before her.

"Come back the lane, I want to talk to you." His face was stern this time, his authority not to be questioned. Kezzie, the hired girl, snorted into the dishpan. Mrs. Goudie paused with her parcel in her arm, to look after them, and Tillie walked silently with Simon. She lifted her chin into the air, but walked in obedience beside the man. The little boys came rollicking out of the bushes, and made as if to follow them. Simon turned upon them with such a terrible ferocity of expression that they retreated at once, sobered and abashed.

Tillie and Simon walked on, without words, through the driveway gate, past the weigh scales, beyond the implement shed and the long low cement piggery. The silence of the barnyard exploded into fearful squeals and terrifying roars as the sleeping Berkshires within heard their footsteps. At one of the small ventilators, high up on the wall of the whitewashed building a black snarling face

22

appeared, white-snouted and squealing like the damned. The little eyes looked so intent and curious and angry, up so high, that Tillie laughed, nervously.

"What a pig! He must be six feet long, to reach so high!"

Simon nodded. "The boar," he said. "He's not safe." The angry tumult quieted as they passed on, ordained to silence.

The lane stretched straight and clean, edged most neatly by stiffly-growing spruce trees, running with scarcely a curve a quarter of a mile back to the tracks. Then a white gate appeared, freshly painted, and shutting off the main farm from the embankment. Across the track another white gate opened to the farm which would be Simon's when he married, and set up for himself.

"When I get to the gate, then I will speak to her."

In the mysterious holy communion of flesh and spirit engendered in the camp-meeting, Simon's words of guidance, persuasion, and love of God for man and man for men had flowed with the ease of heavenly inspiration. There he was the instrument, the vessel, helpless in himself, but powerful in the hands of Almighty God. But, with the paling of the lanterns of the wonderful meeting where so many had been gathered to God, his eloquence had passed. Walking now "back the lane," with Tillie, he was just a tall thin country boy without words.

Daylight robbed him, too, of the mystery which the lamplight and the shadows of the Gospel tent had painted on his face. In the long shafted sunlight of the September afternoon he looked years younger, his brown face shown in its oddly varied construction. The upper part was a delicately boned, flat-planed structure, but the jaw seemed built of heavier timber, underslung and with a thick, long-lipped mouth. His hands, yesterday long and nervous pointers to salvation, today hung square and brutish from shirt-sleeves shrunk too short for his arms. Only in his deeply set red-brown eyes could his peculiar fire still be seen to burn. The haunting quality of his face, which had been so provocative the night before, had planed down flatly to a mere stolidity of conviction, ecstasy giving place to earnestness. The flaming torch had turned back into Simon Goudie, whom Tillie had known all her life.

She had not known how to respond to him in his mystical mood, when the Glory had shone down upon him; but towards the silent, shy man walking beside her she felt a quiet and familiar tenderness. Had she dared, she would have thrust out a hand to touch him. But when she glanced up from the warm crumbly richness of the earth, brown and purple from a hundred years of leafy accumulation, to glance at him, the austere set of his face forbade even the thought. Simon would have been shocked and displeased, she felt. Unwomanly, forward, lacking in seemliness, such an act would be, in his eyes. She walked along, and waited to hear what he had to say.

Somewhere along this lane, then, perhaps at the gate, or beyond it, lay the climax of those swift, unresolved dreams which so quickly ended in healthy sleep. They came when she settled to rest against her coarse linen pillows, thinking, "Now what shall I imagine, to make me happy, and not wakeful?" The dream she made for herself, before she slept, was her marriage dream, very often, and the man was Simon Goudie. Now here it was, perhaps, really.

She considered the circumstances of her being here, walking down this lane, with Simon. Men like Simon, in the Mennonite faith, do not idly take girls walking down lanes, in the broad daylight of a working day, without an end in view. The open sending back of the little boys, the tacit conspiracy of the elders to let them go without the jocose remark so inevitably associated with the early manifestations of love, in the faith—all these things were significant. Tillie knew that her mother, sitting back there on the narrow veranda, with sister Goudie, knitting her endless black stocking, expected that when she came back along the lane again she would be promised wife to Simon Goudie. Her heart leapt, and she waited, but still Simon loped along, and did not speak.

A sudden breeze tossed the crisp tassels of the stooked corn in a tissue paper rustle. For a fugitive moment the sky was dark. Simon looked up at the cloud, and his jaw set in a harsh line. A flicker of alarm touched Tillie. Perhaps she had imagined it all, the seeking, the attention, the wordless messages. Perhaps he had thought to ask her today, but something had happened, she could not know what, and he had decided against her. Perhaps, and her heart was a stone, he had not ever thought of her at all, as she had been dreaming of him.

Yet last night, surely, he had called to her? And again and again? But something had prevented her from going to him; that curious strain of independence which manifested itself in her at moments when she could least expect it, and when it seemed to carry her in a direction opposed even to her will. There was about Tillie a fierce untouchable pride, in those moments, a perfect sense of her own unassailability. Her mother deplored this defect in her character, and prayed that she might be rid of it. A wicked pride, no doubt, a gift of the Evil One, himself, but eradicable by prayer. Last night, in the grip of this pride, she had allowed herself to be carried off for a wild ride with a worldly young man, while Simon had stood on the top of the hill and called to her, without answer.

The spanking drive behind the swift little mare seemed now like a dream ride. The edges of the memory of it were blurred, and yet the central feeling stayed clear and intense. But she did not allow herself to think of it. It was as if she had stored that incident away in the back recesses of her mind, to be searched for, and brought out, if required. It was a wild and unbridled act, of course. But a thing of no consequence, certainly, to any one but herself, at any calculation. She drew her mouth into a firm line. Perhaps Simon had heard of it. Her eyes widened at this thought. Simon would find it hard to believe that she was capable of such loose, unseemly behaviour. That she could come straight from being accepted among the Lord's anointed, and leap into a strange young man's rig, then go hurtling down the road would be, in his mind, out of the question. But in any case it was her own responsibility, and had nothing to do with Simon.

Simon, of course, would be as incapable of thinking evil of her as she would be of performing an immoral act. The distinction was a finer one than that. A delicacy of behaviour, a softness of voice, a gentle submissiveness is required of women. Her act of last night erred grievously on more than one of these counts. An utter acceptance of life as it . is found between the sweet but narrow boundaries of the faith is the first requirement of its members, and the ultimate necessity. It is not enough to avoid evil. Simon's wife must put off the very appearance of evil. Wife? She would not be Simon's wife. Simon must have decided not to ask her. She drew her head high; and Simon, glancing at her, saw cold indifference on her beautiful face.

The train from the north whistled for the level crossing as Tillie and Simon silently reached the gate. It slowed up to take the little grade and blocked their way. Listless heads turned to watch the silent pair, standing together and withdrawn from each other, by the white gate. Across these narrow tracks, separated from them only by the noisy little train now grinding up the hill, lay the pleasant farmlands which were to be Simon's, when he married; unless, of course, the Lord should call him to some other, riper field. The passenger coach had passed now, and the baggage car nosed the engine round the bend and out of sight, the caboose cleared the track, and they could see the square, solid house built of mellowed grey stock bricks, and the red barn buttressed with silo and implement sheds, beyond. Between the house and barns a small orchard stood, in need, it seemed to Tillie, of severe pruning. The garden presented to her eyes rich possibilities which the present tenant failed to see.

Were she to marry Simon, these appurtenances would be hers. Within these substantial physical boundaries Tillie could find a satisfying picture of her life. All the elements of abundant living of which she was yet aware were present. It would be a busy, happy, God-fearing life, with red-faced healthy children and rows of shining boots lining the back stairway, on Saturday night. She could see herself the efficient directing force behind the multitudinous activities of the farmhouse, and the possessor of a garden, there in the little field in front of the house, which should never have been left unfenced.

But this lot was not to be hers. She would not marry. The alternative, within her experience, was dependent spinsterhood. She thought in dreary panic of Aunt Keturah, stretched and gaunt and stern in her spinsterhood, and Aunt Elmina, small and frightened, living in antiseptic grey with her strong hard elder sister, upon the charity of their brother. Long ago Elmina's whimpering kindness had been stamped into the earth by Keturah's force and goodness. The cool virginal grey-green house with the unutterable cleanliness of carpet and walls, the stale faintly aromatic smell of the unused parlour, the hesitant step over scrubbed floors—with these she would be identified. It was a prospect which she could not endure. But what, then? These were her alternatives.

There was nothing to tell Tillie that she was being ridiculous, since she was very young, only at the beginning of things, and a very beautiful woman. It was not possible for her to rest in that assurance, because she had no idea of it. Beauty was not discussed, or commented upon, or even, perhaps, considered desirable, in her life. God made man in His image, and it was not for His creatures to compare His handiwork.

Tillie looked again, across the track to the fertile hundred acres, and thrust back envious thought. It could only

27

have been hers if the Lord had intended it so. Perhaps she was not pure enough to be the wife of one of the Lord's anointed. Had he brought her here to the brink of happiness only to show her this promised land, which she might not enter? Had a sin of hers so angered the Father that this punishment was now to be hers?

Well, there was no need to stand here any longer. She turned resolutely to go back. Simon, looking at her, saw a still-faced girl whose calm bearing gave him no clue whatever to the tumult. All alone with her, back here, in the sudden pool of quiet left by the passing train, he was conscious of a new, alien quality about her, a quality which fed his desire and robbed him of all address. Why could he not speak to her? What invisible but rigid veil hung between them? Austerity and conscious pride, which were so strong, because of his calling, shrank within him. The silence about them grew and deepened. A cool mask of obstinate withdrawal firmed on her face. She had done her share; let Simon speak, or be silent. Tillie turned to walk back toward the house. Desperately, sweat breaking out on his lip and forehead, Simon brought himself to the issue. "Wait!" he said, and pointed across the track to the farmhouse, "How would that suit you, to live in?"

Tillie looked across the siding and saw that the house and the barns had taken on a new look of warmth and tangibility. The sharpness and strangeness were gone and they had become familiar objects, and wore the benevolent features of the known and the beloved.

She smiled at Simon. "There'll be a lot to do in the garden," she said. Warmth returned to her veins and she accepted her gentle destiny with dignity.

Trembling with haste and anxiety Simon stumbled to her, laid hands on her light shoulders and kissed her lips. It was as if a large winged insect had fluttered his wings across her mouth. She raised her arms, and let them fall, without completing the embrace. Simon's face left hers; and they began to walk slowly back, Tillie with her eyes straight ahead, serenity in her gait. Simon glanced furtively at her, from time to time, his hands clenching and unclenching.

Suddenly the lane was full of voices, and the small boys of both families were there, calling to them to hurry, the horses were all ready. Tillie kissed the Goudie girls, passed under the barrage of curious eyes and, blushing deep pink, climbed into the democrat with her brothers and drove out of the Goudie lane. She would not look at her father, and to her mother's speaking eyes she made no response. Until they were out of sight Simon Goudie watched from the gate, waving his long arm in triumphant farewell.

3

TILLIE STEPPED down into the big kitchen, which with its yellow floor and whitewashed walls looked as clean as a new calendar. There was a strong, provocative mixture of smells—fresh butter, rising bread, and sauerkraut and, drifting among these, a diluted stable smell from the short coats by the door and the boots behind the stove. She lifted the thick grey blanket from a bread trough and delicately poked the soft flesh of the bread which now nearly filled it. Her mother stood by in the attitude of instructor.

"Shall I take it out now?"

"Jah, it's about ready. Keep the cover on, though, while you flour the board."

Tillie lifted the thick kneading-board on to the table.

"Out of the draught. Here." Betsey shoved the board

three feet further down the table, and looked at her daughter despairingly. "Not even that, you know. How can you get married?"

Tillie thrust her fists into the deep trough and watched the expiring of the big bubble of bread. She gathered the dough into her arms and laid it on the board; pulling the far half over into a gigantic Parker House roll, she flopped it about, turning a quarter round with each powerful push from the heels of her hands. It was hard work, to knead the dough for a dozen loaves of bread. But she sent it spinning round the board with swift, sure punches, turning it over occasionally, until both sides were satin smooth and creaseless. Her mother watched her, a little grudging of the strength that went into the work, and indignant that she could do so well, without practice or knowledge.

"There now, there now! Not any more, the second time. Put into the loaves. Too much makes it tough, this time."

"Oh."

In the years since she had left school Tillie had gradually assumed charge of the needlework and knitting as her part of the labour in the household. She made the men's heavy work shirts from the traditional pattern and knitted socks for her brothers and father as well as her own and her mother's stockings. She did the ironing, and kept the mending-basket empty. But hers was work without authority, and in the kitchen she had no prestige at all.

She ran up the little set of three steps which took her into the pantry, and brought out an armful of long black tins.

"Where is the butter I should use, for the pans?"

"Butter? Never butter for pans. The salt makes it stick. Get lard from the pail in the cellar-way. Not too much, either. Makes hard crust."

Tillie poised the long butcher knife over the lump of dough.

"Does this make twelve loaves, though? It looks too small."

"Eighteen years old, and never helped with the bread before! Yes, it makes twelve. And be careful you don't stretch them. Cut them clean."

The hired girl made a swift clattering passage through the kitchen, pails of chicken feed in her hands.

"You gotta learn, now, eh, Tillie? Pretty soon you'll have men to feed. No more playing pianos, and getting out of the work then, eh?"

She went grinning out into the orchard, the sound of her foolish guttural laughter trailing behind her. Tillie looked after the girl for a second, and then cut the dough into twelve even lumps, turning them in her hands until they were roundly humped, before she put them lightly to bed in the tins.

Mrs. Shantz considered her daughter, a worried look in her pale eyes.

"It's true enough, though, you know, Tillie, to be married means hard work. And you have never wanted to learn. Now, in maybe less than a year, even, you will need to know so many things. Well," and she sighed deeply, "you must just watch me, every day, and learn what you can. The more you do, the better. When you want to do something, you can learn fast."

Such a remark was as close to commendation as Mrs. Shantz had ever gone.

Tillie spread her hands on the table and jumped up to sit on it. She leaned her back against the wall and looked out of the window over the lane to the orchard, where the first fitful snow fell in delicate white stripes over black new furrows.

"Only tomboys sit on the table."

Tillie smiled, and looked beyond the orchard knoll where the snow thickened in the grey air.

"Simon is going away to the Bible College, for this year.

31

Maybe for two years. There is plenty of time to learn housekeeping, after I come back from Kinsail."

Mrs. Shantz stared at her blankly.

"When you come back from Kinsail! Surely now you will not go away from home?" Her face was full of concern. For it would be a reflection on her, too, if she sent out a daughter to be mistress of a house, all unprepared.

Tillie, still finding something to interest her, far beyond the line of apple trees, responded in a dreaming voice. "Yes, I think I will still go."

Mrs. Shantz tossed her thin hands in the air. "I don't know what you are thinking of! I don't know! Did you tell your father this?"

Tillie nodded. "Yes, I talked to Papa." Still she seemed more interested in the far scene than the near.

"Well, what did he say?"

"He said I could go."

Levi came through the door, humming reverberatingly. "Well, she makes bread, now, does she?"

"Levi. Tillie says she is going to Kinsail, though."

"Jah. There are things she wants to learn, you know, Betsey. And they are not going to be married just right away, you know."

He looked imploringly at Betsey, nodding his head faster and faster. Betsey made a small sign of despair with her shoulders and her hands.

"She can lead you like a blind lamb, always."

"Oh, no, Betsey, now! She wants to learn these things, a long time now. When she is married there will be no time. Now is the time."

He spoke earnestly. "We mustn't make an old woman of her yet, Betsey."

His wife tightened her mouth, and looked at the girl. "I don't want to make an old woman of her, Levi," she said gently, and then smiled, but anxiously, at him. Always it was like this, he could always manage her, always get his own way. He was still speaking.

"Music makes joy in the house, Betsey. It is good to have music at home. And for the children, too, it will be a good thing to have a mother who can play to them, to sing. God gives the talent, and we must make use of it."

"Yes, make use of it."

Betsey stood with her hands limp at her thin sides, watching her husband and daughter. Levi laid a hand on her shoulder, gesticulating with the other big fist.

"When she is tired, or alone, there, at home, it will be a fine thing to have music. And then too, Betsey, we do not have assurance that things will be always like they are now, thanks be to God for His mercy to us, for we have all that we need, and plenty more, too, of His good things. But times change, we do not know what testing He may have in store for Tillie. Perhaps, sometime, it would be a good thing for her to have a little trade. If she could do a little sewing, then, it would be all right for her."

Betsey firmly but gently disengaged her shoulder from Levi's hand. "Well . . . but she cannot go just yet, Levi. No. She is not ready, anyway."

Levi glanced at Tillie, silent in the window.

"After Thanksgiving, Levi, tell the dressmaker. She can come for a little while, through the winter. Perhaps she will not still be at home, next fall, and when is she to learn to do the fall work? Men do not know how it is, in the house, with all the fruit and the meat. She must be at home, this fall, to learn. She does not know anything about how to keep house, Levi! She is always out in the garden, or out in the barn, and playing at the piano. Yes, she can make a pie or cook meat, a little, but that is nothing."

Levi looked lovingly at her, and put his arm around her troubled shoulders.

"Ach, you think she should know all that, just at once, though? Even with you, Betsey, it took a little time. She gets to know something, just watching you, all this time. Surely she must know something that way. Young girls learn from good mothers. They know, all right, but maybe

33

they don't just know they do. And when the time comes, Tillie will think back: 'How did Mamma do that?' And it will come back to her and she can do it."

Betsey flushed. "Well. You two have made up your minds." She shrugged Levi's arm from her shoulder again and went back to her butter, slapping the paddle about in the sludge until spray splashed the walls.

Tillie sat still in the window, almost as if the discussion had nothing to do with her. Her father glanced at her, and back to his wife. "Well, then, Tillie, how is that? After Thanksgiving, when you have learned all that your mother can teach you . . ."

"Yes, Father, that will be the way."

Betsey straightened up from the butter bowl. "When you go to Kinsail next week, Levi, to see about getting the little pigs, you can see the dressmaker. About the end of November, maybe, she can go."

Tillie slid down from the table and looked with new eyes upon the kitchen and its furnishings. She tried to realize the importance of learning, at once, the skills and tricks of housewifery which her mother was so willing to teach her. But she could feel no actual connection between the utensils she handled now and those implements with which she would fashion her own life.

Her life seemed to her unique and glowing. It stretched before her like a pleasant road in a dream of spring. She wanted to go to Kinsail, and to learn those things that she had set her mind upon learning; but in this moment of dreaming it did not seem to matter to her whether she went now, or later. In any case her life was to be lovely, and fulfilled.

"The bread, Tillie!"

Mrs. Shantz's voice broke, sharp and anxious, into her daughter's consciousness; and Tillie lifted the big grey blanket and looked again, indifferently, at the rising white pillows of bread.

34

4

O<small>N THE</small> first Monday in December, Levi brought Tillie to Kinsail. Levi's elder sister Keturah met them at her door.

"Well, you got here."

She pressed her thin body behind the door of the narrow hall to permit Levi to carry in the big box he balanced on his arms, full of presents of food from Betsey. Elmina, the younger of the Shantz sisters, her hands folding and working over her apron, advanced hesitatingly towards them, smiling in tremulous welcome. Levi set the box on the kitchen floor and walked quickly out to the livery rig for the other. Still smiling gently, Tillie stood in the hall waiting for direction, holding the heavy black Gladstone bag easily in her hand.

"I guess you know where your room is, Tillie. Might as well take your things on up."

Tillie walked swiftly up the stairs and was back almost at once.

"Aren't you going to take your coat off?"

"I won't be staying now, Aunt Kettie. I want to see Miss Macklin as soon as I can. I think she expected me to start today. It's half the day gone already."

Elmina's eyes travelled from Tillie to Keturah, to discover what opinion she should form of this behaviour.

"What about your dinner, then? Your mother must think we are going to starve you, anyway, the stuff she sent." Keturah lifted out a pair of roasted chickens, a crock of fresh apple butter, a wooden box of Betsey's special Dutch cheese, and rested her eyes on a bushel of Russets still in the bottom of the box. "She thinks we don't have anything to eat, here."

Elmina's eyes filled with tears, and she looked reproachfully at her sister. "Betsey goes to too much trouble, though, Levi."

"I'll go, then." Tillie was at the door.

Levi stood up. "You want to go alone, Tillie? You're not scared?"

"You showed me the house in the summer, Papa. I remember. When we drove through, after camp-meeting."

"Down the street by the Post Office, Tillie, remember!"

"The brown painted one—"

Elmina looked on with startled eyes. "But she will not go alone, will she, though?"

Tillie laughed. "I'll find it, all right, Aunt 'Mina."

"She's in a hurry to get started, maybe." Levi watched the girl, his eyes moist.

"But she has had no dinner?" The world and its workings, outside the narrow house, were now too strange and frightening to Elmina. To go without dinner was to destroy a bulwark of custom. The dinner was not made for the day, but the day for the dinner.

"We had sandwiches Betsey made, on the train. We are not hungry, yet."

Tillie paused as she opened the door. "You will still be here, when I get back though, Papa?"

Levi pulled out his large silver watch. "Six o'clock, Jake said he would come. I will be here till six, likely."

"I don't know how long Miss Macklin . . ."

"Anyway, I will see you before I go home, for sure."

Levi settled himself in the little house, clothed in his Sunday blacks, and the day became an occasion to the sisters. So rare a visit took on a little the character of a celebration. He waved to Tillie through the window, and she waved again, then turned down towards the business section of the village.

It was the first time she had walked alone, in the village, and she saw houses and buildings which she had not known were there. From the top of the hill as she came down, the spires of six churches, some tall, some low, were visible to her; and the seventh church, her own, with no spire but only a plain gable on the front, she passed at once, just opposite her aunts' house. She made a swift descent into the town, looking about her with lively curiosity. Men and women were coming slowly down the main street now, joining it at the corners of the few small side streets. They walked with after-dinner languor, loath to enter their workshops again. These Tillie noted as she passed, for their pleasant expression, or the height of their hats, or their likeness to Caleb Reesor, or some other familiar figure known to her at home.

Loretta Macklin opened the door for Tillie, giving the girl a shrewd appraising glance before she spoke.

"You're Levi Shantz's girl, eh?"

"Yes," said Tillie, looking squarely into the dressmaker's bright brown eyes.

"Come in, then. It's quite a treat to me to talk to a woman that I don't have to duck down to speak to." She thrust out a long, slim, brown-skinned hand and shook Tillie's with a quick strong clasp.

"Can you sew?"

"I can do plain sewing."

"All sewing is plain sewing. Nobody can take more than one stitch at a time, no matter how fancy she thinks she's doing. If you can sew, what do you want to come to me for, then?"

Tillie looked at the woman. She must be six feet tall, she thought, and so narrow in the shoulders, and I never saw a woman with hair like that before—short and curly like a little boy's.

"Eh, what do you want to come for?"

"I want to be able to make things, right from the beginning. I can't do that. And to learn a trade, so that I could sew for other people, if it were necessary."

"I see. Did you bring your tools?"

"Tools?"

"Scissors, chalk, thimble, line?"

37

"No. I didn't know I should have. I can get them. Do I need them right away?"

"Can't work without tools. Use mine this afternoon, but bring yours along tomorrow, if you still want to come, then. Sit down and I'll tell you how I work it. Here."

Tillie sat on a pin-scarred stool by the cutting-table in what had been the front parlour of Loretta's house. Loretta sat on the edge of the table and ran her thin fingers through her hair as she spoke, then reached for a piece of material and began, with lightning stitches, to whip up a raw edge. Tillie's eyes followed the flashing needle with delight.

"I try them for a week," Loretta said, "and, of course, they try me too." She laughed a parrot's laugh. "And then I know whether it's any use for either of us. If it is, then they agree to stay six months. Any less is no good, for either. Could you stay six months?"

Tillie pondered the question, still following the snap and stretch of Loretta's fingers. She had never in her life spent a night away from home, except rarely with cousins a few miles away. Six months looked like time without end; but suddenly she saw it as a kind of block, solid, three-dimensional, which she might have as a gift if she stretched out her hand for it. Some obscure instinct hitherto unknown to her suggested that she grasp the gift. But she was wary of it.

"Take your time," said Loretta tersely.

Tillie looked about her, and tried to think what it would be like to spend all the winter and spring in this long brown panelled room. Patterns and sketches hung from the walls in sheaves, blown in a soft flutter by the warm air coming up from the big circular register. Bolts of brown linen and striped taffeta, towers of shining white boxes, were piled on top of a cupboard at one end. A homely, yellow-blotched grey cat warmed herself complacently in her basket by the little Franklin stove which heated the heavy pressing-irons. But most important of all, of course, to reflect upon, was Loretta herself. That strange skinny woman with the monkey-like face and the long thin arms had made all those intricate garments which fell from padded hangers on the long wall, and lay in helpless incompletion about the cutting table which filled the window end of the room. Loretta herself, the major factor, was clothed in brown sateen from ankle to chin, her dress fitting as tightly as her skin, yielding only very slightly to fashionable edict, in the bubble at the top of the sleeve. She wore long slender brown buttoned boots, as pointed as pin-oak leaves. Tillie looked at her, and felt a quickening within; the sudden, small, undefinable emotion that comes with the recognition of likeness in an unexpected place. "Tomboy, too," she thought; and swiftly decided.

"If you think I could learn, I could stay six months."

"Well, we'll soon see. First thing, we'll make a bag for your truck, and an apron. Have them for nothing, if you stay. Otherwise, you can leave them here, or buy the material. Always useful."

She pulled down two slender bolts of slippery sateen from the top of the cupboard, and rolled an emerald-green length over the cutting-table.

"Like that, or the fawn better?"

Tillie passed her hand over the shining stuff.

"I like the green, I think."

"Good. Suit you better, too. Have to stick to the browns, myself. Stand up over here to the glass."

Loretta pulled another two yards of the material from the bolt and draped it over Tillie's shoulder. "Take off your hat. And that thing," pointing to the black spencer Tillie wore under her coat. "Won't need it here."

"That green brings out your eyes, and the red in your hair."

Tillie looked with attention at herself in the triple-panelled pier-glass. The girl in the middle glass did seem to have large, bright eyes. The images to the right and left of her, though, were unformed, black creatures, all shoulders, whose faces were obscured by shapeless masses of dead black hair.

"Red in my hair?"

"Just glints," said Loretta absently. "Complementaries. Don't suppose you know anything about colour, of course?"

Tillie shook her head. Evidently she did not.

"Lots to learn, then. Can you draw at all?"

"Pictures, you mean?" Tillie's eyes opened in astonishment. What had drawing to do with being a dressmaker? "I can draw horses and sheep. Cats, too, sometimes."

Loretta nodded. "Well, that's good. We'll see, by and by. Any time you're not busy, make sketches of Florence." She pointed to the cat. "Big ones. Loosen you up. Hang your things in the hall, and I'll start you."

Loretta glanced comprehensively at the black serge dress, as Tillie returned. "If we have any time left, you'd better make a pair of sleeve protectors too. That wool will pick up all the lint in the shop."

Tillie looked at her thick sleeves, comparing them to Loretta's sleek arms. For the first time in her life she felt shapeless and awkward, as if she filled up too much of the world's space. Her boots looked cumbersome and felt heavy. Her beautifully knitted long black stockings suddenly seemed coarse and lumpish.

"Measure yourself from shoulder to knee," directed Loretta, "and forget anything anybody else has told you about sewing. If you're to work with me, I want the work done my way. Haven't much patience with other people's notions. Midpoint to midpoint, and accurate to the sixteenth of an inch. The first thing to learn."

Sitting in unaccustomed idleness in his sisters' home, Levi grew restless, feeling the house too small for him, and filling it the more with his massive frame as he walked about in it, waiting for Tillie to come home with her news.

"The first afternoon, why does she keep her so long?"

"Maybe though she didn't get there, Levi," said Elmina.

Levi pulled out his watch. "Nearly five, now." He stretched out his arms and yawned mightily, tired with the strain of inaction. "Maybe I should go and meet her?"

"Sit down and rest yourself, Levi. Not often you have the chance." Keturah spoke in the tone of one who has seen much foolishness. "The village isn't so big that she can't find her way home. Loretta Macklin will want to get the good of her."

She had lit the lamp when Tillie came in, smiling and fresh.

Levi rose to meet her. "Well, well, and how did the dressmaking get on? I thought you would be home before now."

Keturah and Elmina stopped still in their rockers, to hear what she had to say.

"Papa, she is trying me, for a week, or a few days, anyway, and if she thinks I can learn well, then I am to stay for six months, and she will teach me everything."

"Jah? Maybe you could learn a little faster than six months, though? Your mother did not think you could be away that long, I think."

"She says it is no use, any shorter time."

"Well, now. And you, do you want to stay?"

"Yes, I want to stay."

"You think you can learn, then?"

Tillie looked down at her long hands, remembering the pull of the machine against her fingers, and the long straight seams she had made.

"I know I can, Papa."

Levi sighed. "Well then, do I have to tell your mother you will not be home until the summer?"

Tillie smiled radiantly at him. "Oh, Papa, it is not so long, and I will be home three days at Christmas, Miss Macklin said."

"What about your board, here? Can you keep her that long?" he inquired, half facetiously, of his sisters.

"As long as she behaves herself she can stay," said Keturah. "Seems to me Simon Goudie can't be in any hurry to get married, though."

5

ON SATURDAY mornings Mr. Shardley, the music teacher, came out from the City to give lessons in the Lodge room of the Mansion House, and a stream of young girls flowed through the hall all day, right past the bar itself. After dinner Tillie went down the long hill to the hotel, for her first lesson. She climbed the broad bare steps to the upper floor while the men at the bar looked languidly after her. A girl in the black bonnet was of no interest to them; it was as if a nun had passed by.

Old Shardley shook his head as she left him.

"If that girl weren't a Mennonite, I could make something of her. There's more there than in all the rest of these little pulers put together. But she'd never get out to work at it. They won't educate their children."

He rose from his stool and watched her walk down the street, straight and tall and strong.

"Yeah. Strong, got brains, maybe talent, too. But it'll never come to anything. She'll get so far, and her family will step in. Wonder they let her come at all—she can play well enough now for those bearded cranks to sing to. She'll waste her life playing on some squeaky old organ down a side-road ten miles from nowhere. With a face like that. Lose her figure at twenty-five, and her teeth at thirty, all to the glory of God. Stiffen up her fingers mixing mash for the hogs, and breed as fast as they do. Some lucky oaf."

Mr. Shardley swore gently, took a quick nip from his pocket flask, and had just time to wipe off the drops from his grey moustache before the door opened and his next pupil came in.

Walking along Main Street, with her brown music roll under her arm, Tillie flexed and reflexed her strong fingers. She had noticed her hands, that afternoon, for the first time in her life, as personal attributes, something of which, apparently, she could be proud. Her girl acquaintances had never indulged in the familiar female game of comparing physical features, other than stepping on the barn scales to determine which one weighed the most. Tillie never won that game. It was a new and interesting idea to Tillie that her hands, in themselves, might be of any interest. She took off her double-knitted navy blue gloves, and examined her right hand. The fingers were long, strong, straight, with full cups at the ends. She put on her glove, and smiled. A pleasant, totally new sensation filled her. It was a little as if someone had said, "Look at yourself, now, your hands are good. Not only good, but beautiful, too. Maybe there are other things, too, about you which are interesting and beautiful. What about your face? And your long thick curly hair? You should look at your eyes, too. There's not very much colour in your face. Back at home where red cheeks, the fatter the better, are the most desirable, that is not considered lucky; but out here in the world, now, we think pale skin makes red lips look redder."

A strange shameful feeling came to Tillie. It was more comfortable to be quite unconscious of these things. And surely Mr. Shardley did not mean all he had said. This must be what her father had meant, when he said that away from home she must beware of the ways of the world.

43

Because the ways of the world were not their ways, nor the actions of the world their actions. Tillie deliberately dismissed the thought of her hands, and the embarrassing reference to her complexion. But in spite of their dismissal Mr. Shardley's casual remarks had opened a little window, for Tillie, to the world outside. There was no way for her to close it, and curiosity drove her to look again.

Through the window of Mr. Shardley's remarks she looked into the matter of music itself. She had known that music was divided into two classes. One was sacred music, the hymns in the red-and-black book. The other kind was called classical, and consisted of pieces like the Moonlight Sonata, and Rachmaninoff's Prelude in C Sharp Minor, which a very few people, who had taken advanced music lessons, could play. It was permitted to play such music on Sundays, too, to a quiet and uncritical audience, and it was towards this class of music that Tillie's ambitions ran.

But now it was revealed that there were still other forms. Tillie had listened with deep interest to Mr. Shardley's talk of symphonic music, and opera. At first she had felt a wild, unreasoning desire to go where this music could be heard. But then, when he explained further, it became clear that she could never do that. These musical entertainments were held in theatres, and other forbidden places. It sounded like a very deceptive invitation from Satan himself. How like the Evil One, to hide his sinful temptations under the cloak of music, which was surely a gift of God!

All that kind of thing, Tillie realized, belonged to the World, and she, through the grace of the Lamb, was not of the World. But it was difficult to believe that such a society as Mr. Shardley had described to her, taking pleasure as he did so in the astonishment of her beautiful face, had any reality. She closed her mind to the memory of it, but the thought of Mr. Shardley and his tales returned to her again and again.

The afternoon was free and empty, for Tillie. It was two o'clock. She had no obligation to Loretta, and nothing to

44

do. Elmina and Keturah went out on Saturdays to a sister's home in the country, to help with the Saturday work in a house full of little children. They would not be home until evening.

At her own home, Saturday was a very busy day. There was the baking to do for the Sabbath, when no unnecessary cooking was done, and the big yellow kitchen floors to be scrubbed after it. All the shoes had to be polished and brushed, and the fresh shirts and underclothes examined, all ready to put on for the day of rest. By Saturday night the house shone in every corner, and the little boys were scrubbed until they squealed, in the wooden tub of soapy water behind the kitchen stove. When all was done, Tillie went thankfully to bed, her body tired and her mind and soul rested and cleaned, like the house.

In Kinsail, it was going to be different. Already, on her first Saturday, she walked, lonely, on the streets. There was no one she knew well enough to visit. To go back to the empty house, and sit there, alone in the spotless grey, was a forbidding prospect. She walked slowly along, feeling painfully separated from anything which was hers, or hitherto known to her. Her stiff black clothes were only a symbol of the armour which encased her and kept her from all others who walked the busy street. Mr. Shardley's stories, in retrospect, too, were alarming. If all these things existed, known and experienced by thousands upon thousands of people, in cities where Mr. Shardley said there were *none of her people at all*, what else might there not be, of which she was ignorant? The people who passed her on the street, those people who smiled kindly at her, and said "Good afternoon," and went on, did they know of these great gatherings, where a hundred people played different instruments, and a noise rose to heaven louder than thunder, and sweeter than any earthly singing? She had a fugitive longing to stop someone, and ask him. Somewhere she could, perhaps, get confirmation, or denial. Mr. Shardley had catapulted her into a world where she was without friends, and had no one to ask for direction. She felt herself becoming overwhelmingly homesick. A little boy came along. He had a red-and-black wool toque, pulled down over his ears. He was too sharp a reminder of her own little brothers, and all the bustle and liveliness there was at home this afternoon. But she walked alone, with no one even to talk to, and no place to go but an empty house. Six hours, yet, before the mail would come in, with her weekly letter from Simon.

Two town girls with their skates slung over their shoulders and books under their arms hurried past her, laughing and talking together, their heads bent forward against the wind. They did not glance at her as they hurried by, but turned quickly down towards the market hall, and dived, crowding and gay, into a small brown door, badly needing paint. Above the door at the front of the building, a legend said "Council Chambers." It was here, Tillie knew, that the town council met, upstairs. And underneath the Council Chambers stood the big red fire-wagon, with its huge barrel and reels. The rope from the little pointed bell-tower hung down between the doors, low enough for even a small boy to reach. What lay behind the fire station Tillie had no idea, but the laughter and gaiety of the girls pulled her after them. They could not have been younger than she was, and yet, in the ageless clothes she wore, and because of the invisible armour she carried, they might have been of another generation. She felt herself to be years beyond them, out of all reach of that irresponsible gaiety.

She turned where they had turned, and, more hesitatingly now, was carried toward the door which had closed them in. The glass half of the door, in slanting, greenish, anciently flourishing script, described itself as "Mechanics Institute." It opened, startlingly, and the Presbyterian minister came out, books under his arm. He smiled at her, and held the door open, supposing her to be about to enter. She felt herself to be bolting in like a rabbit. The minister closed

46

the door behind her, and she was in a public library for the first time in her life.

Along the centre of the single shabby room a long narrow table, covered with newspapers and magazines in stiff holders, occupied the attention of three old men. The laughing girls had laid their skates on the floor by the door and were behind the counters now, seriously choosing books from the shelves. The librarian sat quietly on the wide window-seat, looking out into the drifted snow. A box stove sent out grateful heat. No one looked up, or seemed surprised at Tillie's entrance. Evidently she could come in here. She sat down on one of the kitchen chairs which served the table, and looked about her. It was utterly quiet in the room. Above her ranged rows of books in numbers of whose existence she had had no idea.

Tillie pulled off her gloves and approached one of the shelves. Nothing familiar to her, nothing within her experience revealed itself here. The act of reading for just the interest of reading, not to gain information about God and His will for His people, or descriptions of His works among men, was new to her. At home, apart from the Bible itself, which in itself is enough for all, there were no books but a monthly *Religious Messenger* and the *Family Doctor.* When she had finished with school, three years ago, she had finished with reading too. It was more than doubtful whether she should have been using even the authorized school texts. Other books, many of them available in the little school library, had been forbidden to her because they were novels, and not true. It was hard for the brotherhood to see why such books as they put upon the school curriculum should be there. The fathers and mothers of Tillie's generation had not read them, of course, but knew them to be a waste of time, a dilution of truth, if not more evil; so that in reading *Idylls of the King,* and *Silas Marner,* Tillie had been doing her lessons, and nothing more. These strange, extraneous materials had nothing to do with her. Because her people were obedient, by precept, to the laws

47

of the land, Tillie went to school until she was fourteen, driving in the five miles each day to Reesorville Continuation School. But she went home again each night, and it was the home, not the school, that guided her thoughts. And now, by an unreasoning act, she had put herself into this place where, obviously, people were reading, and expecting her to behave as they were behaving. Pride forbade her to make a clumsy escape. She continued to look along the shelves, her heart beating strangely.

The librarian withdrew her gaze from the snowy yard, and spoke to Tillie.

"Perhaps you can find what you want in the catalogue," she smiled, offering Tillie a sheaf of foolscap with the titles and authors of hundreds of books written upon them, in old ink. "And here's a list of the newer ones."

Tillie's eyes mastered the short list. "Could I see *The Princess Passes*, please?" she heard her voice inquire.

The librarian smiled again. "You're very lucky; it has just come in. Do you want to take it out, or had you thought of reading it here?"

A wisp of warning that the Devil works fast and in silence flickered through Tillie's consciousness.

"I'll just read here, for a while," she said with perfect composure.

When the librarian wanted to go home for her supper, Tillie was still reading. "I'll give you a card," she offered, "and you can take it home."

Tillie went out of the door, with the book under her arm, and a card with her name on it jutting out from the top of the volume.

Early winter evening closed in on the village. The deep *pom-pom* from the power-house gave a rhythmic roar, and as Tillie walked rapidly up the long hill to her aunts' house the street lights blinked on. Supper silence dwelt in the village. Green pin-points of stars pierced the winter blue sky. Tillie's steps grew reluctant. At the grey picket gate she stopped, deeply aware of the stars and the snow and the silence, and unwilling to break their harmony with the starchy creak of her feet. For a long minute there was silence still; and then, far away to the east, a thin silver jangle sounded into the frosty air. The sound fell, and rose again, louder this time. There was another losing of the sound, and another crescendo, and then clear definition of a cutter's bells. Sweet and fresh and frosty they sang out, the swift gait of a fast-travelling pacer defining the delicate insistency of their rhythm.

Tillie turned to see the slender swaying animal bank the corner of the town line. The little creature tightened her gait, lightly blurring her music as she swung into the straight, and once more gaily and evenly tossed her bright spangle of sound into the air. Under the street lights the cutter flashed a sudden scarlet, and until the sounds died quite away, down in the valley centre of the village, Tillie stood motionless, waiting and watching for she did not understand what.

A distant shrill note, long and poignant, sounded through the still cold air. The mail train was coming in. Tillie woke out of her dream and went quickly into the house. She would put coal on, and eat a little supper, then go quickly back down the hill for her letter. She had sudden need of the letter tonight. She trembled as she walked into the house, cold from the long day. Certainly she had need of Simon's letter. It was as if she had been pulled a little off balance. The loneliness, and Mr. Shardley, and the book with its strange acceptances, had made her foolishly apprehensive. She had need of word from Simon, to steady her again.

The twilight stillness of the empty house greeted her with cold restraint. She pulled up the draft on the range, shut the damper, and at once lit the lamp. But it seemed to her as if the shadows still lay deep along the walls. She pulled the book into the warm light of the lamp and began to read again. With one long cold hand she brought sausage and bread to her mouth, and with the other she slowly turned

49

the pages. She forgot that the stove needed coal, that the mail closed at eight; and when a stamping of feet at the outer door warned her of her aunts' approach, she had not taken off her bonnet or her overshoes, and it was nine o'clock.

The sisters came in, to spread their cold hands over the fire. In their heavy winter coats they almost filled the hall. Aunt Elmina followed, giving the impression, as she always did, of hiding behind her tall elder sister. Her skin was scarlet with cold, and the swollen blue veins, which seemed to accent her timorous expression, drew double anxious lines on her face.

Keturah regarded Tillie curiously.

"Where have you been?"

"I haven't been anywhere, since this afternoon."

"Sitting around the house with your things on? I don't know how your mother brought you up. What is that book?"

"I got it from the library," said Tillie. The words moved oddly on her unaccustomed lips.

Keturah removed her stiff black bonnet in silence, folding her warm mittens into smooth ovals to place them in the top drawer in the hall stand. Aunt Elmina, moving softly behind her, peered from her shadowy corner with frightened eyes. Keturah hung her fur-lined black broadcloth carefully on its padded hanger, came over to the table, and picked up the book. Her affronted eyes glanced over a paragraph.

"You can't have much to do with your time," she said acidly. "Take it back where it came from, and don't let me see that kind of thing in this house again."

Elmina coughed nervously, rubbing her thick-veined little hands together over the stove.

Keturah lifted the cover from the stove and poured in a scuttle of coal. "And you've let the fire nearly out, I see."

Tillie rose from her chair. There was softness and dignity in her voice and in her attitude.

"Shall I take it back, now?"

"Now! Nine o'clock on a Saturday night? Do you want to be taken for a streetwalker? What kind of preparation is this for the Sabbath? What do you think your mother will think, you running all over the village like any common girl, the minute you are left alone?"

Keturah pressed her grizzled hair still tighter up from her cheeks until they looked scraped thin, her nervous bony hands trembling with emotion. Elmina crouched deeper into her corner, distressed and fearful. Her bright watery blue eyes opened wide in apprehension, and her loose lips quivered.

"Oh, Keturah!"

Her sister gave her no attention, but continued to stare at her niece in uncomprehending anger. What had got into the girl?

Tillie stood motionless by the table, her hand still on the alien book. Thin contempt edged Keturah's voice.

"I should think you'd have more respect for yourself."

The library book made a brilliant spectacular spot in the grey room, fading the blue table-cover into grey about it.

Pasted on the sulphur-yellow cover was a picture of a tall full-bosomed woman. She wore a white, broad-brimmed hat, with a huge pink rose in a cluster of half-opened buds trailing through white tulle from the under side of the brim to her shoulder. Her hair lay in loose molasses-coloured waves about her face. She was smiling faintly, at some person or object invisible to Keturah, and from her delicate white fingers there drifted another pink rose. Her dress was of diaphanous silver stuff, so transparent that her white arms were indicated through huge melon sleeves of most intricate construction. She leaned a little forward over a garden gate, and Keturah saw only evil in her. She represented the wicked womanhood of the world.

Tillie bent easily over and began to remove her overshoes. There was nothing of defiance about her, and nothing of the suppliant either. She moved about the room

51

straightening away her supper things with a poise and aloofness which prevented speech from escaping Keturah as nothing else would have done. In the face of cataclysm, speech is unavailing, but she could not quite leave the proud girl unwounded.

"I suppose you think Simon would like to see you spending your time reading wicked trash like that? It isn't that kind of women preachers are out to marry. Remember that."

6

O N SUNDAY, Tillie woke to the whirr of a driving north wind which sent diagonal sheets of snow across her window. The room was icy cold. She could hear Aunt Keturah downstairs, walking with firm flat-footed steps about the kitchen, and an occasional brief sound of speech reached her. Aunt Elmina's slim but bunioned feet made almost inaudible steps; her voice did not ascend the stairs. The bleak day stretched before Tillie without promise or intent. She felt like a little stream, suddenly diverted from its accustomed narrow bed to run for a while among sweet flowers and herbs, piquant and fresh, and then turned back abruptly into its old course.

The day before seemed empty and cold and grey. There would be a disapproving breakfast with the aunts. Keturah cold and Elmina frightened. Then across the road to the little church as grey as this house, with nothing in its terrible strangeness to suggest the church at home—known and loved, beautiful through association. In the Kinsail church the cold light flowed blue through the naked windows, on to the faces of strangers.

With a distant growl, the wind dropped. The harried snow settled softly in rigid beds, and stillness, Sabbath stillness filled the sky and town and the four walls of the house. They must be reading the morning lessons to themselves, in the grey kitchen. In a few minutes a little stirring indicated that the reading was over, and Keturah was on her sharp knees by the hickory rocker, pleading with God for grace; grace for herself, for her sister, and for others, who perhaps needed it more.

Tillie felt her heart turn cold, cold as the air about her, in conscious stubbornness, and harden against the softening love of Him who was her Saviour. She held herself very still, for a second, almost as if listening for the voice of some evil thing. Carelessness, novel and frightening, strengthened and grew within her. Tillie viewed her reaction with alarm, but as one powerless to stop. Surely just a week of this new life had not so utterly changed her? Why was she not moved at the thought of her aunts downstairs, praying for her, that she might not stray, but be brought home to God's House, in the end, a glorious home, where the Lord's anointed would sing, forever, His praises? But this morning that wonderful certainty brought no joy. She straightened her back and stiffened her shoulders against acceptance, and against joy.

A thin heat and strong smell of varnish from the stove pipe told her that a fire had been lit in the parlour, in honour of the Sabbath. She rose slowly from the warmth of the feather bed and walked over the spotless grey painted floor to the evanescent heat. She held each piece of her underwear close to the pipe to take the chill off at least one side before she pulled it under her grey flannel nightgown which served her as tent and heating system until she was almost completely dressed. With one strong hand she shattered the ice in the tall white china jug and poured a pool of brown slush into the massive basin. She washed her face with tremendous vigour, again and again raising handfuls of ice and water to scrub over her face and then rubbing it joyfully with the rough linen towel. With great sweeps of a rubber-set wire brush she brushed out her thick black braid, bending down so that the hair almost touched the floor and snapped and flew with electricity. Two stout plaits swiftly braided themselves out from her fingers, and were pinned round her head with eight strong pins. Little wiry wet curls spun into shape at the nape of her neck and at her temples. Her hands were stiff with cold now, her usually pale cheeks scarlet with exercise. The rough black serge sleeves of her Sunday dress felt comforting and thick on her arms.

Any other day she would have gone downstairs to lace her high boots in the warmth of the kitchen range; but a new stiff-necked independence was in operation in Tillie this morning. She preferred to be cold alone than warm with her aunts. For this moment, this hour, she told herself, rebelliously, she would do as she, and as she alone, liked. If she chose to be cold, rather than be companionable, she would be cold. Her fingers, stiff as clothes-pins, balked at the laces; but she was beginning to glow, now, and a sense of happiness, almost of gaiety, took possession of her.

She had, it seemed, rubbed out her anxieties with the rough towel. There began to stir within her a kind of rushing exultance for which she could find no reason. From being depressed and anxious she had suddenly become gay and confident. She stood for a moment before her little rectangle of mirror, and smiled brilliantly, mischievously, at her reflection. She felt as she used to feel, sometimes, as a child, filled to bursting with hilarity. At that time she used to go out to the barn and turn somersaults in the hay, run like mad down the lane, leap over fences, give herself to all manner of physical extravagances; all by herself, of course. Such a surge as this she had not felt for years. She stood there savouring the emotion, feeling life tingle through her arms as she stretched them to some unknown compass point, far above her head, in an ecstasy of well-being. And suddenly, in the midst of what would have looked to Keturah like further evidence of a niece gone wickedly mad, Tillie realized that she was hungry, and that the house was utterly quiet again. She came swiftly downstairs and looked out of the hall door as she passed to see the erect, stiff-backed figures of her aunts marching in gloomy superiority across the road to the church. Tillie ought to have been frightened by this utter lack of concern for her behaviour. She realized that she was being treated as an outcast, a pariah, a creature for whom there was, quite possibly, no more hope. And in the mood of the morning she dismissed Aunt Keturah as lightly as a fly from the screen. There would be, she knew, a reckoning for this lofty insouciance, but it was not yet. Always these reckless hilarious moods were paid for by heaviness and despair. But not yet! For this morning, she was removed from responsibility.

There were no signs of breakfast, Tillie's existence was being ignored. Tillie tightened her lips and stiffened her back. For this moment she was invulnerable. The still warmth of the kitchen clothed her in comfort like a cloak. Almost singing with this light inexplicable happiness she cut herself three slices of home-made bread and spread it thick with apple butter, so dark a red it was almost black. She ate the food standing, looking out at the thin dribble of worshippers climbing the snowy steps of the church. When she had finished the bread she deliberately made herself a pot of cocoa, putting in plenty of sugar and heavy cream, fried a thick pink slice of ham, and dropped an egg in to sizzle with it. People passed in a dream before her, going to worship, and she kept herself deliberately away, giving herself over to the pleasures of gluttony. Freedom flowed over her like a warm river. "When I finish my breakfast," she said to herself, "I shall go on up to the top of the hill, walking as fast as I can. Down the eighth is a road which

I have never seen. From the top of the hill I can see where it goes."

In the grip of her invulnerable moment, lost to the thought that it was Sunday, that all her people were in church, that only wastrels and worse walked the streets on Sunday, she set out on her walk. The churches had by now claimed their members, and the long valley street was empty. As she climbed the hill road to the top she glanced back, occasionally, to the narrow vacant village in the sparkling snow.

From the top of the long slow hill where a road branched off to the right, and another, after a little jog, to the left, she stood for a long cold minute, commanding a splendid semicircular view. The road to the left led, after thirty miles, home. That one was soon lost in a downward swoop and a sharp turn. Straight ahead the hill road ended abruptly at the uncompromising fence of a well-kept farm. There was nothing to investigate there. It was just possible, as she stared back at the road upon which she had so gaily climbed to this eminence, to see a broad and, from this distance, unbroken stretch of snow, with sharp fir points climbing up its farther side, which must be Lake Marie, a half mile from the other end of the strip of town land. In the summer a little bunty excursion boat puffed up and down its twenty-mile length carrying seekers after quiet and northern beauty, but now it was still and fast.

The road to the right was the one that concerned her now. From where she stood it ran a mile or two straight and fairly level, for that hilly country, then swerved and fell, and lost itself for unseen miles before the thin line of pole tops indicated that it had again come up out of its secret valley to run along the top of the world. There was no movement on the road; it might have been Tillie's private lane. On one side a narrow sidewalk led past the cemetery, kept clear by the feet of the young of the village walking in couples, seeking solitude. Tillie turned down it, propelled by an odd and urgent feeling, new since yesterday

56

to her, that the world was full of these roads, leading to towns, cities, strange, unknown and perhaps lovely places which she would never see. It seemed to her that she must go down these roads, must see the people in the strange cities, and know what lay beyond the valley. For the first time in the sheltered contentment of her life she knew the fury of haste within her, to see and do a thousand things before—before what? What had she to dread, or escape from? She slowed her pace, and walked less surely along until she came to the last house before the cemetery. A low stile was built into the fence beside the big gate where the funeral processions entered. Tillie brushed off the snow on the top plank and sat down, letting her eyes range over the snowy humps and hollows marking the graves of the newly dead, and those who had long ago given up their search. There was no sadness in her, as she regarded the plot. No kin of hers lay there, of course, since the Mennonites have their own plain garden for their dead. And death was no concern of hers; it could not happen, of course, to her. Old people died, but the thought of death and dying, even as she sat there regarding, pensively, the graves, was not her thought.

Perhaps it is not accurate to say that she was really thinking at all. But she was, at least, the sensitive film upon which a series of new and startling, even painful, sensations were being recorded. A rush of light had been released through the shutter left unexpectedly open, and the brief exposure produced unprecedented effects. The narrow promise of her life had been abruptly expanded. It seemed to her, sitting in the cold winter sunshine, on her lonely stile, that she was heir to a thousand sounds and sights and opening horizons of whose existence she had never even dreamed. The sun, the hills, the wandering road were hers, with a significance for her which they had never had before. A fierce, exultant thrill shook her. In that instant she realized, for the first time in her life, the glorious range of infinite possibility which existed in the world. All her life,

57

she now felt, rather than thought, she had passed in a narrow valley, curbed in a narrow street, where the tall walls shut out the view, and the dark thick trees shut out the light. This morning the walls had been pushed down, the trees shoved aside; she was out in the broad, free, widespread world, and the world was hers. She stretched out her arms to give herself to it, like a young bird launching itself in the air for the first time. For the moment, there was no need to cage this new possession in tangible boards or bricks. The possession was enough. She was ready to laugh aloud with the thrill and excitement. Thought and reason and memory were suspended for this hour. She would travel the world's roads to their ends, she would see people, hear music, sing songs. Light and life and song and the sounds of musical instruments would go with her. There was no physical or spiritual bondage, no duty and no rule, no sin and no salvation. She was giddy, gay, in tune with the universe and beyond the touch of mortal affliction. She was the centre of a radiance whose brilliance dimmed all her past into dull and almost invisible shadow. She could reach out and touch, with a strong but trembling finger, the quivering stuff of life itself, and there was nothing in that fabric to remind her of her own existence, up to that enchanted hour. Beyond care, beyond retribution, beyond reproach, she sat on her stile and felt herself pressed into the rhythm of the world, and rocked in it.

A sudden sound of bells brought her back to three-dimensional reality. In a rapid crescendo the distant sound became a clear, entrancingly gay jingle, and the crisp outline of a scarlet cutter imposed its swift pattern on the unmarked purity of the road. A slender brown horse danced, swaying, down the road before it.

As the cutter came abreast of the stile the driver pulled the horse to a sudden stop, the bells scattering broken shards of sound for a second or two after they stopped. The driver was a young man buried in a buffalo robe, his face grinning under a beaver hat.

"Hello there!" he called in a cheerfully mocking voice. "Looking over your prospects?"

Tillie smiled and shook her head. She was suddenly aware that her legs were stiff with cold, her feet numb and unlikely to bear her weight.

"They won't have to take you far, if you stay there long. You look at least half frozen now!"

Tillie got uncertainly to her feet, her left foot quite devoid of feeling as she put it to the ground. She steadied herself with her mittened hand on the post, and thumped her foot against the gate to stir feeling into it. The driver watched her curiously. The little mare stamped her feet with impatience.

"Come on and jump in. You're really cold." He held the buffalo robe invitingly open and reached out his hand to the girl. "Come on." Tillie hesitated. The mist which had been before her eyes all morning, the mood which had prevented her from going to church, from asking forgiveness for hardness of heart, was beginning to fade a little. She saw that she had placed herself in a highly dubious situation. In a moment she knew that the full significance of her behaviour on this Sunday morning would become clear to her.

"Hurry up," called George. "Maida's getting anxious."

Tillie limped soberly over the culvert on to the road and stepped into the cutter without a word. George threw her share of the robe over her, leaned over it, tucked it in, and pulled it taut behind her. Maida threw her spangle of sound into the frosty air.

"Going down around the Long Block," George informed his passenger. "Do you know this road?"

"No."

"Pretty road."

Tillie nodded. George turned, looking at her quizzically. "What the hell were you doing, wandering around the cemetery, a morning like this?"

59

"I wasn't wandering." Her voice came through chattering teeth.

"Say!" George's voice was full of concern. "You really are cold, aren't you? Duck down." He put his left arm around her, pulling the fur robe up until it almost covered her face. "Stay there, now, till you are a bit warm again." In the same tone he spoke to the mare.

"Come on, Maid! Put them down and take them up, and see how fast you can do it!"

For a few minutes they drove along in silence but for the tunes thrown free on the air by Maida's bells. Tillie felt warmth and sensation creep back into her bones. The road began to drop now, and cedars and pines hedged out the sky from Tillie's view in her smother of robe. She stirred and came to the surface.

"Feeling better?"

She nodded, and looked with interest at the deep green and white road.

"Different weather from the last time we went driving, isn't it?"

George looked impishly pleased to see the red blood rush to Tillie's face.

"You have a good memory for faces, surely."

"You aren't hard to pick out, you know," said George gently. "And while we're on the subject, how did you recognize me?"

"I knew the horse," said Tillie honestly, while George threw back his head and laughed.

"Well, Maida, I guess you're mine for keeps. Can't change horses or the lady won't know me."

"I would know you now," said Tillie, soberly.

"Sure?"

"Sure." They laughed together.

"Are you living in town now? I thought somehow, that you lived a long way from Kinsail?"

"About thirty miles. I'm taking a dressmaking course with Loretta Macklin. And music lessons, too."

"Well, well! Going to be a concert pianist, are you?"

"No."

"I'll have to come round some night and listen to you."

Tillie started. "Oh, no! I really don't play very well, yet, and—and—"

"Oh, I wouldn't mind that. I could look at you, anyway."

Tillie blushed carmine. George was laughing at her, she knew, and there were doubtless words which girls like the "Barbara" in the library book could have said back to this astonishing young man when he talked like that. But Tillie did not know any of them. In this free world into which she had launched herself there was need of equipment which she did not possess. George looked down at her, now, in her confusion; but he smiled in such a merry, amicable way that she smiled too, and settled, with no trace of embarrassment left, back into her buffalo robe. And over the driver and the passenger there fell a happy and significant silence.

Tillie reflected upon the oddity of her sensations, the calm, sure joyous feeling which being with this stranger induced within her. She produced for her inspection the incident of last fall, which she had carefully put aside, and buried deeply, not intending to look at it again. Then too, she found there had been, in that high, strange moment, this feeling of serenity and happiness. Perhaps, then, this is what happened to you, when you left your own road, and stepped, headstrong and wicked, into the world. They had warned her of fearful consequences, yet this was surely innocent joy? Like the discovery that her hands were good hands to draw music from the piano, and the deep satisfaction to find that she could create what Loretta said was "good line," on the drawing-board. It seemed to Tillie, sitting back warm and content in the silently gliding cutter, that her world, in the last few days, had miraculously flowered, and that she knew colour and space and sound for the first time. Although she scarcely stretched out her hand, new gifts daily dropped into it. It was hard to be penitent, to bring to mind regret and repentance for sins, both of omission and commission, which she knew were hers, when she felt herself wrapped about in gaiety and content. She was miles from home; miles away, by a conscious act of her own, from Keturah's disapproving house, and she would taste, exultingly, of new experience, judging for herself its quality.

She smiled up at George.

"Do you think she likes the cutter better than the buggy?"

George pulled Maida in to a walk.

"I don't know that she cares much what she pulls, as long as she's pulling something. I've got a little jogging-cart over at the barn that she'll be pretty surprised to feel behind her, in the spring. Just like a small piece of nothing at all, as you might say. She'll be able to make time with that, all right. Won't you honey?" Maida twitched her ears inquiringly. "Oh she's a wicked girl, she is, just a wicked girl." Maida flattened her ears and jumped back into a furious trot, breaking into her beautiful pace in the distance between telephone posts.

"Do you always go this fast?"

"Or faster," George grinned. "Going to take a flyer at the Kinsail fair, in the spring, just to get in trim, and then we'll maybe do a little touring in the fall, and pick up a ribbon or two."

"Do you mean," said Tillie, hesitating a little over the word, *"horse racing?"*

George looked down at her in surprise at the tone. "Sure," he said, easily. "You know, I always wanted to have a really fast horse. It feels wonderful just to sit behind one, and feel that it's your hand on the reins, and just what you say to them, or maybe how you say it, that makes them go all out, hell-for-leather, with every ounce of strength they've got." He let out an inch of line, and Maida lengthened her stride.

Tillie was silent with astonishment. Horse racing! This,

she knew, from remote sources, was an evil so far out of the range of possibility for people like her that there was no particular emphasis laid upon its dangers. It was a thing not merely representative of the World, all of which was not evil, although all was dangerous, but of the wicked section of the world. Unmentionable sins were connected with it, sins all blanketed under the caption of vice, so remote as to be wreathed in mist, and to have no real tangible body. It was shattering to find that horse racing could be entered into in such a simple fashion. There was a nice young man, and he had a horse, and he tried to make his horse go faster than some other nice young man's horse. It was, apparently, as simple as that. Tillie frowned in concentration. Could there be something wrong, really wrong, with that? There could be no question that it was sinful beyond contemplation, of course; but why? Tillie looked up at George to see if the Evil One had laid some mark upon his face, but she could discover none. It was a thin, smooth-looking face, under the brown envelope of fur, with a straight, unremarkable nose and a large, almost smiling mouth. His eyes were a deep blue, perhaps a little too close-set, and his black eyebrows met in a frowzy peak over the bridge of his nose. His chin was a good square chin; and, as far as Tillie could see, no sign of evil passion or devilish degradation was present in his countenance at all.

Again she felt that odd, vaguely uncomfortable sensation of being pulled off balance. Her world was whirling too fast, and presenting too many new facets to her unaccustomed eyes. A week ago today, just one week ago this very hour, and where had she been? A child in her father's house, a docile, obedient child, content and happy in her life and quietly thrilled by the promise of her future. Within one week she had become a girl who was vain of her hands, wanted to go to great cities to hear music, in evil places, read library books which could certainly not be true, and ran about the country on Sunday morning with a young man who practised *horse racing!* Suddenly Tillie was frightened. What would she be doing next? What other test had the Lord in store for her? It became increasingly clear, as the little mare pulled her so swiftly and so musically along the narrow, steeply-banked road, that these days had been testing days for her, and that she had failed them, every one. Her face grew sombre and still. How subtly had the devil laid his plans and how they must be laughing now, in Hell, to see her, in her black bonnet, and plain black coat, symbols of meekness and humility before the Lord, spinning along this strange road like a wicked woman of the world! The girl in the library book had ridden horses, on the Sabbath, dressed like a man almost, a thing which would be an utter abomination to the Lord; and even as Tillie had read of it, she shivered for the retribution which must fall on such a girl, after such an action. And now, here she was, preposterously, in a very similar situation. There wasn't much difference, and it seemed likely to be a difference of degree, rather than kind. Tillie pressed her hands together, under the buffalo, and tried to think of suitable beginnings to a prayer which would extricate her from this situation. But the words refused to come. She knew that she did not really repent, in her heart, and confession without full repentance is an empty thing. Gay innocence had fled.

Maida slid to a stop, panting a little, and blowing out her nostrils like the petals of a rose.

"Ever come here in the summer?"

Tillie shook her head, and looked at him, stricken and dumb. They were in the depths of the evergreen wood which surrounded Lake Marie. The unpainted wooden pavilion built out over the water for summer dancing was boarded up now, and presented that utterly desolate appearance which it is given to summer places to wear in winter time. The sun sparkled on the smooth stretch of snow out there, beyond them, but where they stood the air seemed dark with the pines, and cold, and above all, unutterably quiet. Even Maida stood affected by the lonely quality in the atmosphere, and held her bells rigidly still.

"We'll have to come down here, in the summer. There's dancing, Friday and Saturday nights. Music always sounds so much nicer over the water, doesn't it?"

Dancing? Tillie felt as if another blow had struck her. As if her cup of guilt were not already full, now had been added this new and devilish ingredient. *Dancing!* Her prayer fled from her throat.

George turned to look at her. She was staring ahead, her mouth held firm as if to keep it from trembling, her naturally pale skin flushed deep pink by the cold. Her dark hair waved crisply out from her bonnet, and sprang from her neckline in a clear-cut curve which brought George's heart into his mouth. He sighed deeply, threw the lines on the dashboard, and put both arms about her before she could possibly prevent it. He pressed his thin cheek hard against her cold rose-coloured cheek, then turned her face towards his with his strong right hand. Wordless, he kissed her firmly on the mouth, for a long minute. His eyes were only inches from hers when he spoke.

"I guess I've been wanting to do that," he said, "ever since last summer."

He withdrew his arms and picked up the reins.

"Come on, Maida."

They drove without speech from the little wood and along the remaining half mile to Kinsail. Tillie's face stung from the spray of icy pellets struck up by Maida's feet. She made no effort to protect her face.

"Which is your aunts' house?"

"The grey one, opposite the Mennonite church."

Tillie heard her words come forth without tremor. It might have been someone else who spoke. They sounded just as they would have before . . . before . . .

As the red cutter drew up in front of the house, a man and woman entered the gate. They both stopped and turned to watch her get numbly out from the rig, refusing George's outstretched arm for support. Tillie was not aware of them until she reached the silent pair, and found that she was looking into Simon's stern and desperate face, while Aunt Keturah watched them both.

7

*T*HE FRONT door closed behind the silent group. With the shutting of its solid panels, there behind the thick white curtains it seemed to Tillie that the sun had gone out, and all the bright beauty changed to an enclosing grey. This house became a kind of cave of refuge from the too bright light of day. She looked at Simon and her aunts without really seeing them. They moved about her in sombre, silent shapes, whose significance seemed scarcely clear. But she could still hear, or thought she could hear, the thin and distant music of the bells.

She moved towards the stairs, and climbed them like a woman in a trance. At the landing she half paused, to see the three faces turned questioningly up towards her. Because she was in this odd impressionable state, she suddenly knew, from their faces, as though they had been illuminated from within, a thousand things which she had never dreamed of before. Keturah's cold red hands, the joints and palms seamed with a lifetime of ceaseless work, became real and important to her. Those hands, and Aunt Elmina's heavily veined ones, stamped on her vision for that brief second before she fled them, on up the steps into her room, had known unceasing and, it seemed to her, unrewarding labour always—to keep things clean, to keep warmth in, cold out, to grow flowers and food, to cook, and scrub floors. Why? Why all labour and no joy? And nothing at the end but this narrow house, this narrow grey pattern, to show for it. And no future but more labour in store. Yesterday she would have taken Aunt Keturah's life completely for granted, only to have been overwhelmingly glad that she was to be saved from the spinsterishness of it. But now she saw that it had nothing to do with the spinster or the married state. It was in oneself that the future lay dormant. She saw her mother's hurried, bent back, and the thin triangle of her face, and asked herself, cast high on the crest of her emotional morning, "Is this all, must this be all there is?" Just the work, and the obedience, and the never stepping outside. The colours, the sounds, the cities, all shut out. And for what?

A tremor of fear ran over her, and she stumbled into her bedroom, shutting the door behind her.

All these earthly experiences were as nothing, less than nothing, compared with one day in the house of the Lord. And she had, for this whole day, forsaken God. His day, and she had not thought of Him, who had given His life for her, that she might not die, but live eternal in the Heavens. Suddenly she saw how easy it was to slip from the heavenly side to the sinners' road. She had forgotten God. She looked at herself with wonder. The face in the mirror appeared quite unchanged. Suddenly she could bear her weight of turbulence no longer. She burst into tears, and flung herself down on her knees by the bed, begging forgiveness for herself, a sinner before God, and before man. In an agony of emotion she prayed and wept, until she was utterly exhausted. She rose, quiet now, shattered but safe, from her ordeal. Her tired peace she had made with God. Now she must make it with man. The fearful, all obliterating surge she had felt, and been terrified to feel, when George kissed her had utterly subsided. She could think of him now, and the cutter ride, and the morning, with nothing but the faint shadow of significant remembrance.

Down in the parlour below her Simon stood and warmed his square hands at the little Quebec heater, glowing and hot now. Keturah came briefly in and turned the damper down.

"She's coming down. You can ask her what she's been doing. Where she's been."

Simon nodded, his face drawn tight, his jawbone working white against his cheek.

"She might tell *you*. You have a right to know, anyway."

Keturah twisted a stray hair up from her neck into the knob at the back. Her thin grey face was streaked red with fear and anger.

When Tillie came in Simon was sitting on the piano stool, fingering the pages of the hymnal with trembling, awkward fingers. Tillie was calm now; still pale from her storm, but composed. She had brushed her hair into a severe sleek line over her broad forehead, and the new style changed her disconcertingly, to Simon. She looked almost like a stranger. There was something in her quiet dignity as she stood before him that snatched his questions from his mouth.

She offered him her hand much as a stranger might have done, too, and her voice, although it trembled a little on the first pair of words, quickly levelled out into unassailable composure.

"Well, Simon! How are you?"

They shook hands abruptly, Tillie withdrawing hers at once.

"Tillie—Tillie—" Simon's voice trailed off in indecision, but the girl's went inexorably and evenly on.

"I didn't expect you this Sunday. How is it that you are here?"

"Didn't you get my letter, though? I thought it would get here last night for sure."

"We didn't get the mail last night."

Simon nodded, comprehendingly, although he was far from comprehending. He knew that he could scarcely wait for the mail to come in, at the College, to see if there would be word from Tillie, or from home.

"There is a big meeting next Saturday, for all the students, and I cannot come then, so I came this week instead. But it is pretty expensive to come. This time, and then not till Christmas again, I guess."

Tillie looked at him gravely. For that moment it did not seem to matter whether he came or went, or came again. She had, in a measure, let go of life, up in her bedroom, washed clean of volition. She could not so soon lay hold of it again. The sweet rushing power she had felt as she pleaded for forgiveness had washed all earthly thought and aspiration from her. Now she seemed in suspension, walking between two worlds, but still nearer heaven than earth.

"I see," she said.

"I wanted to be here for the quarterly meeting, too."

"Quarterly meeting this morning, was it?"

"Yes. This morning was the quarterly meeting. You forgot it was today?"

"I did not remember."

"There was a grand testimony after. Nearly the whole congregation came to the Lord's Supper."

Simon looked at Tillie with stricken eyes. Consternation close to grief etched deep lines from his thin nose to his curiously heavy mouth.

"You forgot the Lord's Supper, Tillie?"

His voice fell gently on her ears, sad, and almost unbelieving. Tillie was silent. After a long pause she walked slowly towards the door. Her face was sorrowful.

"I shall not forget, again."

Simon followed her, speaking earnestly.

"Since I have been away, down there, I find I need more and more to come close to God. The world is too much with us, Tillie. Too much with us, there. For you, though, here, it is not like that." He spread his hands out

69

to include the house. "Here there is not the distraction." He looked about him, uneasily loosening his coat about the shoulders, as if it had grown tight in the back. His voice was low and tense.

"I am glad it is not for long that we are to be apart." He put his hands gently on her shoulders, looking down at her with avid eyes. "Every day I think it is now one day less, till we can be together, for always, praise the Lord."

Tillie looked at him wanly, smiling very slightly. There were so many things which must be said to Simon, but this situation she could not deal with now. She had spent too much, this morning, and her shriving at the foot of her bed had emptied her still further of energy, initiative, and perhaps courage too. Just now she must have rest and spiritual solitude. Simon, glancing first at the open door, put his long arms about her, and pulled her to him. But she resisted, apathetically.

"Not now," she said. "I must help with the dinner."

Simon dropped his arms, and they walked out together to the dining-room.

Cold chicken lay sliced on a big white platter, and with it Aunt Keturah served brown crusted potatoes and coleslaw. Glasses of pepper relish and pickled cabbage with beets made pools of colour on the white cloth. Aunt Elmina nervously pressed her napkin with her little hands, glancing up occasionally in embarrassment at the presence of young people who planned to be married. The pleasant burnt smell of the Shantz brand of coffee mingled with the lovely fragrance of newly opened raspberries. A mince pie warmed in the oven.

Simon's face brightened at the sight of the table. There was little answering lightness in any of the other faces, and he ate through two platefuls of chicken and potatoes in almost absolute silence. Elmina never spoke unless first addressed, Tillie had nothing to say, and Keturah nothing which she could bring herself to say. Simon wiped his mouth, after his first two helpings, and sighed.

"It is not like the dinner we have at the College."

Keturah took up the conversation.

"You do not have enough to eat, down there?"

"Oh, jah, there is enough, if you can eat it. But there is not the taste."

Simon described circles in the air, to indicate the lack in the food.

"There is—" he frowned, to make it clear—"there is no taste. It is all dry, and I am not so hungry, maybe. I am always thinking there of how it is at home. I do not eat well."

"You will stay there another year?"

Simon shook his head. "I thought, when I went, that I would stay two years, but now, now I do not know."

He looked searchingly at Tillie.

"It is a good place, you know, a good place; but there are some things—there are some things there—that, well, I cannot think that in some things there, they are just quite true to the teachings of God."

"But it is the Bible College? They explain its word, and reveal its meaning?"

Simon sighed. "It is hard to know. There are men there who teach, but sometimes what they teach is hard for me to understand. What they say I do not remember, in the word of God. But they are good men. Only, it is different to what I thought, some, and they are not just our own people."

Tillie looked directly at him.

"What will you do then, if you—"

"If I don't go back another year, we could be married, in the spring, and get started on the land?" He looked directly at Tillie, his face grave, his eyes veiling deep desire in the sombre shadow of utilitarian purpose.

"We thought, maybe, when you went away from home, you would not want to come back and just be a farmer." Keturah's voice held a mixture of light scorn and anxiety for reassurance. Simon quickly answered her.

71

"Our Lord was a humble carpenter, Keturah."

"Amen," said Elmina, unexpectedly.

"Mr. Wilson is moving from the back farm, though, this spring?"

"He goes in March, if I am to have the farm. But he could stay, if I do not. There are things that he could do, on the farm, which he does not find time to do. If it is left too long, the land will go back."

Simon spread out his hands, brown and thick palmed, with the thumb as big as the wrist of a child.

"Sometimes I think," he said, "that there is nothing there, at the College, which will show me the way to be a better witness for the Lord than I can be now. Maybe all the study, and the writing, and the setting down of words which are not God's words, is only a hindrance to me. When I am writing down the words, I could be praising God, and bringing blessed souls home to Him, bless His name."

Keturah nodded in agreement, and Tillie looked at him with that strange new detachment which irked and puzzled him beyond endurance.

"Perhaps it is just a waste of the gift of life that is mine. In the vineyard of the Lord I am a worker, and must be out and working while it is yet day, for the night cometh, and no man can work. I think I will not stay there another year. Lest the fire burn and consume me, before the good has been wrought."

Simon stood up and, hands behind his back, his head bowed, walked up and down the room, in complete self-forgetfulness, murmuring words of praise and thanksgiving. Tillie stood by the window, listlessly leaning against the wall, looking out with unseeing eyes upon the snowbound street.

Simon with a great sigh pulled himself out of his absorption, and became aware of her again.

"Maybe we could take a walk, Tillie, and we can talk then?"

Tillie shook her head. "I am tired, Simon. If you don't mind, I will rest a little. Perhaps then, later, we can walk."

"Just as you like, then. I must go and see brother Huber, and you might come with me, I thought." His face showed weariness and disappointment. He might not have been there at all, for all Tillie had to say to him. "You are tired now? So sometimes you are tired, too. I never knew you to say that before. You have been working too hard, perhaps. Sewing all day, and the music is tiring, too, perhaps."

"It is not that. I will be all right a little later. Just now I am tired."

"What is it, Tillie? What is the matter with you today?" He put his hand out to her, but she drew back. "You are not sick?" Tillie shook her head, with an infinitely weary movement.

"It is all right, Tillie, between you and God?"

Tillie nodded. She was conscious of only one desire— to get away and be alone. How long could he keep from asking her what she did this morning, and why she stepped like a drunken woman out of that cutter, instead of greeting him gladly in the house of the Lord? When she told him, she must be stronger than this. His voice was gentle, solicitous, and the unspoken question only the sharper for not being asked. She felt grateful to him, but no more than that, smiled briefly at him, and went soberly upstairs.

Simon, mystified and dejected, reached for his heavy black coat and shrugged himself into it, poking the long fringed ends of his stretched knitted scarf into the armholes of his vest. Keturah, in the kitchen, wiped her hands roughly on the long roller towel, pulling it out to its full length so that she could see into the hall, at the same time.

"Well, what did she tell you?"

Simon's face grew stern and he shook his head. Now that she had gone, the door closed behind her, and there was no sound from her room, he felt himself baffled and

73

frustrated. He stepped out into the street with a curt gesture of farewell. Why should she not explain, simply, how she had come to be away from church, and in the strange man's cutter, on the Sabbath morning? And if she would not, why could he not ask her, outright?

There was always, he reflected, that aloofness about her, when anyone questioned her. A certain lack of humility. He had noticed it before. Perhaps she was humble before the Lord, but she surely was not humble before man. There was an interesting and troubling point here. When she was less tired, she would come to him, and tell him what had caused this sadness in her. He was sure that there was some small grief at the bottom of her trouble, in spite of her cool withdrawal. It was sadness that caused that withdrawing from the sympathy of man. But she must not move away from him. He was all but her husband, and please God, before long he would be that. She must come to him in all her joys and in all her sorrows. Together, at the foot of the throne, they would live in gladness, rejoicing in the Lord.

It would not be long now. His steps became more rapid, his stride increased. He strode on, oblivious to sound and sight, dwelling in visions of the future. Perhaps they could be married in May! He rushed along the street as if in his headlong career he could overtake the months, and bring the time of speechless joy within his grasp.

He would not go back to the college for another year. There was nothing, now, in his way. When he saw Tillie, he wondered how he had ever been so blind as to suppose that he could put off their marriage for two years, until some mythical educational development should be his. Down there, at the students' meetings, he felt himself a stranger, out of tune with their life. Those other men and women could enter into a gaiety and lightness which were foreign to him. Their joking and raillery savoured strongly of this world. They were more of it than he, and less in fear of hell-fire.

74

This morning, back in his own bleak atmosphere, he had felt himself expand and breathe deep again. The touch of the spirit was strong in him, and he could feel fires kindling within which merely smouldered in the city. Down there they dealt with the dry bones of something they called religion, a thing separate from all other activities of life. But the love of God ran through him like a devouring flame. It had nothing to do with church histories, or creeds, or sets of rules, but with the living and being, in the Lord. The breath of the prophet was his breath, and the tongue of Elijah his tongue. He too could call down fire from Heaven, and not because of the books and the notes and the studying, but because the grace of God was working in his heart, and with Him all things are possible. Think of it! *With God all things are possible!*

He was almost running by the time he reached the old bishop's house, in his eagerness to tell him that he was nearly ready to start, after all. All things are possible! No need for fear, or thought of failure, or distrust, or weak wondering. All things are possible. Hallelujah!

The street lights were blinking on when Tillie woke from her long deep sleep. The poles across the street cast long blue shadows almost the width of the road, in subtle contrast to the pale gold snow under the lamps. It was so still that the crackle of the fire in the darkened house made a noise of importance. Unconsciously preserving the quiet, Tillie tiptoed downstairs and lit the kitchen lamp.

Again the familiar areas of the house, its narrowness, and its warmth, seemed security and comfort to her. Within walls such as these, within these grey boundaries, dwelt safety and assurance. These were her birthright, and in these places she was at home. She had wandered ever so little, and her instant reward had been discontent and humiliation. In one day the Lord had shown her His will, and the results of disobedience. Outside these walls, and walls such as these which a gracious God had arranged to

75

be hers, lay dangers which she had been far from realizing. And the greatest of these, the insidious beginning of losing faith—that this seed should have been planted within her heart, after such slight contact with the world—this frightened her. She was ashamed. But now she was safe again. And Simon would soon be back; it was nearly time for church again. She would tell Simon. He would see that she did not escape again, and she could go on, in the peace and gladness of heart which had been hers.

Simon's tall figure, lengthened monstrously by the light from the street lamp, folded its shadow and came in. Tillie greeted him easily, and with her accustomed warmth. He walked swiftly towards her, smiling with satisfaction to see her refreshed and gay.

"Are you better now? That is good. I don't like to see you like that, Tillie."

"I'm all right now. This morning, I must tell you, I think the Evil One was at work in me. I did not want to go, at all, to the meeting, and went out away from the village, to prevent myself going. I sat by the cemetery and thought envious thoughts, and wished for things— I don't know—things that—" Her throat contracted, and she could not go on. She looked anxiously at Simon, but he was silent, waiting. She moistened her lips.

"I was very cold. Mr. Bingham drove me home."

It was done, almost done. What had she been dreading? What was the matter with her, that she had been in such a storm? It was cold, and Mr. Bingham drove me home. No need for more than that, except—except that Simon must be told. But Simon spoke.

"They say he is a good man, although not a Christian. I cannot see how that can be so. But it was a good thing he did, to bring you home. But, Tillie, you must not run from the Lord like that, again. You know, we cannot ever really escape Him, and we must not try. He is our ever present help, in trouble."

"Yes, I know," agreed Tillie, softly.

76

"Keturah said there was a book, Tillie?"

Tillie went upstairs and came back with the library book. Simon looked intently at her as he took it. In his hands the jacket, which had seemed so smiling and attractive yesterday, now seemed foreign to her.

"I got it from the library. And read it." It was hard for her, always, to admit wrong, and this time it was no easier—and still that other thing, hanging over her, to tell, too. Simon turned over the pages, pausing to read a few hard-won sentences occasionally.

"I don't know why you would want to read this kind of thing, Tillie. It will take all of our lifetime to learn to know the truth and beauty of God's work. There is no time to spend on that which is not true." He read on, and then looked at her again. "You have read all, all of this book?"

"Yes, Simon."

His eyes filled with a slow rage. "To touch filth is to become ourselves filthy. I wish you had not seen this thing. I wish your eyes had never read these words. You will never be again the same. Not quite the same as before. Oh, that is how it is, there is no safety, no purity, except in the Lord, and close, close to Him. Pray that you may be forgiven, for this sullying of yourself."

He closed the book violently, lifted off the stove lid and dropped the book in on the glowing coals. Tillie stood motionless, watching him. He dusted off his hands, as if impurity might still adhere, and looked sternly at her.

"It is in just such ways as these that the Devil begins his work. I wish you had not read it. Tomorrow, go to the library, and pay the price of the book, and never go to that place again. Ask the Lord to wipe out from your mind the memory of those words. Let us pray."

They dropped to their knees and Simon prayed for light and the revelation of God's truth, which was their every need.

His face was transfused with a delicate ecstasy when

77

they rose. To pray together, just the two of them, seemed to him an earnest of their life together. He took her hands and looked down at her.

"Tillie, this afternoon I saw the Bishop. I am to start here, after the summer. Maybe, then, we could get married, say in May?"

Tillie looked thoughtfully at him. "I am not through with Loretta until the first of June, though. Perhaps then —we can see what my father says. It seems so soon, Simon!"

"Not soon enough, for me." Simon bent back her head and kissed her, fervently. His face was warm and soft, upon her cheeks. She noticed for the first time that his thick lips pressed out surprisingly flat and thin, as if they had no muscle, only soft tissue, in them. He had not kissed her like that before. She was vaguely disconcerted. But she put her arms about his neck, and kissed him too, and was comforted. Simon tightened his grasp, and his face flushed. A new intent look in his eyes surprised and faintly alarmed her. She disengaged herself firmly from his arms. The time had gone by when she could ever tell Simon that George had kissed her.

"We must go to the meeting, if we are going," she said.

The strong fresh voices of the women, singing without distracting instruments, fell on Tillie's ears as she went into the church like the sweet winds of spring upon a winter-weary heart. She sat at ease in the bare church, at home again. And when the old bishop raised his arms and dismissed them with the words "May the peace that passeth all understanding rest upon and abide with you" she felt that peace was indeed upon her, and abiding with her.

8

*T*WO DAYS before Christmas the valley village of Kinsail lay deep in soft snow. All day sleighs had slipped in from the country bringing fat geese and turkeys and swollen coils of rich country sausage to the famous Kinsail Christmas market. Faint silver traces of bell sound came back down the hill roads into the country as farmers returned home, sleighs lighter and pockets heavier. By five o'clock, Main Street was clear again of the cutters and sleighs. From the power-house down Lock Street a thunderous preliminary pounding set up, quickened, translated itself into a giant hum, and the lights came on.

In George Bingham's drugstore, light flickered and careened off the big blue and red bottles in the window. These insignia of his calling were heavily wreathed in Christmas green which George had gathered himself, out along the swamp road, in the noon hour. Between these giant jewels of bottles lay boxes of silver toilet-sets; beautiful slender combs and squat brushes, long-handled delicate mirrors, shrouded in folds of pleated pink satin. Perfume in cut-glass bottles, slender Venetian glass bottles with a bulb atomizer netted over in pink silk, and handpainted china hair receivers settled themselves provocatively about the toilet-sets.

Billy Davis looped gold tinsel over the branches of a small Christmas tree at the back of the showcase.

"That the last box of tinsel, Bill?"

"That's all, Mr. Bingham. Went out like hot cakes, didn't it?"

Loretta Macklin leaned over the velvet-hung railing and regarded the assortment of glimmering objects with a faintly sardonic smile. She indicated the display with a brusque gesture.

"Getting the suckers with that stuff, George?"

"What do you mean, suckers? Just giving the local boys a look at what it's possible to get the best girl for Christmas. And they've been glad to know, too."

"Anybody buy one of those fancy sets for me, do you think?"

"Well, naturally, they don't always tell me, but I think it's highly likely that you'd rate one, wouldn't you?"

"Might have, twenty years ago. You've just got around too late with the goods. What are you going to do for Christmas, George?"

"Stay here. What about you?"

"Clearing out. Can't take the revelry. Need a family, for this kind of thing. I always go down to the city for a few days, get myself some new sensations to last for the winter."

"Coward, eh?"

"That's right. I'll bring you a report of what goes on, in the bright lights."

"Thanks, Loretta, I'll be looking forward to that."

"Come in and see me when I get back. I'll let you know. Maybe Tuesday night, for supper?"

"Fine."

"We'll kill a fatted calf, and the orphans will celebrate."

"Merry Christmas, then!"

George grinned and opened the door for her, stepping out for a moment into the street.

All the stores on Main Street stayed open for evening hours, this week. There was an unaccustomed air of expansiveness and gaiety in the greetings which passed among the walkers down the snowy street.

"Seasonable weather, George!"

"Merry Christmas, George, if I don't see you again!"

High school girls in groups, with bundles under their arms, happily festive, walked along the street. The Anglican rector had paused under a lamp in conversation with the Methodist minister's daughter, who was home from college for the holidays. He called to George; and the girl, nodding brightly, went on home, her fingers curled around an assortment of interesting-looking mail.

"Wonderful season, isn't it? I was just saying to Miss Ashdown, the best thing about going to the University, I thought, in my young days—and I still think—is going home for Christmas. Don't you agree?"

"Well, as a matter of fact, I don't know much about it. I—well, I'm afraid it wasn't one of my experiences, Mr. Barclay-Thomas."

"Really? Well, sorry you missed it. By the way, I am glad I ran into you. My sister and I were wondering if you would share our Christmas dinner with us? Just a small party, but we would be *so* happy to have you."

"It's very kind of you, sir, to think of including me. Please thank Miss Barclay-Thomas for me, but I'll not be able to accept."

The Rector waited a moment, to find whether any reason would be offered; and since there was none, he prepared to go his way.

"Well, then—I'm sorry. I'm sorry. Perhaps, during the season—drop in on us. Glad to have you. And a merry Christmas to you."

"And the same to you, sir."

This Christmas business had been quite unexpectedly trying for George. It takes time, evidently, to learn to be festive, when one has not had the experience. But he would not intrude on other people's family affairs. He would eat at the Mansion House, and be a trouble to nobody. Nor, and this was another consideration, would he incur obligations by accepting this special hospitality. The Mansion House was the best solution. No obligation there that he could not pay for.

There was something a little bleak and disappointing about it, though. He was too entirely isolated in this flurry of family warmth. Everybody ought to have some real family, for the Christmas season anyway.

Two people stopped to look into the showcase. They were a Mennonite preacher, and a woman of his faith. As George turned to speak to them, he saw that the lovely face under the forbidding bonnet was Tillie's and that she was smiling up at Simon. They turned away without noticing him. He heard a light drift of laughter blow along the street, and they were gone.

An incredibly pretty woman, he thought, even in that rig. I wonder how she'd look in something decent. Walks well too. That man must be over six feet by three or four inches, and she doesn't look any dwarf beside him. She must be five foot eight, I'd say. Just an inch shorter than I am. And looks taller, I expect. All women look taller.

He went in, grinning to Billy.

"One more day, old timer, till the great festivity, eh? Are you having a turkey, Billy?"

"Always have a goose, Mr. Bingham. Turkey for New Year's. And my mother says, Mr. Bingham, if you haven't any place better to go, why we'd be glad to have you at our house."

"I appreciate that, Billy. You tell your mother I thank her kindly, and there's nothing I'd like better, but I can't do it, not this year."

"Oh, well. I didn't expect you could, you know, but I just thought I'd ask. Should I take these prescriptions round now, or can you manage without me?"

"I'll just have to try to get along," said George soberly. "Billy, you know that girl who was looking in the window?"

"Girl? I didn't see any girl."

"Just a minute ago, with a preacher. Looking in."

"Oh! You mean that Minyinite one? I thought you meant a girl. That's Tillie Shantz. Lives up Reesorville way. Peaches Station. Picked fruit up that way last summer, and the year before, too. They've got a helluva great big farm up there. 'Bout the best in the country, they told me. The old man breeds them big black-and-white cows, and there's two hired men and a hired girl, all the time."

"They're well off, are they?"

"Sure they're well off. Nothing to spend their money on, except more farm and more cows. Guess Tillie came in to learn to play the piano, mostly. But she's going to marry the preacher this spring, I hear, so it won't do her no good."

George found himself wondering what a man like that would give his girl for Christmas. Judging from the expression of his back, he thought, he would probably give her a pound of humbugs and a bottle of eucalyptus. The candies in a transport of extravagance and the tincture for a cold in the chest. She'd need it, too, if she kept on spending her Sundays sitting on stiles, overlooking the cemetery.

He whistled softly to himself.

Simon followed Tillie into the crowded train and stood guarding the seat while she put her parcels in the rack.

In the double seat at the end of the coach four boys coming home from the University sat in extravagant ease, singing enthusiastically to the banjo one of them played.

"And o-on my breast ca-harve a tur-ur-urtle dove,
To signify I died of love (died of love)."

Tillie laughed and looked at Simon, and found his face sombre, and his eyes dark, oblivious to the gaiety of the home-coming people, and scornful of it. The dark eyes lit when he spoke to Tillie, but he seemed to find the place inimical to conversation. The boys in the corner with gay abandon had thrown their fur hats up into the wire baskets, and rode the train as if it were their private car. But Simon kept the stiff black hat still on his head, and looked gloomily before him. He looked so stern, as he sat there,

that Tillie had a momentary flick of alarm. Had she done
something to displease him? Surely not, since as she had
walked along the street he had been communicative enough.
But once in the lighted, crowded train he had lost speech.
It was, she thought, looking reflectively at him, often like
this, in the company of strangers. He was so palpably
not one of these. He would give them no words. He looked
with distrustful, almost accusing eyes on the young men
in the double seat, who were blaring forth now:

> "——arbor aevo,
> May she ever thrive-o,
> Tum ti dum de dum de
> Alma Ma-a-a-ter!"

The passengers, with the single exception of Simon,
smiled indulgently at the singers. Even old Tommy Allison,
who had been conductor on this run to the terror of two
generations of schoolboys, relaxed his habitual grim expression. The boy with the basket of candy came lurching
down the aisle:
"Choclitz, megazeen; choclitz, megazeen!"
The boys in the corner fell on him and bantered noisily.
The train slowed for Miller's grade and the thin brakeman,
who had been working this line almost as long as Tommy
Allison, came in with his long pole, adjusting the lights,
and called the station.

Tillie sat quietly beside Simon, speculating on the kind
of life the people in front of her led, in whatever place
they lived. They were just young people, too, like Simon
and herself. But they were married, and the blond elab-
orately-curled head of the wife lay on her husband's
shoulder while he talked to her almost continuously in low
tones. He held her huge plumed hat on his lap, and
under its cover kept her hand in his. Sometimes the fair
curls nodded in assent as the uninterrupted communication
proceeded. Tillie wondered how it would be when she

84

and Simon were married. Soon, now, they would be together like this. Perhaps the other people on the coach thought they were married already. She glanced at Simon, finding it difficult to recover in that stern face, tonight, the Simon who had been the crux of her dreams.

He bent over and whispered urgently, "I wish I was going with you, Tillie."

"It's too bad you have to go back tomorrow," she said, "but for one day you really must see your mother." She smiled at him in a warm and understanding way that almost brought his arms about her.

"Yes. Yes. I know. And the church down there, of course they are expecting me back."

"Perhaps Brother Bricker will be well again, soon, though, and you can come out then, for a holiday."

Simon nodded.

The train stopped to take water, just before the passenger coach crossed Main Street. Tillie pressed her head against the window, to see if she could see her father along on the platform. There was a crowd waiting, but she could not see Levi.

Two little boys stood, half leaning, against a lamp post. Their caps were too big for the small faces underneath them. The older child's ears stood out from his head, the deformity increased in appearance by the ill-fitting cap and the tufts of hair below it. She observed that they shifted from one foot to the other, keeping their eyes away from the faces of the people who waited for this Christmas holiday train with a little heightening of the pleasure they took in waiting for the train every day of their lives. A young cadet from the Military College, resplendent in scarlet-lined cloak and consciously straight as a guardsman, came to stand beside them. While she watched them the children noticed the cadet and walked almost furtively away from his exotic splendour towards the engine end. Tillie unconsciously straightened her own shoulders and held her head higher. The train slowed down and the children

stopped again. The smaller of the two stared now with fixed
attention on the slowing wheels, seeming to remark with
wonder the movement of the shaft and the hiss of the
brakes. The other boy looked into the windows of the
coach, and Tillie realized that it was Lambert. They were
like little strangers in their heavy winter clothes. She was
conscious of a vague irritation that they should look so
alien to the scene, graceless as hobbledehoys.

The brakeman opened the door, called out "Peaches,"
and fastened it back.

Tillie stood up and reached for her parcels.

"One peach, all right," said one of the boys in the
corner. He sprang from his seat and leapt down the aisle
before Simon could move. "Allow me, madam. This yours,
and this?"

Tillie smiled at him. "Why, thank you." She was
blushing furiously.

Another of the quartet bounded up. "Anything else?
Got a bag, lady?"

Tillie pointed laughingly to the blunt-nosed suitcase
between the seat backs.

"Right you are, miss, this way out then." And they
shouldered the suitcase and made off with the luggage.

Simon stood like a pillar of smouldering fire, speechless.

In a minute they were back. "All out, lady!" They
bowed extravagantly towards her. Out on the platform
Tommy Allison pulled out his big silver watch, put one
hand on the rail and called menacingly, "Boa—oa—rd!"

Tillie gave Simon a startled glance, and touched his arm
in farewell. "I'll write," she whispered, and hurriedly left
the train. As she passed the singers they broke with a
good deal of discord into "Everything is peaches down
in Georgia" and subsided into helpless laughter. They
crowded over to the station side, however, in time to wave
to her as the train pulled out. She raised her hand in
answer, and called "Merry Christmas!"

She searched the windows for Simon, so that she might

86

wave to him too, but he had not moved from his seat. The glowering look on his face served only as fuel for the merriment of the boys.

With a quick glance Tillie saw that her luggage was piled on the seat under the notice board. Lambert shambled down the platform to meet her.

Tillie looked down at him, critically loving. "Time I came home," she said, slipping swift fingers under the flaps of his cap and pushing the rough hair back out of sight. "Where's Ben?"

Lambert shifted a shoulder towards the other end of the platform. "Up there lookin' at the train."

The train whistled for the bend and left behind it an exaggerated quiet. Ben wordlessly joined them. Tillie beckoned to him, and gave his hair and cap a similar tidying. "Stand up straight," she said, "you'll be round-shouldered. Didn't Papa come?"

Lambert shook his head. "He had to stay home to finish the chores. Joe, he's gone home for Christmas."

"So you two came all alone, then? Getting to be big boys, aren't you?"

The children smiled with pleasure. "Jah, with Diamond, too."

Tillie looked across the station yard to the hitching-posts, where a tall heavy bay waited under his blanket, hitched to the low home-made cutter.

"Who drives him?"

Lambert straightened up. "I can drive him all right. Papa says I can look out for him."

"Are you all ready to go, then? Not supposed to get your hair cut?"

"We just had to meet you, that's all."

"Come along, then." The little boys stepped down from the platform into the snow. "Aren't you going to carry my grip, though?"

Ben was making the hissing sound of an engine starting up, and describing circles in the air with both hands, and did not hear her. But Lambert looked at her in surprise. "Can't you carry them things yourself?"

Tillie looked for a long minute at the young cadet, laden with the bags that a trim looking woman, who must be his mother, had bestowed upon him. He was laughingly describing himself as the pack-camel of Peaches Station.

She bent down and picked up her things. "Oh yes," she said, "I can carry them."

9

"WHAT DO you think, Betsey, Tillie is all right?" Levi straightened up with a grunt from close observation of his swollen feet. He stood, painfully, in their narrow bedroom off the dining-room. The room was crowded, the big bed against a wall, a massive dresser against another, and a heavy hand-made cradle still resting, empty, at the bottom of the bed. When there had been the children, one after the other, in the cradle, they had been even more crowded. But it had not occurred to them to use either of the bigger rooms at the top of the closed stairway. A farmer must be near the barn, must be able to reach his animals quickly. And in the winter, he must be near the stoves, to feed the fires, late and early. Before grey dawn faded white over the orchard which he could see through the single small window, Levi was out. Always first, before the hired men. That made a good farm. It was a long time since either Betsey or Levi had really seen the cradle. It was like a wall, or a ceiling, that it was not possible to move.

Levi struck his ankle sharply on the rocker.

"Ach! That thing! We must take it out from there, Betsey! Soon, perhaps, Tillie will have use for it." He sighed, heavily. "It does not seem long, does it, since she was there, herself?"

"It seems long enough, in some ways."

Betsey laid aside the little white house-bonnet and took down her greying fair hair. She braided it into a thin short braid and disappeared under a long-sleeved flannel nightgown.

"But there in Kinsail she has not got fat, Betsey, do you think?"

"She is fat enough. A woman does not need to be like a sow."

"It is a good thing, though, for a young woman not to be too skinny."

"Tillie is not skinny. She is well enough as she is. You worry about her too much, Levi. She is well enough. Though she might be better fed, at home, here."

"You were fat, Betsey, do you remember it? Before we were married, though. It is living with me, maybe, which has worked it off you?" Levi smiled at his wife, putting out a big hairy hand to pat her grey flannel shoulder.

"When there is so much to be done, someone must do it." Betsey spoke without emotion, stating a simple fact. "There is always work, when there are men to feed, and chickens, and children in the house. Put some of that liniment on your feet. It is on the top shelf of the sideboard."

"They sting some, tonight." Levi hobbled out into the dark room, lurching to save the tender spots on his bare feet. The house was quiet now, and black, save where a long strip of pale winter moon stretched through the window over the brown painted floor. A whispering laughter came from the room above. Levi smiled to himself, in the darkness. "Tillie is talking to Bertha, and telling

89

her all about Simon, I don't doubt, and filling her head with envious thoughts, of being a married woman, and a big house all her own. Thank God he is a good man."

Betsey knelt in the strip of moonlight, when the lamp had been doused, and prayed her silent prayer. Then she climbed up on the high feather mattress, and worked her way on her knees, to the other side. Levi sat on the edge of the bed, rubbing the aromatic stuff into the hard calloused skin of his feet. The moonlight found him, now, and illuminated the big grizzly beard and the heavy round shoulders.

Then he dropped carefully to his knees, too, and prayed, but not in silence. He prayed loudly for the good and the salvation of all in the house. And for a special blessing on the daughter who was again under her father's roof. He made acknowledgment that she was, after all, only a gift and a loan to him, and that he was less her father than was her heavenly one. He could trust that the Lord would care for her, since, if he, her earthly father, loved her so much, how much more must her heavenly father.

"All the same, Betsey," he said, as he climbed into the bed, obliterating the hills and hollows already formed by Betsey's thin passage, "All the same, about Tillie, now, I don't know—"

"Well, it was you who let her go, Levi."

"Jah, jah, I know. It is right to learn—but—"

"She can't have come to any great harm," said Betsey, drily. "After all, she's only been away three weeks."

"Is it only three weeks? I thought it was longer. Oh, Betsey, you know, I wonder, maybe, if she isn't too young—"

"Go to sleep. And let other people sleep."

The voices ceased to sound from above, and in a few minutes the moonlight shone over the farmhouse with none awake to mark its progress.

In the morning the house was full of movement. Two turkeys, perhaps a little over twenty pounds each, stuffed to bursting with bread and onions, hissed and sang in the oven. Tillie and her mother and Bertha stepped quickly about the big yellow-floored kitchen, peeling potatoes, and scraping carrots, and running down to the cellar for pumpkin and mince pies, all ready to be warmed. They dished out apple butter and schmierkase, chopped winter cabbage into salad, sent the little boys to the pits for the reddest apples, and supplied them with bags of black walnuts to hammer out on the stone steps.

By noon three visiting teams of horses were tied in hospitable stalls, and three sleighs rested in the driveway. The boys brought in the summer tables from the shed, and at one o'clock twenty-four people, closely related to each other by marriage or by blood, sat down to Christmas dinner. Beside the children's places lay brown paper bags, saved for the purpose, and filled with home-made candy. After the meal there were exchanges of gifts. Simple things like hand-knitted mitts, for the men, double knitted and surpassingly ugly, in dark brown and red mixtures. Women received bottles of hand lotion, made by special recipe at home, and bottles of pickles and jellies, as from one house to another. Levi gave Betsey a pair of leather fur-lined gloves, to keep her chilly hands warm on the long drive to church. Tillie brought her mother a warm black spencer. Extravagance in any form was contrary to the teaching of the church. Lavish giving of presents to people who had, thanks to the goodness of the Lord, all and more than they needed was contrary to custom, and considered in bad taste.

But for Tillie, this Christmas, it was a little different. The women went into the dark spare bedroom off the parlour, and came out with clumsy parcels in their hands. Nodding mysteriously, and with significant smiles, the visiting aunts and married cousins presented Tillie with heavy sheets and pillow-cases. The old ladies, whose faces were bland and smiling, their furrowed hands clasped over swelling stomachs, watched her as she opened the unwieldy bundles, inexpertly wrapped in newspaper, and tied with coarse string. A woollen quilt made of sombre patches from men's winter suits and coats, and a bright cotton quilt star-patterned in white and turkey red, added strong notes of utility to gifts not noticeably erring in the direction of frivolity. They were lifetime presents, these; a pair of hand-woven blankets weighing twenty-eight pounds to the pair, and a length of homespun white linen cloth which would make a man's Sunday shirts to last into his old age. Fingers creased with the spinning of coarse brown flax felt the white linen appreciatively.

"Jah, it is good, Keturah, this piece is a good piece."

Those hands were capable of judging, and they had earned their rest on the black billows of Sunday skirts. These were the essential accoutrements of life that they were handing on to Tillie. Of these things, and things like them, strong and useful and good, without ornament and disdainful of design, a rich life could be made. The Lord will provide for His children; but not unless they show themselves worthy of His care.

The men passed into the parlour and ate the nuts that the little boys had shelled, leaving the presents to the women. It was fine, it was fine to give the girl things like that, but it was women's work. Levi smiled and rubbed his red mouth with his hand, to see his daughter standing there, blushing lightly, at the receipt of these things.

Old Fanny Bricker, almost blind now, and not to be trusted to walk across the room alone, called out loudly, with the imperious toneless voice of the very deaf.

"When are they going to be married? Who is it the girl is marrying?"

Levi bent down and shouted in her ear. "It's brother Goudie's boy, Aunt Fanny. You remember Simon Goudie?"

The old lady nodded. "I remember him. How old is she, now?"

"Tillie's eighteen!"

"I had two children when I was eighteen. When are they going to get married?"

Tillie blushed a deeper pink. Her father winked at her. "What'll I say, Tillie?"

A hush fell on the group.

"When did you say?" Fanny supposed that, as usual, they had forgotten her and her question. In another minute she would have forgotten it herself, she knew. She would just put it out again, and hang on to it, till she got her answer.

"Well, what shall we say, Tillie?"

They were all smiling now. Tillie shook her head, as though to disperse a mist before her eyes.

"Spring, tell her."

"In the spring, Aunt Fanny." Levi's voice reached her.

"Spring. Spring. In the spring." The old woman rocked herself back and forth in twilight contentment. "In the spring," she mumbled to herself. "Jah, that will be it."

"Something for you, Aunt Fanny," Levi said, and laid a parcel in her hand. Gently he untied the thick linen string which bound it, and guided her hand to the mouth of the sack. Rough squares of maple sugar and large smooth peppermints met her knobby searching fingers. She picked out a crumbling square of the candy and brought it to her mouth. What was it, though, that was to happen in the spring? She paused for a moment in her rocking; it had gone. But the candy was sweet and strong, and that was all that mattered. Tillie watched her as she mumbled and sucked and rocked. This, then, she thought fleetingly, was the end of it all. This the end of which Aunt Keturah, stretched and thin, was the middle stage. She looked down at her own strong hands and dismissed, lightly, the dread that had visited her.

"My girls never got married," said Aunt Fanny, suddenly and loudly. Her faded eyes were fixed on no particular point; she seemed to be talking to the darkness, her companion. "The boys didn't like them, I guess!" She laughed a little. "No. They never got married at all."

She noisily finished her candy and reached for another. Her elder daughter, Ruth, standing behind her chair, quietly closed the bag.

"That's enough, Mother, you'll make yourself sick." Her face was flushed in humiliation. The younger daughter stood, stout and rebellious, waiting for more reference to her ignominious status.

"Tillie's not going to be an old maid, anyway, are you Tillie?" piped Lambert; and the little boys looked at her with wide pale-blue eyes under their cream-coloured brows.

"Go and wash your dinner off your faces," she ordered.

She could not look at Ruth or Lois. For her that slim and steep divide which separates those who marry and those who do not was crossed. She, a fortunate one, was on the further side. Fat Lois, her face still burning, stepped back to help lift from the table the blankets and sheets which were the outward and visible sign of the distinction. She laid the things heavily on the couch, and the moment passed.

The little boys recovered soonest from the heavy dinner, and while the old men dozed, in their shirt sleeves, on the parlour chairs, and the women washed the dishes, they put on their new caps and went out to play in the barn. A faint jingle of bells announced the coming of the mail man, and they trudged down the lane to seek treasure in the mail box. On top of the box they saw, to their intense excitement, a parcel too big to go inside and leaning up against the post itself, in a kind of occult balance.

"Is it something from the catalogue?"

"But Mamma did not send in an order, though."

"Maybe it is, likely, the viola for me."

"You are not to have the viola until you can buy it yourself, from your calf, Mamma said."

"And it is not long enough, yet, for my viola."

"Is it heavy? It could be seed."

"No, it is not heavy."

They lifted it down from its precarious perch and bent over to spell out the name.

"Ach, it's only something for Tillie, anyway. Quilts, or something."

All interest in the box evaporated. Dangling it between them, they carried it indifferently back to the house and tossed it on the dining-room table without comment.

In the parlour there was music, now, and the little boys sat quietly outside the door to listen for a while. Tillie was playing the piano, and the good rich chords and the strong loud melody of "Joy to the World" reverberated through the house. They began to sing. The young men and girls gathered around the piano; and with great enthusiasm and no discrimination they sang of the death and suffering of their Lord, and of their triumphant joy in His resurrection. To the birth of the baby God and the call of the old rugged cross their lungs accorded an equally loud response. The oldsters, Levi and his brothers, rested in their chairs but raised their voices too.

No need for Levi to look at the words. He knew them all, years ago. "Sing that one again," he called. "Betsey, you sing the verse, there."

The others were stilled, and Betsey sang alone. Her voice rose, thin and high and querulous; but when she came to the repetition, "The Christ of the Cross, Oh the Christ of the Cross," she closed her eyes and gave herself up to the grief and melancholy of it. Then the youngsters sang again, joining happily and with full throats in the chorus, and the sadness passed. And although the old men, rocking in their chairs and tapping out the measure in grey-socked feet, *bump, bump, bump* with their heavy heels on the bare floor, were saddened for a moment, it did not last long. For now they sang of Beulah Land, and the treasures laid up there for them. In the midst of the snow and the cold of Christmas they could see that high hill, full of the

95

bright promise of summer, and the filled ear, and the flow of milk and honey. Praise the Lord!

"Play something, now, that you have learned by the music teacher in Kinsail, Tillie."

"Jah, play now. We have been singing here long enough."

Tillie smiled, and gave the stool another whirl. "What shall I play, then?" She leafed through a thick white book. "Here is something." The women sat up in their chairs, their hands folded, and the men looked out of the window, watching the slow gathering dusk, and thinking that they should soon be on their way, while Tillie played. When she had finished there was a murmur of approval.

"It is too bad, maybe," smiled an uncle, passing her on his way through, and patting her gently, "that you are going to be married? Maybe you could get to be a music teacher, too?"

Tillie shook her head. "No, I could not, Uncle Chris, I have started too late. He says I should have started when I was five, or six."

"No! Does he? Well, well, you can play good, anyhow. Good enough for us to hear."

"It is good, the classical music, yes. But the singing of the Lord's praises is better."

"Jah! Praise the Lord, it is better!"

"Chris, we must go now. It is getting dark."

"Jah, we must go. The cows do not like to wait. And the fires, too."

The women rose, sighing a little. It was over, the visit, and the conversation; and now there was the long drive home, and the milking to be done, and the chilly house to be warmed up, and the good skirts taken off and hung in cold closets, and the big denim aprons put on again. They walked to the bedroom with the slow and natural dignity belonging to the class of woman whose whole life is motion, so that she never hurries. Soft sibilant sounds came from them, and affectionate words of farewell, as the

96

heavy wraps were found and put on; and then they came back and stood in the dining-room, reluctant to leave. Tillie lit the hanging lamp.

"What's on the table there?" Mrs. Shantz bent sharply over and read the address. "Is this something you have sent to yourself, Tillie? The postmark is Kinsail. Or from Simon, maybe?"

The black-bonneted heads nodded, pausing on their way to the door, curious. They moved back, to the light and the table. "Is it a present from Simon? A big one, he sends! Ah, the young men, when they are going to marry, they send presents!"

Old Martin Reesor smiled beneficently down from his great height, fingering the beard that gave him such a distinguished look, had there been anyone to see it so. "Open it, Tillie, or we won't get our wives home tonight, and they won't rest until they know what it is."

"It is not from Simon, though, surely," thought Tillie. "Simon gave me my Bible, and he would not send me another thing, a big box like this." Something caught at her hands as she untied the string. She moved awkwardly.

"I have no idea what it could be," she said.

The brown paper cover rolled back from her hand, and a tinsel-tied package was revealed. Suddenly Tillie blushed scarlet, and her hands were cold and numb. She saw again the yards of tinsel in the drug store. George Bingham had sent her this. A card slipped off the table to the floor. One of the little boys caught it and carried it to the light. The silent gathering waited to hear him read it. "Tillie from George, Merry Christmas!"

"What is it? Open it." Mrs. Shantz's voice was sharp. Tillie drew off the tissue paper, and two tinselled boxes burned on the table like slow fire. One was an enormous box, holding three pounds of sweets, built with an extravagant overhang which made it look as if it held five. It was upholstered in dull gold paper, and bore a diagonal ribbon of what seemed to be pure gold across its padded bosom, reminiscent of the Order of the Garter upon some royal breast. In delicate beautiful purple script the upper left-hand corner bore the imprint "Private stock." Unable to stop, Tillie unwrapped the accompanying parcel. A slender gilt perfume bottle emerged from the tissue paper. Attached to its long neck by a pink silk rope was a fabulous pink atomizer, netted and tasselled in pink. The unsubstantial confection struck a note as exotic in that house as would an orchid in a window box.

For a moment no one moved or spoke. Then the older women turned and set their faces towards the door.

"Well, we'll be going now, Betsey."

"Good-bye, good-bye. Next time, now, you must all come to our place." The women kissed Betsey with the kiss of love, and filed silently through the open doorway. Outside they combined in little silent family groups, to wait for their respective sleighs. It was characteristic that no word was spoken of the thought which was foremost in their minds. In a few minutes the lane was full of the music of the bells, and all the visitors had gone.

Tillie still stood in the dining-room, looking at these strange, unprecedented gifts. It was her father's unspoken inquiry that affected her more than her mother's quick, suspicious question.

"Who is George?"

"George Bingham, the druggist in Kinsail."

"What is this that you have then, from the druggist in Kinsail? Why does he send you a present at all? Does he send a present to every girl in Kinsail?" Her voice grew scornful. "He must have more money than brains, then." She looked at Tillie with apprehension. It was time the girl was safely married. "And what is this rubbish he sends you?"

"Open it, open it, Tillie!" The little boys, wide-eyed with astonishment, were able to be even more astonished when Tillie drew off the padded cover, revealing the rows of tiny chocolates, framed in their white waffled cushions;

round ones, square ones, and special bottle-shaped ones. Some had little purple flowers moulded on them, and some intricate designs in hard white sugar lines. There were also lumps of pure, rich milk chocolate.

"Are they good to eat?" They did not quite look like a thing to be eaten.

Tillie felt herself to be close to tears. Her father looked from her to the shimmering articles on the scrubbed table. He picked up the atomizer and examined it curiously. With a thumb almost as big as the bulb itself he squeezed it, tentatively. An infinitely delicate mist sprayed out under the lamplight.

"It squirts!" The little boys were captivated. "Let me squirt it?" The perfume of attar of roses pervaded the bleak, unadorned room.

"It stinks." They crinkled up their noses, accustomed to the smell of pigs and horses, and now acquainted for the first time with a smell for a smell's sake.

"What's it for, Tillie?"

The man's face became grave. "Women put it on themselves in vanity, to lure men to them, to sin. I never had such a thing in my hands before.—How is it, Tillie, that this man sends you this? I don't know him, surely? How do you know him so well as this? These are dear things, and why does he think you need them? It is not for a stranger to be sending you chocolates."

He flipped the open box with the back of his big hand, so that the elegant little confections jumped in their cushioned coffins and a few leapt to the table. The little boys would have scrambled for them, but the look on their father's face was so stern and so set that they dared not. Perhaps there was some spell on these things; they were without doubt some wicked thing—and they put their hands behind their backs and stood as still as stones.

Levi's eyes flashed with the frightening anger of the good-natured and loving person. He had never been among men as men, except with his own sect, and the few to

99

whom he sold his grain and milk. What the operations of these other men were, out in the world, he had little idea. There was no interest in him for such things. His life was full, abundant, satisfying. Lo, the Lord had promised him abundant life, and he had it, even here on earth. That Heaven would be better, he had no doubt, but his life on earth was good too, good. And now this vague cloud appeared. A man whom he did not know, and whom, surely, Tillie could know but very little, sent his daughter rich gifts. And his daughter stood there, looking at them flushed and speechless, with that proud upswing of her head which he had learned to respect, even when she was a little girl. He was exasperated beyond words, his exasperation acting only as a thin veneer for his unnamed fear. "Why does this druggist send you presents?" He was roaring now, shaking his fists on the table till it rocked. "Betsey! Take these children out of here. I must speak to Tillie."

Betsey opened her mouth to add a word, but was brusquely waved out. The little boys went quietly out before her, in silent awe. The thin scolding of their mother was chronic, but neither of them had ever seen their father in real anger before.

"It is time for the cows," she said, "go up the kitchen stairs, and change your clothes." The little boys took off their good shoes at the bottom, putting them carefully on the shelf where they would stay until Sunday, and skimmed up the stairs in their stocking feet, talking in scared whispers when they had got right to the top, and shut their bedroom door.

Betsey drew herself into a corner of the kitchen where she could look through the window on to the darkening orchard. It was almost dark now, in the unlit room, except for the grey light of ending day and the flash of an occasional spark from the range. She drew her mother's old rocker over to the window, and watched the dark come on. Upstairs there were the slight scufflings of the little boys. Now they had run down the stairs and shot out to the stables. Levi's voice reached her, raised in anger; and the rustle of paper; but no sound from Tillie. "She has gone stubborn on him. Well." Betsey's mouth set in a thin line. "Let *him* try, now."

For years she had had to deal with Tillie when pride and stubbornness and stiff-neckedness overcame her. Levi thought she was the perfect one. Let him see what he could do with her. She sighed. It was hard, just the one girl. And she thought again with sorrow of the two little ones, between Tillie and the boys, who should have been here now to comfort her. Perhaps one of them might have been a real daughter to her. Tillie had never been quite that. Even when she was a baby she preferred Levi. He was so proud of her, too. Among the fat and slumbrous girls of her own age she seemed wild and quick. Her father had given in to her. When she should have been spending time in the house, helping her mother, where was she? Out in the field, riding the horse for the corn cultivator, or driving the team for the hay-raking.

Darkness dropped like a cloak over the trees as Betsey sat there alone, holding herself very still so that she might hear without listening. And at last Tillie's voice came to her, clear and proud.

"I do not know why he should send me a present. If you like, I can send it back tomorrow."

Levi persisted. "But how do you know him, at all?"

"He gave me a ride home, one day, when I was walking by the cemetery, and cold."

"Walking by the cemetery? Why do you walk by the cemetery, then? And cold?" Levi's anger had given way, in part, to bewilderment.

Tillie drew a deep breath. There was no way to explain it. She tightened her lips. Why did she have this guilty feeling? She had done nothing, nothing. She was eighteen; she was to be married. If someone sent her something, it was her own affair, and the sender's. At that moment reaction set in so strongly, from the childish position she had been put in, that she could have dealt with a situation which included Simon, George, her father, her mother, and Aunt Keturah.

"We shall send it back tomorrow," she said crisply.

Her father looked at her in surprise and apprehension. "Jah," he said, heavily, "that will be the thing to do. Send it back."

"From the dressmaking shop," said Tillie, a tide of anger rising in her, "people buy silk things and lace for Christmas presents. Not just sheets, and blankets, and thick quilts."

At that moment Betsey opened the kitchen door, and they both started at the sound.

"Well?"

"We are sending it back, tomorrow," Tillie said sternly. And there was a look in her eyes which her mother dared not meet. But she had to make one thrust at the proud child.

"Simon will think it—"

"What Simon thinks he may keep to himself," said Tillie, and gathered up the parcels. Blinking back tears of anger and spent passion she walked up the stairs, gold box and tinsel and attar of roses. Levi and Betsey looked after her.

Levi thrust out his hands helplessly. "But what a thing!"

Betsey listened to the sounds from the upstairs, and was rewarded by the bang of a door which resounded through the house like the sound of blasting, not too far away. They looked at each other, Levi alarmed, Betsey exhibiting grim resignation not entirely free from complacency. "She is a wicked, rebellious child," she said, "and it is because of you, and the way you have spoiled her."

There was silence, now, from above, and Levi walked into the bedroom like a man who has been struck a great blow between the shoulder-blades and must carry himself low, crouched, almost, to protect himself from another.

He changed his clothes. "Ach," he said, "jah," and walked heavily out to the barn.

Lanterns set upon the wide dusty window-sills in the cow stables produced light within and without. Levi closed the stable door behind him and felt again the peace that laid its wings upon him here. The silky sound of expert milkers streaming jets of milk into tall pails, the comfortable shifting of heavy bodies from one pillar of leg to another, and the anxious bawling of the young cattle, made for him a wholly satisfying symphony. One of the hired men whistled between his teeth as he milked, and the little boys were staggering along with their pails to the separator, bending almost to the ground with the weight. A thin and anxious mother cat strained her deflated body towards one of the men, who said "Here you are, then, old lady," and shot a thin stream of milk into the air. The cat sat up on her haunches and, lapping furiously, drank from the hose-line. Levi laughed to see her frenzied efforts to clean up after the fountain had ceased to flow. "Lambert!" he called. "Get a good dish of milk for the black cat. She has a lot of babies to feed yet."

He stooped down and stroked the anxious creature. She turned big staring eyes on him, and raised her back to rub against his hand.

"You've got your troubles too, haven't you, kitty? Jah, we all have our troubles. Who's left to be done, Jake?"

"The Mooley, and the Anderson cow, and Whitey."

"I'll do Whitey and Mooley. Get over, Whitey." He sat with his big beard reaching almost to his knees as his head rested on the smooth, warm comfort of the cow's flank. The rhythm of the familiar process, and the warm placidity of the beast, induced a feeling of peace. What then was he worrying about? Customs were different, out there, among these people. The man did not mean any harm, surely. His heart was sore, that he had been so cross with Tillie. He had treated her as if she were a hardened sinner. He was ashamed. Tears rolled down the big red face, and twinkled off into his beard. When he had finished the cow he drew a bandana hastily out of his pocket, and blew his nose and wiped his eyes.

The boys and the hired men finished with the droning of the separator, and carried off the milk and cream to the milk house. Levi walked up and down the aisles of the stable in the light of the one lantern they had left with him, talking to the animals and repenting, in his heart, of the sin of judgement of which he was guilty. Not by might, nor by power, but by my spirit, saith the Lord.

There was a cold draft upon him, and the door opened, with Tillie standing there.

She could not see him, in the brown shadows of manger and feed bin and stall. "Father!" For a minute he did not answer, enjoying the sound of her call. When she was a little thing, coming out often to seek him, she called like that—eager, and also a little frightened to be alone in the big barn. In those times, he knew, with a guilty feeling, she had come to escape some household task which Betsey had prepared for her. He was a partner, in those crimes. But then they had been such friends. "Father!" It had not changed, her voice. He knew just where the two notes of "Father" were, on the piano. A and F sharp. Jah, she had not changed that. And in a sudden rush he knew that she had not changed at all. This thing from the man in Kinsail, how was it her fault? And the story Keturah gave Betsey, full of head-shakings and suspicion of his little girl! It was woman's way, always to be wondering, and waiting for the Evil One to catch up with another. The sound of her voice as she called him was lovely to his ear. "Jah, Tillie, is it you?" There was nothing but love in his tone.

"Where are you, Father?"

"Getting out the roots."

She slipped down from the sill and came quickly to

him, passing now with the ease of a blind man in his own room through the long aisles, and pushing open the hand-smoothed wooden bolts without needing to see them.

"So you came out to see the father, did you?"

In the near-darkness words come easier to people who are never articulate about their feelings.

"Tillie, come here now." He looked at her closely, lifting up her chin in his big hand. Her face, in the light of the lantern, was white and still. "You have been crying? Ach, Tillie, there is no need to cry. There is no need. I have been thinking, it is an awkward thing, this, and if you send it back you maybe will hurt his feelings. He must have meant just to be kind. Although still I do not understand it. But this is what we will do. Tomorrow you are going back, and leaving us again?"

"Yes."

"Well, then, I will go with you, and we will take the thing back, and I will see the man, and tell him. I will tell him, now, that it is a kind thing for him to do, to send you these things, but that, you see, with us, we do not quite—we do not— A perfume, now, is not for a girl like you, and anyway, anyway, I will say, that you are going to be married, soon, now, and the young man would not have you taking such fine presents from another."

"Very well, if you think so."

"It was kind in him, and he meant well, no doubt."

He looked at her, kindly, and a little troubled. "You are all right, there in Kinsail, Tillie? You do not miss your own place, too much?"

Tillie sighed. "I like the work," she said, "and the music, too. It is good to be learning to play. But Aunt Keturah—"

"Jah, I know, Aunt Keturah. But she is a good woman, Tillie, and—well, she is a good woman."

"Father."

"Jah?"

"I am not just sure that I want to be married, this spring."

"No? You are not sure? Well, then, you must wait. I think, mind you, myself, that you are too young, maybe."

"I would like to come home, when I have finished with Loretta. And stay for the summer here." She stretched out her arms to include the whole of the floor of the barn. "In fact, Father, if I had not promised Loretta the whole six months, I would like to just stay, now."

"Ach! Then you really like it better here, with us, than away in the town?" Levi's big face beamed. "That is good, that you would like to be with us."

The comfort and security of the old barn seemed, to Tillie, to hold her like a fire-warmed easy chair. She rubbed her hand along a curving heavy chain.

"But it will not be long now. And I think it is good that you should stay at home, for a few months, anyway, before you marry and leave us. The time will not be so long, now. When are you finished with the dressmaker?"

"The end of May."

"Well then! That is the day we will look for!"

Tillie turned again toward the door. "Simon will be disappointed, I am afraid."

"Simon is young, too, a few months will not matter to him, in the long years ahead."

He watched her walk slowly the length of the passage, and heard the heavy door close behind her. For a long minute he stood there, reflecting upon his daughter, and the man she was to marry. Then he sighed and turned to throw another load of mangels into the barrow. They grew up too fast, these children. Just a little while ago, now, there was that little fella of Abraham's running around barefoot like Lambert and Ben, here. Then, suddenly, he was a young man, and a preacher, too, and Tillie was ready to marry him! Soon now, she would be Simon's wife. He felt that he knew the little boy who was Simon, but of the grown man he knew little. In the summer, when

Tillie came home, they would have him here, some, and all get to know him better.

But there was no need to be uneasy, about Simon. He was chosen of the Lord. That was the thing, though! Chosen of the Lord! There was no need to know more than that. And Tillie wanted him. Well. Anyway, there is no way to know another man, really. Each one lives so lonely, to himself alone.

10

ON HER first day in Kinsail, after Christmas, Tillie felt an inexplicable necessity to see George again. When she thought of him she could not remember how, exactly, his face was made. Across the counter she could really look at him and see what he was like, at a safe distance and in the security of his knowing now that she was an engaged girl; for her father would by this time have taken back the presents. She thought to look at George much as a child will look at a strange creature in a cage, from a southern country. It is lively, and beautiful, and only desirable at the outer dreamlike fringes of desire. To touch it, to hear it sing, or purr, or squeak, would be an agreeable adventure. But there is no thought of acquiring it as a pet, or household ornament. It is a creature to touch, and to pass by, keeping only a piquant little memory of contact with an exotic whose eyes have rested on other skies than this. The passing by forever would bring no regret, more than that ever-present regret in the heart that one man cannot see and know all, and go every-where, before he dies.

Unfinished sentences jostled and scattered in Tillie's mind: "I just came in to say that it was very nice of you . . . Thank you very much . . . I think it was so kind of you . . . " But none of these would do. What she really longed to know she could not ask. After all, since it was over and done with now, she could scarcely walk in and say, "By the way, did you send every girl in the village a Christmas present like that? And if you didn't, why did you send one to me?"

Tillie's eyes brightened, as she crossed the road, and her mouth fixed itself into a smile which plainly announced that she was mistress of this situation, and meant to enjoy the taste of it. Pleasant anticipation stirred her. The rehearsed sentences were driven back. She would be able to think of the right thing to say, when the moment came. In just a minute now, she would see his face clearly. For a second she halted, her breath coming quickly, and her hand to her throat. Was she really prepared for this meeting? Her confident, merry smile faded, and a grave dignity of expression replaced it. But she went firmly on. Her eyes searched the window for a sign of him. She opened the door. There was no one in the long narrow shop. All seemed utterly still. As she quietly closed the door behind her a bell jangled harshly in the back room. It startled her, and she could feel her heart pound. She held her breath. Still there was no movement in the store, although it seemed to her that she could hear the sound of deep breathing, somewhere. She stood irresolute, un-certain, robbed of her sensation. Was that a sound of breathing, or was it not? Why did he leave the store without anyone there? Where was he? From the green shadows at the back of the dispensary a low shape, noise-less in effortless motion, padded along beside the wall. Georgette the cat lifted illuminated eyes to the stranger, and escaped under the counter. Silence again.

She walked a few paces down the quiet aisle. A faintly antiseptic smell came pleasantly to her nostrils, and her eyes quickly ranged the shelves and showcases. There in the lower one, out of the window, now, were those glittering bottles, like the one he had sent her. There were yellow netted bulbs too, and green, and blue. The pink was the nicest, certainly. Were there beautiful boxes of candies here too, like hers? She searched rapidly, with her eyes, for them. In the small showcase under the wicket to the dispensary were piles of chocolate boxes. Glossy paper covers and bows of red ribbons trimmed them. Ladies in wisps of floating materials and very red lips decorated their tops. There was no gold box. Tillie smiled with a new confidence, and a satisfaction which she would have been most perplexed to explain.

The town clock bonged out nine. What was she standing here for, now? Loretta would think she was not coming back, this morning. She put out her hand, and rubbed it gently along the smooth rounded edge of the counter. She must go. She must go, now. But she did not move. She would wait another minute. Supposing he had been there, what was it she had arranged with herself to say? What were the words now? A vague feeling of guilt and apprehension awoke within her. She stirred, suddenly a little frightened lest she should be caught there, without reason. What would he think? What would anyone think? She swallowed in a dry throat. "Let me get out of here! Oh! Let me get out of here, before anyone comes in!"

She turned and stepped swiftly to the door, let herself out and heard with unmeasured relief that the bell clanged again and the door was shut behind her. She strode down Main Street, her face red and set, fleeing from something or someone unknown. The men in front of the barber shop turned to look with mild surprise at the tall hurrying figure. George, inside, emerged from a hot towel to catch a glimpse of her as she all but ran past the window.

"That one's in a hell of a hurry to get wherever she's goin'," observed Buzzy, leaning over George and bending his head after the retreating figure.

"Came out of your place, George, as if she was shot at."

"Did, eh? Well, we don't shoot 'em, yet. Maybe young Bill gave her a scare."

"Yeah. Good kid, isn't he?"

"When he's awake, he's good enough."

"Sleep much?"

"Not while I'm looking at him."

The barber grinned. "There you are, Mr. Bingham." He flicked his towel in the general direction of the back of George's neck, and bowed him out.

"Feels fine now, thanks, Buzzy."

"'Bye, George."

Billy Davis met his employer at the door of the shop, a dazed expression on his face.

"Did you see anybody come in here, Mr. Bingham? The bell rang like anything, but there wasn't anybody there when I came through."

George looked at the boy. His hair stood on end, and his cheeks looked rosy and warm. "No," he said, "I didn't see anybody come in. Run along now and finish your sleep. I'm here for the day."

Billy reddened to the ears.

"I just sat down for hardly a minute, Mr. Bingham, I couldn't really been asleep."

"No?"

"I don't think so, Mr. Bingham."

"Didn't see anybody in the store, eh?"

Billy shook his rough head vigorously.

"People can't come out of places unless they've been in them, can they, Bill?"

"No, I guess they can't."

"Well, somebody came out of here, all right, just like a bat out of hell."

"Did they?"

110

"They did. And might have taken the till with them, for all the good you are, looking after things."

Billy's face set in misery. "Aw, Mr. Bingham."

"I mean it, Bill. A drug store has a lot of valuable things in it. Worth a lot of money. See what I mean? A man who works in a drug store has to be right up on his toes all the time."

"I see."

George waved his hand towards the back of the store.

"And all those things back there! Why, you might have half the town dead or dying, with what somebody might pick up while you weren't watching."

Bill surveyed the shelves with anxious enquiry.

"Is anything gone, do you think?"

"Not as far as I've noticed yet. Time alone will tell. Scud across and get the mail. And the next time you sleep, you're through. And I don't mean maybe."

Billy shot out the door on the double.

"I'll put the fear of the Lord into that tousle-head and he'll be some good to me yet."

George looked about him, as if there might perhaps be something new and different in the air, since Tillie had been there. He was amused to realize that he was almost as annoyed at missing her as if she had really been his girl. Since he had sent the parcel he had been piqued by a nagging curiosity as to how she would receive it. When a shadow fell across the bar of sun on the floor he looked up, a dozen times, to see if it were Tillie, tall and shy, and yet with something which was not shyness, in her manner. When he dropped the parcel into the mail bag he had called himself a fool, and if Cora had not been looking at him so curiously, obviously trying to read the name and address which he had carefully arranged to be upside down, for her, he would have carried it back with him. But when it had actually gone, and the whistle of the mail train told him that it was now irrecoverable, he began to enjoy his little escapade. During his enforced

Christmas holiday her face as she was opening the parcel appeared to him several times a day. Sometimes he conjured up the scene; always, of course, with delightful surprise as Tillie's role. He could see envious sisters, an approving mother, and always the Mennonite El Greco, smarting with injured pride, biting his lips in the background. So, when she came in to thank him, blushing prettily, of course he had to be out.

"Damn, damn, and *double* damn!" said George, pounding the counter. Georgette came bounding out, ruffled and affronted.

"P-P-Per—aouw?" she inquired, in an anxious voice.

"Peraouw yourself," said George sourly, and pulled out a sheaf of invoices from the till tray, to check.

The door opened again. George looked eagerly towards it. A tall, burly Mennonite farmer in a broad black hat and furred coat, advanced towards him. Among the refinements of the shop's fittings, the precise placing of the bottles, the exquisiteness of the labelling, the farmer seemed unduly blurred in his modelling. It occurred to George, always sensitive about his size, that the two of them meeting there resembled the meeting of a medium-sized fox terrier and heavily built Newfoundland.

"Good morning, sir. What can I do for you?"

The big Mennonite carefully laid a parcel on the counter, as if it contained a number of soft-shelled eggs. He cleared his throat with a reverberation as of thunder.

"I want to see Mr. Bingham, please."

"I am Bingham," said George, pleasantly.

"How do you do. I hope you are well? But it is maybe your father, then, I need to see?"

George shook his head. "My father has been dead for twenty years, sir. If it's George Bingham you want, I'm your man."

Levi looked at the young man, puzzled, and yet reassured, too. Why, he was just such a young one! He had seen the girl, and, why, he wanted to send her a present. Perhaps, now, that was how they did. He was a nice young one, too. Look how clean and neat he looked, and the shop, how tidied up!

"Well, well. Excuse me, then. I thought you were much older. Surely you are young, though, to have a store, all by yourself?"

"Maybe I'm older than I look."

"I remember this store better when Josh Bolendar had it. It did not look like this then. No. It looked a little as if, maybe, somebody put in a fanning mill, for just a few minutes, and left everything where the wind blew it. Jah! But it is nice, now!"

George smiled. "I'm glad you think it's improved. Lots to do yet. But it takes time. All takes time. This summer, I hope, I'll get things organized a little better."

Levi brought his eyes back to the parcel, clumsily tied in extra paper to hide the original wrapping. It was a difficult thing he had to do. That nice young man there, he had not meant any harm. There in the showcase were a dozen more of these bottles, with the little squirt thing. But in the window too, were boxes of cigars, and tobacco, things which must not be touched. How did this young man not realize? Truly they were blind, who did not wish to see. And yet, it was all there, in the teaching, that he who runs may read.

He shook a kindly but reproving finger at the slanting tobacco case. "Why, though, do you keep that kind of thing here? With us, you know, it is forbidden. Surely you would not put a stumbling-block in thy neighbour's path?"

"Well, Sir, you know, we do not all think alike, in these matters, do we? I don't smoke much myself, but there are better men than me, who do."

"But these men, though—"

"A different point of view, sir, a different point of view."

"Jah, that's it, but the difference, there, it is a very important difference, though. A very important difference.

113

It is all the difference, maybe, between eternal life, and eternal damnation."

George shook his head. "I'm afraid I can't see it that way, sir."

Levi sighed. "No. Perhaps not now. But perhaps the time will come, when the spirit of the Lord will speak to you, speak to you as it spoke to the Prophet in the wilderness. And then all will be made clear. Praise the Lord."

"Grand old chaps, these, riding their pet horse," thought George, "but why is he saying all this to me?" He glanced at the parcel on the counter. The newspaper wrapping revealed a familiar shape below. He flushed to the roots of his hair. In the pictures he had made, all to his own advantage, of the reception of the parcel, he had not included the father. And here he was, nodding earnestly and pleasantly enough now but probably, when the question of the box came up, ready to turn into a figure of very stern aspect indeed.

A group of high-school girls came swarming in, to buy films and chocolate tablets and, quite obviously, to chat with George. Levi waved them forward; he could wait. He watched them bridle and giggle and cavort, as the Newfoundland dog which George found him to resemble might have watched a batch of kittens. When they had crowded out of the door, laughing still, he turned with a twinkle in his eye which was reassuring. "Can't be quite out for the shot-gun, anyway," George reasoned, amused at his own half-formed apprehensions. Levi indicated the door with his arm.

"It is wonderful to be young. They do not know it now, but they will know, when they are no longer young and frisky, maybe."

"They're certainly full of high spirits, anyway."

"Jah. When we are older, we forget, we forget how it is, to be young, like that. But you too, you are still very young. Perhaps what I have come to say to you is all wrong, after all." He put his hand on the parcel. "You

114

know what this is, don't you? You see, I am bringing it back to you. You know my daughter, Tillie, a little. She told me that you were kind to her, and drove her home, one day. Jah. But the thing is, you see, these things,"— he flipped the parcel delicately with his long finger—"she could not have them, from you. These are dear things, and anyway, the perfume, a Mennonite girl does not use that. And she is going to be married, you know! Yes, she is going to be married, not so far away, now. The young man she is to marry, he would be angry, I think, to know that another young man had sent her a present, like that."

George opened his mouth, and closed it again, finding no words.

"No, no, he would not like it, at all, you know." Levi waved his big beard over the counter, bringing his eyes down to the level of George's, and speaking with great earnestness. "We do not want you to feel bad, you know. It is not that we have anything against you, though. No. How could we? We do not know you."

George shook his head like a tongue-tied kindergartner.

"Well, I'll say good-bye, then. God bless you, and give you eyes to see the beauty of His ways. Good-bye."

He struck George's shoulder with a smart double stroke which left him slightly rocking, and went out of the store. When he had gone, the shop seemed larger and more airy. Where his shadow had filled the showcase there shone a broad bar of light. George hitched his shoulders as if to rid them of the pain of strained muscles.

"Well, I'll be God-damned!"

The parcel sat on the counter, and seemed disposed, he thought, to sit there until he did something with it. He put his hand on the scuffed brown paper, thinking that it had done some travelling since it had left him, and feeling a momentary ridiculous sense of envy that the inanimate object should have been where he could not go. When he had shrugged off the feeling of childish inferiority which the big man's kindly attitude had induced in him, he found a residue of frustration. He had put out his hand, in a friendly fashion, he assured himself, and it had been slapped. Not with a vigorous, resounding kind of slap, either, which could be returned with a hearty punch, but with a kind of gentle, admonishing wrist-slap which had to be accepted, and which, in some odd way, left no room for animosity. And here was the damned thing back on the counter. What in hell was he to do with it? Unparcel it, sort it out again, sell the perfume, urge the beautiful box on cross-eyed Frank Casey to take to old Kate Joicey, whom he had been calling on once a week for twenty years, and no nearer to marrying her than he ever had been? For some unidentifiable reason, he could not do that. He stood there, and felt as dejected and miserable as if his play-acting had been real, as if there was a girl whom he loved, and for whom he had selected these things, and she had sent them back. He looked about for the villain in the piece, someone whom he could blame for the frustration, and could find none. Certainly not Tillie, with her beautiful, gentle face, and odd, not quite submissive bearing; she would not do. Nor would that amiable giant her father. There must be somebody, or something. His mind presented him with a picture of the El Greco preacher, and immediately he felt release. Of course.

Tillie was going to marry him. And he would be angry. With his long, awkward legs, and his big full mouth, and the gait, when he walked, of a barefoot, knock-kneed ploughman; he would be angry. Forsooth! There he was, there was the man who had broken this delightful fantasy. For the first time, George gave Simon full consideration. He gave Simon perhaps five minutes' unbroken thought, before the next customer came in. He picked up the box carefully, and put it on a low shelf in the dispensary, address-side down, before he came back to the business of selling his goods over the counter.

ILLIE FINISHED her letter to Simon and laid it
aside, ready to post in the morning. She felt that
she had snatched back into her keeping some
precious thing which had almost escaped her. It seemed,
recently, that the girlhood which she had been so anxious
to be rid of had become suddenly a valued possession
which she had been foolishly ready to discard before she
had realized its worth or significance. She looked in some
doubt at the letter, however, lying there on the white
dresser-cover, inanimate but powerful. It did not say
just what she had expected it to say, somehow, but she
did not know how to amend it. She took Simon's letter,
which had been waiting for her when she returned, and
read it again. It sounded as if Simon already felt the
year at college to be behind him, and himself to be practically on the way home to her, to the church here. Why
then, since this was what she had wanted of Simon, did
she not send that kind of letter back to him? Sometimes
she had felt that she could, that she must, to still some
inner urging, write down to Simon the kind of words that
he sent to her; but when she started, the words would
scarcely form from the pen, and the impulse languished
when they took reluctant shape on the cold white paper.
Any attempts to express her half-resolved emotion were
failures. And yet, Simon was to be her husband? To
marry Simon was what she wanted most? Yes. Yes, it was.
But she would not be hurried. Perhaps, if she had never
left home, she might not have felt the necessity of coming
to, as it were, a working agreement with herself. Since
she had been away from her own people the need to
become articulate had grown upon her. Back there, where

she was surrounded by people who had known her from birth, there had been no such urgency. But out here, where so much that she had taken for granted all her life seemed to be in question, she had strong need to put into words, or at least into intelligible thought, the factors which made up her life. And now she had new need for companionship and conversation.

Endless topics for speculation grew out of the workshop; and Mr. Shardley and his tall stories of mountains and villages filled with music needed talk. But there was no one to whom she was an equal, here. She was a pupil to Loretta, a niece to Keturah. Perhaps, if Simon had been there, she could have talked these things over with him. But the thought of such intercommunication was chilled by the remembrance of conversations suddenly concluded before they were well begun. There were some things which it would be difficult to explain to Simon; even, she thought, when they were married. They would, of course, be one flesh, but she could see that within that holy union there would inevitably be barriers. This, too, was a thing she must consider.

She slipped sighing into her bed, and turned to her pillow. Consciously she sought again the marriage dream, closing her eyes and invoking it. But the images would not quite form, as they used to do, in bright unblurring clearness. She was vaguely discomfited. Perhaps she would need the long summer for the decisions she must make before she gave herself quite into Simon's keeping, to be forever his submissive wife before the Lord. A long summer, one last one, to keep the "grozmutter's garden," much as the grandmother had kept it herself for fifty years; a long summer, before she took over the rough garden of her new home. She thought with interest and pleasant imaginings, of the new garden and the problems it would present. With this one she would work out new plans, instead of keeping it as the grandmother had. The special gifts which she was acknowledged to have inherited would work in new ground. But not this summer; this summer, still the cabbage-roses of the old garden; time enough in September to start the new one, over there.

She lay comforted and relaxed in her bed, watching the shadows and lights from the street lamp divide her ceiling and walls into patches of grey and gold. It seemed to her that the room was more spacious than before. All about her there was air and light and a long view to the edge of the world, where before there were high walls about to shut her in. The feeling of somehow having pushed back the walls eased and contented her. Tomorrow she would post the letter.

A treacherous, sudden flash of memory came to her, of the curious, flattening, thinning out of Simon's full lips, when he kissed her; and involuntarily she drew an erasing hand across her mouth.

Surrounding the Bible College, and lining the streets about it, were the large houses of just vanished splendour. Into these houses, at the time when Simon Goudie sought revelation and instruction from the fountain head, young men and women with bulging valises, packed in country towns and villages by anxious mothers, walked with lonely steps. These were the boys and girls, the bright ones from the little centres, whose ambitions lay not quite within the range of university education, but who sought a little more than could be given them in their own native settlements. Small, unauthoritative institutions, lying on the thin out-skirts of the great and approved universities, welcoming them in without benefit of entrance qualifications, claimed these travellers. They went from the cold tall houses to short-course and big-diploma schools, drawn by little insid-ious advertisements in weighty weekly papers designed for the unlettered.

The tall houses presented an impregnable front of solid red brick and red-brown stone. As the curious and wonder-ing eyes of the visitors glanced upwards, they saw an astonishing outcropping of cupola and ornamental gable, among the elms. Occasional wispish bushes peering through the narrow alleyways on the clear sides of the houses indicated that behind them existed gardens, of sorts. The country strollers speculated as to what could possibly grow in such deep shadow, in such black sooty soil.

When the snow came, and the streets were bare and windswept, the tall elms empty of leaves and birds, it was like living on the outer edge of a fortress.

Simon Goudie lived in one of these high houses, walked the cold streets, and bettered himself for the service of the Lord, in the Bible College. His room on the third floor looked into the branches of an elm tree, half a block from the school. The little mission church where he preached, as supply, lay just two blocks west of his boarding house. His physical world was bounded by the slender isosceles triangle whose apex was the church, and the base-points boarding house and school. He very rarely strayed beyond the limits of his plot. There was nothing to draw him out of it, into new fields. He had no curiosity concerning the life of the city, and felt neither desire nor need to extend his experience of human living. The life of the city he knew to be wicked, its practices so foreign to his that there was no use in his investigating them. The wickedness he deplored, and included in mechanical prayer, but at the same time knew to be no immediate concern of his. He was quite separate from this world. The Lord had not called him here to save souls. He might, for this winter, have been a solitary actor, walking about among stage properties. Souls were to be his harvest, yes, but not just any souls, thrown loose upon God's great, minutely planned canvas. The paper city was not his field, and the people at the boarding house, the people whom he passed on the street, had for him no real being.

Even in the little church his congregation was a congregation of foreign, inimical beings. They were more alien to him, with their sand-papered, citified faces, than if they had spoken a foreign language. Their dress was the same, almost, as that of his own people, but their speech was undeniably different, smoothed over with the standardized city glibness. They were harder, drier, laughed briefly, loudly, and talked too fast. The men looked pale, in comparison with the rich full-coloured faces of the farmers at home. They seemed to him slack, too, in the fulfilment of the Lord's commands. But mere slackness hardly merited the powerful denunciation he thundered at them. His fire was too fierce for the members of the Mission. They appreciated the quality of it, none the less, and felt that they were having a time of rich blessing, and thanked the Lord for his gifts, remembering for a long time after the meeting the strangeness of his appearance, and the sudden fanatical lighting up of his eyes when the spirit moved in him.

But they did not come to the front, and Simon was starved for a meeting in which God would come down, and touch the very hearts of men. He was conscious, too, at the back of his mind, of a vague distress that, all this time, although he had striven well, he had had no special call from the Lord. He was content, oh, more than content, to go back, to serve near home; but sometimes, when he heard of wonderful experiences, related to him by those who had received definite calls, he longed too, to feel a certainty, as they said they did, that he was just where the Lord intended him to be. But, Praise God! He was safe in the assurance that He had His plans for him.

He sat in his cold bedroom, worrying out alien interpretations of simple Biblical statement, feeling the matter in hand to be of no real significance, and following the argument with difficulty, since thoughts of home and the dreams of Tillie which were always with him pressed continually upon his attention. They presented themselves to him as miracles of warmth and desirability, and he longed to go home. But he resolutely struck these enticing images from his mind. Tomorrow there would surely be Tillie's letter.

She would write to say how disappointed she had been
that he had had to go back to the city for Christmas, and
how she had missed him, perhaps. Ten days now, since
his lonely, frustrating holiday, so tomorrow, certainly,
there would be a letter. He would put off thinking about
her. He could wait till then, and show himself a man
worthy of his great calling.

But in the morning his agitation and longing were so
great that he ran to his boarding house between periods,
to be sure of the letter, to have it in his hand. He read it
like a thirsty man drinking, as he strode back to the College.
Then his footsteps slowed, and he read it again, trying to
find another meaning in it.

Kinsail, January 7,
Friday night.

Dear Simon;

It is Friday night, and I am all alone. Aunt
Keturah and Elmina are visiting Mrs. Nighswander, who is not expected to be better. I am
afraid you will think that I am a long time
answering your letter. Your father was up town
today, and is well. He heard from Brother Bricker
that it will be maybe two months yet till he can
preach again. So you will have a lot of practice.

Simon, I know now, a little, what you mean
when you say that the world is full of dangers,
and temptations are to be found in unexpected
places. I nearly always go home the back way.

We had a nice Christmas. In a way, I was
sorry to leave home again, so soon. But of course
Loretta was expecting me. We are very busy now,
starting to make a great many things for Miss
Percy's wedding. The wedding dress itself is
white silk poplin, with a deep pointed bertha,
and ruching all around it. Today Loretta let
me sew some front seams, which are important,

122

and pin some tucks. Twenty-four tucks in a
square, in the front of a waist. She said they
looked professional, when I got them done. Next
week perhaps I can start to cut. It is very interesting.

Simon, I have something to tell you, and it is
that I do not think we can be married so soon,
after all, if you don't mind. I think I had better
just stay at home for a while, after I finish the
dressmaking course. I hope you don't mind.
Perhaps the fall, instead of the spring.

Tillie.

At the door of the building he crumpled it in his strong
hand and hurled it into the snow.

12

URING THE winter months, until the snow had gone,
and the high round maples up and down the
streets were misty with buds, Tillie seldom passed
the drug store during open hours. She slipped out of
Loretta's house and along Montreal Street, which ran
parallel with Main Street, until she could turn along the
park road, and join it again far past the drug store. She
made her purchases at Bowman's, at the east end, where a
few small shops constituted another tiny business section.
She understood that the Tempter had been at work, with
her. She must give him no further opportunity.

Sometimes, searching among the sprinkling of black

anonymous Mennonite bonnets over the streets of the village, George thought he had seen her, but could not be sure, and a strange reticence prevented his asking any questions of Loretta. He stopped expecting Tillie to come in to the store, and she sank from the surface of his mind. Yet occasionally, with no warning, memory brought her lovely face sharply before him, as he had kissed her by the frozen lake. Then he held his breath and bent over the counter, pressing his knuckles on the hardwood until they hurt.

George had no business with women, he told himself. Not for marrying them, certainly. What had she wanted to tell him, the day she flew out of the store? Whatever it was, it couldn't have mattered much or she would have been back. He smiled to remember the drive they had had, that Sunday morning a few months ago. Odd girl. Might be interesting, if she ever got to talking. Must be something behind that smooth wide forehead. George warmed at the memory of the kiss: "So shy and quiet about it," he thought. "Didn't say a word." He glanced involuntarily at the low shelf where the parcel still lay, face down, under a pile of boxes. He gave it a light touch with his toe, and turned again to his work.

With the coming in of the spring stuff, and the idea he was working on, of bringing in ice-cream on the little ship "Bluebell," he busily made his summer plans. Back of the dispensary was a big store-room, opening into a rough patch of grass with a few cedar trees around it. When Josh Bolendar had the store, he and his family lived over it and had a kind of green garden there. A few of Mrs. Bolendar's iris still bloomed on the sunny side, and the lilac trees at the entrance were purple in May.

It was full of rough packing-boxes now, but George had been giving it thought. It could be cleaned up, and if the grass were looked after (Billy Davis could do that; keep him awake), it would be a nice spot for half a dozen round metal tables. What better, for all these summer

124

people with nothing to do but spend their money, than a nice dish of ice-cream at Bingham's Garden Parlour? George looked out at the rough yard and saw it full of straight-backed old men in white flannel trousers and nautical blue coats, leaning back in his graceful chairs and ordering cherry sundaes and sarsaparillas. It would be in use longer than just for the summer people. Hot-faced baseball players fresh from the diamond in the park would find it right on their way home. They would have to come in from Victoria Street, of course. He couldn't have them trailing through the drug store. And in the peaceful empty time, when the summer people had gone, it could still serve the village. He planned for Newt Kribbs to build a big insulated ice-chest in the store-room. There would be no more in overhead, and a sure profit. And besides all that, even without considering the profit, there would be the pleasant hum of life out there, organized by himself. The only thing to be sure of was that it didn't interfere with the drug store. He had the jealousy of a parent, for the store. But the parlour would certainly be the thing to do. He would put a long white apron on Billy Davis, and rake in the money.

It might be, a little later, that he could make a big thing of the summer business. Nobody here had thought, yet, of the importance of summer business. It all streamed past, up the lake to Port Rossing. He would make a Port Kinsail that would stop the traffic up the lake. What did Rossing have, that Kinsail had not? Well, ice-cream, for one thing. You could buy it in Kinsail, of course, up a flight of dirty stairs, in beside the bakery. You could even sit down to eat it, if you didn't mind overlooking the baker's garbage cans, and the baker's family life in full swing beside you.

Some day, and not too far on, either, if his hunch was right, there would be a full-fledged soda fountain here. Pennants and coloured lights could be strung about. Perhaps there would be a little restaurant along with it. A shell of a building would do; he could close it up for the winter. "Make a packet at that kind of thing," he assured himself.

He spent the evening in the dispensary, drawing plans, and opening boxes of summer goods that had come up on the night train. There was something particularly satisfying to him, at this hour of night, in finding himself alone, locked in with his kingdom. In the glow of the lamplight a thousand bottles glittered and winked. They were all adorned with the neatest of white labels, edged in brown, and they were all his. His was the hand that had printed those mystic signs upon them, and his was the sole hand to administer their contents. Upon his shoulders lay the responsibility for the dispensing of powerful specifics, which taken otherwise than by his careful measuring might deal painful death to the trusting community. But he was neat and accurate; no one need fear that he would be less than meticulously exact.

He cleared out the show window and put in bathing-caps and rubber shoes and cameras, films and sponges. He draped pennants, which said "Kinsail" in orange felt against black, along the back counter, and regarded his summer display with satisfaction. Nobody had as yet seen a pennant bearing the name of this town. All this kind of thing was new. The old druggist had never thought of handling articles so extraneous as these. But George had proved that he knew what people liked to buy. The extreme neatness of his store, and the invariably courteous reception to all comers, had been as attractive to the natives as it had to the increasing numbers of summer visitors. George had made a place for himself here. He was a member of the local Oddfellows lodge, and on the library board. He was a sidesman in the Anglican church, and played right defence for the Kinsail hockey team. He felt himself grow into the village, and the sensation was deeply satisfying to him, city-bred as he was, and accustomed to transient existence. The sense of belonging here was very strong in him, and became an important factor in his every move; and tied in with it was a lusty ambition for the freedom that money can bring. The memory of early poverty, the barrel-scraping, and the small but timely legacy which had permitted him to buy this business, were a constant sharp reminder of what the lack of money means.

When he had come, he reflected, just a year ago, fresh from city habits and city services, he had thought it riotously amusing that the lights went off at eleven o'clock, and didn't come on again until dark fell the next day. But now he was accepting it, as he was accepting all the other idiosyncrasies of small-town living. He set his square chin and said, in effect, "I'm doing all right here, and I'm going to do all right here. Whatever will help me to get on, that will I do, and nothing else." He saw his course as lying straight before him, and he was busy trimming his sail. There would be time, later, to look into a scheme for an equally satisfying domestic life. He had plans for that, too.

George recalled the distaste with which he had sat down to the evening meal at the big draughty boarding house up Church Street. Pale peaches had lain in flattened despondency in a shallow pressed-glass dish. The bread on its oval silver server buckled in staleness. There was a platter of sliced meat-loaf, dry at the edges. Over the whole picture was a faint shadow of discomfort, of a vinegarish, withholding way of life. George contrasted with this the image he had made of his own house.

There would be lights; beautiful, gleaming lights. Imagine having oil lamps, when for the pressing of a button he could have whole rooms gloriously illuminated! The brownish carpet with its all-over pattern he tossed out of his picture. He would have lovely, bare, polished floors; floors which would reflect his lights in a thousand soft shimmerings. Here and there, perhaps, a rich, jewel-toned Oriental rug, he would have, to pick out the deep reds of his velvet curtains. He curled his lip at the skimped lace curtains in the dining-room. There would be something else for that. Something which he had perhaps not even seen yet; but he would make the money, and get it.

He tossed out the shabby cruet and the stained steel knives. Solid silver flatware; and crystal for the peaches. And no boiled-over peaches, either. His peaches would be done whole, in brandy, or something, a lovely delicate rosy colour, and white napery and slender stemware to go with them. There would be no cold air, either, creeping up from the floor and blowing gales down the stairs, as it did in the winter. A lovely, even warmth, every day and at all times, in his house. In the summer, of course, a delicious coolness, when the music-room would be open and his wife would, perhaps, be playing in there, on the grand piano, with the sun coming through the slatted shades, making bars on the shining floor as golden as the notes which would shake from her fingers. The big music-room would be bare, but for the piano and the fur rug on the floor; but it would be sweet with the scent of flowers grown in his own garden. In the winter they could be supplied from the green house. It need not be an over-elaborate greenhouse; just big enough to keep them supplied with roses.

George grinned a little, to find himself thinking in these fanciful terms, but the grin faded quickly. There were people with no more equipment than he had, who lived that way, thought nothing of it. Why should not he? The thing was to know what you wanted, and get after it. People didn't get what they thought they wanted, in this world, because they did not want it hard enough to believe they could.

He had lots of things to think about, plans to make, schemes to carry through. And in the end, the middle, or perhaps, not too far from the beginning, no scrimping life for him. Freedom to come and go, play or work, see and do all that there was, on the whole earth. People in Kinsail, and lots of them in the city too, lived their whole lives out, never experiencing anything at all but the muddy little ruts of their lives. And all the world went by, without their seeing anything, let alone owning anything beautiful, precious, or desirable. Think of the horses, beautiful horses, to be had, the swift boats to be run, the magnificent mountains to be climbed, and the oceans to sail. But there had to be money. First of all, there must be the money. You had to set your course right, and keep to it, or you didn't get these things. Or, perhaps, you got them when it was too late, surely, to matter. George didn't intend to be sixty before he set his hand, for instance, on a fast boat which was his own. But there were things, naturally, which you had to do without, when you were making your freedom-giving pile. And for a young man like him, serious dealing with any woman was one of the things to let go.

He carefully locked the front door and went out by the back, considering the rough garden by the light of the high moon. In the morning Billy Davis could start to get those packing boxes out of there.

"Must take an evening off, and run down to see Loretta. Haven't seen the horse-faced preacher around, lately, either, now I come to think of it. Married by now, likely."

George struck the lilac tree a blow that skinned his palm.

13

THE PERCY wedding, so long in preparation, was arranged for the last Thursday in April. Loretta and Tillie had made a complete trousseau for the bride, and dresses and petticoats for what Loretta described as a whole tribe of fire-eating relatives on both sides. The day before the wedding there were still adjustments to be made.

"Fussy as a bunch of ring-tailed baboons," Loretta muttered, twisting a length of cream-coloured silk braid in her clever fingers, to make a frog for the corded silk sack; the bride elect had decided as lately as yesterday that she couldn't be married, lacking it.

"Holy smoke!" she grumbled. "You'd think you could tie up with a man for life without making all this splutter about it, wouldn't you? Just as well nobody ever asked me, I guess. I might have put up with the man, but I couldn't have stood for all this pother."

She cast an appraising eye over Tillie's iron. "Have to be hotter than that, for that sleazy stuff. So they thought it was a little too full, did they? If I was goin' to all the trouble the Percys are, to get rid of my daughter, I think I'd let the quality extend to the petticoats, too. Drawers might as well be potato-sacking as that stuff they gave us to do them with. Fancy on the top, these brides are, but rapidly deteriorate towards the centre. Take the other iron."

Tillie's new iron hissed and spat, and Loretta nodded approvingly. This girl was good. Been a great help to her, these months. Could do with her, well do with her, for another six. Pay her a little, any time now. She could take direction, intelligently, and there was a lot more to her, too, than you usually got, in these country girls. Some kind of pretty good cerebration might be imagined to be going on behind that serene broad forehead. But you couldn't get anything out of her, Loretta thought, with a crowbar, if she didn't want you to have it. She smiled in appreciation. Her own head was made of the same intractable stuff, and she respected the quality. The girl's hands were good, too. The dressmaker watched her for a minute, noting with artistic approval the unconscious grace of the tall figure bent over the pressboard, the gentle fall of the shoulder line, and the strength of the profile as she turned her serious gaze on the slippery grey stuff. "Take a girl like that and dress her up in the Percy clothes, and people would be looking for the Percy girl behind the backhouse."

Tillie straightened and shook the perfectly pressed skirt. Loretta felt a stir of pleasure in the look of her, and the satisfaction of a teacher in the work of a good student.

"Look at these sketches," she directed, pointing to a sheaf of coloured wash-drawings just arrived from the wholesale house, "and pick out something that you think would do for Lois Boynton."

"I don't remember the look of her, very well, I think."

"No great loss to you, but she has to be clothed. Tall girl, about your height. Mouse-coloured hair. Slightly swaybacked. I sold her that fawn-coloured crepe with the satin stripe in it. Handsome enough material."

Tillie gravely regarded the drawings, discarding and eliminating until she was left with one.

"Do you think she would like this?"

"Do you like it?"

"Yes. Although it looks a little top-heavy, perhaps. It might not, made up in the stripes, and on the figure."

"Umhum."

"It has a pretty line from the elbow to the cuff, hasn't it?"

Loretta looked at the paper and flicked through the other pages with a knowing hand.

"I think maybe you've picked the best one, at that. By no means the easiest, though. Brand new, too. They'll like that."

Tillie smiled with pleasure. The whole idea of colour and balance and proportion and line was still so new to her that she felt a little intoxicated when she had recognized values of which, such a little while ago, she had not known even the names. She found herself, since working with Loretta, seeing shape and mass and blocks of colour which she had been blind to before, in the house, in the street and in the formations of cloud and tree. In her mind she pulled down, reconstructed, rearranged these masses and patterns, until they seemed perfect to her. It was a little glimpse into the possibility of creating, and a taste of the ultimate human satisfaction. She might so easily have missed it.

Loretta held the pattern up to the light.

"How'd you like to wear a dress like that? You'd look a hummer in that one. Done up in a salmon corded silk, with ten yards of Cluny around the gimp line, and dripping down the front."

Tillie laughed. "I'm not likely to dress that way, as you ought to know!"

"More fool you," said Loretta, abruptly. "Well, that'll do, then. They can't expect too much, with the figure we have to go on, anyway. Get that parcel second to the last on the third shelf, there. With the black shoe-lace around it. You can start cutting on the underdress for this creation, tomorrow."

Tillie unrolled the parcel, lifted out a bolt of cream-coloured sateen, and awaited instruction.

"Watch this for a bit, Tillie, I'll show you how to fold these fool frogs. Case you ever have to make some. I'd have you practice on this, but she has to have it tonight."

Loretta's fingers arched and twisted over the gleaming braid, turning and nipping it in until she had made four most elaborate fastenings, with whorls of smaller loops forming what might have been fleurs-de-lis around the main button-holder. Tillie examined the fasteners closely, memorizing the order of the loops.

The clock in the distant dining room boomed out six. Loretta looked startled. "Six? I promised this contraption for six. Wonder the old lady hasn't been down here before this. Where is the woman, anyway, so anxious to have the thing that she works me to death to finish it, and then doesn't even turn up to get it? And me going out to supper, for once in my life, too."

"Could I take it over?"

"Be much obliged if you would. I'd like to enjoy myself, out, not worrying about giving the Percy family collective heart failure, if they found the house in darkness."

"What shall I do with the sateen?"

"Cut the selvages and hang it over the rack to stretch till tomorrow. Do you know where the Percys live? Third house north of the Methodist church, on the west side."

Loretta sighed, and reached for a suit-box and tissue paper.

"Well, that's the Percy wedding, and I'm glad to see it out of the place. Good notion to go and see how it looks on the figure, though! What about you and me shutting up shop tomorrow, and going along?"

"Oh, I'd like to do that! Shall I take the parcel now?"

The six-forty whistled for the grade crossing as Tillie came down the Percy steps, having handed in her parcel. George Bingham heard the whistle and opened the boarding-house door. So that they met, without any warning at all, on the sidewalk just in front of the church. They faced each other with startled eyes.

Tillie's face grew cold and she set her lips in a stiff line, to keep them from trembling. It seemed a long time before George spoke, in such an easy pleasant voice that it instantly warmed her, and her embarrassment left her. She might have been an old and valued friend, one with whom he had long been on easy, even affectionate, terms.

"Hello there, stranger, so you haven't left this neck of the woods after all? Where have you been keeping yourself?"

He laid his hand on her shoulder as he might have laid it on a child's head, or his mare's neck. Its weight and warmth were exquisitely thrilling to Tillie. His fingers grasped her slender shoulder, giving it a little tight press, till she could feel the strength in them. A wave of dizziness spread over her body, and she closed her eyes briefly, to recover.

"I've been here all the time."

"Right here, in town?" George's face turned towards hers in surprise, as they slowly walked down Church Street.

"Yes. I'm nearly through my course. Just another month, or so."

"You don't spend much time on Main Street, do you? Loretta keep you caged up?"

Tillie shook her head, smiling now. George noted with pleasure that she was not as nearly his height as he had thought. Could show a couple of inches, anyway.

"What were you doing up our street?"

"Taking a parcel in to the Percys'."

What if the next thing he asked was "And what were you doing in my store, and why did you rush out like a loon, before I got there?" But he said, merely, "Oh, yes, great shines up there. Going to the wedding?"

"I think Loretta and I will go. We made all the clothes."

"How do you like the dressmaking business? Will you be going in for that yourself, one of these days?"

"I don't expect so."

"No?"

"No."

"Nobody could call you a chatterbox, could they?"

Tillie smiled, and said nothing, for there was nothing in her mind that she could put into words. She was looking at the gaunt lilac bushes that made a hedge for the church-yard, the dead-white fretwork on the parsonage veranda showing the red brick through like embroidery, and the stable door opening right on the street, as though she had seen nothing of the kind before.

"How much longer are you going to be here, then, did you say?"

"I'm to stay till the end of May. Then I'm going home."

"You sound as if you are glad to be through with us, are you?"

"I'll be glad to be home again."

"I guess you will. Coming over for the mail?"

The girl in the wicket threw open the grill just as they came in. "Hello, George. And Miss Shantz, there's something for you, as usual. Doesn't often miss, I can tell you, George. Pretty faithful, all right."

Tillie blushed, and reached for the letter. George opened his box and found nothing at all. "Nobody seems to feel that way about me," he said. "Just a trifle nosy, our Cora, isn't she?" he added, as they left the office together.

Tillie was silent. George looked at her with an amused smile which served to brighten the fresh pink on Tillie's face.

"Do you know you're blushing as red as a poppy?" His tone was teasing and provocative. "Sorry I can't walk along with you, but Billy hasn't had his supper yet."

"I haven't either," said Tillie, inanely. "Good-bye."

"See you at the wedding!" Whistling gaily, George crossed the street to the drug store which was his own beloved possession.

Aunt Keturah and Aunt Elmina rocked on the narrow veranda, as Tillie came along.

"You're pretty late," said Keturah, looking severely at her. "We've had ours. Yours is on the table."

"Thank you, Aunt Keturah."

Tillie walked past her and straight up the stairs to her room. There was a noise of vigorous splashing. Keturah sighed. Elmina eyed her nervously, and coughed her little apologetic cough, as if in that way she could atone to Keturah for the noise and the broken routine which Tillie's presence had occasioned, ever since she came.

"Washing," said Elmina, diffidently.

"Splashing, you mean. I must go and see to things."

The sisters left their rockers and went into the house.

Tillie ran down the stairs, shining and rosy from the water, her eyes bright and distant, a secret smile on her face. She looked with evident distaste at the cold supper spread out on the table. "I don't think I'll have any supper," she announced. "Don't seem to be hungry tonight." She cleared the table briskly, clicking plates on to their piles with a precision that seemed in itself defiant.

"How's Mrs. Nighswander?"

It was obvious to both of the older women that there was something, and very probably not Mrs. Nighswander, on her mind.

"Worse," said Keturah.

Tillie stopped her swift progress. "Poor old Jake. What will he do?"

"She's not dead yet," said Keturah coldly. "I was there all day. He can only pray. She may get better, yet."

Aunt Elmina's eyes suffused. Poor Martha! But yet she, Elmina, she was not sick, in her bed. She looked brightly at Tillie. "I'm older than Martha," she said.

Tillie nodded. It seemed to matter so little, once you were old, surely? She smiled lovingly at the little woman. "Were you alone, all day, then?"

Elmina nodded. "Yes, nearly all day."

"Warm, isn't it?" Tillie stepped quickly to the door, as if to fan her flaming face with cool breeze. "I think I'll put on a cooler dress."

"Have you got a cooler one here, except your best one?"

"No. But I'll put that on."

The aunts stared at her in astonishment.

"You'll put on your best dress, to sit around the house with? You go on at that rate, you'll come to want."

But Tillie ran upstairs without answering, and changed to the navy-blue lustre. Comfortable and cool, she went out and took up a position in a rocking chair on the veranda. She passed her fingers through her thick hair, enjoying the feel of cool air passing through it, and stirred it up from her head.

Keturah watched her from the doorway.

"You're as restless as a hen on a hot griddle, lately. Better come in. This hot is unseasonable. Treacherous weather. Getting dark, too."

Tillie carried the chair inside and sat down again. But

she did not seem able to light, anywhere, for more than a few minutes at a time.

Keturah looked at her in exasperation, while Elmina watched her with hands half raised, as one waiting for a strong wind to blow.

"Can't you find something better to do than squirm around in that rocking-chair? Have you finished your practising? What use there is spending your time and money in learning to play these outlandish pieces, and you going to be married and settled down, right away, I don't see. But as you've paid for them, you might as well get something out of it, I suppose."

Tillie got up from her chair, tossing carelessly to the table the letter she had been flipping up and down in her hand. Keturah looked at it sharply.

"Any special news from Simon?"

She was answered by a series of smashing chords from the piano. With strong relentless fingers Tillie played a Chopin prelude, ignoring the strange abbreviations advising softness and languor. Then without any warning transition she broke into a bold, scandalous variation on "The Holy City." Keturah sat transfixed in her chair, her hands clutching the arms, her whole being outraged by this misuse of a sacred theme. Elmina's little hands worked at her throat, and her eyes bulged with fear as Tillie's fingers spread over the keys in crashing arpeggios; for Tillie was playing like one possessed.

Keturah rose unsteadily and advanced towards the parlour. She could not see Tillie's face, but in the light from the street she could see the strong fingers flailing the music out of the hidden strings—loud, aggressive, fast, fearful music.

"Stop that! Stop that! It is wicked!"

She laid her bony hand sharply on the girl's shoulder. Tillie winced as though she had been struck. All the colour was washed from her face and she looked inexpressibly weary. She regarded Keturah as if she were a stranger, and then looked past her to Elmina, and the dark hall. The bounds of the little house became suddenly intolerable to her. For a moment, in the wild music, she had found release for something within her being which demanded freeing. Just as she had pushed away her intangible burden, the presence of Keturah, cold and disapproving, had cast it again upon her. The gentleness which she carried like a cloak deserted her, transformed into inexplicable urgency. Somehow, somewhere, surely, she could find a balance, and this quivering uncertainty which she had felt often, lately, would leave her. But the solution was not here, tonight, in this house. She stood trembling and taut, by the piano.

"I'll go out for a while, Aunt Keturah. I think sitting all day is bad for me."

"Out? It's nearly ten o'clock!"

"I'll not be long." There was pleading in her voice. Somehow she must escape this house, be really alone, for a while.

"You are not to go out!" Keturah stood before the door.

Tillie moved past her with a strong and silent step, into the little hall, and put on her coat and bonnet. She smoothed on her gloves, and stood before her aunt.

"I am going out." Her voice was as cold and even as ever Keturah's had been.

"If you go out that door," said Keturah, "then you need never come in it again. I'm looking after you, while you're here, and if I'd had any idea that you'd turn out the way you are doing, then I would never have told your mother I'd have you. It'll be a good day for you when you get married, if you keep out of trouble long enough for that. And I doubt if you will. What do you suppose Simon would say, you running around like this?"

Tillie stared at her, sudden contempt and a release of unexpected power in her eyes. But she was so angry that her voice shook.

"Perhaps I am a better judge than you of what Simon

may say. And if Simon—" But then the tears, stupid unreasonable tears, began to choke down her throat. "If Simon can't trust me to take a walk by myself in the evening then he'd better—" She could not quite say the words.

"A fine wife he's getting!" said Keturah, resorting through fear to sneering. There was nothing in Keturah's experience to consult. What had happened to the girl, and what must she do? She almost cowered as Tillie walked past her, head held high and voice cold.

"Good-bye," she said, conclusively, and opened the door and went out.

Keturah followed her on to the narrow veranda, Elmina peering behind her to see Tillie gain the sidewalk and stride along in the soft yellow light without a backward glance. They watched in silence. The proud black figure walked with increasing speed up the long hill, until the cone-shaped cedars swallowed her up.

Elmina anxiously bit her red loose lips, and whispered, "You won't really lock her out, Keturah? Surely not?"

Keturah pulled the screen to with a click, fastened the hook and shut the inside door, bolting it to with an angry thrust.

"She's a wicked, rebellious girl. It won't hurt her to have a good lesson. It's a hot night. She can sleep in the barn."

Elmina trailed into the parlour and searched through the window for the wanderer. "Shouldn't we wait just a little while, though?"

"No. It will do her good to have a good scare. There's a pair of horse blankets in the stable. She can sleep there, all right. A night on hard boards will straighten her up, maybe."

"Oh, Keturah!"

Keturah picked up the lamp. "Come on now. And if you hear her, don't move down. Somebody has to teach that young one something."

139

Keturah stretched herself, painfully, in her tall wooden bed. In a few minutes she was asleep, while little Elmina in her room fretted and worried. In the early dawn Keturah started up, thinking she heard the door-bell jangle. But the sound was not repeated. It was not Tillie, humble and repentant, imploring admittance. It was nothing at all. But now she could not sleep again. When it was really light, and surely it could not be long now, she would get up and see if the girl were on the veranda. But most likely she was in the old stable. By now she might have come to her senses. She struck a match and looked at the alarm clock on the chiffonier. Only four o'clock, still. She turned to rest her back, and tucked her thin feet up in her flannel nightgown, seeking relaxation and comfort which might give sleep. The door bell rang commandingly. There could be no doubt, this time. Keturah smiled with satisfaction and relief. She lit the candle, and another ring, imperative and startling, vibrated through the house.

"In a hurry, now," Keturah commented. "Getting anxious."

She felt under the bed for slippers, and with deliberate movements was putting her long arms through the sleeves of a grey cloth wrapper when the bell rang again, prolonged and sustained and loud. Keturah picked up the candle in a shaking hand, now more with anger at the imperative summons than relief, and walked with slow, deliberate steps down the front stairs to the door. Over the banister she noticed Elmina's thin figure bending down. "Get on back to bed, you'll get cold." She set the candle down on the hall rack, carefully pushing her coat away from the flame, before she opened the door.

Old Jake Nighswander stood in the open doorway, his eyes helpless and frightened, his loose mouth all puckered up and quivering toothlessly over his round white beard. He tried twice to speak, before any sound would come out.

"Martha—she's worse, Kettie. She won't say anything

140

to me, at all. I'm all alone, over there, now, with her. I have to get the doctor."

He hitched up his trousers, and with his elbows pressed down to the long coat he wore, to keep them up, looked imploringly at Keturah.

"You will come and stay with her, there, while I get Dr. Percy? Jah?"

"Have you got the fire going good? Get it going, good, and put the kettle on, with lots of water. She'll need heat. I'll be there, just as soon as I can."

Jake stretched out his hand, in gratitude. "Oh, thank God, thank God." He hurried off back across the empty road, in the beginning of the dawn.

Keturah wound the long braid into a nest at the back of her head, on the way upstairs. "You might as well come too," she said tersely to Elmina. In five minutes she was dressed and watching beside Martha Nighswander's bedside, while the heavy feet of Jake's old driver made rhythmic music down Main Street, going for the doctor.

It was afternoon before Martha was easier, and Keturah could come back, for a little while, to her own house. There was no sign that Tillie had been there, and the heavy brown cobwebs hung undisturbed over the top of the stable door.

14

TILLIE walked through the town on the dark side, her long legs covering the ground with satisfying speed. She made her way straight down Main Street, and when she had reached the dark post-office she stopped and looked steadfastly across the street at the light in the window of the drug store. A door opened in the block beyond, throwing a brief rectangle of light on to the sidewalk. Somebody said "Good-bye, then," and the door closed; a man's figure dropped into the shadows, and his quick footsteps clicked away. Tillie gathered herself closer into the post-office platform and stood there paralysed, watching the glitter of the light on the bright objects beneath it, and the mystery of the green shadows beyond the velvet curtain. Four people passed, two men and two girls, their light clothes quick blurs, their voices gay and bantering. One couple turned down Lock Street, and the other went on, more slowly now, gay voices giving place to low, and whispering words to silence.

She began to walk again, suddenly overwhelmed with loneliness. The storm that had gathered in her head was spent. Presently she would have to consider Keturah, and come to some decision. A shiver passed over her. Suppose she should go back, and find the doors locked against her? Her feet brought her to a stop; for a second she felt impelled to rush back at once, and demand to be let in, to be given the security of walls and roof. But pride prevented her. "I am not a child. I can choose for myself, surely, what I shall do. I can't bear to be shut up, so, never to breathe but there." Her days were happy, filled and satisfying, always learning, and solving problems new as each day to her. But, lately, the evenings were empty parcels of time, to be done with, and thrown aside.

The purring of the electric power-house became louder, the beat slower and more insistent. There were three final heavy thumps, and the light flickered and went out. A final deeper silence spread heavily over the village. Not a pin-point of light seemed left, up and down the street, or in the township, or, perhaps, the world. A light cool breeze played over the tops of the budding maples, as if come in answer to the sudden dark. The air grew quickly cooler.

In a moment the tiny indistinguishable night sounds would start, but now, when the breeze stilled in the maples, there was soft, distilled quiet, hanging from the sky, and growing up from the earth.

The darkness grew so thick about her that she might have taken an armful of it and tossed it over her shoulder, but that there was a cloudlike darkness there, too, to bounce it back to her. In another minute she would begin to see outlines and shapes, as one darker than the other, when the stars in the deep black of the sky should begin to advertise themselves as more stable sources of light than the street lamps; but not quite yet. Now the cool comfort of the utter darkness and quiet soothed her, calming her restlessness. It was as if a cool and competent hand had been laid upon the hot tangle of her undefined misery. Perhaps, here in this quiet, she could find peace within herself. To be totally honest, in the spirit as in the letter, was a cardinal point in all her training. If she were restless and unhappy, then there must be a cause for it, and she must find it. To go on as she had been doing was weak, if not sinful. To blame Keturah, or anyone else, for her lack of satisfaction with her life, was stupid. It came with a shock of realization to her that she herself, and she alone, was responsible for herself. What Keturah did, or did not do, had no reference to her life at all. If she was to be happy or wretched, free or bound, it was her own doing. Walking slowly, still west in the dark village, she searched her heart.

Through the darkness, familiar phrases recalled themselves to Tillie's mind, until she could almost hear her father's rich voice, pleading with those in darkness to seek the Lord. "Open your hearts to the sweet sound of His voice. Ask, and ye shall receive. Knock, and the door shall be opened unto you." Perhaps the source of unrest lay just here. Had she neglected God? She went to church, it was true, with Aunt Keturah. But sitting there in the cold blue light she had allowed her thoughts to wander

143

into these new paths which had lately been shown to her. There had been no comfort in the Word. But it was not true that she had forgotten God. He had as much forgotten her. She had prayed, these quick, hot spring nights, for deliverance from this oppression which plagued her. There had been no help from on high. Sometimes she felt the pressure within her to be intolerable. Was she to go on like this, then? In this strange world where she had strayed, so innocently, it seemed that the manners and customs were too unreal for her to understand, and yet, while she could not behave as the inhabitants of this world did, her own customs were useless to her too. And Simon was not here, to help her. Perhaps he could have; but the thought of Simon, so much a man of unimpeachable principle, gave her no help. The weeks stretching between her and June, when she could go home, seemed without end. "If only I could go home now!" It was the one thought that had any hope in it. Once at home, her mind, bruised with baffling blows received from the little excursions she had made beyond forbidden doors, would be healed. But even as she thought of it, she grew impatient that there should be so much forbidden. She felt herself between two currents, whirling like a witless thing. "I must go back. I'm so tired." She leaned against a tree trunk in weary resignation.

She was beyond the tracks now, where the lone lamp of the station-master burned its misty yellow oval into the green darkness. She fixed her eyes idly on the mass of the Mansion House, across the way. Silhouetted against a suddenly illumined hall was the full figure of a woman, her hands upraised from her plump, well corseted figure, to the hanging lamp. The hands worked with the chains for a minute, jockeying them up and down until the pulley caught, and the lamp reached nearly to the ceiling. She stood directly under it, so that her face lay in the shadow; and into the ring of yellow light surrounding her there stepped a slight young man. Tillie gazed at the two, drawn irresistibly from her cloister to those who lived. The woman in the hallway lowered her arms slowly, still looking up to the circle of light, as if by act of mind to steady the lamp after her hands had let it go.

The man moved into the penumbra and encircled the woman's body in his arms, drawing her to him, and kissing her passionately. The woman dropped her arms about his head, and seemed to press it to her with tenderness. Tillie drew in her breath sharply, hunching her shoulders and closing her eyes, not daring to look, and then not able to keep from watching. The man and woman kissed again and again, under the lamp. Tillie felt her stomach muscles tighten; she held her breath, and turned away. When she looked again, the lovers were drawing apart, reluctantly. The door opened. The man crossed the long narrow veranda and ran down the side steps, still keeping his eyes on the woman who stood laughing in the doorway. Finally he waved at her and walked briskly down the street, whistling lightly. Tillie noted mechanically that he was flat on the D. The lights in the Mansion House went softly out. Tillie's breath left her in a gasp, and she leaned heavily against her tree for support. She was unutterably exhausted. The pride and power she had felt an hour ago were gone. She might have been having some unthinkable nightmare, sent from the Devil himself. She had seen herself, since the man kissed the woman in that lighted hall, for what she was. Weak, wanton, no better than a harlot. As a man thinketh in his heart, so is he. Her stomach felt sick; her knees trembled. She stood away from the tree and put out a hand to steady herself, and prayed.

"O Lord, help me! Help me! Take this from me, and let me be as I was before."

But surely, she was still a good and faithful child of God? She was among the most fortunate of people still, surely? A good man loved her; she was secure in that. Her future was joyous and serene. What unreal cloud had she imagined to lie between her and her happy life? She would go back, now, and ask Keturah for forgiveness. And, above all, she would never permit herself to think again of the strange, sweet, weakening power of a man's hand on her shoulder—a stranger, whom she had seen only twice before. Never. Her mouth was hard.

Up the long hill she walked, past the drug store, past the corner of Church Street where she had walked with George, and through the dark village to her aunts' house. She paused at the gate to look up at it. Oh, why was she not safely inside that steep small structure? She softly lifted the latch on the gate and crept up the steps. No light, of course; and no sound. She lowered herself wearily to the floor and sat still there a few minutes. Then she rose and gently tried the screen door. It was hooked. Stepping with care, on her toes, as if afraid of waking someone—and if she did not wake someone, where would she be?—she went around to the back door. It was bolted. The thought of raising a window, and crawling in that way, occurred to her; but she dismissed it at once. The windows were probably locked, from the inside, and in any case pride would not permit her to climb like a thief through the window of a house which she had had, at least until now, a perfect right to enter by the front door. She looked longingly up at her own window. How happy she would be, to be inside there, sleeping her innocent sleep, on her own bed. She was so tired, now. But she had chosen this way, and she must do what she could with it. The way of the transgressor is hard. She hesitated, looking at the old stable, and then back at the house. She was defeated and worn, but pride had not quite left her. She would sleep in no stable. She went wearily out of the gate, closing it softly behind her, and started back down the hill.

The tune from "Kiss Me Again" which the whistler had left on the night air circled foolishly in her head.

Down Lock Street no light burned in any house. Tillie's slow footsteps sounded light and hollow on the board walk leading to the brown frame house where Loretta lived. She mounted the front steps firmly and sent a purling ring through the darkness of the house as if it were broad noon and she Miss Percy herself.

"Who's that?" Loretta's voice came from behind the house, and was followed in a minute by Loretta, who drew up in amazement as she heard Tillie's reply.

"Well, Tillie, for the love of the crows! What are you doing here, this hour of the night?"

"I'm locked out. Could I stay with you?"

"Keturah out?"

"No."

"Know where you are?"

"No."

Loretta's quick ear caught an undertone which prevented any more questions, burning though she was with curiosity.

"Sure you can stay. Come on round the back. Front door's locked. Just got home myself, sitting out back here enjoying the sky. Telling myself I ought to get in there."

The two women walked in the shadow of a tall cedar hedge to the broad porch on the back of Loretta's house, overlooking a few apple trees and pasture land beyond.

"We'll pay for this warm spell, I shouldn't wonder. But no reason not to enjoy it while we have it, is there?"

"I was afraid you'd be in bed."

"Should be, too. Just waiting for company, I guess. Did you get the parcel in all right?"

"Yes."

"Screen door opens from the south side. Awkward, but never seem to have it fixed. Have a light in a minute."

She reached down a small oil lamp from the shelf above the stove, and felt for the matches on the warming-oven.

"Always keep this handy. Don't seem to be able to get to bed as early as some people."

She lit the coal-oil burner with the same match, and put a small kettle of water to boil on it.

Tillie's face was white and strained, in the lamplight.

"Awful glad to have company. Just sit down and make

147

yourself comfortable. You can sleep in the front room, upstairs. Nothing fancy there, but plenty of room. We'll have a little snack, first."

She went to the three-cornered pantry off the big kitchen and brought out a box of date cookies, a bottle of raspberry cordial and a small platter of dried beef curls.

"Cheese, if you'd like some, and here's biscuits."

She smiled, unusually and warmly, at the girl.

"Give me the bunnit. Cup of tea in a shake."

She directed Tillie to a deep chair, noting with concern her white face and tense mouth.

"Glad you came down. I do get lonely, once in a while. People say I ought to put a boarder in some of those rooms, upstairs, but I don't want the bother of it. Can't think my own thoughts with a nest of magpies chattering in the house."

Tillie smiled briefly. "I'll try not to be a nest of magpies."

Loretta nodded. "I'm not worried. Smell these; nice, eh?"

Tillie bent obediently over a crock of apple blossom, in full bloom, standing on the floor. The pure scent filled the big dark room.

"Always bring a branch in, about February, and force them."

She handed a thin china cup with a frail gold-and-brown pattern to Tillie. The tea was strong and scalding hot within its delicate walls. The gaiety of the little meal, the pretty plates and the wonderful crimson light thrown on the white cloth through the raspberry liquor, coupled with Loretta's unquestioning friendliness, warmed her. She might have been another person, enjoying this unexpected kind of hospitality. It was the first time she had seen any of the house but the work rooms. Was this, then, how some people did? Apple blossoms in the house? Suppers at nearly midnight? Decorated, delicate china, sure to drop and break at a touch? In the edge of the yellow lamplight she could see soft glittering objects on the long sideboard. There was a six-inch lace edging on the tablecloth which someone must have spent months of time and eyesight doing. Decorations, vanities, extravagances, all of these. And yet—

The lamplight found the soft gleam of the backs of books, rows and rows of them, apparently, right up to the ceiling, on narrow shelves each side of the door. Open on the table, as though Loretta had been reading while eating a meal, lay a book with many lines of fine printing. Two or three volumes were piled up under the apple blossoms, where the light would be good, in the day-time, and a stack of magazines flanked the couch. Tillie put out her hand, and awkwardly touched the open book.

"Take your time with your supper, Tillie. I'll just run up and fix your bed. Excuse the lamp, a minute. I'll leave it on the landing, so you won't be quite in the dark, till I get a light up there."

"I'm being a trouble to you, Miss Macklin."

"No trouble at all, only too glad to have you stay."

Tillie could hear her quick, nervous footsteps, clicking on the bare floors of the upper storey; she sang a tuneless, hoarse-voiced song as she worked, and presently shouted down to Tillie that all was ready.

Tillie drew herself reluctantly from the comforting warmth and colour of the dining-room, and slowly climbed the stairs, the smell of apple blossoms trailing her up to the landing.

"You look tired, Tillie, time you had some rest."

"Yes. I am tired."

"Bathroom right at the back of the hall, candle at your hand, here. Towels on the foot of the bed, nightgown, wrapper, slippers, too. And good night to you."

Loretta laid her hand for just a moment on Tillie's arm as she paused before going down. "You won't be nervous, up here all alone? I sleep downstairs."

"Oh, no, no!"

"Good night then. Breakfast about eight. I'll call you, if you sleep in."

A door closed, definitively, and Tillie was alone in a big bare room, with three windows wide open and sending in drifts of cool, pleasant air. The bed looked wide and deep, and on the foot of it lay a nightgown which had cost Loretta twelve dollars for material alone. It was shell-pink crepe satin with long sleeves, edged at cuff and collar with the narrowest of double ruffles, and hemstitched with blue along the opening in an elaborate Italian style. Sixteen pearl globes made buttons for the creation, and Tillie opened the door twice, to ask Loretta if it could possibly be a night-gown. But downstairs all was dark, and she did not dare disturb her. She slowly folded her own garments on the back of a chair and put it on. There was nothing in her whole experience to prepare her for the sensation her body received, as the silk slid down over it.

Loretta turned in her bed, laughing to think of Tillie's astonishment when she saw it. "Change from the sugar bags, anyway," she told herself with grim delight. "Imagine that old bat shutting that child out. Ought to be tarred and feathered and run out of town on a rail. This one's got more spunk than old Ket's used to handling, in spite of her pretty face and lovely soft manners. Notion to ask her to stay with me, till her time's out. Kind of comfortable, having somebody in the house, for a while. Bet Keturah's having some hard thoughts, just now. I wonder what the trouble is, really? Just plain cussedness, probably. Man in it, likely. Usually is. But I thought Tillie was all fixed up with that lantern-jawed preacher from Lemonville. None of my business, anyway, but if she wants to stay here she's welcome to. Fun to see how old Keturah would take it. I'd kind of like to show the girl a few more tricks, anyhow, before she buries herself for life."

Up in the big bare room at the front of the house, Tillie knelt despairing, at the open window. Her long crisp hair hung over the slender trappings of the silk gown, and she prayed for a light from her Saviour, to show her on her way. She was so lost, now, she told Him, and utterly without help. She was a sinner, in countless ways she had sinned; and now she was in black confusion, and knew not where to look, or what to do. The lure of the flesh had overcome her. What now, should she do, and where look for help, but from Him? Ask, and it shall be given to you, seek, and ye shall find. But something still stood between Tillie and her God. The words she could find were wrong, or she had not deeply repented. There was no answer from the night air. Finally she ceased to pray, and just knelt there, looking out into the darkness, until she was stiff and cold, and her knees hurt. She got up and slipped into the big bed, flung herself on her face, and slept, with her hands curved above her head, like a child.

15

D OWN THE aisles of the Methodist church, broad white ribbons had been looped from pew to pew, marking the places for the invited guests. Tall black iron standards holding pots of blooming Easter lilies formed avenues down the church. Under the golden oak pulpit, where the light through John Wesley's face shone red and blue and yellow, a bank of lilies was arranged. Green mosquito-netting in loops and swirls concealed the pots, so that nothing could be seen but the big, long-throated lilies, blooming in this strange garden. Their scent was overpoweringly sweet, and the stealthy voices and unconscious tiptoeing of the ushers suggested that a funeral would take place here, rather than the brilliant marriage of the village's most socially prominent daughter.

The back seats were almost full of the village itself, not invited to the wedding, with no prospects of cake or reception, no responsibility for gifts, but welcome to gaze and enjoy. Each bedizened guest who claimed the right to sit within the white-ribbon area was an object of interest and critical inspection. Necks unaccustomed to public appearance grew red under the scrutiny, and the women moved self-consciously in the long procession from the door of the church to the chosen seats.

Tillie and Loretta slipped into opposite aisle seats, almost at the back. "She'll come out this way," Loretta whispered, "my side going in and yours coming out." She sat back and let her bright eyes rove mischievously over the congregation. "Enough stuffed birds here to fill a taxidermist's shop," she added.

But Tillie scarcely heard her speak. She looked with amazement on the little church. In her eyes the stained-glass windows, John Wesley on the right of the choir loft, and Shepherd Jesus with His lamb on the left of the organ, the streaky red carpet and the simple Gothic carving were decorations of the most elaborate and exotic kind. The scent from the lilies quickened her senses, her heart beat suddenly too fast, and she felt an apprehension of popish danger. For what were these windows but graven images?

As the thin grey-haired organist came in, keeping her eyes strictly upon the organ and her music, a flutter went through the congregation. She settled herself comfortably on the bench, and pressed her bony red knuckles over the sheets; but in pulling out the stops she touched the keyboard with her elbow, and a discordant squawk startled the people. A flush spread over her face; she straightened her back, and dropped her fingers squarely on the keys, and the solemn, dream-filled music of the Intermezzo from *Cavalleria Rusticana* swelled out into the little church. To cover her embarrassment she played louder than she had meant to, and the volume was startling. Then, recovering, she began to play with conviction. Tillie felt the tears spring to her eyes. The church and the flowers and the people were blurred with tears. The vestry door opened, and two men walked delicately across the church to the altar.

"Here's the victim," Loretta whispered hoarsely, and Tillie looked through her tears to see a strange young man, thick in the shoulder, with a red face and an amiable, stolid expression. Standing beside him, head held nervously high, was George Bingham. "If I had the choice of those two," confided Loretta, leaning over, "I'd take the best man, myself."

The organ ceased, and for what seemed to Tillie a long time there was silence in the church, with only the lilies alive and breathing. What had happened? Was something wrong? The organist fidgeted on her bench, her eyes glued to a small mirror fixed on a bracket by the music stand. The young men stood utterly still. Someone coughed, and it made a frightening sound. There was a rustling just outside the red baize doors; they opened an inquiring crack, the organist nodded, and the wedding music of *Lohengrin* filled the building. The bridesmaids' dresses which Tillie knew so intimately, first the fawn one which had given trouble with the matching of the stripes, and then the green watered silk with the cream collar, passed in review. She noted with appreciation that the left sleeve stood up at exactly the same angle as its twin, although the shoulder was distinctly lower on that side. The whole pageant for the moment was reduced in Tillie's mind to consideration of that sleeve.

Now the music grew louder and louder, until it seemed that the sounds were bouncing back upon each other, when they hit the walls, so that the melody was lost in a knitting of the echoes. Tillie saw that Miss Percy had entered; and watching the young man at the altar, now, she saw him turn and look at Miss Percy with such a warm, loving, welcoming expression that again she felt tears burning in her eyes, and stood there, until the bride and her father came to a stop before the altar, with tears dripping from her cheeks unchecked.

These tears were the manifestation of a new emotion. She was conscious of a feeling of lightness, of gaiety and joy. It struck her as immensely wonderful, and as a matter of the most extraordinary importance, that this kind of thing could occur in Kinsail. Celebrations, such as this—affairs of the greatest possible gladness, obviously—must be going on, she supposed, in villages and towns all over the country. She had never known any of this before. It seemed to her that she had found a new ingredient in the make-up of her native land. Perhaps people like Dr. Percy's family lived in this kind of atmosphere always. Not that there would always be weddings, of course, but in their daily lives this acceptance of gaiety and music with gladness was, with them, the usual thing. All memory of Keturah—the disagreeable, inevitable interview still before her, since she had had no stomach to face her aunt this morning—all memory of her weary disillusionment of last night, dissipated in the joy of the music and gaiety of the wedding. She felt herself expand, and knew that she could embrace this abundant way of living.

The vestry door opened, and the bride, smiling in a way which looked to Tillie almost like the smile of triumph but was, she supposed, only the expression of supreme happiness, came down the aisle, leaning on her husband's arm. He was almost laughing; and the bride passed so close to Tillie that she could have touched the heavy cream silk of her dress. There was no suggestion now of the funeral. All was laughter and happy relief. Triumphal Mendelssohn carried the procession through the church. The bridesmaid in the green silk followed close behind the bride, leaning on George's arm. They might have been blown along the aisle by the rich volume of music that followed them.

Just as the green bridesmaid passed, George found Tillie and gave her a broad good-natured wink, as if he would

154

say, "Well, here I am, all ascot tie and striped pants, but you know me for what I really am, don't you?" Tillie smiled radiantly at him, carried out of herself. She might have said farewell to all her old life, and made herself a new one, just for this moment. There was for her a kind of enchantment about this little span of time that allowed no memory and no anticipation to spoil its perfection. She was lulled into pure happiness. When she and Loretta reached the church steps, and stood with the others to watch the bridal procession walk along Church Street to the bride's home, she was still smiling, included for the moment in a new world in which, for her, it was overwhelmingly necessary and wonderful that she should be.

They walked slowly down Main Street, turning reluctantly into Lock Street, loath to take up with work when other people seemed just setting out to play. The streets were full of these loiterers, too. "There's the Percy girl and her new husband," they seemed to say, "off to a grand reception and a party. Why should we have to work?"

Tillie was quietly basking, against all resolve, in the new sense of communication set up between her and George, when she raised her eyes from her pleasant contemplation and saw that it was Aunt Keturah who approached them.

The old woman stopped abruptly, as they met. She passed over Tillie with a cold glance, and spoke to Loretta.

"So you took her in, did you?"

Loretta greeted Aunt Keturah with cool amiability.

"And this is how you teach her a trade, walking the streets by day, as well as by night."

"We've been to the wedding, Miss Shantz." Loretta spoke cheerfully, in determined good humour. "No way for a poor man to get to a wedding, in this town, but by walking. The Lord didn't supply wings, you know!"

"A blasphemer, too," said Keturah, drawing in her breath, and carried away now to a state of mixed emotions quite unlike any previously experienced. She was reduced to coarse, abrupt, fearful words, by the nameless fear which gripped her. She looked searchingly at Tillie's face, as if to find a mark there.

"When did she come to you, then? Or did she come in at all, last night? Wandering the streets like a homeless cat!"

"It occurs to me," said Loretta, beginning to enjoy herself, "that you have not very much right to enquire. After all," her voice hardened at the thought of it, "you shut her out, it seems."

Tillie's face grew white and troubled. Loretta, glancing at her, recalled the tired strained look of her when she came in, last night, and went on. "What did you expect the girl to do? Lie down in the street to sleep?"

Tillie looked from the one to the other in helpless inaction. There must be something she could do, or say, which would stop this altercation, but she could find no suggestion within herself. The older women glared at each other, and she might have been both blind and deaf, for all the attention they paid to her.

Keturah's words fell on her like showering stones. Since for Keturah there were no intermediate steps from good to evil, there was no possibility of innocence in the girl before her. A girl was good, and by good she meant unquestioning and obedient, or she was a bad girl. That one step outside the familiar, accepted boundary must result in instant disaster had been her teaching, and her imagination permitted no mutation of this idea. Safe within, and in desperate danger without. Inevitable fall followed even the most seemingly innocent flight. With the brutal speech of the inarticulate, she approached her niece as if she were a proven thief and harlot.

"Walking the streets," said Keturah, laughing with thin contempt. "I'd have thought *you'd* be old enough to know better, if she doesn't."

Loretta, her bright eyes brighter still with unbelieving anger, stepped closer to Keturah.

"What do you mean by what you're saying?" Her voice was low and menacingly quiet.

"She's a streetwalker! Nothing more or less than a woman of the streets!" Her voice rose in a thin, uncontrolled screaming.

"Strong language there, Miss Shantz. Tillie could have you up in court for that remark." She suddenly lost her temper. "And serve you damn well right if she did!"

Keturah raised her hands, as if by a physical act she could ward off the profane word. It was possible to revile her niece, and to accuse her protector of any depth of depravity, but one forbidden word might be (who knew?) the unpardonable sin. She must separate herself from this sinful atmosphere at once. She turned to go on.

"I'll send word to her father," she said.

"Ought to cheer him up no end," said Loretta, anger running bright, like one of her metallic threads, through her voice, "if you give him a touch of what you've given us this afternoon."

Keturah looked at her from the depths of bewilderment. This wicked woman evidently felt that she, Keturah, had done something wrong.

"It's some Levi's fault she's as she is. From this time forward she will be an outcast, from her people. I'll tell him to come and get her. You can keep her till then. She can't come in my house again. Jake Nighswander will bring her grip."

"Tell him when he comes," advised Loretta, "after you've finished sending the poor child to hell, that he'll find her with me, playing dominoes with a few of Satan's imps. Good afternoon."

She strode forward again, grasping Tillie's unresisting arm with her brown gloved hand, and marched down Lock Street for twenty paces, then turned. Keturah was still standing where they had left her, looking after them. "Wait here," commanded Loretta. She walked swiftly back to Keturah. "And as for you and your kind," she said, impressively, "may the Lord have mercy on your soul." She turned her back on Keturah's consternation, and walked rapidly back to Tillie.

"Well, that seems to be that. You're staying with me for a while. I'm delighted to have you."

"I feel that I'm putting you out, though."

"You're not. I'd thought of suggesting it, from time to time, but I didn't get round to it."

Tillie hesitated at the door. "Shouldn't I go and get my things, if I'm going to stay?"

Loretta unlocked the door and looked with distaste on the pile of unfinished sewing in the workroom.

"Old Jake's bringing them over," she said, absently. "That fool wedding has got me all upset. I don't seem to care if I never do a tap again—Oh, hell, let's just shut up shop for the day, and rest and play like the idle rich."

Tillie smiled uncertainly. She had scarcely recovered from the storm loosed over her head, and was not sure what she should do, in this house, if she were not to work in it.

"Hang up your hat and stay a while!" Loretta was warmly gay. "I'm going to put on the kettle, and we'll have tea out on the porch. Pick yourself something to read, on your way through."

When Loretta came to find her, the tray in her hands, Tillie stood helplessly before the bookshelves, scanning scores of titles, all completely strange to her eyes.

"Find anything you like there?"

Tillie shook her head. "I haven't read many books," she said. "We don't believe it's right, you know."

"Nonsense!" barked Loretta. "Can't be kept back by that kind of thing, this day and age. You've got to read, and read plenty. Since your aunt thinks you've gone to hell anyway, you might as well enjoy yourself there." She laughed her characteristic, hoarse laugh. "Give you a real taste for literature, if they'd let me have you for a while."

Tillie turned her back on the books. She had expended too much emotion for one day. "I must not," she said.

"Don't let me persuade you."

Tillie moved to the porch with the slow grace and pride of carriage which gave Loretta such pleasure to watch. "Don't dance, either, I suppose," she said abruptly. "Too bad. Great waste. You've got exceptional balance. Sit in that basket chair. And if I were you, I'd put my feet up."

Loretta knew herself to be exhibiting maternal solicitude, and was amused and startled. "Well," she told herself defensively, "I might have had a daughter myself, about her age, if any man had asked me. Maybe not so good looking, but I hope she'd have looked happier than that one does."

"Your aunt certainly goes to a lot of trouble, to bring you up right, doesn't she?" Perhaps if she made light of it, a little, Tillie would take it easier. She laughed softly at the remembrance of the old woman's rage.

"She feels responsible for me," said Tillie, seriously. She had fallen into humiliation, through pride, but she could not allow Loretta to make fun of Keturah.

"People run into a deuce of a lot of trouble, trying to keep other folks running straight, according to their own notions."

"I seem to have made a great deal of trouble for her, this year," said Tillie, regret at least, if not full repentance, in her voice.

"Better be troubled than bored," advised Loretta, flippantly, passing a plate of lemon biscuits, and reflecting that Keturah really did think Tillie was bound for fire and brimstone. Pious old ignoramus.

"I suppose your father'll come down like the wolf on the fold, will he, and snatch you from out this burning?"

"He will come, of course."

"Well, damn it all, just when you're really useful to me, and I used to you, and depending on you, too!"

Tillie looked startled. "Of course, I am going to stay until my time is out!"

159

"What about your father, though?"

"I can explain, to my father."

There was a pause, during which Loretta looked curiously at Tillie.

"What's the objection to reading books, with you?"

"Because they are not true."

"True? What is true? Doesn't it depend a bit on what you mean by true?"

Tillie looked astonished.

"But how could it mean anything else? If a thing is true, it is true. If it is not, it is not!"

Loretta flipped up her brown skirt to display a flounced petticoat.

"What colour is that?"

"Blue," said Tillie, promptly.

"I bought it for green," said Loretta. "Becky Smithson sold it to me for green. Which would you say is true, blue or green?"

"I don't know, then. It looks blue to me."

"Umhum."

"But that doesn't make any real difference, does it? But to read lies, and to fill the mind which should be filled only with the thought of God, with foolishness—that is what is wrong."

"And is it all foolishness, then, that brilliant and gifted men and women have taken thought on, and written down so that others may share their findings?"

Tillie looked gravely at Loretta. "I don't know. Perhaps there are things which would be good to read. But we feel that to know and love, and then, perhaps to understand God's own word, will take all our life. It is more than enough."

"Do you honestly find that it is, for you? Are you never more curious than that? Do you really find all that you need in the Bible?"

"I know that I shall find there all, all that I would ever

need. It is in myself that I am lacking, if I do not. It is all there, I am sure."

"Why are you sure?"

"Why?"

"Yes, just tell me why, now."

Why? Why the sun, why the moon, why the spring and the fall, the seed-time and the harvest, the flowering and the waning? There was no answer to this question. There could be no question.

"I can't tell you why; I just know, that is all."

"Marvellous piece of literature, of course, the Bible. The men who thought up the King James version had wonderful sense of rhythm. Their sentences are magnificent—'Though I speak with the tongues of men and of angels, and have not charity, I am become as sounding brass, or a tinkling cymbal. And though I have the gift of prophecy, and understand all mysteries, and all knowledge; and though I have all faith, so that I could remove mountains, and have not charity, I am nothing.' Well, perhaps you'd better stick to it. You won't improve much on that. Just listen, though, for a minute, and see how you like the sound of this:

'The quality of mercy is not strain'd,
It droppeth as the gentle rain from heaven
Upon the place beneath. It is twice bless'd:
It blesseth him that gives and him that takes.
'Tis mightiest in the mightiest; it becomes
The throned monarch better than his crown;
His sceptre shows the force of temporal power,
The attribute to awe and majesty,
Wherein doth sit the dread and fear of kings;
But mercy is above this sceptred sway,
It is enthroned in the hearts of kings.
It is an attribute to God himself;
And earthly power doth then show likest God's,
When mercy seasons justice.' "

Tillie listened in bewilderment. "But that is not God's word, is it?"

"No, my child, that is William Shakespeare's word. He had what you might call a gift with words that some of those early Hebrew fishermen and lawyers that you are devoting all your reading time to might well envy."

"I don't know any books written by Hebrew fishermen, though. I just mean the Bible, Miss Macklin, not any other books."

"Tillie," Loretta spoke impressively, "who wrote the Bible?"

Tillie set down her cup and looked at Loretta, shaking her head from side to side. "It is God's word, God wrote it, I suppose. I never thought of it, that way."

Loretta impatiently continued, "And where was it found then? Did God write it up there in the sky, and float it down to the pulpit of the Mennonite church, all ready in beautiful English, to be read?"

The fervour and intensity of her words was almost frightening to Tillie. "I don't know," she said, slowly, "I never thought of it." The possible blasphemy in Loretta's tone seriously alarmed her. "Let us not talk of it any more, please."

Loretta sat down, sighing. "Well, Tillie, you must know that somebody wrote the Bible, if you'd give it a moment's thought. A good many hands, and minds, at long intervals of time, worked on that great book before it reached us in its present state."

"Men wrote it?"

"Of course, who else? And they didn't all tell the same story, either, as you will find, if you look at it, carefully. Take the apostles, for instance, who wrote the story of the resurrection. All different, every one. Which is true?"

"I didn't know that."

"Ask your young man. He's been studying the Bible, hasn't he? He'll know something of the problems of people who insist on believing every word, literally, as read. I suppose they must take some kind of lukewarm critical approach to the Bible, down there."

Then Tillie realized what she had been hearing. There was a thing called Higher Criticism, which had attacked the Christian church, like a dread disease, even affecting ministers of the gospel. This was some of the same kind of thing, and this too, she must earnestly guard against. Dangers, everywhere she walked.

"And listen to me," Loretta proceeded, thoroughly warmed to her subject now. "If you were a cabbage, you could sit on your stalk in your field till you rotted, for all of me. The back concessions are full of animated cabbages, and a good many of them wear Mennonite bonnets, too. But you are not a cabbage, or you would not be here. Shardley says you have real talent. Cabbages don't play pianos. Look at your hands. Made for creation. More to be done with hands like that than scrubbing floors and pressing work-pants. Some people were intended to be cabbages. You are not. Don't go through life pretending to be satisfied with a mumbo-jumbo which, as you are finding out for yourself, is empty and unrealistic, when you look into it. And what about this abundant life—even your Bible makes out a case for that. Is it an abundant life to cut out from it all or nearly all the gifts of sight, and sound, and human expression? Come in here. Listen to this."

Loretta wound the gramophone and inserted a black cylinder into it. There were a few preliminary scratchings, and then the golden voice of Caruso filled the room until the curtains seemed almost to shake with the power of it.

> *"Questa o quella*
> *Per me pari sono*
> *A quant 'altre d'in torno*
> *D'intorno mi vedo."*

163

Tillie sat like a woman in a trance. Her long fingers stretched free into the air before her, as if she could feel the vibration running through them. "Play it again," she commanded. Loretta shifted the needle bar and the music poured out again.

"That kind of thing," said Loretta tersely, "was not thought up by pretending to be a cabbage, with neither eyes nor ears. Wake up, girl, and find out what there is in this world. Nobody's very sure about the next one, anyway, and you'll be a long time dead."

16

*L*EVI SAT down a little gingerly on the slender chair and looked appreciatively, in spite of his concern, at his daughter across the sunny long room. She looked so brisk, neat and swift-moving a woman, in her long green cover-all, that he found it a problem to identify her completely with his little girl. The weeks since Christmas had altered her greatly, it seemed to him. But he could find her at once, when she smiled. There could be nothing really wrong.

"So this is where you do your work?"

Tillie regarded him lovingly.

"We spend all day here, usually. Except for meals."

She looked about the room as though to see it through his eyes, and found it bright and inviting and comfortably familiar.

Levi leaned forward and whispered conspiratorially, "Where's Loretta?"

"Uptown for the mail."

He nodded, satisfied and happy that they were alone.

Tillie sat down in businesslike fashion before the machine, lifting the shuttle slot to inspect the bobbin for thread. Levi's big brown finger moved in a six-inch orbit over the work table, carrying with it slivers of pink mull. Scraps of the material found their way to his feet; his arm moving from table to chair dislodged a pile of pinned patterns which fell across his knees, trailing snips of pink haze with it. He looked up in comical dismay, and would have got to his feet but for fear of causing further damage to these delicate and unpredictable objects. Tillie, meticulously tucking on the machine in the window, watched him with mischievous eyes, not offering rescue. Florence, the cat, extricated herself from her basket of clinging blind babies, stretched and yawned luxuriously to be free of them, and leapt to Levi's knees. She examined them, kneaded them for a few seconds, and settled herself comfortably along his thick thigh, purring with pleasure. Levi looked down at her and laughed.

"She don't want me to go, I guess. You fixed it right, so I can't move at all now, kitty, didn't you?"

He bent down with a grunt to pick up the patterns, leaning sideways from the chair, so as not to disturb the cat.

"Pretty thin stuff, this, isn't it?"

The light shone through the voile with imperceptible change.

"It's strong, though. Made of good strong cotton thread. Mercerized. That's what gives it that shiny look."

"Jah? But nothing in it to keep you very warm, already."

"It's not meant to be warm."

"No? Isn't it? Not to keep warm?"

"Just to be pretty and fresh. That kind of dress has to be washed every time it's worn, nearly. It washes well."

"But it would be always in the wash, surely? Don't the women have other things to do too?"

"Some of the goods is heavier. Look."

Tillie brought down the satin stripe.

"I've done everything to this one, so far."

Levi considered the half-finished dress with interest and ignorance.

"Yes, did you? Pretty soon now you could make for your mother, then? Like the Sunday ones, those big skirts?"

"Yes, I could, Father. But only with a pattern, still. When I finish with Loretta, then I will not need a pattern. She is teaching me what they call designing. Then I can make my own patterns."

She gave the fawn stuff a competent and affectionate sweep of her long hands and arranged it on its padded hanger.

"That's what I really want to be able to do. Every day I learn something new. The longer I stay, the more."

"Jah, I see, then." With this new grown-up competence and assurance facing him Levi found it hard to put the question uppermost in his mind. And Tillie was not making it easy for him. He thought perhaps she might bring it up first. He shifted his shoulders uneasily and fixed a stern look on his face.

"Tillie."

"Yes, Papa."

"What I came for now, you know. You know, I guess. I got your letter, and then word from Keturah, too."

Tillie straightened up from her machine and looked soberly at him.

"I cannot go back there, to live with Aunt Keturah."

"No? Why not, then?"

"Because I cannot."

She flushed in remembering the meeting after the wedding, and the fearful words that had been said. But she could never bring herself to repeat the terms of the altercation. Nor could she tell him that Keturah had locked her out. That was Keturah's information to impart, if Levi

166

was to know it. The act and the raw revelation of Keturah's suspicions had affronted her so deeply, had so offended an innate fastidiousness, that she could not possibly have discussed the incident. Rather she would be wrongly accused, forever, than engage in humiliating defence.

"She does not want me there, either, Papa. Only to find fault."

Levi stirred uncomfortably. "Your mother is worried, though, Tillie. She wants you to go back there, for sure, right today. I think so too, you know."

"No, Papa, please."

"Whatever was the matter, then? It could not be so bad that you could not be friends, again, surely? They are your aunts, Tillie, you must think of that!" Levi's eyes were troubled, and he looked with concern into his daughter's grave face.

Tillie pulled the spent bobbin up from its bed, whipped an end of thread around it and clicked it into the filler.

"Have you been up there, yet?"

"No. Not yet. I will go up and take dinner with them. And I can say that you will come back, and be a good girl, Tillie?"

She slowly shook her head, resting her cheek on an idle hand.

"But whatever it is, you cannot go on, like this, with unforgiveness in your heart? Perhaps she spoke a little hasty?" Tillie was silent, looking through the window to the empty street.

"Or maybe you did? Then you cannot be at peace, surely, until you speak again, and ask pardon?"

"I cannot ask forgiveness. I did nothing wrong."

Tillie treadled furiously and the bobbin flashed full.

"No? No, I am sure not, Tillie. No real wrong. But sometimes, you must understand, it is hard for an old woman to just see what a young one wants. There is going to be misunderstanding then; and Keturah thinks she must be even more careful of you than if you were her own. Your mother and I, who know you better, we know that always you can be trusted."

Tears sprang to Tillie's eyes.

"Some ways, it is hard, for Keturah."

"Hard for Keturah?"

"Jah. She has no husband, there, no little children of her own, ever. Women need children, and a man too. For her it was always somebody else's baby she came to look after, when the mother was sick. All her life she has been a great one for where there is sickness, children or old people. But it was not her own home, you see."

Tillie stopped her whirring machine and listened with attention.

"When she was younger, oh, a lot of years younger, she was not like she is now. No. Sometimes, a little, you make me think of how she was then. When I was just a little fella, she was like you are now, some."

Tillie turned involuntarily, to find herself in the pier-glass, seeking reassurance.

"In the family, we cannot have mistrust for one another. We must live in love, together. How can we teach the love of God, if even in our own hearts we do not have it?"

"I do not think Aunt Keturah loves me, Father."

"Ach, she does though. She is afraid for you. And it makes her cross, because she is frightened."

Levi laid a heavy hand on the cat and leaned over her in grave earnestness.

"That is how it is, Tillie. Oh, I am sure of it." He passed his fingers down his long thick beard. "Sure of it."

Tillie recalled the wild bruising words, the thin blotched face and the upraised red hands of Keturah. She felt again the shame which had filled her at the humiliating scene, and could find no conviction for her father's explanation, in the memory of it. But she trusted him so completely

168

that the stubborn look in her face gave way to serene inquiry.

"Is it that, do you think, really?"

"Jah. I think it is. And another thing too," Levi lowered his voice, as though keeping his remarks secret from invisible listeners. "We give her some money, you know, a little bit, to board you. She will not have it, if you stay away. She needs to have that little bit. This way, I can know that she has some. It is a help to me, Tillie, when I know that."

Tillie looked at him in surprise. "I didn't know that!"

"Jah. Always, when we can make an excuse, we must make it, to give her money, not just things to eat. You see now, it is you who must go to her, and stay. It is easier, not, than for her?"

"I see, Papa." The machine sewed a slow seam. "Yes. I will go."

Levi smiled. "Can we go now, then?"

Tillie looked over the room, folding the mull lightly into its shining cardboard box. "When Loretta comes back we'll go, right away." Her mouth and jaw were set with determined purpose. Levi, dissolved in relief, sat still and hummed like a gigantic insect, in accompaniment to Florence. The weight of half-guilty misery lifted from Tillie's heart, and the cloud which had hung between her and her father rolled away. They sat in glad and comfortable conversation until Loretta's step sounded on the veranda.

Loretta greeted Levi with a crisp nod. "Glad to see you. Come to see how Tillie's getting on, eh?"

Levi put out his hand, first brushing Florence gently from his lap. "Good morning. Yes." He smiled warmly. "She is doing well, then?"

Tillie became again for a moment a little girl at school, learning to read.

"Getting to be pretty useful," said Loretta, throwing her

169

parcels on the table. "All the way up to the tailor's, for five cents' worth of beeswax," she added irritably. "Nobody this side of the hill had any to spare."

As Tillie took the covering from the little hive-shaped parcel, Loretta turned again to Levi.

"Your sisters gone away, have they? Noticed when I went by, the house looks shut up tight as a drum. Blinds down."

"Away? I did not know. Where would they be away, except for a day, maybe?"

"Papa thinks I should go back to Aunt Keturah," said Tillie, gently, and with her own peculiar dignity. "I was going to ask you if I might go now, for a few minutes, to arrange things."

Loretta looked sharply at the girl.

"Do you want to go back?"

Tillie hesitated for a second. "I think I had better."

Loretta turned to Levi. "I was hoping you'd let me keep her. Very good company, she is."

Levi reddened. "Well, well, that is good. That is nice. She is all right here, we know that. But with her aunts, now, that is where she should be."

"I see. Well, I don't think they're home. But certainly you may go and see, Tillie."

In less than an hour they were back.

"You were right. All closed up. They're moved over to the Nighswanders' while Martha is sick there. Keturah is looking after her now, and Elmina doing the cooking, for them. Poor Jake, he cannot do alone there. If you still can keep Tillie, for a little, we would be obliged."

Loretta stood silently considering. Tillie studied her face with anxiety.

"Well," said Loretta, "I like to know where I stand, and what I am doing. Can she stay here until her time is out, or do I have to let her go when Martha Nighswander gets out again, maybe in a week or two?"

Levi remembered the soft-voiced apology which Tillie had offered Keturah, and its grudging acceptance. He looked at her as she stood, serenely waiting, beside him, and came to his decision.

"I guess she can stay."

17

FROM THE open windows of his attic bedroom Simon could feel the spring. Boys and girls walking the narrow grey streets, so soon to be blotted out from the sky by an impenetrable canopy of leaves, called to one another in higher, shriller voices now. Excited whisperings came from the rooms adjoining Simon's. About everything and everybody there seemed that quickening tempo which spring brings to the northern, winter-locked world. Soon now it would be summer, and the end of Tillie's time with the dressmaker. In her letter, Tillie had not said that when the longed-for summer ended, their marriage would crown this year which had been so strange and revealing to her, and so lonely for him; but Simon understood that she meant it, and was content that he had been guided to be considerate of her wishes. Sometimes God moved in quiet, curious ways, which it was not given to man to understand. But to find out what was God's will, and to do it, that was man's privilege and duty.

Since the sharp disappointment of the winter, when Tillie had decided that they must wait until the fall, Simon had felt within himself a sensation of suspension, a kind of lying fallow, of his being. The knowledge that he was waiting, obediently, for the revelation of God's will for him had induced a kind of ecstasy within him. Now all that was almost past. The winter was over, spring here, and Simon began to feel assurance that his way was to lie just as he had hoped it would, always, of course, if pleasing to God. Nearly the end of April, and he had had no call. In another month, then, he could go home. He was given to the Lord—oh, yes! All, all was His, to do with as He would. He would serve Him, and only Him, to the end of that little space of time which men call Life; but which is, to our heavenly father, only as an instant, a drop in the waters of eternity. He would serve Him through all time, and go wherever He willed him to go. "Where He leads me I will follow, I'll go with Him, *with Him,* all the way!"

A sudden breeze through the tree-tops stirred his farmer blood. He could see the wide quiet fields and the deep spring bush of his father's farm. The black land would lie cool and fertile beyond the creek, and surely by now the forty acres between the orchard and the bush must be almost cleared of snow. He could see the bent grey figure of his father, gnarled like a beech bough, but shapeless under several coats of unremembered origin, the brim of his straw hat curled up, feed measure in hand, walking about the barnyard. Small boys darted around him, the hired man busy in the stables.

"I should be home, now. The animals get restless, too, in the spring. Something gets into them. The horses, sometimes, if you speak to them sudden, just shake. And the old boar, you can't trust the boar any time, but he's worse in the spring. Did they mend the top boards in the pig house, though?"—It seemed to him, as he thought about his home, that nothing right would be done until he got there. The young ones were too daring; they took chances with the animals. And Father was getting old. He sighed deeply, closed the text-book and reached for his Bible, opening it for comfort and strength at the psalms.

"Say among the heathen that the Lord reigneth . . . Let
the heavens rejoice, and let the earth be glad; let the sea
roar, and the fulness thereof." He read aloud now, drinking in the sure promise of the beautiful words. "Let the
field be joyful, and all that is therein: then shall all the
trees of the wood rejoice before the Lord: for he cometh—"

When the supper bell rang he was still half reading, half
praying. He scarcely noticed the people at the table as
he mechanically emptied his plate, and he walked down
to the meeting in the college still in a kind of trance-like
exaltation.

The principal of the Bible College lifted up his hands
and prayed. The visiting evangelist rocked in his chair and
moaned "Jesus, Jesus," over and over again. The missionary home from Portuguese East Africa, and his white-
faced wife who had lost nearly all her hair with sand-fly
fever, sat bolt upright in their hard chairs, their eyes
rigidly tight, and memories of desperate dangers and scant
delights played before them as the principal prayed. The
man could think now, safe here in this warm hall, of the
little outpost with the grey-painted hospital, and the black-
footed nurses with the white gowns; the shallow and sluggish
rivers, miry and fever-ridden, where lions crept down.
Once, when they had just crossed the river, on their trip
out, there were screams from the other side, and a lion
had eaten a native child. Now that he was here he could
see it as he saw it before he went, as the great field of
unharvested wheat which it was the Lord's wish that he
should be given the privilege to pluck for him. And his
wife, through her closed eyes, could see only the grave of
her eldest child, just a baby he was, only two, alone there
now. Had she the strength left, she could have clawed her
way back, to be near the grave, but her strength had been
culled by the fierce winds and the heat and the fever. Her
face was still, and only her pale mouth worked a little
when she thought of going back. And the Lord had blessed
her with three more children; pale little girls, these. Only

the son was there, alone. The children, except the baby, who was in the mission rest house where they were staying for their furlough, sat beside their mother, pale little exhibits whose blue eyes had seen the wonders of Africa, and the steeps of the oceans between their home and this bare hall. Their dresses were too long for them, and of summer print. There had been neither the time nor the money to buy suitable ones, since they came home. One of them kicked her boots wearily against the rungs of her chair; and the missionary fixed her with a warning eye, as the long prayer finished and the principal began the introduction.

". . . have been blessed by the Lord in bringing to us, this evening, a message from the dark continent. Dark, but lightened by the lamp of God's word, carried to them by our brother here. Brother Heise will tell us of his work, which by God's grace, and to the glory of Him who is our redeemer, he is privileged to carry on. Let now your hearts be open. It may be that someone here tonight will hear the voice of God call to him, out of Africa, and Brother Heise will talk with him, after the meeting. Brother."

The missionary rose, nodding briefly at the principal, and leaned over the pulpit. He looked searchingly over the group of students, and up at the ceiling, cleared his throat heavily, and began.

"Tonight, as I look around me here, I see a happy, comfortable people; people who are well dressed, who have had a good dinner, and whose hearts are right with God. Surely I am right in thinking that you are all, men and women alike, right with God. But I can see, too, another scene; perhaps if I close my eyes I can see it better. It is a group of students too. They are under the coconut palms; they are tall, those trees, sometimes more than a hundred feet; and these students are waiting to hear some word of hope, perhaps from you. Yes, perhaps it is for you they wait. For Satan is never idle. If there is no one there to tell them about Jesus, they will not know. They come to learn; whole families come. But they do not come alone. No. The wicked witch-doctors come with them, always ready to show that they are more powerful than Jesus. And to teach them that the air is full of evil spirits, which cause them to be sick, and to die. The witch-doctors teach them that they alone can keep the evil spirits from them. They do not want them to know about Jesus, for then all their power would be taken away from them."

His eyes flew open as he remembered the people he had left behind him there. Safe now in this hall in the promised land of home, he could still hear the sound of the marimba, bats' wings stretched on hollow gourds, weird and snarling and as frightening as sin. He could see the mad wicked ceremonial celebrations when the men covered themselves with tents of grass clothing and, rearing tall ostrich plumes on their godless heads, the women danced. Then sadness veiled his face, and he thought and spoke of those poor benighted ones, out there, as children, looking to him and to his God for salvation out of certain Hell. The little ones squirmed in their hard chairs while their father, his voice now in an imperative whisper, evoked picture after picture of the terrible, urgent need for men of God, to bring the ignorant ones, who somehow had been left out of God's illumined areas, to a knowledge of Him.

There was a warm hush in the hall. The eyes of the students rested on the speaker with a dumb eagerness. The visiting evangelist waited only for him to be through. Simon Goudie sat on the front bench, his red-brown eyes burning up to the speaker. With the tongue of a lover the missionary spoke of the people and their necessity, the danger, and the wild beasts. Simon could see the Kaffirs, safe from their murderous brothers beyond the river of salt water which no other tribe dared cross, but not safe from the Evil One, and knowing nothing of God. Among the wretched and the damned he could see his own tall form walking, administering and admonishing, saving and sanctifying. Like Paul, he thought, on the road to Damascus; it was even like

Paul. When the missionary, suddenly weary, had finished, and they knelt to pray for those lost souls in that lost continent, Simon's heart was flushed and full. He had had his call.

A call so clear had come to Simon Goudie that he could hear nothing else. No other bell, however sweet, could sing in his head, that night. He thanked God, humbly, and yet exultantly, too, for having made his path so clear. And he was still on his knees when the visiting evangelist began his shouting. He was deaf to his exhortations, wondering why he was speaking thus, to them, as they sat there. It was the people of Africa to whom this message must be carried. He could hardly wait, in his new burning zeal, for the end of the meeting. When the sweet words of the benediction scattered the crowd he went at once to the missionary and offered himself, as a candidate for the mission fields of Africa, to go whenever and however the Church, as a function of the Lord, could arrange it. The missionary's eyes brightened. He shook Simon's hand, holding it a long time, and looking up searchingly into his eyes as if he could perhaps see there, in some degree, a promise of the future and the gifts which he would bring to Portuguese East Africa. The visiting evangelist, imagining him to be a conquest of his own, put his arm about his shoulders, and spoke gladly in his ear of the rewards of serving the Lord, here, or in East Africa. The principal joined the little group, and when he heard that Simon Goudie, whom he had thought of as rebellious and more than usually uncouth material, had decided for Africa, he ran to the piano and sounded a great crashing chord on it, so that all the multitude was stilled. Then he raised a quieting hand, mounted the platform, and announced the great decision. The visiting evangelist led out, as soon as the principal had finished, with a great booming "Praise God from whom all Blessings flow," and the meeting broke up in praise and exultation. The missionary's wife extended a cold, thin, bony hand and smiled a little, with her lips. Simon scarcely saw her.

"Come to the Mission House tomorrow," said the missionary, "and we can talk a little." He nodded to Simon, gathered up the thin-legged children, and left the hall. Simon followed him out. His dream was bright and strong; the fire which had burned in him in the camp meeting would burn still brighter in the lush cornfields on the shores of those muddy rivers in the depths of Portuguese East Africa. His eyes saw rows of suppliant blacks, kneeling towards him with outstretched hands, hailing him as messenger of a Saviour whom, without him, they would never know. He was exultant, he was fulfilled. This then, was the reason that he had been guided to come to this alien college. God, moving in His mysterious way, had brought the wonder to performance. There was no trace of doubt in his mind, or heart. He walked in his dream through the streets of the city, still and warm in that April dusk, faster and faster until he was suddenly utterly exhausted, and crept home to bed, falling asleep with his clothes on, stretched diagonally over the bed which was so much too short for him.

18

THE BEAUTIFUL warm sunny days brought release to Tillie's spirit. Sun poured into the workroom and Tillie felt herself expand and delight in the promise of summer. She had laid aside her white house-bonnet, at Loretta's request, and wore under her sateen cover-all a shantung dress which she had designed and made, as part of her course. Loretta smiled with a smug satisfaction at Tillie's obvious pleasure in it.

"Nothing your family could object to, is there? Plain material, plain pattern. You can dye it black, when you leave, if you want to; but while you're here, let me see you in something light."

Tillie had bought a pair of low shoes, made of fine kid; and Loretta gave her, and insisted upon her wearing, some pale fawn-coloured silk stockings. "I like to have a little life in clothes. And if I'm going to have you right here, for a month, then let me enjoy looking at you. Aesthetic appreciation. Part of your course."

Tillie laughed. It would be an adventure for these few weeks, and there could be no real harm in it. Anyway, she was there to do as Loretta said. Perhaps, with her people, there was too much of the letter, and not enough of the spirit, in many matters.

During these days Loretta's words worked on Tillie's consciousness like the irritation within the oyster which produces the pearl. In spite of doubt, and that suspicion of new things which was a natural reaction of her family and in her deliberate tradition, she was developing a sense of inquiry. Her native intelligence asserted itself, and she saw that much of Loretta's illuminating comment must indeed be true. She read again with new interest, and for the first time in her life with anything like an analytical approach, the first three gospels. It was true. They were different. Each said that the Lord had indeed risen, but they differed as to who had seen Him, and where He had been found, and how long after His death. Her new spirit of awakening scepticism advised her that if this was so, then other, more important discrepancies might be found, throughout the rest of the huge book.

She fingered her Bible listlessly, these evenings, turning over the pages and falling upon phrases familiar to her since babyhood, which she must now question. But the thing that most disturbed her, and caused her to doubt the Word, was the picture which Loretta had drawn of fishermen with gnarled and dirty hands, writing down their impressions of our Lord. She supposed the fishermen to have been like Joe Reesor, one of the hired men. In the summer time he was a fisherman too. When the work on the farm allowed, he went along the shores at the upper end of Lake Marie, where a little string of lakes lay full of fish. If Joe Reesor had seen the miracle of the fishes she would not be disposed to be sure that he had been right. Lawyers, too, Loretta said. She thought of Lawyer McPherson, who rode through the village, Sunday mornings, on his black horse. What she had thought was God's word, straight down from Him, turned out to have been written by men like these. How could anyone be sure that they had written it right? Or that if they had, even, after all the translations, and the losings and the findings of the scrolls that Loretta said they were first written on, how could anyone know that hundreds of mistakes had not been made?

The Bible had lost its reality for her. She looked at it curiously, now. This was the fount of all her hope, for this world and the next. What was it, really, that she held in her hand? When she went to bed, and did her reading, she thought of Simon and how, when she could speak with him again, since letters seemed so difficult, she would ask him. Perhaps he would have an answer that she, by her own light, could not find. She began to consider, too, from this new approach to a printed word, the verses which she had had to memorize, during the three years at the Continuation School. A word or phrase Loretta used sometimes brought back a stanza that she had learned with such ease, those few years ago, to state correctly, and not think of again. Now she was startled into realization that some real person, somewhere, was behind these words. She looked down at her hands. Some of the names that she remembered, now, having to learn, were women's names. Some woman with hands like these had taken a pen and written down those words. By some process beyond her conception these words had been caged and brought to their neat prison. She thought of the harried, fuddled old man who had taught all three classes of the Continuation School, including science and Latin. He had had nothing to say about these strange women. And now she would have liked to know. When she sat alone she tried to stir from her memory all that she had heard and read. Sometimes in the morning she would wake with a whole section of a poem fresh on her lips, and then find to her amazement that Loretta knew who had written the words, and talked about the writers as if she had known them personally.

There was little enough time in her days, now, to consider these things. During the daylight hours she and Loretta sewed with speed and intensity, and the pleasant evenings, when the light had gone, they spent listening to the music of the gramophone, or Tillie practised on Loretta's heavy old piano, upstairs in the store-room. Several times she had come down to find George Bingham sitting in the dining-room, talking to Loretta and smoking, like a man at home. The evenings ended with food and drink, and light, gay banter. Tillie went half smiling to bed, on these nights, accepting this little interlude in her life as she might a gift. It was as if she were a spectator enjoying a performance which was none of her own making and which would pass, leaving her to go home and continue in her own way. She would, of course, disobey no express ruling, but neither would she withdraw from experience and knowledge. She felt herself to be in complete mastery of her situation, and looked back with wonder and contempt on the folly of the girl who had wandered through the town under the stress of uncontrolled emotion. She thought of that night with humiliation as she sat now at her machine, confidently tucking. Then she removed the memory from her consideration, and sang as she sewed, from pure contentment with the lovely day, her pleasant occupation, and the novelty of her costume.

Florence the cat, and three variegated kittens, argued the relative merits of "in" and "out" with reference to their basket at her feet. Florence loudly expatiated on the desirability of "in" while the kittens, equally loquacious, described themselves as "outers" to a cat. Unsuspected dust-motes in their thousands rode sunbeams to the floor. Through the open window the strong scent of mock-orange blew in.

Tillie was in charge today, and conscious of a nice feeling of competent responsibility. Loretta had gone to the city by the eight-forty-five last night, to the wholesales, and would return by the nine-ten this evening. Tillie looked at the clock and was surprised to find that it was already six. She pulled the piece of moiré from the machine and inspected the banks of tucks with critical eyes, taking it over to the window to see it more perfectly.

There was the sudden stilling of a clatter of wheels just outside the window, and Tillie raised a face so startled that George, jumping from the buggy, laughed aloud.

"You kind of look as if you're seeing tigers!"

"I wasn't expecting to see anybody."

George slipped Maida's halter around her neck. "Loretta in?"

"No. I'm all alone today. Loretta went down to the city last night."

"Oh, Lord, did she?"

George looked disappointed, and faintly worried.

"I'm a man with a problem, I am, and I thought maybe she'd have a sensible idea for me. I can't make up my own mind, apparently." He pulled the leather down and slid it into his pocket.

"Steady, darling—we're off in a minute." He laid his hand reassuringly at the base of the mare's mane, pulling the black stubble through his fingers.

"Well, she'll be back tonight, will she?"

"Yes."

"I'll come back, then." He looked inquiringly at Tillie. "Unless you could come out for a little spin? Whoa, girl."

"Where are you going?"

"Going out to look at an idea I think I have. Come along and I'll tell you."

"Give me a few minutes to tidy up."

"Don't be long, then. Maida wants to get travelling, don't you, little one?"

Tillie unbuttoned her apron and hung it up, pushed her hair back from her face, and locked the workroom door. In the hall she stretched out her hand for the black bonnet, hesitated, and dropped her hand to her side. Smiling mischievously, she closed the door behind her and stepped into the buggy.

George gave a little pull on the reins and Maida leapt. He might have been talking to her, with his hands, Tillie thought. She watched them a little as if she had never noticed a man's hands, separate from himself, before. They were square, smooth, sharp-cut hands, she found, with crisp knuckles and strong fingers. The hands paid out the reins, and pulled them in, turned them very slightly to the left or the right, gave two little jerks, or three, and Maida understood his slightest intention, perfectly.

"She's a good girl, isn't she?"

"She's lovely."

"And getting faster all the time, too."

"Have you raced her yet? You said you were going to."

"So you remembered that, did you?" George's voice was teasing, and Tillie laughed.

"Yes, I remembered."

"No, I haven't been racing. Just warming up for the 24th. Will you come to the Port Rossing fair, and see her get her ribbon?"

Tillie shook her head. "We don't go to horse races."

"Don't you? Why not?"

"We do not mingle with the world."

"With your hat off," said George, "I almost forgot that you were half way to heaven."

They climbed the long hill, Maida straining to fly over the long grade.

"No sense at all," said George. "Up hills, dearie, you go just a little bit slower. You'll wear yourself out before you're properly grown up, this way."

"Oh! There's the crape on the Nighswanders' door!"

"Sure. Old lady Nighswander handed in her checks, this morning. Old man running around like a hen on a hot griddle all day. I guess your aunts have been looking after things over there, haven't they?"

"Yes."

George looked curiously at her.

"Don't see much of the relatives any more, eh?"

"No."

"Isn't that Keturah now?"

Tillie glanced towards the grey house. Keturah stood by the gate, half turned towards the road, and they passed close beside her.

"Good evening, Aunt Keturah," said Tillie, evenly, bowing gravely.

Keturah looked after the flying buggy until it was out of sight, unbelief in her eyes. George pulled up his coat collar with an exaggerated gesture, and shivered. "If you ever think of speaking to me in that tone," he said, "just give me a word of warning, and I'll put on my fur-lined shoelaces."

Tillie smiled and said nothing. George looked at her with interest.

"You're the damndest kid I ever saw," he announced with affectionate patronage. "Maybe you'll do instead of Loretta, to tell me what I ought to do. You people all feel yourselves a cut above ordinary humanity, anyway, don't you? Maybe you could give a little advice to a struggling mortal."

"I never thought of it, like that. We do not think ourselves above anybody. We are just not part of this world, and the amusements of this world. Our hearts and minds must be on the things of God."

"I see. Well, then, didn't God make the horses?"

"God made everything that moves, breathes, and has its being."

"He made them able to run like billy-o, didn't He, then?"

"Of course He did."

"All right. Now, all I'm trying to do is just show God that when He made this little baby with the long slanting ears, out in front there (one Saturday afternoon, I think it was), He made a lulu of a stepper. What's the matter with that?"

Tillie was inexpressibly shocked by the blasphemous way George used the holy name, but she was amused by the utter novelty of his talk, in spite of herself.

"I scarcely think that is what you are trying to do, really."

"Surest thing you know. And then, when the Fair is all over, do you know what I'm going to do? Settle right down to business, and make myself a packet, and buy another mouse. Or, at least, up to this morning, when I had this other idea, that's what I was going to do."

"Isn't it very dear, keeping horses, when they do nothing but run?"

" 'Tis very dear, very dear indeed. But out of this life, dear Tillie, I aims to get what I want, and if it takes money, which I'm pretty sure it will, somehow, then money I shall make for the purpose. And I don't know but what I've hit on a notion that will do it faster than the drug store."

"What is it?"

"One mile and one-quarter farther along this road, which we travelled once before, I seem to remember, and round the corner, and I'll tell you all about it."

George put his hand on her knee, pressing it slightly, to emphasize this point. Tillie felt the faint, sick stir within her that she had felt before, at George's touch. But it was gone in a second. George withdrew his hand, and settled over into his corner of the buggy with a faint frown between his eyes.

"Wish to God I knew if I'm being a damned fool or not."

Tillie waited for enlightenment. The buggy negotiated the side-road corner on two wheels and they were beyond the swamp and among the giant cedars, travelling the dusty sand of the lakeshore road. George turned Maida sharply in to the hard-packed track to the pavilion and drew her to a sudden stop. He jumped out and tied her to a tree.

"I'm thinking of buying a farm," he said. "Come and see it."

Tillie walked hesitatingly among the big trees, feeling the sand firm beneath her feet, held in immutable contour by the tough running roots of pine and cedar, so close to the surface that they broke through, here and there. It was growing dark, among the trees, and the quiet was the silence of a pasture field at night.

"Come down to the water."

A gentle, long slope studded with cedar brought Tillie to the beach. The rustic oblong of the little dark dance-pavilion, with canoe storage underneath, hid the north shore and the entrance to the long narrows from her. The east shore, half a mile across the water, cloaked in untouched evergreen, lay black under the bald-headed hills beyond. To the south there was a farmland clearing, an old black house half way down the rise, and fields above pricked with unpulled stumps.

George stood beside her. He pointed to a tall pine with a twisted top, across the lake. "See that jack pine? That's the start." He described a semicircle in the air, including the high land on the east and the old farmhouse on the south, pausing to end his arc a few hundred feet short of the pavilion.

"That's the place. What do you think of that, for a farm?"

Tillie looked doubtfully at him, to see if he meant to be funny.

"Well?"

"You don't really mean it, do you?"

"Sure I do. You know all about cows, and alfalfa, and rotation of crops, don't you? Maybe I'll take you on as my technical adviser. What kind of cows grow best among those stumps, please?"

Tillie laughed with relief. "For a minute I thought you were being serious. I know old Mr. Armstrong has been trying to sell his place for a long time, but of course nobody will buy it. You couldn't grow anything but potatoes and pine trees in that sand. It wouldn't be worth your while to take out the stumps, let alone clear the rest of it."

"I'm thinking of buying it, all the same."

"Oh, no! You're not even a farmer. No person could make a living on land like that."

"Plenty of water, though."

"Cows need more than water. Don't let the Armstrongs persuade you."

"How do you know all about the Armstrongs?"

"They have a farm near home, and I know they have been trying to get rid of this for some time."

"What do you think it is worth?"

Tillie studied George's face. "There are only about ten acres cleared, I think, and they're not stumped, either. That would only be good for pasture. Good pasture can be bought for four dollars an acre. The rest would only be worth the timber. If you really want to buy a farm, why don't you buy a good one?"

"Maybe I haven't the money for a good one, though."

"You will lose what you have, on this land. It's no good. No good at all." Tillie's face was distressed.

"Armstrong wants two thousand dollars for it."

"Two thousand dollars!"

"Two hundred acres, about, all told, and frontage on this end of the lake. About a mile and a half of shore-line.

186

Difference in depth. Craziest looking blueprint you ever saw, anywhere from a hundred feet to six hundred."

"Two thousand dollars for sand and stumps!"

"Sixty miles south," said George soberly, "people are paying a dollar a foot for land like this. And a lake not so pretty, either. Lots. For cottages. If I had the ready money, I could make a little fortune out of Lake Marie."

"Oh! Cottages! For people to come and live in, in the summer time, you mean?"

"Yes. I could make this into eighty lots, easy. Good big lots too. If I didn't do anything else—and I have other notions—and sold the lots for even a hundred dollars each, that'd be eight thousand, wouldn't it? Four hundred per cent on your money. What would be wrong with that?"

"But — why would people come here, though?"

"Why do they come down the lake, and past us to Rossing, too? Somebody is going to think of this, within the next ten minutes, and make a mint." He turned abruptly. "Come on. It might as well be me. Surely I can get two thousand on the store. If the bank won't give it to me, I'll have to find somebody that will."

They drove silently back through the quiet damp roads, drawing aside occasionally to let another buggy pass in the cool of the swampy, cedar-scented air. The lights of the town like a string of badly strung pearls glowed in the distance before George spoke again. "I don't see how I could be wrong," he said.

At the post-office, George handed Tillie the reins and went in for the mail. A minute later he tossed her a letter and then went across the street to the drug store. Tillie saw that the letter was from Simon, and written in the upper corner was the word "urgent," heavily underlined. She turned it face-down and watched George come out of the lighted shop with a parcel under his arm. He jumped into the rig, and Maida leapt.

"Well," he said, "I'm doing a lot of clearing up, tonight. I'm going to buy that damned land. Doc Percy will give the money, maybe, for a chattel mortgage on the shop. If I have to do it that way. I have some that I can use. And I've brought you your Christmas present. Maybe I had a nerve, sending it to you, but I didn't think you'd mind, and I didn't seem to have many people I could send presents to. I kind of liked doing it."

"Oh!"

"Yeah. But your father had the idea I was trying to beat your young man's time, or something."

Tillie sat in silent distress.

"It wasn't just like that, Tillie. And anyhow, I don't know what to do with the fool thing, now. I can't very well sell it, and it's just cluttering up the store. Couldn't you take it, now that you know me better?"

"Yes, I think I could, thank you."

"I don't want you to think, or your father, either, that I butt in where it's none of my business. Another man's girl is perfectly safe, where I'm concerned. So you take it, with no hard feelings, eh?"

Tillie stretched out her hand. "Thank you," she said numbly.

"If I lose my shirt," said George, far away already from Tillie and her words, "I'll pitch a tent out there, and live there myself. Nice place for a house, where the old shack is."

"It would be," agreed Tillie. "Right overlooking that little bay."

"Nice, eh?"

"Yes. Good night," said Tillie. "You won't come in to see Loretta, then?"

"No. No, I don't think I will. I've just about made up my mind. I'll go home and do a little figuring now. Well, good night. Come on, Maida."

The buggy clattered away into the darkness. Tillie stood for a long moment, in the shadow of the house. She held the box close to her side, and with her free hand smoothed the light springy silk of her dress over her breast, again and again, until the sound of the wheels had died quite away.

Loretta, in her checked taffeta travelling suit under the sudden glare of the dining-room chandelier, for a second seemed a stranger.

"There you are, then. Was that George?"

"Yes."

Loretta yawned. "He might have come in, for a while. I'm so glad to be home I could pat the walls. Where have you been?

"Up at the lake."

"Not going to bed so soon, are you? I'm as restless as a coot, tonight. One day in the city and a jangle of nerves. I was hoping you might feel like playing."

"I'll be right down, then."

Tillie withdrew with a strong feeling of relief to the shadows of the upstairs, hesitated beside the electric switch, and then lit the candle in the big bare room. She opened the package and drew out the atomizer, setting it to glow attractively beside the candle. She experimentally squeezed the little netted bulb, and a fine spray bent the flame, releasing in instantaneous evaporation a sweet and spicy fragrance through the room. She smiled with sudden delight, and put it carefully down. Her reflection in the pier-glass, as she looked up again, startled her. In the strange light dress, with her thick hair roughened by the wind, she saw herself as a stranger, and smiled to see the beauty in the picture.

She took the cover from the gold box, and passed her hand over the ranks of jewelled candies, selected one and ate it, astonished to find that it was filled with hot, sweet juice. Another one, quite different in appearance, held another thick, stinging sweet liquid within. Still smiling, she sat down and took the pins from her hair, shook it out, and put it up again, parted chastely in the middle but with the loose waves less severely brushed, and the long black hair coiled about her head, instead of tightly braided into her usual coronet. The girl in the mirror approved of the change. She sprayed perfume on her waves, and laughed at herself. She leaned far out of her open window to reach a branch of the mock-orange, and broke off a pair of long flowered twigs. These she thrust into her belt, then picked up the candy box and went downstairs.

Loretta stared at her. "Holy bananas!" she said.

"Have a candy?"

"I will, indeed, thank you."

Tillie smiled, appreciative of the unspoken compliment. "What shall I play?"

"I don't care. Anything you like. Sorry you still have to climb into that old barn of a store-room; if I'd known how much use you were going to make of the piano, I believe I'd have had it brought down."

Tillie turned pleasantly to her. "I like it up there. I think it's good to be alone, when you're playing. Perhaps it sounds better, too, from a little way off."

"It sounds good, anyway."

Music poured from the open window into the village air. People walking along Main Street, a block away, could hear, and it heightened for them the quickening joy of the spring night. Tillie played for an hour, first for Loretta, listening from the dining-room, and then for herself. And at the end of it she was intoxicated with the sound, and the perfume, until it seemed to her that there could be nothing that really mattered, in the whole of life, but music, and the fragrance of flowers. She rose from the stool, in an enchantment.

After a little listening silence Loretta called her.

"Come down, if you're through, Tillie, you've got an audience."

Tillie walked in her dream down the hollow stairs. George and Loretta stood at the table, watching her. George's voice trembled, a little, when he spoke.

"That was lovely. That was really lovely, Tillie."

Tillie smiled at him as from a great distance. It was as if she had not quite come back to them yet. For a minute they all three stood motionless, Tillie smiling in her listening fashion, and George and Loretta staring at her. Loretta laughed nervously.

"Well, we might sit down, I suppose. But thank you. Tillie. Thank you."

"I'm glad you liked it." Tillie sank into a deep basket chair.

"I ought to be going," said George, reaching for a chocolate and settling into his chair.

"Stay for a while, I'll put the kettle on. Tillie looks worn out."

Loretta went briskly into the kitchen, whistling aimless little snatches as she cut bread and cake.

"I ought to help Loretta."

"Sit tight, little one," said George with easy affection. "I'll buttle. Well, there go the lights! Bring you a lamp in a minute."

Tillie regarded him with surprised eyes, and sat still. It was novel to see a man offer services in woman's work. She sat in the dark dining-room and waited while George and Loretta laughed in the kitchen, feeling a rare content in the atmosphere of gaiety which George managed so often to produce in the house. She gave herself up this evening, almost without reserve of mind or sense, to the alien life she found here. It was as if she had made a deliberate movement of acceptance. When George brought the fringed lamp in she was smiling and gay, and joined easily and successfully in the light chatter which constituted conversation between Loretta and George. She was like a swimmer trying out new waters, finding them free from currents, and unexpectedly buoyant. When George lit his pipe, in happy relaxation, after the supper, for the first time she accepted it as natural, and perhaps good, that a man should smoke. What could it matter, after all? There were no good reasons for her people to object, if they would only think a little.

Loretta, long and elegant, slim as a twist of paper as she sat on the stairs, her small curly head bent over her cup, was not essentially different, surely, from any tall, thin, middle-aged woman of the faith. It was imagination, it was ignorance; there was no difference that mattered. They were all the children of God, created in His image. Tillie trembled with the force of the truth that she felt herself to have discovered. Earlier in her life, there at home, and when she was a child, she had not been quite ready to be as the other girls were, and content with those things which so completely satisfied them. But now, here was life offering to her, at every turn, new richness and satisfaction. She would take what she could of this way of living, and make it her own, add it to her own tradition, and here would be an abundant life. She was hungry and thirsty for knowledge and sensation.

Fragrance drifted about the room. She had filled herself with music until she was perfectly satisfied. Her friends were with her. With no reserve of judgement they had accepted her, as she was, to be one of them, approved and loved. She knew there was no holding back of affection because of a flaw in her, as there had been, always, with her own family. She was free, as she had never been free, to say what she thought or felt without fear of sharp reproof. She felt the fabric of her life to have grown richer, strong colour now showing through the grey. She smiled, as she sat there, a lovely warm happiness welling up within her.

"George," said Loretta, "is going to make a million, I hear. What do you think of it, Tillie?"

Tillie smiled gently. "I expect he will," she said, "if it works out that way."

George laughed and stood up. "It's going to work, all right. What I came back for was to give you this, Tillie." He handed her Simon's letter. "And now I'll really be gone."

Tillie followed him to the door, leaving it open so that light reached the steps.

"Not walking, are you?"

"I'd put Maida up before I found the letter. Then I was in an awful hurry, so I walked."

Loretta called out from the back of the house, "Ought to get a fast horse!"

"Perhaps I really will, some day. Good night, anyway, and thank you for a very pleasant evening indeed. Good night, Tillie."

"Good night, George."

With a tender smile George took Tillie gently in his arms and kissed her. "You darling," he said, in a low voice, held her to him for a silent minute, and was gone. She stood in the open doorway. George's heels clicked briskly along the board walk, and he whistled with cheerful energy, over and over again, the first few bars of "Kiss Me Again." Loretta joined her at the door.

"Hasn't much of an ear himself, has he, Tillie? For all he enjoys it so much, hearing you play."

"Goes flat on the D," said Tillie, in a dull defeated tone.

She picked up her letter mechanically and slowly climbed the stairs, leaving the candy uncovered, the table uncleared. Loretta looked in perplexity at her slack figure. She seemed to have to steady herself by a hand on the wall.

"Do you feel all right, Tillie?"

Tillie turned on the top stair and looked down on the remnants of the properties of gaiety.

"Oh, yes, thank you," she said in a voice drained of all vitality, "I think I am. I'm very tired, though, now." She passed the back of her hand over her eyes. "Good night, Loretta."

"Well, good night, then," Loretta said doubtfully, and watched until a light flared and the door shut it from her.

Tillie held herself motionless, in silent misery, before the open window of her room. She felt her heart to be gripped by a hand so powerful and cold that she could not move. They were right, then; her people were right. There was

193

frightening truth as basis for the admonitions of her brotherhood which she had lately come to believe unreasonable. You could not mingle with the world, and not be hurt. You must be of it, or not touch it at all. And she could never, never be of it. She had scarcely pushed aside one curtain, to look a little way into the ways of worldly living, and swift almost unbearable pain was her instant reward. She thought of the sweet-faced unquestioning women at home, safe and pure and happy, and passionately wished to be one of them. She had been so sure she was right. Where she thought she had found grace and beauty there was revealed brutality. What else might she not have found, had she looked further? What secret thoughts and acceptances might there not be, among the people of the world, not discoverable by superficial acquaintance? She recalled maxims which she had dared to doubt. "Satan is very crafty, and can transform himself into an angel of light." She pressed her hand to her heart, and pulled herself up, holding her breath to see if she could ease the pain.

The night airs blew the strong scent of orange blossoms into the room where the spicy fragrance of the perfume lingered still, but she was unresponsive to it, now. She pulled the flowers from her hair and belt and tossed them lightly out of the window, then pulled it down, shutting out the sweet treacherous air. Moving stiffly, she reached for the Bible, which she had presumed to find unrewarding of late, and almost at once found the promise she was looking for. She read it avidly, gathering balm from the words.

"Thou shalt also consider in thine heart, that as a man chasteneth his son, so the Lord thy God chasteneth thee. Therefore thou shalt keep the commandments of the Lord thy God, to walk in His ways, and to fear Him. For the Lord thy God bringeth thee into a good land, a land of brooks of water, of fountains and depths that spring out of valleys and hills; A land of wheat, and barley, and vines, and fig trees, and pomegranates; A land of oil olive, and honey; A land wherein thou shalt eat bread without scarceness, thou shalt not lack any thing in it . . ."

The disregarded lamp smoked heavily up one side of the chimney, and darkened the room to a half light. Tillie turned the flame down and sat on the end of the bed to read Simon's brief and almost incoherent letter.

Gradually the smell of burning oil overcame the last vestige of flower fragrance.

19

AT THE Shantz farm snow still lay in the corners of the fields, where the old stumps met the newer rail fences. But the rest of the land was clear of it, and in the noonday sun lay black and crumbly, drying for the seed, at last. Levi stood, contrary to custom, on the front veranda, looking through the arch of elms over his fields to the road. The land and the trees were still bare, but he felt the new, miraculously recurring sensation of spring in the crisp air. The warm winds of a few days had created a semblance of summer, in the country. Levi drew long, noisy breaths, smelling out new summer smells from the breast of the earth. Now he could see the shape of the hills to the north of him, and the roof and buildings of his neighbour. His friends seemed near to him, not far on the other side of snowy fields, as in winter, or beyond the obstacle of heavy green bush as in full summer. The trees between looked thin and sparse, contracting the distance between him and his brothers. He felt, in the swelling fulness of emotion within him, remorse that he had not visited these men more.

Their smoke curled up from their roughcast houses, white against the dark earth, not grey by contrast with the snow. The big red barns across the road stood larger and nearer than they had all winter. A swift surge of love for his neighbours rose up in Levi. The love he bore them, and the love he bore for Betsey his wife, and Tillie and the little boys was too great to be borne within his broad chest, and in silence. He knew himself to be filled with warm compassion for all men, and felt lacking in commission, that he had not done more for these brethren whose houses, when the leaves came, would be hidden again.

But the main well of his emotion was the thought that there was Tillie, coming home soon, now. He laughed aloud, when he thought of the richness that was his, in Tillie. He pulled his big blue handkerchief from his overall pocket and violently blew his nose. He smiled broadly to himself to think what Betsey would say if he went in, like that, and said he was full of love for her! She had never been one for words of love. Never one for that! And since Tillie had left, the house was too quiet, and somehow lacking in comfort. All winter, there was no music. The front room with the piano in it was all shut up, ever since Christmas. Too far from the kitchen to heat, and no need for it. But now, soon, though, it would be different! The spring came, now, and the front door would soon be open, and there would be loud glad music in the house. Albert Fretz would tune the piano, a little, when he came soon now, to do the clocks.

The sun warmed Levi's head, and the warm wind blew his beard apart in the middle, as if he had combed it. He shrugged his shoulders in pleasure to feel the air warm on his chest.

"Ach, but it is nice, the spring!"

How fast the winter goes, once it starts! Already there must be dust on the road, since there was a faint brown spiral lying out there behind the buggy stopping at the Reesors' lane. Usually one of the hired men went down the lane for the mail, but today Levi, in his love and loneliness, welcomed the chance to speak to the driver. Likely there would be nothing for his box, but he could speak to Abe, a little. He strode down the lane, still damp under the shading maples, singing loudly to the empty air.

"I'm living on the mountain,
Underneath a cloudless sky (praise God)
I'm drinking at the fountain
That never shall run dry.
Oh yes, I'm feeding on the manna
From a bountiful supply,
For I am dwelling in Beulah land!"

His voice boomed out over the fields. "Yes, bless His holy name forever, dwelling in Beulah Land."

The mail man drew up at the gate.

"Warm spell."

Levi nodded and smiled. "Jah, feels like summer, today."

Abe leaned down over the box on the seat beside him. "Something for you, in here some place."

"That so? Thank you. Thank you."

Levi beamed on the driver. "Well, it's warm. Late coming, but sometimes it's better, that way. Most times we're out on the land two weeks ago, though.

"Lots of work to do, on a big place like this."

"Jah, lots of work." Levi looked back towards the house, nodding his head. "Lots of work."

"You got good help just now?"

"Pretty good help. My little boys, though, they're too small, yet, to do much. But they all help some."

"How many acres would you work?"

"Two hundred, but pretty nearly twenty-five in bush, yet."

"Yes. You've got a big place to look after. Takes a lot of feed, for all that cattle, too. Daughter home yet?"

"No, not just now. She's coming home soon. Getting married, about harvest time, maybe."

"That so? Well."

"These girls, they don't stay with the old folks."

"Not the good-looking ones, anyway."

Abe handed Levi a thin letter, and picked up the reins. "Got to get along." He clicked to his horse and started at a slow trot up the road. Levi lifted the letter in salute to him, and started up the lane, peering at the handwriting on the envelope. Betsey met him at the door, curious and a little fearful, as always, at the arrival of a letter.

"'What is the letter?"

"In a minute, when I get my glasses."

Levi reached up to the high cupboard and pulled his steel-rimmed glasses from a brown pitcher that also contained receipts and bolts and an old brush for cleaning separator parts. The hired girl stood still to listen; a hired man paused on his way out of the door. Levi opened the letter clumsily, stopping to pick up a bit of paper torn from the envelope and place it carefully on the table before he began to read.

Dear Brother:

Greetings in that Name which is above every name!

Simon has decided for Africa. I have a letter this morning. It is hard to lose our children from us, but to give them to God is not to lose them. They are but lent us. And only for such a short time, our sojourn here, and then to meet above, where there is no more parting. Praise His name. Simon comes home soon now, to stay nearly all summer I think. September, he says, is the likely time to go. How does Tillie say, I wonder, to you about this?

My heart is very full, brother. I am short of

help. If you could come to see me, in love, we could talk then.

Yours in Christ,

ABRAHAM GOUDIE.

Brother Brubacher has just been here. He brings news that Sister Martha Nighswander died. The burial is here at Lemonville, Saturday. If you can, stay over with us, for Sunday.

There was silence in the big kitchen. For a long minute the four figures might have been made of wax, so rigidly were they poised, the hired man with his foot in the doorway and the girl suspending her hands over the dishpan. Then Bertha laughed, suddenly and harshly, and dropped her hands to the dishes.

"Africa!" She flung a thick white plate into the draining-pan, and followed it up by another. "Tillie won't go to no Africa, I guess."

The hired man stepped quietly outside, and closed the door softly behind him. Levi looked across at his wife with the big, sober eyes of a child who has been punished unjustly, then got heavily to his feet, folding the paper carefully in its creases, and handing it to Betsey. "You get the things ready Betsey, and come with me, too. We'll go, first thing in the morning, to Lemonville. Bertha, she can look after things here."

"Take for the night?"

"Jah. Abraham can tell us. Tomorrow we will talk to Abraham."

Betsey watched him go slowly across the yard to the drive shed, his back bowed a little, as if he carried an uneasy burden. When he had passed from her view up the ramp towards the granary she turned abruptly to Bertha, and began to tell her, in sharp scolding tones, what she must be sure to do, since for two days she would have charge of the household. All afternoon she worked quickly, cooking and arranging, making provision for the meals, with Bertha

199

muttering beside her, "Leave her folks and her good home here, and go away off there, with all them strangers. What's Tillie to do that for? Way off there, none of her own folks. She don't want to go way off there, with just Simon Goudie."

But Levi sought the silence of the grain bins, and letting the smooth cleft grains of wheat run through his thick brown fingers, knelt in the lengthening shaft of sunlight from the high dusty window and wrestled with the Spirit, until victory was won.

20

T HE BURYING ground at Lemonville lies high on the southern slope of a sand-hill whose tall pine trees close round the three sides of the little cemetery to make a burning sun-trap of it. The grass does not grow well, there, and now, in the spring, the sacred plot lay bare and yellow in the sun.

Martha Nighswander, in her rough box, attended by no single bloom, although in her lifetime she had grown such beautiful gardens, sank with a harsh rattle of gravel into her appointed resting-place. Little Jake, her husband, his circle of white hair lifted into ridiculous points by the wind, stood sobbing beside the grave, to see her go. His face was red with weeping, and the piteous, quivering red mouth made aimless shapings and circlings over his white beard. He held his broad-brimmed hat in his hands, as did all the brethren about him, and found no comfort in the words of the preacher.

"For since by man came death, by man came also the resurrection of the dead. For as in Adam all die, even so in Christ shall all be made alive—And as we have borne the image of the earthly, we shall also bear the image of the heavenly. Amen. Praise God. We shall not all sleep, but we shall all be changed. In a moment, in the twinkling of an eye, at the last trump. For the trumpet shall sound, and the dead shall be raised incorruptible, and we shall be changed. For this corruptible must put on incorruption, and this mortal must put on immortality. Death is swallowed up in victory. The grace of the Lord Jesus Christ, and the love of God, and the communion of the Holy Ghost, be with you all. Amen."

The preacher put on his hat, and turned from the grave. The women wept and looked with commiseration on the little widower.

It was over now, the last words had been said, committing their sister to her Lord, and only little Abie Morningside, with his twisted neck, left to fill up the open grave. The black figures moved slowly towards the gate, the women talking in gentle voices as they walked. The old preacher grasped Jake's hand, pressing it warmly, offering comfort and hope based on the assurance of salvation which had been Martha's. He bent down lovingly to the little man, holding his hand still in his own, and striking his shoulder with the other one, to emphasize the undying hope which was his, in Lord Jesus—the resurrection from the dead, and the glorious meeting there beyond, in the house which is not made with hands, but is eternal in the heavens.

Little Jake nodded his head in agreement, whispering wildly, "Yes, yes, it is so. Praise His Name. Yes. Yes." But it did not seem that he was really grasping the meaning, since the tears rolled still, uncontrollably, down his face. Abraham Goudie came over to him. "Brother," he said, and kissed him on both cheeks, then held an arm closely about his shoulders. "What are you going to do, now that she is gone? Will you come and make us a little visit, for a while?" Mrs. Goudie came too, and asked him to come to them, to stay, so he would not be alone, just yet. The women talking apart in little knots, said, "Where is he to go, now? There were no children, ever, it is lonely for him. He should not go back to that house, and be alone." They questioned their husbands with their eyes, and several men came to him, shaking his hand in sympathy, and inviting him to come home with them, for a visit.

Levi, his nose swollen with weeping, started over to Jake, meeting his sister Keturah on his way. He stopped to shake hands with her.

"Well, Keturah. How are you? Poor Jake. He won't know just what to do for a while. Tillie—Tillie did not come?" He was hungry and thirsty for news of Tillie. "Of course, she cannot always get away any time."

"I don't know what Tillie does, or does not do, since she left my house, Levi."

Levi opened his mouth to speak, but his throat tightened so that he could not utter the sounds.

"If it was my girl, I'd see to her," said Keturah, grimly, and marched on. "I've washed my hands of her."

"Keturah!" All the heads in the burying-ground lifted, at the boom of his voice. Keturah paused.

"What did you tell her, to make her go?"

"I will not have a girl in my house to walk the streets."

"To walk the streets? Tillie?"

"Bring her home, Levi, while there is time. If there still is time." Keturah looked with satisfaction at the big perplexed face, and went on her way.

Levi looked after her, and beyond, to where little Jake stared about him in bewilderment, and as if the power of choice were taken from him. All these people asking him to go here, go there, and it did not matter, really, where he went, now. Since Martha was not there, how should he know where he would go? Even at home now, there was nothing that he need do. Except for the horse. Someone must feed the horse. Soon he must decide something, everyone was going, now. All had somewhere to go.

The hearse backed carefully down the grade, almost into a row of very old, small tombstones, to turn around. The black horses, once on the road, broke into a trot and started swiftly for home. Horses hitched to buggies were untied from the railing on the fence, and the little yard was cleared, except for a few close friends. The livery man in charge of the chief mourners' democrat, respectful of Jake's sorrow, waited in silence and self-effacement to drive him home. His tall black team neighed indignantly to see their stable-mates start off before them.

Keturah laid her firm hand on Jake's arm. "Are you coming along, now?"

Jake looked at her, waveringly. "Are you going back now, Keturah?"

"Yes. We're going now. You'd better come, too."

It seemed to Jake that here was direction. And he had his horse to feed. "Thank you all, but I got to get home," he said, in a voice husky from much weeping. He climbed up into the democrat, assisted by the black-gloved hand of the livery man. In its turn, the democrat veered into the ancient stones, and whirled back down the road to Kinsail. The fifteen miles passed in the deepest of silence, since the mourners in the back seat were deterred from ordinary speech by the presence of the widower, and he had nothing to say for himself.

The Goudie rig turned last out of the churchyard. The four friends talked quietly and compassionately of a sorrow which was not theirs, and could not speak of what was resting so heavily on each of them. But after supper, when the men went out to finish up the chores, Abraham and Levi spoke together.

"They will go, for sure, Abraham?"

"Jah, I guess they will go."

"We have no word, yet, from Tillie."

"There has not been much time, though."

203

"No, not yet."

"Simon says, in his letter, that he had great joy, and knew that the Lord spoke to him."

"Jah, jah. The voice of God. He spoke to him, then."

"So clear, he says, so clear, yet."

"With us, the old ones, left behind, though. It is hard to give them up."

Abraham stood still, and looked about the shadowy stalls. The lantern in the high window of the cow-stable threw a warm, shadow-etching light on his thin lined face. "Yes, for us it is hard. There is plenty to do here, and with the other farm, too."

"He could have served God here, too."

"But it was not to be, Levi. And it is a wonderful thing, though."

"Jah. He is chosen, then. He heard His voice."

"He called him, and His voice was like the voice of many waters. The voice of God." Abraham's tone was low, and the men stood listening in the quiet stable, almost as if the presence of God might be about them and they must not be loud.

"Tillie will be a good helpmeet to Simon, Levi. A strong woman."

Levi sighed deeply, his breath almost shuddering into a sob. "To me, though, it seems she is just a little girl, yet."

Abraham nodded. "Jah, the girls seem younger than the boys. Simon never seemed like a child, for long. He was always anxious about the things on the farm, here, and now for a long time busy with the things of the Lord."

"He will be a faithful servant to Him, out there, and gain rich reward. Tillie, though, she is so young."

"Simon will see that it is not too hard, for her. And it is not quite yet. Until September, likely. The boat leaves in September."

Abraham hung his barn coat on the nail outside the kitchen door, and in silence they walked through the darkened dining-room to the parlour, where the lamp was lit, and the women sat quietly knitting in the yellow pool of light.

"We have been talking of the children, a little," said Levi. "You are thinking about this call to Africa, too?"

Mrs. Goudie nodded her head. She sat very still, her fat little hands quietly resting on her lap, the stocking hanging limply from the ends of her fingers. Her fresh plump cheeks were pale, in the lamplight, and her grey fair hair hung limply over her ears. "She looks older, right away," thought Levi. "With her, it is as with me, we mind it more than the other father and mother."

"It is hard for you, Josephine, to lose your boy to a far country. Jah, I know. But when it is the Lord who calls—"

Mrs. Goudie stirred into life. "He is not strong. He was never strong." She shook her head, again and again.

"She thinks of him still as a little one. Ach!" Levi smiled gently upon her.

"In the winter," she went on, "In the winter he coughs. All winter he must take care, that way."

Abraham smiled indulgently at the Shantzes. "She likes to make a babbie of him yet. But he is a man now, and can look after himself."

"He is not so young as Tillie, surely that is so," said Levi, "and sometimes they do not seem to us to grow up."

Mrs. Goudie seemed not to hear, and talked on in a low, brooding voice. "He is a child, too, in some ways, and does not know how to take care of himself. In the city he does not eat, even, and comes home starved and white. Who will see that he has a good feed, and does not wear himself out, over there?"

"Tillie, she will then," said her husband, in a gentle joking voice. "He will have his wife then, Josie. You must not think you are the only woman who can feed him, now!"

"Well," Betsey said, crisply, "there is nothing we can do. Once they leave home, it is not the same. They will have to learn to look after themselves now. They are old enough. And they are in God's hands."

Levi looked at her. "You have brought us back to sense, Betsey. They are in God's hands. Why should we concern ourselves so much?"

After a few minutes they knelt in the parlour, chilling now, and Levi prayed aloud that they, the parents of the chosen children, should learn to bow with utter acceptance to God's will concerning them. And that they should realize when they were worrying, that it was selfish worry, and that they should be given strength to cease from fretting. He commended the children and themselves, in their human weaknesses, to the grace of God, and stumbled behind Betsey up the narrow stairs to a broad and clammy bed. It was hard to sleep, up here in this strange room, the sheets seemed to take so long to warm, and then he was conscious too, of a strange weight upon his heart. What was it that made him feel so heavy, when he thought of Tillie? He had washed himself clean of resentment and fear about her going away—but there was not yet a feeling of complete ease, about her. And then he remembered that Keturah had been telling him that Tillie was not behaving well. That was the thing. She was a severe woman, and full of alarms, usually. But Tillie was gone from her house, now, some time. He moved heavily and uncomfortably in the cold bed. That was it. In the other, bigger thing he had forgotten Keturah's message, for the moment.

21

GEORGE BINGHAM came down Lock Street twice, before Tillie left Loretta's house, to ask her to go driving, but she gently refused, and heard his wheels rattle off down the gravel without regret. She was persuaded that there was nothing left of the old ungovernable emotions she had experienced because of this man of the world. From now on her life was to be of the spirit.

"The wind bloweth where it listeth, and thou hearest the sound thereof, but canst not tell whence it cometh, and whither it goeth. So is every one that is born of the spirit." She felt herself beyond doubt, now, to be of that miraculous company. She had been snatched from the burning. Loretta watched her with interest during these days.

"You ought to have been a Roman Catholic, Tillie," she said, "you have a good face for a nun."

Tillie smiled in her new, uncommunicating fashion, and made no answer. She would not be involved again in fruitless speculation. While she had been defying Keturah, and trying in her feeble earthbound way to reconcile the world with her people, this call had come to Simon. God had had to strike her hard, to make her see. But the scales had fallen from her eyes. No longer was the call of the flesh for her. While she was complaining of her circumscribed horizons, He had prepared this plan for her. She who had begrudged the trifling obedience to His laws had been offered the opportunity to travel farther than anyone she had ever known, across the world. She gratefully understood that again she had been shown God's great compassion, and the wonder of His ways. Her old unbridled impulses toward fresh experience and new landscape were to be satisfied, but within the certain boundaries of God's will.

She dreamed now that she walked through Africa, which was in her dream a kind of duneless sandy region, surrounded by the very blackest of high mountains. The broad golden sands were of an unimaginable brightness, crowded with suppliant figures. Two white-clad figures moved, radiant, among the blacks. At the foot of the high hills, sleek galloping shapes of lions and tigers loped tireless along the margin of the plain, while over all shone the heavenly light.

Although it was through Simon, of course, that this bright life opened now to her, she knew it to be God's own doing, on her behalf, and she seldom thought of Simon in direct connection with it. The letters he sent her were ecstatic, almost distraught, evidently written under pressure of time and emotion. There were many more negotiations, apparently, that he had to see to, before he could be free of the city and come home. Now it seemed that it would be into June, before all would be complete. She must make herself ready to come to the city too, not later than the first of July, and be prepared to stay for several weeks. There was a good deal she could learn, about the place they were going, right here. People would advise her about preparations. She wrote to say that she was going home the first of the month, and would be glad to see him, and would be ready to go to the city.

Tillie came home on a soft evening in early June. She stepped down from the train on to the cinder path to meet her father, still moving in the atmosphere of unreality which had surrounded her since she had read Simon's letter, God-sent to reach her when she needed it most, and knew that she was bound for Africa.

Levi, who had been ready to laugh and sing, and find life better, when Tillie came home, found that he was looking into unseeing eyes. He complained to Betsey.

"Tillie is not like herself, now."

"She is grown up some. That is all I see. Now she knows it is not just all laughing, and singing, and playing the piano."

"Certainly it is not playing the piano. Hardly at all she plays the piano. It is like a stranger in the house, Betsey."

And because she was so soon to leave them, it was harder still, not to have her like herself. Levi shook his head.

"I wish Simon could come home once, and she could talk things over. Maybe there is just something that worries her."

He tried again to get at the root of her remoteness.

"You have not seen Simon, then, since he decided this way?"

"No."

"But he will be coming soon here?"

"As soon as he can."

"Jah. For the service, anyway. Two Sundays away, isn't it?"

"The last Sunday in June. He cannot come before that."

It was not so easy to talk things over with Tillie, now. She had become, in the eyes of her family and all her people, not just Tillie Shantz, any more, one of a score of girls to be found in the meeting place, but Tillie Shantz who was to go to Africa, on the blessed business of the Lord. She went swiftly and competently about her work, so that Betsey was stripped of any criticism. In any case, even if it had not been so, there would have been no scolding possible, in the face of that calm, aloof gaze. She might have been wearing a mask, from morning to night. Only the children and Bertha were unaffected by her new status. Bertha followed her about muttering her disapproval of the whole African scheme.

"Down there in Africa there's all these here black people, though, aren't they? All them people without no clothes on? I don't know what you want to go away down there for."

"God is not interested, Bertha, in the colour of the skin that people have. It is their souls which we must bring to him."

Bertha acquiesced dubiously. "Jah, I guess that's right. But they're pretty funny-looking people, alright. There was a man back home, he was down there. He had some pictures, and they was awful funny-looking people, only aprons on."

Lambert led Tillie out to see the new all-black calf which was every bit his own. A heifer, too, and when she had a calf it was to be his, too. Tillie pulled the little creature's ears. The calf bowed her throat and backed, frantically reaching out a long searching tongue to suck at the caressing fingers.

"When I come back, then, you'll have quite a herd."

"How long are you going to stay away?"

"Seven years, Lambert."

"I'll have a big lot of cows, by that time. I'll be nineteen, then, and maybe Papa'll give me a farm, by then."

Tillie withdrew her hand from the calf's reach, and wiped it, tomboy fashion, on her skirt.

"She won't hurt you, Tillie!" Lambert looked disapprovingly at his sister. She must have been softened, by town life. "Scared of a little calf. Look." He reached out his fingers to the calf who whisked her tail in pleasure and sucked vigorously at the hand.

"Thinks it's a tit," said Lambert informatively.

"Your hand will be all slimy."

"I don't care if it's all slimy. I don't care, about anything like that. Ben does though. I got to feed her every time, myself, and look after her all the time. Then she's mine."

"Has Ben got one too?"

"No. He had one, but he hasn't got one now. He doesn't want one."

"Doesn't he? Why not?"

"He only wants a bull calf, then he can sell it. He doesn't want any heifer calf, though."

"Why doesn't he?"

"He's not going to be a farmer, like I am. He wants to be an engineer. But that's too dirty, Papa says. You got to leave home, too. I don't want to go nowhere."

Ben came across the barnyard, a look of intense interest on his serious face, a big egg in his hand.

"Give me a hairpin, Tillie?"

"Is it a duck egg?"

Ben nodded, cautiously scrutinizing the egg for a thin spot. With sober concentration he pierced the egg.

"Hope it isn't bad," said Lambert, "I did a bad one once, it tasted awful."

"I can do it so I don't taste it, though. Look."

Tillie watched them affectionately, as they stood there by the straw stack, tow-headed, bare-footed children, with all their lives before them. Since she had come back this time, they seemed to look younger than she remembered them. Perhaps it was the overalls, the faded blue that gave them that touchingly young, vulnerable look. But they were not babies, any more, now. They had responsibilities, already. When she came back, they would be grown men, almost. Lambert would be all right, though. There would never be anything he needed that he could not find here, or in some similar place. But her heart went out to little Ben, standing there dusty-browed and tense, fiercely working at his egg, his cheeks blown out to their utmost capacity. Ben would want more than this farm life could give him. She closed her eyes and prayed fervently, as she stood there, that he might not find his way too hard, before he came to his place of peace.

On the day before the service, when in the afternoon the unleavened bread had been lifted from the bake-oven, and set to cool on the great zinc sheets in the summer kitchen, and there was nothing more to be done till supper time,

Tillie brushed her hair up from her hot face, pulled down her sleeves and buttoned her cuffs, straightening her dress as though expecting guests. Her mother watched her almost with apprehension.

"You don't think Simon is coming here, though, today?"

"No. He will get home tonight, and drive over tomorrow."

"He should have come here, maybe. It is a long drive, from near Lemonville."

"His mother will want him home, first. He will make an early start."

Tillie opened the kitchen door and looked across the orchard rows to the fields and the green bush beyond.

"I'll be back in a little while."

She stepped through the doorway and closed the grey door gently behind her. Through the window over the table her mother and Bertha watched her walk slowly across the driveway, pause a little, looking about her, and then open the gate into the orchard. She turned back, looking intently at the house, slid the bar back to bolt the gate, then walked more quickly into the shelter of the apple trees. The women watched from the window, without words. They could see that she lifted her hand, now and then, and touched a tree along the row. Once she laid her head against the warm rough bark, and rested it there for a few minutes, looking a long way off.

"What's she doing that for?" Bertha whispered as though Tillie could possibly have heard her.

Betsey shook her head. "I don't know. I don't know." Tillie straightened up and resumed her walk and was lost to their sight beyond the elderberry bushes.

She lightly vaulted the fence between the orchard and the cornfield, feeling the grass margin pleasant to her feet. This afternoon she meant to go alone, for the last time, perhaps, to her old favourite spots over the whole farm. She would not be at rest here, for long, ever again. By this time tomorrow she would be launched into her new life, wherein this place would forever after be just a beloved background. Tomorrow she would renew her profession of faith, and publicly accept her destiny.

She paused in the back pasture field, down by the bright small trickle of spring water over black earth that as a child she had thought of as the most pleasant place of all. She bent and put her hand in the icy water, smiling with pleasure at its intensity. It never failed, grew no larger, no smaller, was always as cold as this. The children thought it must be ice, melting inside the earth forever, that made the spring.

There would be good corn, this year. Already it was as high as her waist. She walked the length of the cornfield, feeling the swish of the ribbed leaves against her dress, and remembering the games they had, with the visiting cousins, hiding in the corn. Down there, where the train came close to the back field, was where they used to put crossed pins on the tracks, for the locomotive to manufacture into scissors for them. There lay the hardwood bush which they tapped in the spring, for syrup and sugar. All that now, she was putting away. She was going out from it to a strange country, where there was nothing familiar, nothing known, except her husband. Just now, out here where every foot of earth and bush and tree had been known and loved, all her life, her spirit faltered at the thought. She was near her testing time. It was harder than it would have been if Simon had been there, to tell her more, per-haps. There was never, had never been, any doubt in Simon. If she were weak sometimes, then he should strengthen that weakness.

She thought of Loretta, and the small considered expla-nations she had been able to give her of the creation of the world, and the fallibility of the Bible. She saw that men had gathered together a little knowledge, and it had made them bold, contemptuous of Him whose mysteries were far too great for the human heart to understand, or even hope to grasp. The thing to do was to have faith. Faith would remove mountains. It had nothing to do with reasoning, or the accumulation of evidence, to prove or disprove. Men had made tight little interpretations of the word of God— written by men, she knew now, but inspired by Him. That was the thing. He had inspired every word, it did not matter that men had put down His words. That was probably the way it would be with all the doubts—behind the obvious discrediting a vast and valid truth. It had all sounded so reasonable, when they spoke of what they knew of the origins of man and the word of God, that she had been convinced. But what they could know, what anybody could know, was only the merest fringe of the mystery. It was better, perhaps it was the only way, to accept without question, as her people did, to believe all, resting in the assurance that God did not work with man's reason or attainments, but only with his heart.

"Verily I say unto you, except ye be converted, and become as little children, ye shall not enter into the kingdom of heaven." There was no room now for doubt, and the time for questioning was over. Among all the multitudes in the world outside, of whose existence she had only lately become dimly cognizant, there might perhaps be other paths than that her people trod, to lead to the throne. She could see now that it must be so. But this was to be her way. She bowed her head as she began to walk slowly home down the back lane, and prayed that she might be made steadfast in her faith.

22

OWN AT the Reesorville church, the Sunday that
Simon Goudie was to be dedicated to his mission
and sent out from his people with their blessing,
Tillie stood at the door, and the people looked at her
curiously. She might have been a stranger, whose mode of
life and manner of being was foreign to them. To be chosen
by the Lord, to go to speak for Him to those dark-skinned
brothers on that far-off golden shore, must surely leave a
mark on the face. They looked at her, as she waited there,
to see if they could see the mark. They formed in little
groups before the unpainted planks of the entrance platform, and in their delicacy and instinctive politeness, left
between her and them a circle of respect. To her brothers
and sisters in the faith she stood there as a chosen vessel of
God, ready to be sent into the farthest land to serve Him.
She was conscious of, and grateful for, their loving support.

The groups about her were quiet, as is the gentle custom
of the people, and the women smiled tenderly upon her.
The girls of her own age looked down, and wondered how
it had come about that Tillie Shantz, who so recently as the
last camp-meeting, even, had been running about red-faced
and laughing with them, should now have been so elevated.
But that was the way, with the Lord. He called, when it
was least expected, and we must be ready. Today it might
be Tillie Shantz who was being called, but tomorrow, or
next week, or this evening, it could be Martha Hoover, or
Mildred Burkholder. When the others saw her standing
there, looking so tall now, and with that remote, almost
proud look upon her face, they listened carefully for the
voice within themselves which should say, "Bertha Wideman, come now to Africa, and serve Me there." But for the

most part the women were glad that it was Levi Shantz's girl, and not their own fat and useful daughters, who had been called. And yet, there was something about it, maybe, which would make the girls restless, for a while. The women looked with reverence upon Tillie, as God's choice, and with strong relief upon their daughters. The men, well out of sight and earshot, by the driving sheds, spoke of the wonderful thing which had come to Simon Goudie and Tillie Shantz.

"To think that Tillie Shantz is to go so far from home, though!"

"Jah, and just now she was a little girl, yet, like Adeline, here."

"Brother Goudie will feel the loss of Simon, too."

"For a long time now, though, he knew he would go. He gave himself to the Lord, I remember the night, when he was just a little feller, there at Lemonville."

"I remember too. It was a wonderful victory for the Lord, that night. About twelve sinners brought into His fold, then."

"Simon was always ready. Is he here yet?"

"Isn't that the Goudie black, coming now?"

"Here's Levi."

The men walked slowly, deprecatingly over to Levi, and put out their hands. They shook his hand hard, and said nothing, but in the calloused grip was both sympathy for the man who was losing his daughter, and congratulation for the glory which was to be hers, through the grace of God. The group of men with Levi passed silently by Tillie, each man giving her a quick, shy nod as he passed. They cleared their throats and walked with squeaking shoes down the men's side of the church, and fell into fervent prayer on their knees before the benches.

Tillie waited for Mrs. Shantz in the empty churchyard. She and the lame Sister Wideman crept along the road, still forty rods from the gate. Simon, alone, drove on a tight rein, jerking involuntarily at the sight of Tillie so that the horse slithered round the gate-post, scraping the hub as he went. The rangy black almost leapt past the platform. But in the flashing moment they had clearly seen each other. Tillie caught her breath with quickened excitement, and something else that might, in another woman, have been fear. In a swift, subtle realization she knew that this was a meeting with a stranger. Suddenly she saw that within the dreamlike atmosphere which she had created about herself, Simon was the real and cogent being. It was into Simon's keeping that she was to deliver herself. The nun-like serenity which had carried her over the last six weeks was shattered.

Simon came bounding around the corner like a man who has been driven, and driven hard. Uncouth and violent, his long face almost haggard, he came panting up to Tillie, clutched her hands and pressed them against his chest. His eyes blazed, and his long lips worked, speechlessly. Abruptly he threw down her hands and pulled her close to him with a fierce, convulsive movement, pushing his mouth on hers until she could feel the shape of his long strong teeth behind his lips. In a few seconds it was over. Simon's breath came in gasps as he spoke to her. "Oh, Tillie, Tillie! How long—it has been so long!"

He turned as the women's footsteps sounded on the boards behind him, nodded briefly to Mrs. Shantz, answered Tillie's full gaze, and then plunged down the basement stairs to prepare himself for the pulpit. Dazed and numb, Tillie followed her mother down the aisle into their seat.

The women's side of the church was filled with rows of mild-faced girls and women from whom, as they entered the lovely atmosphere of the house of God, all thought of worldly care was washed away. Even the babies, hooked under their mothers' arms, became for a little while solemn and still. Little black-bonneted girls sat beside their mothers, the smallest next to her commanding knees, with the others rising in some cases, by steps and stairs, to the eldest

217

daughter pressed against the wall. In corresponding benches on the other side, the sons were ranged beside their fathers.

The church was almost full. The people of Reesorville had come out in all their numbers for the dedication service which was, in a way, to seal the contract that Simon Goudie had made with God, for his life service among the black brothers. Whole families were there; the very oldest among them, the frail old women and deaf and shrunken men, those who lived in the old people's side of the big comfortable houses which God had provided for His own, came that day. People who, because of infirmities of the flesh, did not often have the joy of entering His house, came, that lovely June Sunday, and warm expectancy filled the church.

Shadows from the delicate new leaves dappled the sunlight through the open windows, and fell on the eager face of the preacher who ran up out of the room below to speak to the people. Levi studied his face, and turned, heavily and deliberately, to see what Tillie, across the aisle, saw in it. Tillie looked ahead, her mouth held tight and straight. It seemed to her father that her face was too pale. He saw, too, that many curious glances rested upon his daughter. If Tillie knew that the eyes of the people were upon her, she gave no sign. She appeared to be utterly composed, looking, with the others, impassively at the face of the preacher. As the congregation rose to sing, she gave her father a loving, swift and childlike smile.

Simon read the first verse aloud, mouthing the words almost as if he could taste them, and repeating the last lines over again, his head thrown back, his eyes closed.

"Jesus, Saviour, pilot me
Over life's tempestuous sea;
Unknown waves before me roll,
Hiding rock and treacherous shoal;
Chart and compass come from Thee,
Jesus, Saviour, pilot me."

Sister Burkholder, a baby in her arms, struck the note, and led the singing in sweet, sure tones. The men's side brought in the strong bass and tenor parts, and the hymn rolled on to its solemn conclusion:

> "When at last I near the shore,
> And the fearful breakers roar . . .
> May I hear Thee say to me,
> 'Fear not, I will pilot thee'."

The preacher buried his face in his hands for a few minutes' private communication with his God, and then he spread out his long arms and prayed for the sure and certain salvation of all who knelt together there, before Him. He did not touch at all upon his own fresh problems, but dwelt upon theirs, asking that they might indeed have a pilot, in Lord Jesus. And these men and women who had never seen an earthly ocean in their lives, and who never would, felt themselves to be travelling precariously in frail ships among fearful storms, requiring only the certain knowledge that Jesus would guide them through. Very few of them had ever set foot in so much as a row-boat; but Simon and Tillie would know of these dangers, and the spiritual metaphor became clear and enriching.

Tillie knelt by her mother, her eyes open, staring fixedly along the aisle to the open doorway. Her strong fingers were clasped under her chin; her head was unbowed, and the preacher's words rattled over it like pebbles. Soft moans of approval came from the men's side, and sibilant agreement whispered up from the women. "Yes, Lord, yes."

The preacher prayed on and on. The buzzing of a few bees on the windows accompanied his words, but that was the only other sound. Then a delicate, double staccato note came to Tillie's ears from the outside. There it was again, lost for a second, but now stronger; very faint, but insistent. The boys in the back seats heard it, too, and raised their heads to see what was coming. It sounded like the hoof-

beats of a galloping horse, but surely no horse could go so
fast. And there was no sound of wheels. The horses tethered in the shed stirred and stamped and rattled their rigs.
Then it became clear to the listeners that it was not one
horse galloping down the road, but two. Tillie kneeling
high now, saw two rubber-tired racing sulkies flash past the
church, their drivers bent double over the horses' tails, legs
spread wide and stretched along the shafts. The sound had
been misleading. The horses were not galloping; they were
trotting. The horse on the inside flew over the ground with
that light, swaying, dizzy motion which Tillie already knew
too well. She rose, like a woman in a trance, and stared
out of the church. A few curious young eyes followed her.
Betsey looked up in wondering disapproval. She pulled,
frowning, at Tillie's skirt, and Tillie reluctantly knelt again.

The soft quick sounds that the feet of the flying horses
made on the sandy road telescoped into a purr in the distance, and then all sound ceased. Only the pale beige dust
settling in feeble puffs on the bracken and blossoming
raspberries at the edge of the road was indication that she
had not imagined that swift passage.

The congregation rose from its knees, and the testimony
began. The querulous voice of old Chris Lehman, who had
been a strong and true singer in his day, but now, since he
was so deaf, could not hear himself, was raised in tuneless
praise, as testimony. Old Sister Reesor, up across from
Chris, almost blind, gave her testimony in a high shrill voice,
at the same time. Ben and Lambert were in convulsions of
silent laughter, looking over to see if Tillie were enjoying it,
too. But her head was low, her eyes shut. The old voices
ceased, almost at the same moment, and she heard her
mother's voice, thin and remote.

"I want to say, here today, that the Lord has been good
to me. Often I have slid back, but He has caught me in
His strong arms, and brought me back to the fold. Praise
His name."

"Amen, amen, sister."

Strong, approving throats groaned out their gratitude. A young girl spoke now.

"I am glad to say that I belong to the Lord Jesus, and He has saved me from my sins. I want to love Him more, every day." Her voice broke with a little sob, and then came the answering chorus, "Yes, Praise God, only Love Him, only Love Him."

"Yes, Lord, yes."

Simon's voice sounded an obbligato, pleading, praying, exhorting, in small ecstatic phrases. From time to time he thundered his unqualified denunciations. His voice, to Tillie's ears, was the voice of a stranger, speaking a foreign tongue, dealing perhaps with a matter long since dead. An impassable chasm had opened between herself and Simon, and she removed him from her consideration. In the over-whelming discovery she had made, the resolve she had formed, there was no question of Simon. It was as if she had found herself the possessor of a little island, fabulously rich with treasure. It was inconceivable that she should reach her island, and claim her treasure, since there were obstacles which appeared insurmountable between her and it. But within her there was welling warmth, even to know of the existence of the island. She saw Simon now with new and penetrating clarity; sat in indifferent judgement on him as if he had been a stranger, appraising him as such. He was an earthbound spirit, held down to the narrow plot which would be his essential proportion, no matter where he went, or what fantastic soil he trod. There was some-thing she had heard, once, at the school; she deafened her ears and sought the words:

"I am a part of all that I have met,
  Yet all experience is an arch wherethro'
  Gleams that untravell'd world whose margin fades
  For ever and forever when I move."

That was it. There was much more, too, but she could not remember more. She felt the truth of it. It was true for her, but for Simon it would never be true. Simon took his horizon with him. She saw, as in a revelation, that the confines of the spirit are not to be described by a circle as large as the universe, but that narrowness of mind can effectively confine the boundaries of the whole world. She had been prepared to follow Simon as a spiritual leader, as a consecrated man of God. In the splitting of a second she had seen the fallacy in that childish dream. She put her hand to her mouth, and closed her eyes in revulsion. She was as cold as the moon, for Simon, now and forever more. The sound of the quick feet of the horses, the glimpse of the flying wheels, had revealed her to herself.

Someone now began to sing, and she heard her father's big voice join in; and then, when the song ceased, he started to speak, finding it hard to choose the words in his deep concern to give proper thanks for God's care. His usual flow was halted, today; there were long pauses between his sentences. It is hard to give the heart's treasure, even to God. Tillie's throat tightened. Where could she go, to escape the grief of hearing this? The punishment would be hard, and this was the beginning of it. The words seemed to burn her, as they fell. She wept silently, helplessly, not seeing or feeling anything now but the pure flame of grief.

Levi ceased to speak, and began to sing again, the congregation joining tenderly with him. "All the way, my Saviour leads me." Fervent responses rose murmuringly: "Amen, amen, brother, He will go with her. All the way, all the way, praise His name."

There was a shuffling pause. Simon looked over the people to see who next would speak for the Lord. His cheeks flushed deep red as Tillie stood, pale and trembling, supporting herself in her nervousness with both hands on the back of the pew. Simon nodded.

"Sister," he said, regarding her pale face with avid eyes.

She began in a clear voice, keeping her own eyes fixed on some distant hill not visible to the people.

"I thank the Lord for His loving kindness to me, at all times. But I now feel no longer worthy to be called His child, in His eyes, and in the eyes of this congregation." She paused, swallowing a heavy sob. "I want to say before you all, that there has been a great mistake. I have no call to go to Africa. I—I am leaving the church. I hope that the Lord will forgive me. There is nothing else I can do."

Her voice broke beseechingly on the last words. There was the quiet of death in the building. Tillie stood for a long minute, her shoulders tight, her arms to her sides, holding herself utterly rigid. Then, unable to endure any more, she dropped her hands from the back of the seat before her, turned, and with head bowed walked out of the church. Simon's face greyed like the sky after a swift sunset. Betsey did not turn her head. Levi sat perfectly still, as if under a spell which it was not in his power to break. Into the silence came the voice of the preacher.

"Let us seek the Lord in prayer."

23

FOR A long time after he had come out of the stricken congregation to see nothing but the empty road where he had expected to find Tillie, Levi could not be persuaded to start for home. The little boys found her black bonnet swinging from a post, and brought it to him. He hurried down the road to where it had been, convinced that she must still be somewhere here. But when they went into the light bush and called her name there was no answer. All along the roads leading out from Reesorville, the home-going buggies drove slowly, so as to find perhaps some trace of her, but there was nothing. With apprehensive sidelong glances at Levi the young men crossed the mill-race and peered along the margin of the water for a footprint, but they found nothing.

"Home, yet, Levi. She has just gone home, somehow. We must go back. Somebody has given her a ride, maybe."

But Levi shook his head. "Who would there be, though? No, she has not gone home."

"We must go, Levi. Come, now."

Levi stood in the middle of the road, twisting the strings of the bonnet aimlessly through his fingers. Betsey signed to the little boys to get the rig.

At the top of the bald hill behind the church, Simon's tall figure seemed blown at random by heaven's winds, as he looked this way and that over the steep sandy hills and tried to see into the deep small valleys where the roads disappeared under cedar swamp. From his vantage ground he stared unbelievingly into the sky, too, as if somewhere above there might be written a message for him. He could see nothing but the gathering clouds, fold after fold of grassy hill, dark irregular streaks and blotches of bush, and the tops of telephone poles marking hidden roads.

Nowhere in all the landscape was there any unknown vehicle moving, or any unknown house which would harbour, without question, a wandering girl. He paced up and down the brow of the hill, demanding of God to know what had become of her. He shook his head in violent refusal to follow the Shantz rig home, when Betsey called to him; but he came down to see them off, and they heard the church door crash behind him before they had got through the gate.

Betsey glanced at her husband, but he was neither seeing nor hearing. He lifted the reins mechanically and the team turned gladly homeward. Clouds gathered above them as they reached their farm in a silence unbroken by words. Even Bertha was quieted by fear and wonder, and hustled the little boys off to change their clothes. A hired man came out of the warm darkness of the barn to reach for a horse's head.

"We're nearly all through, Levi. Not worth you coming out."

The light shafts dropped with a shiver to the road and the horses trotted eagerly towards the stable so that the man behind them had almost to run to keep up. The only noise in the hushed evening was the slap of the reins and the muffled plop of the horses' hurrying hooves on the soft earth. A smell of rain was in the air, a flash of lightning to the south. Then there was the sound of iron shoes on the cement floor, and of cowbells from the lane; and the giant insect hum of the separator became a scissor-sharpening tone. The women went into the house, taking down lamps from the top of the cupboard and silently lighting them from matches groped for in the dusk.

Levi stood still on the veranda, his eyes and ears strained for sight or sound of Tillie. Surely now, that was a buggy coming? The wheels came nearer, must now be at the gate, slackened their speed, then picked it up again and passed. He sat down on the bench, his knees apart, his big hands spread on them, helplessly waiting for he scarcely knew what.

It was not possible to believe what he had seen and heard. There was no way that he could realize it. All that was really clear to him was that his daughter had gone. When he tried to remember what she had said, it seemed that the pain was too great, there around his heart, for him to bear the recollection of it. He could not have heard what he thought to have heard. No. All this weight of grief was because she was gone. Of, if only she were still there, as she used to be! What if she were still only a little girl, there in the kitchen with her mother, though! What if he went out there, now, and there would be the white table

225

with the plates on it, and Tillie, too, stepping about so quickly, and laughing as she told some funny thing to Bertha. Always she liked Bertha. And Ben and Lambert with their tow heads, following her around to make her sing to them, or draw pictures on their slates, maybe. And then, perhaps after supper she would play to them, and they would all sing, there in the parlour. He smiled to think of the good times they had. Then he looked down at his side. Tillie's bonnet, what was it doing here then? A flood of bitter, scalding remembrance broke over him, and he knew afresh that he had lost her. Worse than lost her, now she herself was lost. To this world and to the next. Even if she came down the lane now, well and happy, it would be no use. Better that she were dead than to live the life of the damned. This afternoon she had renounced the church and was gone—no matter, really, where. Since it was from God she tried to go, no matter where. But he started up at the sound of wheels again. He held his breath to listen. Yes. Surely this time they would turn in. Surely, now, there would be news of her.

The buggy turned into the gate and a tired horse walked stubbornly the length of the lane. Drooping with anxiety Levi started for the lane. It was quite impossible to remember that Tillie had said—had said those things. He could not grasp them then, and he could not remember them now. The years themselves had vanished, had never been, the years that turned her from his little girl to the young woman with the newly remote face. He hurried stumbling to the buggy only as a father looking for his child, with nothing but love in his heart, and longing for relief from this intolerable burden.

The women in the kitchen looked up with startled eyes at the sound of the wheels, and moved swiftly to the window on tiptoe, as if there were reason for secrecy.

"Maybe that's her! Maybe that's Tillie, now!"

Bertha pushed her long-jawed face through the open window. The slow wheels stopped at the side stoop.

"There's Levi. He's coming." She peered into the dusk. "It's raining. 'Taint Tillie, though. Just Simon Goudie, all alone. Been driving that horse pretty hard, I guess. Well. Put on another place, will I?"

Betsey nodded, her face grey and drawn under the thin hair which she had not thought to comb since she came home. The untidy wispish greying locks about her ears gave her a slatternly look so foreign to her that Bertha noticed it with alarm. She pushed her own hair back, fiercely, as if by her action she could induce Betsey to return to herself.

"I guess Simon Goudie, he got a call all right, but I guess Tillie, though, she didn't. But don't you worry, Mrs. Shantz, she'll come back all right. She'll be all right."

Bertha's voice wavered off uncertainly, her bright wild animal eyes keeping furtive watch on Betsey's face.

Betsey gave no answer, only stepping to the door to beckon the men in. "Come and have your supper now. It's nearly bed-time, or after, and no supper yet."

Levi spoke to Simon. "Where did you go?" Simon raised his hands in a gesture of defeat, outspread to indicate the breadth of country he had fruitlessly searched.

"To Charlie Bricker's and brother Davis's and Ben Reesor's, and down the eighth a mile and a quarter. In by Chris Taylor's there. Nobody saw anything. Only two men racing horses, the only strangers. Nobody with them. Only little carts. Nobody saw anything strange, at all."

Levi looked at the young man as if in sudden anger.

"Do you know more about it, anyway at all, than we do? Did you know, ever, of a change in her heart?"

Simon shook his head. "In her letters there was nothing. She seemed to be all right, and ready to go, and that."

Levi growled impatiently. "But she cannot be far, if nobody took her. And where would she go by herself, but home here?"

"Today all the people were on the roads. And only in

a few minutes, wasn't it, she was gone? Somebody would have seen a buggy."

"It was not long, surely."

They thought back to the time when the sun had gone in, and the church door closed behind Tillie.

"Unless she went into the bush," suggested Simon, wearily, "for to hide."

Betsey came through the door and stood quietly before them, her hands hanging before her, lightly linked.

"She cannot hide from God," she said.

The men looked at her in wonder. In an afternoon the quality of her voice had changed. She drew herself into the deep shade of the grapevine by the steps and spoke to them. In the kitchen Bertha stood still to listen. The little boys crouched behind her, afraid to move lest they be sent supperless to bed.

"She has gone. It seems to me sometimes that I always knew that she would go. It is no use now for us to look all over for her. She is not a little girl, any more. She is a woman now. She has taken everything into her own hands."

Betsey held herself straight, pushing her shoulders back and stretching up her chin. Her voice trembled a little, but she controlled it and went evenly on.

"Now it is between the Lord and her. We can pray for her, that is all, that her heart may be softened. But from now she is lost to us. Maybe, Levi, you were too easy with her. Or perhaps it is my punishment for feeling bad and so rebellious when the babies died. Maybe the Lord didn't mean for me to have any daughters, and then when I pleaded so hard he let me keep one for a little. But it was not to be. We must forget Tillie now, Levi." Her voice hardened. "And you too, Simon. You must forget her too. Wipe from your mind and heart all thought of her. She was not worthy. Levi, tell the men to come. The supper is ready now."

228

With a gesture unique in all their married life Betsey drew Levi's head down to her with both hands and kissed him tenderly on the forehead.

They ate their meal in the quiet of a house of mourning. When they had finished, Levi reached for the Bible, saying, "We'll have the reading in the other room tonight. Bring the lamps, Bertha." He walked stiffly into the parlour and sat down before the table, stretching his sore feet out to the side. "The heat," he said, rubbing his hand over them. Before the reading started, Bertha suddenly spoke to the gathering in general.

"Tillie. God didn't snatch her up to heaven off that road there. She's got a fella in Kinsail. She's there now, likely as anything she's there now. That fella sent her them chocolates, last Christmas. That's where Tillie is, all right." She laughed softly to think how clever she had been.

In the shadowed fringes of the room the hired men sat upright on hard chairs, looking at the floor. Simon kept his big hand over his face, and Betsey's face seemed more tired still.

"Be quiet, Bertha," she said, glancing at the little boys, half asleep on the sofa.

In a voice full of tears Levi began to read. "I will lift up mine eyes unto the hills, whence cometh my help. My help cometh from the Lord which made heaven and earth. He will not suffer thy foot to be moved: he that keepeth thee will not slumber. Behold, he that keepeth Israel shall neither slumber nor sleep. The Lord is thy keeper: the Lord is thy shade upon thy right hand. The sun shall not smite thee by day, nor the moon by night. The Lord shall preserve thee from all evil: he shall preserve thy soul. The Lord shall preserve thy going out and thy coming in from this time forth, and even for evermore."

24

*T*ILLIE STEPPED tremulously out from the sheltering church into the hazardous world which she had chosen of her own free will. She was shivering as if with cold, and her bonnet-strings tightened on her swelling throat. She pulled at them, feeling relief when they slipped out of the knot. She lifted the bonnet from her head and hung it without thought on a fence post.

The road was bathed now in empty silence, but in a few minutes would be full of curious people. She stood uncertainly for a long minute on the high crown of the road, then, lifting her full skirts, jumped the ditch and landed lightly on the steep bank beyond. She made her quick way through the bush by the children's short-cut path to the disused crossroad corner. Only a few hundred yards and she would be at the schoolhouse, safe from encounter. As she stepped out of the bush into the road, three crows, flashing their torn taffeta wings, dropped into a triangle at her feet. The sign of death. Could she still believe that, or was it just superstition too? What could she still believe? Certainly not that it was only in the world that ugly passions dwell in the hearts of men. Each man has his mask, in the world or out of it.

The crows flapped harshly up into a dead pine tree beyond the schoolhouse, then down again, and dropped from her sight. Tillie followed their flight with her eyes until the sky was as empty as she felt her heart to be. Her legs trembled under her as she crossed the road. It took almost all her strength to step up to the high platform. She sat down upon it, resting her head against the well-remembered door, staring before her in the stunned fashion of a man who returns to his home to find it a smoking ruin. The bright blurred vision of a life given to the glory of God on the other side of the world vanished as though it had never been.

A light breeze blew down from the tops of the pine trees, seeming to shake the cedar wax-wings out of their nests, and filling the air with soft sound. Thin and far away there came the sound of singing. Tillie raised her head to hear them, releasing slow tears from her eyes. The service was over, then. But she had cut herself off from the singing, and the people who sang. She had parted herself forever from her people, from everything that had been incontestably her own. She closed her eyes in pain, and her throat filled again.

There was the sound of a rig down on the town line. She got heavily to her feet and tried the door. It was bolted from within, but the worn latch-hole permitted her little finger to enter, and she easily shot the bolt. The acrid school smell compounded from the generations of mice that came to eat the crumbs from the lunch pails, the dust, the chalk, and the smell of little boys who are not washed quite enough, assailed her familiarly, as she entered. Tillie went into the Continuation room.

There was little change since she had been here. The old man had gone, but the hard little couch he had introduced because of his mysterious spells of illness remained, and the low green-baize curtain which hid it from the class still hung. Perhaps the new teacher needed it too. Tillie smiled a little wistfully at the innocence of the people who did not recognize the illness. The wall bookcase, unpleasantly comb-grained by an unsteady hand, still lacked a catch, and offered the same selection of literature. The big box stove held traces of its winter ashes, and half-dissected crayfish clouded in bottles on the science table.

The seat where she had sat was near the front. She went on tiptoe down the aisle, afraid of disturbing she knew not what, and slid into her old desk. There was one boy, she remembered, a Mennonite too, who had sat across the way.

231

He went to school until he was sixteen, and some said to the university afterward. She had been at the church the day he withdrew from it. The dreadful words he had said stayed with her. It was unthinkable that she had used them herself. Could he, so harshly judged, have been so full of grief? Perhaps not. He had no father or mother, any more. It would not be quite the same. Perhaps he too, in the end, had had no choice.

Once when she was a little girl the thought came to her that some day her father must die. She could remember just where she sat when she realized it. There would be a day and an hour when he would no longer be there. For a few days afterwards she had thought she could not want to live, if her father should die. And now she had put a gulf as wide and as deep as death between herself and him. She rested her desolate face on her hand, and gave herself up to grief. The far-off rattle of iron on gravel came increasingly often. The people were going home; but there was no message for her now in the sound of home-going wheels. There would be no place in her father's house for a backslider from the house of the Lord.

In the capricious manner of the hot days of early summer there gathered a great black cloud over the sand-hills, and while the afterglow still lingered on the tops of the hills, slanting rain slashed down from the shining rim of the cloud. The sun lost touch with the valleys now; there was cool darkness, and heavy rain fell.

Tillie searched the cupboard for paper, and found a pad of dusty foolscap and a pencil. Sitting at her old desk she wrote laboriously, a long letter to her father. When she had finished she read it carefully through, and signed it. After a long search she found a brown envelope saying "Ontario Teachers' Manual" in the corner. It was empty, and the glue unused. When the rain stopped she would walk to Siloam by the Lemonville road, and give it to Abe before she took the train to Kinsail. Her father would have it tomorrow.

232

But when the storm was over it was quite dark, and the evening train long since gone. She felt her way to the teacher's couch, and in the wakeful night she acknowledged fully and without qualification that she must go back to the world, and accept it, because of George. She forced herself to see again the picture of the embrace under the swinging lamp in the Mansion House hall, and to know that it was George there, acquiescent, more than acquiescent, in the fat woman's arms. She closed her eyes, when she had made the picture come, too pained to bear it, but then again and again brought the image to her mind. And in the end she could say to herself. "Yes. It was so. There is no mistake. It was like that. I know it was like that, and I must bear it." Perhaps there were circumstances which would explain it, a little; but even if not, she knew she could accept it. In the new road which she had deliberately chosen to walk she knew that she might expect great grief. Well then, she must learn to take the grief with the delight. She felt herself grow eager and strong.

25

THE LEMONVILLE road lay ribbon-straight and washed clean between its cedar bindings, under a sky so blue and cloudless that to believe it capable of rain and cloud was quite impossible. The packed sand surface struck leather-hard under Tillie's striding feet. She walked her road in quiet rapture, free now to remember every moment she had spent with George, measuring out parcels of distance in terms of permission to recollect. She called up the memory of his arm about her and his quick, shy but not furtive kiss as they stood in Loretta's doorway. She stopped, drawing in a quick breath at the recollection. Then she resolutely washed her mind clean of all reminiscence, feeling a necessity to discipline herself in recollection, lest the flavour should in the slightest degree be lessened. Until she reached the next crossroad, until she was right at the top of the third hill, until she saw a red barn, she would not think of him again. The goal reached, she gave herself up to the ecstatic moment of memory, closing her eyes to recall the sudden lifting of her heart as she felt his arm lightly enclose her, and the quick, warm kiss, so soon over as scarcely to be felt, but as a kiss in a dream to be remembered. "Not till the first cement bridge; not till I turn the corner at the cheese factory; not till I see seven crows."

But the ecstasy did not diminish, and the remembering filled her with such happiness that she could scarcely believe it was really true, that it had really happened. He had put his arm about her, and wordlessly kissed. Fresh, undiluted, amazing joy came as she said to herself, "He must really love me, though!"

It was nearly seven o'clock now. Another hill and the first road past the gravel pit would bring her to the turn. Then only a few minutes more and she would be in the village. She was ravenously hungry. The smoke from morning fires in the farmhouses she passed reminded her forcibly that there were people there sitting down to porridge and ham and pie. She swallowed her hunger down and went swiftly on. There would be nothing open in the village, at this time of day; unless Gill's general store at the four corners, a quarter of a mile before the country road turned into the main street, might be open for milk. A light team with a load of forty-gallon iron cans met her at a trot on its way to the cheese factory. The driver looked curiously at her, turning his head to look again until she turned off the road. The fields one by one within her range became inhabited with doll-like figures. An inquisitive youngster in a ramshackle buggy, on his way to the mill with a bag of grain for shorts, pulled up beside her and asked if she wanted a ride. She made a quick decision.

"No thank you. I'm not going far."

The boy nodded and went reluctantly on. The empty world seemed suddenly to have been filled with people. Tillie became conscious of her bedraggled skirt and the rough braids which were all she could make without brush or comb. But she had smoothed them out with her hands, and they stood in a strong coronet above her smooth forehead. When she passed the mill, the boy and the miller stood on the platform in silent curiosity and watched her swift passage.

A man with heavy rubber boots and a grub-hoe over his shoulder gave her a bleary-eyed "Good morning." It took him the length of his cornfield to wonder what that one was doing on the road in that get-up at that time of the morning. He turned and gaped at her, shaking his head.

Unless she could get something to eat at the corners it would be another two hours before she could expect to find food. The little milk-train stopped at every flag station in the twenty-five miles to Kinsail. But at least in the train she could rest.

The store at the corners commanded a view of all the four roads. There was some activity there, evidently, since a horse and buggy stood outside. Tillie hurried on. A box of biscuits, or some bananas, or a handful of dried meat; any kind of food would do. The tall buckskin horse at the hitching-post turned to look at her nervously as she went past. She noticed automatically that he had three white stockings and a curiously mottled blaze on his face. "One more stocking and he'd be no good at all," she thought to herself, and opened the double door into the shadowy store. A small copper bell jangled harshly as she shut the door behind her. The horse backed the length of his halter and pushed his legs straight in front of him, flattening his ears.

"Here she is!" a man's voice said from the back room, and George Bingham, smiling broadly, walked slowly towards her. "Heard you were lost," he said. "Where the devil have you been hiding yourself?"

"I saw you go by, yesterday," said Tillie.

"By where?" George looked intently at her.

"Reesorville church."

"Oh, yes. Having a little brushing with one of Chris Taylor's boys. Where are you staying, here?"

"Nowhere. I'm going to take the train to Kinsail. But I want some food, first, and to leave a letter for Abe."

Mr. Gill came silently out from the back room, full of unspoken questions, tying his apron behind him. Tillie nodded pleasantly to George and walked over to the glassed cupboard which held a few cooked meats and on Saturdays, for the idle wife, a plate or two of home-made cookies and biscuits. Half a bologna sausage seemed to be all, today.

"Not very much in, yet. Monday's a bad day. Early yet." Mr. Gill watched her narrowly, with small blue eyes lost in folds of brown skin. "Father'll be glad to know you're all right," he ventured.

"Have you any bananas?"

"Not very good, I guess. End of the bunch."

"I'll have half a dozen, and a pound of arrowroots."

She handed Gill the brown envelope, and money for a stamp. "Be sure to give this to Abe, will you? This morning, for sure."

"Sure, sure I will." He nodded rapidly. "Comes along about ten."

George watched the transaction in silence. When she had paid for her purchases and started out the door he followed her. "Wait a minute, Tillie."

"If you hear any more," he said to the man, "tell him I might be interested. He can come and see me if he really wants to do business. I'm not over anxious, though. She's pretty small." He waved his arm and closed the door on the curious face.

"If you're in a hurry to get to Kinsail, Tillie, you'd better come with me. I'm going to try to get there some time today. You can't say that much of the train."

He laid his hand on the halter of the tawny horse.

"Is he yours?"

"As of yesterday. Like him?"

"But you haven't sold Maida?"

"No ma'am, no ma'am, I have not. 'Member I told you I'd make a little money and buy another little hoss? This is it. I'm leaving Maida out to grass, for a couple of weeks, maybe. Running a wee bit lame, this morning, I thought. Till I get acquainted with this one, anyway."

"But I saw her yesterday, surely?"

"Oh yes! Well, come along, let's try Tiger. You can eat your buns in the buggy."

Mr. Gill's face was two inches from the glass in the door. Tillie looked at him, gave her parcels to George and climbed into the buggy. Mr. Gill called loudly to his wife to come on down out of that and see what there was to see.

George untied the horse slowly, keeping up a low-voiced running conversation with him and letting his hand rest soothingly on his neck.

"Not very sure of me yet, are you, Tiger? It's all right, boy. Somebody's treated you pretty rough, I'd guess, but we're going to get on fine."

The horse picked up his silk ears and unfolded them. Still in a quiet voice George spoke to Tillie. "Just get the lines in your hands, will you? In case he gets ideas. We had a little argument on the way down."

Tillie unrolled the lines from the whip stock, gathering them short in her hands. The horse stood quietly now, but listening with every muscle. "I don't think there's a bad bone in his body, but he's got a few ideas we'll have to iron out. And then I think I'll have a real horse."

George kept his hand reassuringly on the horse's neck,

and looked closely at Tillie. "Don't you think we ought to have more than bananas and baby-food from here to Kinsail? When did you have your last meal?"

"Yesterday noon, I guess."

"You guess! For God's sake don't you *know?*"

Tillie flinched at the name of the Deity, but straightened her shoulders in remembering that she was adopting a new criterion. Such a thing did not mean just what it sounded as if it meant. It was a manner of speaking, and not a sin. She smiled.

"Dinner, yesterday, then."

George waited to hear what she had done since, but she said nothing more. Tiger stamped his white socks impatiently.

"Do you think you can hold him for a bit? I'm going to see if Gill can't dig up something else to eat. And maybe a bottle of pop. Back in a minute."

The thought of the long drive home with Tillie was pleasantly provocative to George. He was already tasting the sweetness of possessing a little more money than he needed. There seemed to be full promise of more to come. He had bought the lake land at the most propitious time, evidently; already there were three cottages going up, and talk in the township council of opening a road through on the south side to the Ransom road. He was considering moving for the summer out to the old house, and camping there. He would be on the spot, then, for discussion with the campers and any new prospects, and it would satisfy a primitive urge to be actually living on his own land. On the drive home he would talk about these affairs to her, and find out, too, what she had been up to. Yesterday in the sudden rain, up at the farm where Maida was boarding, and where he had picked up his new horse, someone came in driving like Jehu, demanding of Chris whether he had seen anything of her. She must have run away, surely! He had not seen the man, but he looked like a Mennonite preacher, they said.

238

George glanced at Tillie through the door. She did not look now as though she would run away from anything, sitting there erect and watchful and composed. Tiger backed suddenly, but she had him standing squarely on his feet in a second, before the wheels had time to scrape the platform. In the six weeks since he had seen her there had been a perceptible change in her face, surely. There was less of the baby, more of the woman. Perhaps it was just that; the childlike roundness had suddenly given place to well defined, delicate planes. What in the devil, he asked himself irritably, would that smug-faced gospel-fighter want with a lovely creature like that, anyway? Surely to God that kind of girl wasn't standard equipment for every mad man off to Africa to convert the natives to red flannel pants?

The milk-train screamed for the crossing and Tiger left earth, pawing frantically for refuge from the noise. He plunged and then kicked, furiously determined to loose himself from restraint on all sides. Bucketing the buggy like a matchbox behind him he took the bit in his teeth and ran snorting like a fool back up the road towards home. The men ran yelling out of the store, after the rig, but there was no hope of catching it. They saw the light wheels bounce from the tracks, the top waver and tip. It leaned precariously towards the ditch on the right side, scraped the wooden railing of the bridge and went right off the road into the ditch on the left. It was a miracle that it did not overturn. The pale horse ran like the devil's own along the ditch, and then they saw that he was climbing out and running up the steep bank, his head high in the air, pulling his mouth hysterically. Swaying wildly, the buggy hurtled over the hill and dropped out of sight.

"By daddies, she'll be killed if she ain't already," said Gill, soberly.

"Get out your horse and go for Doc Sylvester," George

ordered him. "I'll get to the top and see if I can find her."

"Yeah. Yeah. That's the best way."

For a moment shock held them paralyzed, staring up the empty road. "Tell him for God's sake to hurry."

Gill nodded. "I'll send one of the boys horseback, that'll be faster." He ran shouting back into the door. The empty road became busy with people. The excited chant of "Runaway! Runaway!" passed from child to child. Little boys dropped their playthings and young men their tools, and ran up the hill. The women came out of the back doors of their houses near the corners and gathered in little questioning, fearful groups by the side of the road.

Gill caught up with George half way up the hill. "Delbert's went for the doctor. If he's out he's goin' up to the telephone office and get through to Doc Wilmot up to Lemonville. Times like this it'd be handy to have a telephone, I expect."

The party walked in silence. George looked with an agony of apprehension at empty skyline just before him. Once up there, what shattering sight would they see? The bright morning in just a few seconds had been transformed from a set for a gay and provocative adventure to a back-drop for almost certain tragedy. Why the hell had he taken a chance on the horse, anyway! Couldn't be content with one nice little driver; oh no, he had to be the big noise. And somewhere over that hill, little Tillie Shantz, through no fault of her own, lay perhaps dead, because of him and his fool ambitions. Oh God! Let her not be dead!

They called in inquiry to the men at the mill, but they shook their heads, pointing with a fling of their arms up over the hill. The miller and his son came down from their platform and joined the climbers. On the brow of the hill George stood still, gathering courage to lift his eyes. But the long slope was empty. Gill pointed to the deep narrow ruts carved harshly into the sloping shoulders of the road, up from the ditch. "She got this far, all right."

Half way into the dip, little strips of bark hanging fresh from the old cedars on the other bank showed where her rough passage had been. Here the tracks merged into the roadbed, and they looked in vain to find where she had left it again. They walked more slowly now, searching with careful eyes for the splintered fence or break in the cedars where she might have gone through.

"No sign of her, that I can see."

"Nothin' at all. Nothin' at all."

"She must have got him up the other hill."

"Here comes the doctor, isn't it?"

"Yeah. That's him."

The men divided into two quiet groups to let the doctor pass. He drew up to speak to them.

"Seen anything of her?"

"No."

The doctor nodded. "Who owns the horse?"

"It's my horse, Dr. Sylvester."

"Better come along with me, then."

George put his foot on the step, but Gill stopped him with a yell.

"Lookit! Lookit!" He dropped his voice to a whisper. "Lookit that!" He pointed to the far hill. "Ain't it him? Ain't it him, coming back?" The men searched the hill with unbelieving eyes. "Ain't it, though? Sure it is. Sure it is. Tell that gait anywhere. Walkin'. He's walkin'. She's got him walkin'!"

Over the edge of the hill the long thin head nodded into view, ears twitching. Tiger walked with a little twisting jerk, flinging his feet petulantly high, as if still unwilling to submit to the voice and the hands behind him. He was still unsure of the advisability of coming back to the place where he had been so frightened, but he was coming. The doctor pulled his horse as far off the road as he could take him, and they waited in silence for Tillie to bring back the horse. They heard her speak to him in a voice at once kind and convincing.

241

"Step up, Tiger."

She flapped the lines very gently on his back and he broke into a relieved trot. "That's the boy. That's fine now. There you are. All right, then." Her voice came to their ears, steady and sure. Tiger seemed to gain confidence from it. She signalled George to keep away from the horse's head. The men gave her a wide road.

"I'll be back in a few minutes," she said quietly, "I don't want him to have to stop just yet. Be ready."

His pale hide was streaked with dark sweat; he was shuddering, and flecks of foam fell from his mouth. She seemed, as she passed them, to be urging him on. The men turned as on one pivot and walked rapidly back. The horse and rig fled past the corners and turned on into the village. Gill spoke first, when girl and horse and buggy were just a postage stamp for size.

"Well, ya can't say she scares easy."

"Nothin' broke, apparently, either."

"I guess not."

"She's turning him round by the warehouse."

"Here she comes, then, hell-for-leather."

Tillie brought the horse almost to a stop in front of George.

"Get in," she said, tersely, and they bowled rapidly along the first mile on the road to Kinsail. When Tiger seemed to have settled into his swift steady dog-trot she handed George the lines.

"Think I can be trusted with him now?"

Tillie smiled brilliantly at him. "He went so suddenly I couldn't hold him. Where are the bananas?"

"Bananas! Good God, I don't know where the bananas are. I threw them into the ditch, likely. We expected you to come back in pieces, not in any shape to be having your hand out for bananas! Whew!"

"He's very frightened of noise, isn't he?"

"Evidently he is," said George, drily.

242

"But you could coax him to do anything, though, and he's a clever horse."

"And you're a hungry woman, aren't you? After what you've put me through this morning my breakfast has turned to vinegar, inside me, probably. Going to do me irreparable harm, too. We'll turn down the tenth and drop into Mrs. Badgerow's and see if she'll fry us an egg."

"Aren't you in a hurry to get back to the store, though?"

"Not in such a hurry as all that. I told you, didn't I, I've got a student there now, third-year man? He can manage all right, till I get back. He doesn't expect me till noon, anyway."

"Billy Davis gone?"

"No, Billy's still there. But he's working out behind, mostly. Wait'll you see the changes around there!"

"You've been busy, then."

"First time I've been out of town except up to the lake for months. And look what I got landed with! Bought myself a pretty doubtful proposition of a horse and picked up a wandering woman. And a hungry one, at that."

"I'm sorry to be such a trouble," said Tillie meekly.

"Yes, you are. You look it, too. Scare a man half to death and then sit there looking as if butter wouldn't melt in your mouth. When are you going to tell me what you're doing on the road at this hour of the day, anyway? Why aren't you at home where you ought to be, sewing up fever tents for Africa?"

George's voice was rough. He spoke almost as if he intended to hurt her. She glanced at him in surprise, then looked quickly away across the flowing fields.

"I have changed my plans," she said quietly. "I'm not going away after all."

"No? How's that?"

Tillie's mouth quivered. It was much harder than she had supposed, to say these words.

"It was a mistake. It was all a mistake." Red flushed

243

her neck and cheeks. "I am going to ask Loretta to let me work with her again. For a while."

"Well, that's good. She'll be tickled to death."

"Yesterday—yesterday at the church, I told them."

"Your father too? What did your father say? Does he know all this?"

"Yes," she said, in a whisper.

George opened his mouth to say, "What about the preacher fellow, then?" But he looked at Tillie's withdrawn face and was silent. Her hands lay trembling in her lap.

"Well, lady, it's good to see you again. I can hardly believe you're whole."

Tillie parted her lips, nodded brightly, and said nothing; and George looked about him at the dwindling hills. Already the sand belt was giving way to more productive country, where the earth showed black instead of yellow. Perhaps it was just a growing sense of belonging to the country, the knitting of his bone after the break from city life, that caused in him now a vague uneasiness. Perhaps he had passed this way in another form, eons ago, and it was his indestructible ego that recognized its old haunts, and stirred uncomfortably! He grinned to find himself thinking such nonsense.

Now Tiger was content to walk, hitching his slender long bones along in apparently effortless locomotion. George slackened his lines.

"Seems easy enough in his mind now, doesn't he?"

"He covers as much ground walking as most drivers do trotting."

George smiled with swift pleasure. "You think I picked a winner, then. Were you very scared when he lit out with you?"

"Yes. For the first minute or two."

"You don't ever look scared, though, do you?"

"I don't know."

"And if you did you wouldn't tell, either, I suppose. You'd get first prize for clams at any county fair."

He looked at her with affectionate interest, and saw with consternation that the colour had drained from her face and that she was shuddering as if from sudden chill. He took her hands in his free hand and found that they were marble cold.

"Tillie! What's the matter? Are you all right?"

She turned her pale face towards him, smiled slightly, dropped her hands to her sides and fainted.

"Reaction, emotional exhaustion, hunger. No wonder. I should have known this would happen, but she always looks so damned cool. What in hell has she been putting herself through? Half a mile to the Badgerows. Better get there before I do anything to bring her to. Lord, the poor child."

He slipped his arm about her, drawing her to him so that she would not slip to the floor, and urged Tiger to show what he could do.

But the grey pallor frightened him, and he turned the horse into the first lane. For a moment he was held in unreasoning fear. Suppose after all there was something the matter with her? She would be capable of sustaining injury without mentioning it. His reason told him that Tillie must be all right. She had just fainted. Heaven knows she had had enough to make her faint. But could he be sure? It became overwhelmingly necessary to George that there should be nothing wrong with Tillie.

A yellow collie came bounding out, and his mistress withdrew her fat soapy arms from a wooden wash-tub to follow him. She watched in open-mouthed astonishment as George tied Tiger to the gate post and lifted Tillie's dead weight out of the buggy. A little boy in overalls and nothing else ran delightedly up from the hen house.

"Is your wife gone dead?"

"Fainted. Have you some place she can lie down?"

The woman opened the door for him. "Bring her through to the room."

Moving rapidly in spite of her pudding-bag stoutness the woman indicated what was evidently a spare room off the

245

dining-room. Swiftly she lifted the white crocheted spread and unfolded a blanket from the box at the end of the bed. The room was dark and smelled of moth balls.

"Put her down here and I'll get water."

Almost at once she handed him a jug and a cup of brown cool water.

"Thank you."

Tillie stirred and seemed to pass from unconsciousness to sleep. The fat woman looked with embarrassment from the sleeping girl to George. But she was more curious than embarrassed, and determined to know.

"That ain't Tillie Shantz, is it?"

George nodded, keeping his hand on Tillie's wrist. The woman's eyes glistened.

"Well, well. I kind of thought it was. Used to see her up to the Reesorville school there. I heard she was going to get married, but I thought it was a preacher she was marrying."

Her eyes rested on George's gay checks. He said nothing, and she talked on, reluctant to let the story go without conclusion. "Yes, I heard she was getting married this summer, but I thought it was a preacher she was going to marry."

Tillie sighed deeply and turned under the blanket.

"There! She'll be all right now." George's voice shook with relief. "It's just that she's been too long without anything to eat. There's nothing the matter with her."

"Oh, huh?" The woman was obviously skeptical. "Yes, I see."

"Could you possibly make a cup of tea for her? Or cocoa; and if you happened to have a little bread and butter, perhaps? I think she'd be glad of anything at all, in a minute or two, now."

The woman nodded comprehendingly. "Yes, sure. Tea will be the best, though. I remember when I was that way, every time. I couldn't stand cocoa at all. Seemed to just turn my stomach. Too rich. I'll get her something. You just stay here. If she gets ready to open her eyes she'll maybe be glad to see you there. In a strange place. I thought she was going to marry a preacher, though. I was the same way. Couldn't stand the sight of my breakfast, but about nine o'clock I could eat raw horse without salt."

It was warm and green-dark in the little bedroom, the close camphor-filled air pungent and sweet to the nostril. George stepped quietly to the window but it was nailed down. Thick lace curtains and peeling green blinds effectually shut out the day, creating an illusion of isolation from the working world. Tillie lay still on the bed in childlike sleep. She looked forlorn, vulnerable. George felt a sharp sense of responsibility for her. He reached for a chair and drew it up to the bed. Holding her limp hand in both of his he leaned over her, surprised at the tumult within him. There was such abandonment in her pose, such a careless surrendering, that he felt he must turn his eyes from her, or bring her at once back to awareness. It occurred to him that he had never before seen her less than mistress of a situation.

He began to murmur her name, rubbing her chilly hand in both of his. He felt her fingers grow warmer, and take voluntary hold of his. He slipped from the chair to the floor, still cupping her hand in one of his, and with the other tenderly pushing the rough hair back from her face. She opened her eyes briefly, and smiled at him, and was gone again.

"Tillie, can you hear me? Are you listening, darling?"

Tillie nodded her head in a tired fashion, without opening her eyes.

"Do you know where you are? You fainted. Come on, honey, open your eyes. We're in a farmhouse. Somebody who knows you, Tillie."

The quiet face gave no indication of interest. "Aw, you

247

can wake up now, dearie. She's getting you some breakfast. She thinks we're married."

Tillie's mouth curved. She opened her eyes again, focussing more successfully this time, to find George's face just a few inches from hers. She lifted her free hand and hesitatingly touched his cheek. They looked at each other in silence. Caught and crystallized in one image, the other moments they had been alone together within an isolating frame of darkness or distance appeared in George's memory. Here it came again, the tremulous, vibrating sensation that had haunted him like half-heard music; the curious sense of fatefulness, in their being together.

This then, was how it happened. George half smiled to see the vision of the splendid house with the bare polished floors and the statuesque exotic woman, his musician wife, fade like the boyish fancy that it was, in face of the warm substantial reality. He looked almost with wonder at the calm face.

He marvelled at the fate that had picked him out of the rattle and hurry of a city street to throw him into the quiet of these hills, and show him as his overwhelming desire this calm-faced girl in the nunlike clothes. But perhaps he was over-confident. What of Tillie? Would she wake from her sleep and find that she could accept this throw of fate too? She had meant to marry the preacher. But if she still expected to, why was she here? She should certainly not be permitted to marry that shambling dolt. George brought his thick eyebrows together in a scowl. He laid his hand on her clumsy skirt, gently pressing the wrinkles out of it with his closed fist, and looking for the words he would say to her, when she could hear him.

The woman in the kitchen changing stove lids might have been in the moon. But at any minute now she would come in and break this frail enchantment.

"Tillie!" he whispered. "What about that lad you went home to marry?" She turned her face abruptly from him.

"No!" she said sharply. George laid his cheek to hers and whispered.

In an hour they were on the way again, driving silently through the empty roads. Tillie felt tremble in her mouth words which had never come to her at all, when she walked with Simon, words foreign to her ears, which she had perhaps not ever even heard uttered, in her whole life. Love you! Darling! Oh, my darling! To say them, to let them free, would give her exquisite pleasure. Never before in her life had she felt even remotely like this.

It was as if between herself and this man there existed no matter at all, visible or invisible. She felt herself sway towards him like a young pine bent by a strong wind. When they were together he was always quite without barriers for her. She could reach him without having to push aside the thinnest veil. His very physical being drew her irresistibly towards him. To touch his coat sleeve was enough, almost too much. There was no need or capacity for passionate embrace, at this time. She had not the strength or desire for it. She could feel the touch of his hand on her sleeve through all of her being. She could not have borne more.

The drive through Kinsail took on the nature of a triumphal entry. The people and the houses fell into a proportion which was no longer strange to her. They made a crowded and lively picture of which she was a conscious part. She was aware of a shivering sense of homecoming, a joyous delight in recognition of places and of people whom she could see and meet, for the first time, without conscious reservation. Now she could receive them and welcome them fully, without raising the old invisible barrier. She could judge them by her own reactions alone, free from the necessity of considering their appearance or conduct with regard to its probable sinfulness. So free, so sure, so just she felt, so happy and so tolerant of all mankind, that as the scarlet wheels spun down Main Street she smiled with radiance upon all that they met. In the late afternoon the street seemed full of friends and acquaintances who turned their heads to look wonderingly after the flying buggy with the smiling people in it.

As they turned down Lock Street, George looked quizzically at Tillie, threw back his head and laughed in sheer loving amusement.

"Well, by the Lord, you certainly look the part!"

"What part do I look?"

But he would not tell her, only laughing more, until she laughed too, for no reason that she knew of, except perfect joy.

Their faces were towards each other, still smiling warmly, when they reached the corner of the unnamed lane where Tillie used to slip through the town by the back way, when she could not trust herself to go through Main Street. George drew aside to allow a topless old-fashioned buggy to pass. It was drawn by a tall black horse unknown to George. Tillie did not even see it, since for this moment she could see nothing but George's face. George glanced at the driver, and quickly back to Tillie, wondering if she had recognized him. He was almost sure it was the lantern-jawed preacher fellow. There was no doubt that he had remarked them.

Tiger stopped willingly in front of Loretta's brown house. He stood with his head down, sobered by twenty-five miles. But George made him fast to the maple tree. He came back and laid his hand on Tillie's, looking at her with a secret, loving look, with only perhaps a trace of relinquishing, was it, in his eyes.

"Do you want to wait here, while I see if she'll take you in?"

Loretta answered the bell herself. She had a length of pleated lavender linen in her hand and a mouth full of pins. She took the pins out and stabbed them in the pincushion on her wrist as she prepared to speak.

"Tillie—" George began, but she interrupted him.

"No, she's not here. This town is crawling with young gents looking for Tillie. I wish she was. I could certainly do with her right now."

"If you stopped talking I could start," said George, impudently. "I'm not looking for her. I've got her, darling. I know when I'm licked."

26

SIMON, pounding at Levi's door at midnight, was almost beyond speech. Levi looked out of his bedroom window, and called to him. "Wait, I'll get a lamp, once." When he opened the front door, Simon was standing there as one in a trance. Levi pulled him into the light. His face was white and stricken, his brows knotted, his thick lips apart in astonishment. He looked at Levi for a while as if he hardly knew why he had come. Levi shook his arm.

"Where is she, where is she? Did she come back with you?"

Simon licked his lips, and shook his head as if to clear it. Betsey thrust her head out from the bedroom door, in the shadow. "Simon," she whispered, "Simon, where did you find her?"

"Sit down, Simon." Levi's voice was intended to soothe.

"No! No! *No!*" Simon's voice rose in a shriek. He drew himself up to his full height and struck at the chair Levi offered him. It fell against the stove and clattered to the floor. Simon watched it, his eyes glittering, his nostrils wide. For a moment it seemed as if he might pick it up again, for the pleasure of hearing another crash. Levi told Betsey to go back to bed. He would have laid a hand on Simon's arm, but the young man stepped out of his reach, and began to speak.

"Bertha—Bertha got it right. He has had her. When I was looking for her, all over the roads, calling her name, although she refused the Lord. Calling her name. She was with that man. She is Alohah. She plays the harlot, when she is mine. She doted on him as a lover. The Lord will break the jaws of the wicked, and cast them into everlasting darkness!"

Levi's breath escaped him in a whispering groan. "Surely, Simon, surely not, with the man!"

Simon turned from the room and was gone into the darkness. The black horse started wearily homewards, too tired to respond to the urgency of his driver. It was after two when they reached the sleeping farm. Simon automatically unhitched the horse and took off his bridle so that he might drink. Head down, the horse stumbled into his stall. Simon picked up a pail and carried it towards the feed room at the end of the piggery. He fumbled for the latch with an unsteady hand, and failed to lift it free. Angry at the resistance, unable to tolerate yet another blow of circumstance, however slight, he struck the door with his fist. The latch jumped and the top half of the heavy door swung back, reverberating against the wall. He wrenched the lower half open and started down the passage. The big boar, asleep until this moment in a pool of moonlight, leapt to his feet, squealing in panic and excitement. The long bristles on his backbone stood up in a razor edge. For a second he steadied himself on his delicate hooves, his pale eyes lit with fear and rage. Then, with his mouth open, his sharp tusks working up and down, he charged. Simon had time to scream and throw his bucket, but it bounced off the boar's back unnoticed. Simon went down, the boar squealing over him. The sharp little feet travelled over his stomach, and chest, and head.

In another few seconds, but for the ecstatic chop and muffle of the boar in the feed bin, there was quiet again. Back in the horse stable the tired black shivered and waited in vain for the hot mash that should have been his.

Levi and Betsey drove over, the day after the accident, and walked white-faced and silent into the house. Abraham Goudie put out his hand to them, and they shook it in silence, then passed on through the dining-room to the bedroom which Abraham indicated. "Doctor's just gone," he whispered. Simon's mother sat by the bed, not raising her eyes from her son. Lizzie Goudie walked on tiptoe about the room, picking up bits of linen and keeping steadfast watch on the bandaged head, for a sign of regained consciousness. The group in the doorway stood for a while in mute contemplation of the scene, and then turned away. Levi laid his hand on Abraham's shoulder, looking tenderly at him, while tears flowed down his face. Abraham tried to smile at him, and spoke in a whisper.

"Did you find her, Levi?"

Levi nodded. "Simon found her. Did he tell you, though?"

Abraham shook his head. "Nobody talked to him yet. He must have come home in the night. It was only in the morning Lizzie found him."

Levi controlled his tears and spoke in a low firm voice. "He will get better, though. And if, even, he does not, his soul is with the Lord. Pray for us; we have lost our child. From now she is dead to us, Abraham. We have no daughter. Betsey, she told me, but for a little while I could not think it. It must be so. Only wickedness could do this thing. Sometime, perhaps, the Lord will bring us joy again. It is not easy, yet, what we do, brother."

They shook Abraham's hand in loving silence, and went out of the house.

He was too long recovering speech, the doctor said. Sometimes such a shock, and with such an injury, might last a few days. But not like this. They came to understand that he might not speak again. Perhaps in some other ways, too, they might find him changed. Often he worked his mouth, and looked at them imploringly, but no recognizable word issued from his lips. He made himself understood with violent gestures and fierce expressions.

Old Fanny Betz, who had special gifts and could charm sickness away, came with her little bag of magic—the walnut shell and the piece of black cloth, small, but cut to her purpose and touched, so they said, with a substance that only Fanny knew. She went privately in to Simon, and closed the door behind her, so that no one should break her spells by looking or hearing. The children were sent out to the barn, and all the blinds drawn in the dining-room. Fanny used all the charms that she had brought with her; but when she came into the light of the kitchen again they could see that she was troubled. She was very quiet and tired and would not stay to supper. She shook her head doubtfully.

"If he is not better seven days from now," she said, "then come for me again, and I'll try once more. I have still another one yet." But she drove away looking discouraged. "It is harder, when I haven't got any name."

But that charm was no good either, and Simon's speech was gibberish.

In five weeks he had almost completely recovered the use of his legs and hysterically insisted on leaving his bed, staggering out into the dining-room in his nightshirt, the red seams of his wounds vivid in his white skin. They tried to moderate his excitement, and explained that the doctor thought it was bad for him. He must be quiet, always. But they were not sure that he understood them. He appeared to be listening, but from the rapid chase of expressions over his scarred face it was clear that what he was hearing was not their admonition. Perhaps there were some other voices, which they could not hear.

His sister Lizzie, seeing him in anguish one morning, because they could not understand him, handed him a slate which the children used at school, and a slate pencil. He looked at the slate in seeming comprehension, then picked it up in his powerful hands and broke it over his knee. He smiled in pleasure at the clean split, and examined the splintered frame in his hand. Then he lost interest and threw it on the floor, and was content to drowse again, for long hours.

Out of his bed he was impatient, to the point of violence, of any restraint. He became sulky and obstinate with all except his mother. Usually, when he sat at table and refused to eat, or else ate so greedily that there was no meat left for anyone else, his mother could put her hand on his arm, saying, "Now, Simon," in her gentle voice, and after a moment of glowering he would make an effort to conform.

The oddest and most frightening change in him was in his flesh. He had always been so thin. Now he began to gain in weight. The thinly covered bone structure of his face disappeared gradually in a heavy mask of flabby flesh, with black beard growing sparsely where the tissue had not been injured. His clothes in a few weeks were too small for him. His mother made him new long smock-like shirts which he could pull on over his head, to save him trouble in buttoning, since he did not appear to want to exert himself in small precise matters. He did not like to wear boots any more, but went barefoot, and liked best to use only the long shirt for clothing.

For days together he scarcely noticed his family, sitting for silent hours in the hot August days with his back against the smoke-house, his feet straight out before him, cooling himself in the shade of the walnut trees. He took his Bible out there, some days, but his mother could not see that he was really reading it. He opened it listlessly, sometimes, and turned the pages over, rubbing his fattening hands down one page or another without seeming preference.

Someone had always to keep him in mind, and watch, every few minutes, to see that he was still there. If he suddenly made up his mind to walk away, it was hard to persuade him to stay at home. He wanted to go somewhere, along the road. Several times they had missed him, and found him a mile or two away, walking very fast. Once he went south, once east, and several times he was going straight north, when they reached him. They brought him back protesting and crying like a baby. But he soon seemed to forget his frustration, and was quiet and good again.

27

GEORGE LOOKED at the big red barns with a first touch of misgiving. Since he had asked Tillie to marry him he had had the glow of a giver upon him. He was a prosperous young man, a business man of vision, who might, perhaps very soon now, according to the standards of the town, be a wealthy one. Beside the excitement, the anticipation and the joy in the prospect of marrying a beautiful woman there was just the pleasant trace of patronage. After all, she was one of a curious, faintly comic set of people who wore long beards and no collars and funny hats. It was not the usual thing. There would be wisecracks and snickers in the livery stable and pool room. He was prepared for that, and he would make

them eat their words, he and Tillie together. He loved
her, and smiled even to think of her. She was a gentle,
lovely, exquisite creature. She could give any woman in
town half a lap and step up to the post before they saw
the ribbon.

In the ten days since she had come back to Kinsail,
George had been unable to persuade her to visit her
people, and he came alone now to the Shantz farm to
tell old Levi of their plan to marry, and to ask his
blessing. Tillie had looked at him sadly and inscrutably
when he insisted that she should come with him. He
would marry no girl in a hole-and-corner fashion. Her
family should be told, and properly told, by George himself, and Tillie with him. She shook her head. "I cannot go." She had written to them, again, explaining her
position as well as she could, with dignity and love and
deep regret. There had been no answer. George thought
lightly of this. Of course they were expecting to see her,
any day. That was why they had not written. She must
come with him. They could take the train, and a livery,
and be back the same night. She laid her hand on his arm,
and tried to tell him how it was, but could not convince
him of the gulf which she had placed between herself and
her family by proposing to marry an unbeliever. And
that was the least of unutterable griefs which they were
suffering, because of her. He could not understand, at
all. That they should be upset at her unconventional
departure from the church, and perhaps sorrowful because
of the abrupt change in her plans, was only natural. It
was fearfully bad luck, too, that the preacher should have
been so mangled, just at the same time. But that had
nothing to do with her. He did not know that she could
not bring herself to even think of her father. She could
not endure the thought of meeting Levi and finding in
his face what she knew she would inevitably see in it.
She raised her arms as if the gesture would explain, and
dropped them again in resignation.

"Go if you want to. Maybe it is the thing to do. But they—they will not want to see me."

On the train and behind the bony livery horse he had been busy with problems and plans for the lake and the store, purposely relegating to the back of his mind the thought of the approaching interview. It might not be pleasant, it might even be humiliating for him, he considered, as he remembered the look of the big man in his narrow shop, but it was the thing he had to do. Tillie, undoubtedly had exaggerated the reaction they would have, anyway. What could they possibly have against him? Religion, of course, but nothing that made any real difference. He felt little doubt that he could make things smooth again, and right whatever wrong they imagined Tillie to have done them. As he turned what must be the last corner before he would come on the farm, he felt upon himself the sheen and gloss of an exotic magnanimous stranger bringing benefits and the glimpse of far places to an insular people.

But when he consulted the mail-box, and then looked up the lane to the house, doubt stirred in his mind. The house stood a quarter of a mile from the road, in a gentle slope of lawn and garden, flanked on the left by a smooth drive and seven acres of apple trees. The love of all green growth which was so strong in the first Tillie Shantz who came to live on this land had spared a score of pine trees which still studded the grass, here and there beyond the house. Down the southward slope from the house, bounding it from the spring wheat field beyond, the "groz-mutter's garden" spread riotous in the sun. For three generations after the first Tillie, the great wide border which she had planted with lilies of the valley, mignonette, lobelia, alyssum, poppies, and bushes of great pink cabbage-roses was tended by her daughters and the wives of their sons, and their daughters. When, back in the seventies, the squared timbers of the house were covered with rough white plaster, still solid and free from cracks after more

258

than thirty years, Tillie's grandmother had planted roots of purple clematis, which climbed and spread and now pasted great purple stars on the white walls to the south and west. A little grove of butternut and English walnut trees lifted their slender dull parasols above the black roof of the house. The red brick of the smoke-house glowed through low sweeping hemlock branches.

George filled his eyes with the mellow beauty of the farmstead. On the field to the right of the lane perhaps thirty great black-and-white cows raised incurious heads to see him pass. The young cattle beyond the orchard whisked their tails and leapt gladly by the creek, under the shade of a few old elms left standing for a hundred years. There was that in the house and fields before him which spoke of a century of growth and development and sunny maturing. He knew himself, as he was carried through the arches of the maples planted eighty years ago, to be a rootless creature, new and raw and unfinished. The temerity of taking the daughter of this substantial dwelling away from here, to be the wife of a man without even, in all honesty, a decent roof over his head, struck him with force. His eyes ranged beyond the broad black chimneys of the house to the bell steeple on the summer kitchen, the arched and buttressed roofs of the red barns. This kind of holding, he knew, represented prosperity of the solid, unassailable kind. His little scheme of speculation in summer-cottage property would be insignificant, beside it.

The unpeopled look which the house at first presented altered as he came nearer to it. Fresh smoke lifted in plumes from the summer-kitchen chimney. A thin little boy in shrunken blue overalls and a doughnut of a straw hat ran after the rattle of a lawn-mower up the front lawn, making a satin stripe. In the broad vista between the house and barns a sober nodding horse with his ears thrust through his own straw hat picked his way along the rows of corn, guided by the word and hand of another little boy. A long-skirted grey figure in a black sunbonnet bent to the ground in the long green rows of beans, out from the berry bushes. Two bent backs hacked at the ground with short-handled hoes, too far away to have their crop identified. A team of matched bays stepped down the ramp of the largest barn, stopping at a shout from inside, then pulling again until a sharp satisfying clack from within brought them to the halt.

There was an air of competent efficiency about the place that George could admire as he might have admired the shining dustless equipment of a model dispensary. He looked with wry amusement at the two thin rockers on the narrow veranda.

"Guess nobody in this house spends much time out here," he conjectured. Between the rockers stood a heavy wooden bench made by axe and plane from lumber cut on the place. The furniture was pale blue, incongruously gay, having received the paint left over from the last traditional painting of the ceilings. It, and the wall behind it, and the doors and windows and the slate-coloured floor, gleamed in apparent dustlessness, in perfect accord with the absolute order of the whole. A black hump-backed trunk, roped and labelled, stood irrelevantly on the step end of the veranda.

The little boy with the lawn-mower stared at him, for a minute, then dropped his machine and ran like a colt for the kitchen, skirting the long ell so as not to have to meet the stranger. A bobtailed collie, stretched half asleep on the kitchen stoop, shook himself and walked soberly down to meet him. George tied the driver to the post and stood undecided as to which door he should approach. The door by the bench and the rocking-chairs looked as if no one had knocked there for years, if ever. It stood so far from the work section of the house that it seemed unlikely that any noise from there would be heard in the back part. He had not yet learned that the correct approach to a farmhouse is through the stable door—or the granary, or the root cellar, or the cornfield, or wherever the man of the place is working.

The door behind the Dutchman's-pipe vine seemed an appropriate entrance. He reviewed quickly what he meant to say, rehearsed a few words in his throat, and knocked nervously on the dining-room door.

For a fleeting tender second George permitted himself to think of Tillie walking tall and light about this dark square shining room beyond the screen. It looked almost unused, too, although it must be a thoroughfare. He wondered where Tillie's room was, and found a quickening and tightening about his heart, to think of it. Strange and lovely to think that in such a short while now, just time to get the house a little bit livable, she would be his wife. Of all these years of her daily life he knew nothing. He was divided in his feelings. At once he felt curiosity to know how it had been, living here, accepting all the oddness and restraint as natural and right, and a petulant desire to draw a curtain over the picture, not to think of it again.

In the garden which he could see now, through the window directly across from the open door, she must have spent long childish hours in play. Or did Mennonite children not play, but begin at once to work and worship, fat gnomes under their black toadstools? He shifted his shoulders in conscious resentment at being connected with oddity. The flower garden was Tillie's work, she had said. She had all kinds of ideas of what ought to be done, up there at the lake, for a garden. Where was everybody? Not all out in the fields, surely? He knocked again. The little boy had run to tell somebody. It was hard to see how Tillie had thought they could live in the old house, even for the summer, when he saw her own home. But she had insisted. Well, it would save him money, in the long run. And perhaps she was right. They could fix it up. He smiled at the romantic idea of living with Tillie on the fragrant shore of Lake Marie.

There was still no answer to his knock. A peacock with his tail half spread grumbled discordantly in the shade of the elderberry bushes, but there was no other sound of life.

George turned in growing irresolution from the unresponsive silence of the house to see Levi in full Sunday blacks, with two women, walking slowly towards him from the front of the house. There was a careful formality in the full black skirts of the women and the freshly smoothed tight hair under the crisp film of the white house-caps. George glanced down at his smart grey and green diagonal check, and found it frivolous. Levi walked a little in front of the women; they kept their calm eyes on George's face, and they walked in silence. Levi raised his hand when they were a few feet from their visitor, and they paused. By some subtle sense George was aware of eyes in the open window now, people listening and watching. He started to walk eagerly towards the three, but the same gesture stopped him. Levi regarded him gravely for a minute, then came on, appearing less large viewed against the broad canvas of his home ground than he had in the shop. He seemed to George to be much older than he had thought, the thick thatch more grey than black; and he was thinner, surely. But the most terrible change was in his face. From an amiable giant he had turned into an accusing judge. His eyes were netted with the lines of distrust and suspicion; there was threat and anger in the tightened muscles of his mouth. The words which had seemed to George appropriate and easy dissolved in his mouth. The man advanced towards him now with an almost menacing gait. George became alarmed. In spite of his determination to be resolute and urbane, he knew himself to be shrinking back, while Levi walked slowly towards him. The big man raised his fist, then looked at it, in astonishment and shame. He murmured to himself in a low voice, as one in wonder. "I would have struck him. God forgive me, though, a little boy, with perhaps not sin in his heart, but only silliness. But she is gone. Gone because of this young one?" Then he raised his weary eyes and spoke to George, with the anger all gone from his voice, and only a tired tonelessness remaining.

"It is from Tillie you come."

"Yes."

"It is you, then, it is for you that she has forsaken her God?"

"Oh, no," said George, "I wouldn't say that, sir. People do change their ideas, you know—"

But Levi was not listening. "We have had a letter from her. Tell her unless she has something better to tell us, never mind writing." He looked at George's slight flamboyant figure and shook his head in mystification and sorrow.

"Our daughter, that we had, is gone." He pointed loosely to the front of the house. "In the box, there, are the things that belong to her. Take it with you. And go now. Go!"

George walked in silence past the women, recognizing the grey face of Keturah. The other must be Tillie's mother. He did not dare to speak to them, feeling the awful eyes of Levi upon him, and noting the sad severity of the faces. He picked up the box and carried it in guilty silence to the buggy. The three people walked into the house, sparing not another word for him, obviously unwilling to hear him try to justify his presence there. He turned the rattling rig around and drove down the lane, trying to understand how he could have behaved differently, and why he could say nothing more to Tillie's father than he had. The power in the man's voice had sent him scuttling home like a guilty schoolboy found trespassing.

A thin figure under a big black sunbonnet ran across the field to stop George at the gate. He drew up the

263

horse and waited for her. She had a narrow pock-marked face with a twisted chin and a look of intense scrutiny.

"Are you the one Tillie's going to get married to?"

George smiled in relief. It seemed a long time since any one had spoken to him in kind inquiry.

"Yes, I guess I am. Why?"

He felt himself passed in judgement under that bright unhuman eye.

"Well, you tell Tillie that if she wants any hired help away down there where she's goin' to live, why I'll come way down there and help. She ain't used to doin' so much, around. Maybe you didn't know that? Maybe I shouldn't be telling you that!"

She laughed her high uncontrolled laugh. George had a sudden picture of the revolution he had effected in his life. What kind of establishment of his could contain an ill-wrought piece of humanity like this girl, and himself, under one roof? But there was kindness and acceptance here, and he was grateful.

"That's very good of you. Bertha, isn't it?" he said. "And I'll certainly tell Tillie." The girl grinned widely.

"Yes. You tell her I wouldn't be afraid to come away down there."

She looked back at the house and shook her head.

"Levi, I thought he'd get over it all right. But I guess he won't ever, now. Not with Simon Goudie."

She looked furtively at George, as if perhaps in mentioning that name she had betrayed a knowledge which she might not be supposed to have.

"If she wants any help, you tell her I'll come."

She turned and ran back to the bean patch. As George jogged along the road with the trunk pressing him uncomfortably in the ribs he took a last look at the farm. The little boy ran his mower, the horses moved up and down the ramp, the bent figures hacked at the ground with their short-handled hoes, and the horse with the straw hat continued to cultivate his corn. Nothing had altered on the land. His passage had been as unremarked and unimportant as a fleece of cloud hung for a second across the sun.

But the rough pale-blue bench had been put to use, and the thin rocking-chairs held rigid rocking figures. George saw that it was Levi slumped on the bench, his head bowed, hands over his eyes. It must be Betsey and Keturah on the chairs, black-clothed, gently rocking, speechless. They were watching to see an end of him, perhaps forever.

28

GEORGE'S CAR was the third to be bought in the village. There was no assurance in Kinsail that they were a safe thing, at all.

Tillie swathed her big white straw hat, shaped like a beehive with a flower-blanketed deck, in fawn veiling three yards long and a yard wide. Over the white linen suit with the fine-tucked net blouse and forty yards of cream soutache braid, she put on a sidewalk-skimming fawn duster with deep raglan sleeves, and was ready for the trip. Loretta kissed her, her face flushed with pride and affection and excitement. The Rector stretched out his white clergyman's fingers and said, "Well, God speed you, Mrs. Bingham," and waited for the inevitable start which all brides gave at the first mention of the new title. Tillie did not disappoint him. She waited for a moment to hear some invisible woman respond, then smiled and held out her hand. Miss Barclay-Thomas followed them all out to the car, watching Tillie get in, and obviously admiring her courage, if not indeed temerity, in setting out on such an important journey as a honeymoon in such an unpredictable invention. The broad brass band on the hood gleamed in newness, the horn and the lamps were glorious in brass. George pulled his duster from the back seat, exchanged his black derby for a checked travelling cap, and bent to crank the engine. The three on the sidewalk watched him with concentrated interest.

"Careful of your arm, George," advised the Rector, who had a theoretical knowledge of the dangers of motoring. "It can fly back and strike a heavy blow. I heard yesterday that Doctor Percy himself got a nasty shock from his. A nasty shock."

At the fifth spin the engine turned over with a satisfying roar, and the car quivered. The forgetmenots in Tillie's hat trembled over the brim. George waited for a minute, then worked the crank loose, put it carefully in the box on the running-board, and climbed in under the steering wheel. He slid the gas lever up and there was a deafening noise. Farewells other than nods and smiles and waves were impossible. Then a little lessening of the vibration, a little jump forward, and the wheels turned. Backfiring only occasionally, the car rolled successfully down Church Street, turned the corner and proceeded noisily through the hot unpeopled main street.

"Be better when it gets warmed up," George shouted over the engine. Tillie nodded and smiled, the pink cornflowers and blue forgetmenots casting little bouquets of shadow over her happy face.

Once out from the village and bowling down the dusty August roads the riding was smoother.

"It's lovely!" Tillie called to George, and outspread her hands to indicate that she meant the car, and the wedding, and the day, and himself. For a daring moment he took his hand from the wheel and laid it on her white gloved hands. The car turned impudently towards the ditch, and he clutched the wheel again.

"Once you get used to it, better than a rubber-tired buggy!"

Tillie nodded. The wind carried her veil streaming out beside the car. Dust rose in thick plumes behind them. It seemed to them that they were flying through space.

"Do you like to go fast like this?"

Tillie pulled her duster over her white skirt and smiled in enthusiasm. The needle of the speedometer shot up to twenty-seven miles. George kept both hands tight to the wheel and coaxed the accelerator along notch by notch with his thumb until they were going over thirty. The engine was quieter now, but they felt speech to be impossible at this speed. The wind would wipe the words from their mouths. They drove a breathless mile and a half, then George pushed the lever down and drew a little off the road. He let the motor idle and listened attentively to it for a few seconds.

"Sweet as a nut," he said, with satisfaction. "We'll just wait here till the rig gets past. Some horses shy." Tillie looked at him in mild inquiry and with a shade of apprehension.

"Are you sure you can start it again?"

"Sure I can. I took it up to the lake last night. It's going to save me a lot of time and horseflesh, Tillie. First time I had a really good chance to try it out by myself. So I stopped her and started her up about a dozen times. Just to be sure!" He grinned boyishly at the thought of it, and Tillie's heart leapt.

"Just a little knack to it. Do you think you'd like to learn?"

"Yes. I think so."

"They aren't scared of trains, anyway, these contraptions."

They looked at each other and smiled in recollection.

"You'll find this a good deal easier to handle than Tiger." He looked at her with tender eyes and laid his gloved hand on her knee, turning so that he could see her face, squarely. "We'll manage, all right. I wouldn't take my wife out in anything I wasn't pretty sure I could handle."

Tillie's face bloomed into delicate pink and she laid her hand on his.

"I'm not forgetting, either, that it's your car really," he said soberly. "It was your money that went into this, you know." Tillie nodded in satisfied agreement. George looked at her, as if she might still clear up the mystery of how a father could refuse to communicate with his daughter, refuse to recognize the man who was to marry her, and still give her ten thousand dollars when she left home. All in bundles of bills, in the little black trunk, when she opened it. "It is my share. It was to come to me," she said, "when he died. It is the same, now, for him, as if I had died. They do not think of me, any more."

"In time, though," George said, "in time he will come round, surely?"

"No. He will never." She looked a little desolately, George thought, to the north, where the distant sand-hills stretched in blue haze.

"Tillie, did you know how it would be, with him, and all your people, before—?"

She nodded. "Yes. I knew." George felt the blood beat in his temples. He tipped her face back with his free hand and leaned over gently to kiss her. Her mouth, warm and soft, received and returned his kiss. When she opened her eyes the buggy was only the length of a field away. Already the horse looked with suspicion on the shining stranger in the road. He shied nervously towards the opposite ditch. The young Mennonite driver brought him to a stop and went to his head to lead him past. He motioned to his wife and child to get out too. In silent and apprehensive procession the people in black walked past the car. The man was busy with his horse, but the little boy stared with curious eyes at the car. A sharp word from his mother brought him away from it. The woman looked straight ahead of her, moving no muscle in her sombre face, walking modestly and righteously and without resentment along the road, put out of her conveyance by a godless pair. The machine itself, probably, would be revealed to be outside God's plan. Her flat-heeled boots with the bulging capless toes raised little puffs of dust with each step. Her thin shoulders drooped a little, almost abjectly, as she followed her husband.

"Do you know them?"

Tillie looked after the walkers.

"All my life," she said, keeping her eyes fixed gravely upon them for a moment.

"They didn't speak to you, did they?"

She shook her head, her eyes shadowed.

"They think I am responsible for Simon, you know, besides— Most of them don't speak, any more," she said, gently and with resignation.

George turned to look angrily after these disdainful persons, treading a dusty road in their ugly boots, with holy superiority in their stupid countenances. He looked sharply at Tillie, sitting in calm loveliness beside him, almost smiling now, the people on the road forgotten.

"It had nothing, absolutely nothing to do with you at all. You know that, Tillie, don't you? You *do* realize that?"

Tillie nodded.

"Do you care if these black freaks pull their damned witches' skirts away from your side of the road? You don't care, do you?"

It was incredible and distasteful to him to remember that such a little while ago she was one of them. He looked down at her slim kid slippers, the white silk embroidery on her ankle, involuntarily comparing.

Tillie parted her lips in the curving suggestion of a

smile, and laid her hand lightly on his shoulder. She had made her decision, and accepted in full its consequences.

"No, no, I don't mind."

Her eyes rested on the gold filtered through the white silk gloves from the broad wedding ring and the opal-set keeper. More than anything else, in this new life wherein she had launched herself, the rings on her hand reminded her that she travelled a strange road. It was the very badge of worldliness.

George reached for the hand, rubbing the brown gloves hard over the white. He slid his forefinger through the palm opening of her glove, softly moving it to and fro through the cup of her hand.

"Man and wife," he said, looking at her as though marvelling. "Man and wife."

It was early evening when they came to the city. The long hills had flattened into level rich farmlands, and the farms in turn broke into market gardens. Villages and hamlets and strange country lay between them and home. There were more cars on the roads now, and the horses took them with indifference. George did most of the talking, during their dreamlike passage along the dusty road. Maida's leg was a little stiff yet. She'd better stay a while, up at the farm. Chris would have the vet, if she didn't improve the next few days. Perhaps they'd see some racing in the city, if the meeting had started by now. Was there anything else, specially, that she would like to do, now that they were away? Harder to get away, from now on, likely. They'd be busy at the lake, and the student would go, in September. But Tillie had no ideas, except perhaps, if there should be one of those musical entertainments that Mr. Shardley talked about? There was such a constant purling of happiness within her that spoken communication was superfluous, conversation scarcely heard or heeded.

The hot summer night brought the city women out in

clusters of light dresses under the soft yellow gas-light. Tillie looked with quickening pleasure at them as they strolled negligently by the clanging street cars and stared with animated gestures into windows full of sparkle and light.

"Do you know the city?" George took his eyes from the traffic for a moment to watch the bright face with pleasure. Tillie shook her head.

"I was here once, when I was a little girl. With Father. I don't remember much. Not to know my way." Her eyes travelled from brilliance to brilliance. "I don't remember it like this, at all." Images ten years old came to her; the slow train with the dusty red-plush seats, and the houses in the city all back yards, evidently. Stuck together, most of them, it seemed, with thin slices of red brick on the fronts, and all the rest dirty roughcast backs.

"No. I don't remember it like this at all."

"Have to show you the town," said George, smiling fractionally at her, engaged in the business of guiding the car through the curving crescent of the park. "This is the University campus."

Tillie looked with concentration at the park and pointed towers thrust up through the trees.

"Where you went?" There was warmth and quick interest in her voice. The very sidewalks where his feet had walked grew intimate and worthy of special note.

"Which was yours?"

George pointed dangerously. "Can't see it very well, in this light, of course. We'll come back here in the morning, if you like."

"I'd like to see the house you lived in, too, and the store."

"Would you? Why? They don't look any different to all the rest, but I'll show you, if you like."

George introduced the city with a proprietary air. "Those are the Parliament Buildings." Tillie obediently noted a black mass terminating in flat, bulb-like forms, reminiscent of the drawing on the "Holy City" music sheet. She had supposed it to be some eastern temple, and was conscious of both surprise and discomfort to find it in Toronto. For a flashing second she realized that in adopting the world for her own, she had laid herself open to much obligation in the matter of education. There was much that she should have laid hold of, back there in school. Now she must make up for that lack. The little sum of practical knowledge which was sufficient for living within the narrow circumference of her former life obviously would not do now. She glanced back over her shoulder at the minarets, and the long sweep of garden.

"That's the hospital. If we kept straight on going down here we'd run into the lake." They turned east on College Street.

Tillie filled her eyes with the great turreted bulk of the hospital. Did every one of those lighted windows indicate a sick person? "All that place," she marvelled, "full of sick people?"

George indicated a rank of windows. "In that one room," he said, "there might be twenty beds."

"All in one room?" She looked again, and thought she saw a white-capped figure bending over a bed, and was filled with pity. The poor people, to have to go to a hospital. To be away from home like that, when one was sick. To be among strangers. She wondered who these people would be, who would not have someone to look after them at home. In the upper floors of the hospital were greenish lighted windows, she noticed.

"Operating rooms," said George, carelessly.

Operating rooms! Helpless, abandoned people, up there, with knives being used on them! Tillie looked down at her beautiful clothes, considered her swift and happy passage, her utter fulfilment in this marriage. But while all this was going on, the world was full of men and women in desperate pain, pitifully at the mercy of strangers. At home, when people fell sick, they lay quietly away in some room reserved for them, with all their own people about them.

"You've never been there, have you?"

"Oh, yes. Couple of times. Glad to get there, too. Not that one, that's just for children."

Children! Where were their mothers, that they must go to a place like that? Tillie looked again at George. There was so much that she could never know about him, that she would have been so glad to know. What was his mother like? What did he do, when he was a little boy? The life of a little boy, in a city like this, was incomprehensible to her. There didn't seem any place for children to be, in a city. She would have liked a procession of pictures of George from curly-haired baby to young man.

George fingered the accelerator. "Hard to get down to ten miles an hour, after the country."

There were at least as many cars as carriages, down in the heart of the city. "This is King Street. This is where the good tailors are, and the best grocery stores in Canada. In the morning we'll take a walk down here, and see."

Tillie looked up and down the strange streets, taking possession of their mystery and richness. The front of the hotel was as bright as day, with the fierce crackling arc lights, and the lamps of the brass-bound cars waiting at the entrance.

"Here we are." Tillie stepped stiffly out into the glare. A button of a boy with a scarlet pill-box seemingly glued to his head leapt for the luggage. Overhead an opalescent fan-shaped glass canopy spread from hotel to carriage-way. White awnings stretched out from what seemed to Tillie a thousand windows, and a score of little iron balconies were filled with waving Boston ferns. At the curb a man in a scarlet coat, blazoned with brass braid, his shoulders heavy with fringed epaulets, consulted with George. But George refused the suggestion that an attendant should garage his car.

"No. No, thank you, I'd prefer to take it round myself."

Revolving doors swung them through into the great rotunda full of people, all talking or smoking or laughing, it seemed to Tillie, all busy with strange ploys the nature of which she could not hope to guess. Little gay groups of young men in long-tailed coats and white ties stood about among the veined brown marble Ionic columns, waiting for their parties to assemble. The palm trees springing up behind huge green leather couches, and the long aquaria filled with goldfish, produced an odd effect of heavy southern landscape. Under the unquestioning feet of all these people a strange and beautiful mosaic pattern swirled in blue and green and white. Here and there rich rugs in jewel-like blues and reds interrupted the swirling circles and softened the blow of leather on stone.

As George signed the register with a firm hand, smiling at the new signature, Tillie cast her eyes up to the coffered ceiling, rich in misty oil-painted landscape. The walls, she noted with interest, in the recesses between the pillars, were made of pictures too. There was music, somewhere, but she could not find it. Strings, it seemed to be, with a piano too.

The elevator moved slowly up. Already their bags were in their room, and little Buttons standing respectfully at the door.

George gave the rooms a swift inspection. "Sitting-room, bedroom, bath; all right?"

Tillie stood by the pile of luggage, slowly untying her veil.

"Lovely." She pulled, finger by finger, at her gloves.

George stepped to the window and drew back the velvet curtains. "We can see the lake." Around Toronto's black island the lake lay silver. Pinpoints of light marked the yacht club and the amusement park, over there. A small checkering of yellow and black moved through the silver to the dark.

"Ferry going over. We must do that, while we're here."

"That would be nice."

"Come see."

They stared out of the window into the straggling street below, the black of the harbour and the silvery water. George gently drew the long pin from Tillie's hat, lifted it from her head and tossed it on the sofa. He wheeled her gently round and slipped the long duster from her arms. They put their arms around each other and kissed; then drew apart and looked with wonder on each other, for a long minute.

"Wash your funny face," said George, in a thick voice. "I'll put the car away. Just a couple of blocks, the doorman said. Then we'll see if they'll give us some dinner. I don't want you fainting on me, again."

Most of the diners had gone when George and Tillie went down to the tall beautiful room with the clear red carpets and white walls. Deep red curtains hung on the long, long windows, between the delicate gold mouldings which panelled the walls. Tillie looked with appreciation at the slender spindled white banisters leading up to the musicians' platform, and the huge plaster cornucopias which swung out to the corners of the room from the central chandelier in the ceiling. As they came into the room the musicians were wrapping their instruments in velvet cloths. Tillie watched the pianist gently close the piano, and pick up a sheaf of music. The violinists and the man with the cello followed him down the little flight of stairs and into the corridor.

"Was that the music I heard?"

George held her chair for her. "Probably was. They play for dinner, but it's over for tonight." The little electric lamp with the frilled white and silver shade picked out the blue and pink and gold in Tillie's opals as she looked at the long list of strange food on the menu card. But her mind was still on the men with the music.

"Let's have everything on the ticket, eh?" said George.

"I wish I could have heard them play," she said, wistfully.

"Maybe they haven't left the hotel. Likely just gone up to the ballroom. They have supper-dancing, one or two nights a week. We'll go up after dinner and see, shall we?"

George ordered a sherry, green turtle soup, veal cutlets with mushroom and roast young turkey with cranberry sauce. "I didn't know people ate turkey, except at Christmas!" Tillie looked with delight at the rubber-tired cart with nearly a whole bird on it. Lemon sherbet came on in cut glass bubbles, and a small flotilla of side dishes arranged itself before them. George explained to Tillie the drinking of a toast, and they lifted their fragile glasses to each other.

George noted the native grace of Tillie's long fingers on her glass, the dignity of her attitude, the grave pleasure in her flushed face. "If there are hayseeds sticking out of anybody's hair," he thought wryly, "it'll be mine."

Tillie had never seen people dancing before. She felt herself drawn into the ballroom by invisible strings towards the source of the music. Under the dim yellow lights from the chandelier the slowly waltzing pairs melted and swayed towards the shadows of the alcoves and back into the pool of light in the centre of the huge room. The sweet provocative music of the violins and piano soared and sifted among the dancers. Sudden swift tears sprang to Tillie's eyes. George looked at her in surprise.

"Anything the matter?" he whispered. She shook her head, unable to speak. It was impossible for him to know anything of the swift emotions that the shift and shuffle of the dancing feet, the flow and sway of the skirts and the bodies aroused in her. The bows of the violins hidden behind the palm trees might have been drawn across her quivering heart. She knew herself to be in the midst of one of the manifestations of the Evil One himself, in his workings among the children of men. And she was straining after it, feeling certain answer to the rhythm and vibration of the music, in her own being. The orchestra stopped and the smiling dancers pair by pair reluctantly felt the spell withdraw from them, to leave them standing at rest on the dance floor. There was a quick clapping of hands. The musicians rose and bowed, and played again. The shadow of remembered, determinedly discarded superstition passed from Tillie's face, and she smiled.

"Ever dance?"

"No," she said regretfully, watching the easy graceful swing of the soft full skirts and the circling toes of the men's glistening dancing shoes.

"Like to try?"

"Do you think I could?" Her feet and ears and her whole body told her that she could.

He smiled encouragingly at her.

"Sure you could. Come on." He felt her light hand on his shoulder and they waited for the beat. "Don't try too hard," George said, in a low voice. "There's nothing to it, if you just let yourself go. We'll stay on the outside, till you get used to it."

Tillie felt herself caught in the golden net of the music.

29

"YOU DON'T mean you think we should stay here all winter, though?" George held his paint brush suspended, in his surprise. The little barn on the lake farm had been repaired, the soft boards replaced and a shining tin roof laid. Now George himself was spending a sunny Sunday giving it a lick of scarlet paint. The old wood was thirsty for it and he was on his third coat. Tillie sat on an upturned bucket beside him, leafing through the sheets of a seed catalogue. She could not quite bring herself, with full freedom, to the doing of unnecessary labour on the Sabbath. There was something in her bones which prevented her, although she would have defended George's painting job, or anything else he might have decided to do, to the end. George finished his brush-load, and hung his brush on the side of the pail by the tack trick which Tillie had taught him. He came to sit on the ground beside her.

"Don't you think we could, George?"

"I don't know. I never thought of it, though, as being more than just a summer place. Wouldn't you get lonesome, all by yourself out here, all day? It won't be like this in the winter, you know." George waved an arm to include the bright lake, calm today in its perfect reflections of pine and cedar and occasional flaunting crimson maple. The little birches by the very brim were already pale gold, and would soon not show leaf at all. Although it was now well into September and the people from the city who had built nine cottages on Lake Marie had shut the doors of their little habitations, and boarded their windows for another season, the local people had not abandoned their summer playground. The white patch of the bank boys' tent still showed through the trees behind the bathing-house. This morning three red canoes drifted on the still water, shattering the precision of the reflections with the cut of their paddles. Across the water on the north shore somebody played the old piano in the little grey pavilion. The tinkly music was sweetened and softened by the distance. Maida and Tiger, out to pasture in the newly fenced field behind the barn, stepped delicately among the stumps. George scooped up a too inquisitive kitten from the side of the paint pail, and he and Tillie looked at each other and laughed at the fun there was in being together, here, with all these creatures and objects of their own.

"I don't think I'd be lonely here. Anymore than I would

in town. Why would I?" It did not seem to Tillie that she could ever be lonely again, anywhere in the world, if she knew that George would come back to her at the end of the day.

She looked with loving eyes on the old house, all fresh now in its new covering of sweet-smelling cedar shingles. It looked like an oddly shaped nut dropped on the slope of this shore. There was new white trim on doors and windows, and the sash had been refreshed with white paint. A big square bay window opened off the dining-room to the outside, in place of a sagging porch. The cracked fretwork had been stripped off and replaced with broad straight-edged facing boards, painted white too, and giving the whole structure a trim, severe line which was most satisfying to Tillie. George was not quite pleased with it. It caught his eye now, as they sat there looking over their possessions.

"Looks a little too plain, that way, doesn't it?"

"I think it's right, like that. When the planting gets done, it won't look so raw." She found herself thinking "Papa would like that," and felt a sharp contraction of her heart at the thought that he would never see it. "Vines crawling through fancy woodwork rot it. It looks untidy, too."

"Have we got any vines?"

Tillie pointed to about twelve inches of dried twig, which she had planted at the corners of the veranda, and under each post.

"Are those things vines? It'll be quite a while till they reach the woodwork, won't it?"

"They're fairly quick growers. We'll put up a trellis for them, next spring. That would take off the plain look a little, till the green gets up. It takes a long time to make a garden. You have to start slowly, and think things out."

"But it's going to be winter soon. What about these little scraps then? They won't grow in the winter, will they?"

279

"Roots. They are starting to make roots now. In the spring they'll start to climb."

"Well, you're the doctor. If you think it's going to look all right, that way, then that's the way we'll have it."

"I'm just looking to see what else we could put in this fall, before the frost comes. In the spring we'll bring up some little pines, and start them. I wish they hadn't taken them all down, leaving it bare, like this."

The old house had been stripped of its resigned antiquity, wrenched from its peaceful prospect of decay into a raw, uncomfortable newness. Tillie looked at it with the eye of a creator, her fingers itching to complete the picture she had made in her mind's eye for it. She saw it settle again in a glory of garden and trees. It began to seem to her that it would be an act of desertion to leave it there alone, its transformation half complete. To break up the setting they had created for themselves in the first lovely weeks of their marriage, too, was perhaps in some obscure fashion an ill-omened act. They were building security and growing roots on the shore of this lake, she thought, like the little grey vines.

As if at a signal the horses suddenly turned and trotted down the hill to the fence, running together like a team. They hung their heads over the railing and turned their faces to Tillie and George in an amusing kind of bright enquiry. George looked towards them and laughed. "They'd like to come right in and join the party. Come on over and talk to them."

Tillie slid her arm through George's and walked whistling up the grade. The horses pricked their ears to listen. George deposited the kitten on a low arm of a beech tree behind the stable. "There you are, Columbus, work that out." Tillie smiled at the little creature scrambling up and up.

"He'll be sorry when he gets to the top."

"Maida is frightened of them. I'd be afraid she might

step on him. She's not used to this kind of community life."

"But she likes Tiger."

"Yes. Just a little bit jealous though. Always see that you have something for her, too, eh, when you give Tiger his treat?"

"I always do. But Tiger needs it more. Maida knows everybody loves her, but Tiger isn't sure yet."

"He's getting to be nothing but a big baby. Look at that."

The tall horse stretched his long thin neck over the fence and fumbled at Tillie's skirt with strong flapping lips.

George put his hand through the rails and ran his fingers down Maida's hocks. "Step up, dearie." He seemed not to be pleased with what he found there. But he gave both horses a clip on the flank which sent them snorting back up the hill. "Nothing for you this morning. Go and scrounge for yourself." He watched the little mare narrowly.

"Do you think she's still favouring that leg a little?"

"It looks like it."

George frowned. "I was hoping you couldn't see it, and that I was just imagining it. Damn. If she's really got something there, then the Bingham silks will be seen not at all, this fall. Tiger certainly can't go yet, where there's any excitement."

"He went beautifully this morning, though."

"Yes, didn't he? I think he likes you to drive him better than me."

Tillie smiled provokingly. "Knows when he's in good hands."

"Just as long as things are quiet he thinks he's Dan Patch."

"He's quieting, though, a lot."

"Well, maybe we won't take any horses out this fall. By spring he'll be calmed down, maybe. There's talk of having a big Dominion Day affair, right in Kinsail, next summer."

"Is there?"

"With racing, and baseball, and reunions, and all the works. Maybe we'll have two horses on the track."

George watched the slender little mare trot up the rise.

"Well, I'm disappointed about Maida. But I guess I'll live. I've got plenty to do, anyway, with a wife on my hands, and a new clerk to break in."

They came back to the little barn, walking in slow content. But George's mind was still on Maida. He turned to look again at her. "If she's determined to hold that leg stiff, then she'll have to have a baby. She's so spoiled that she thinks she can just eat her head off, and do nothing."

Under the brilliant September sunshine Maida's coat shone like a freshly peeled chestnut. Little ripples of sunlight broke on her flanks when she twitched the flies off. George considered the beauty of her, standing up there. He spoke hesitatingly.

"Gill says he has a man with a stallion that would be just right for her, he thinks. Papers, and everything. A dandy horse. But golly, I don't know."

"From here," said Tillie, "she doesn't look much bigger than a colt herself."

"She's pretty small, isn't she? I'd hate to have anything happen to her.—Doc Davis can't find any reason for it, except a few old scratches where she's crossfired. But they were all kept clean, all the time. I don't know. Doesn't seem sore enough for a tendon, do you think?"

"She'll likely be all right," said Tillie, comfortingly. "She doesn't act as if it really hurts her."

"She doesn't, does she? Maybe we're just seeing things."

"If we extended the fence along a line from the big cedar to about here," said Tillie, dreamily, "to keep the horses out, we could have a lovely border that I've always wanted to make. A cedar hedge at the back; there are lots of little cedars along the swamp road. Then we could have a thick line of larkspur, with Madonna lilies in front."

She pointed with an eager hand. "Then down in the very front, clumps of blue cornflowers. And at the ends, pale pink cabbage-roses. Wouldn't that be nice?"

"That would be lovely," said George. "Especially if I had any idea what you're talking about. I wouldn't know a cabbage-rose if I met one in my soup. Is a cornflower a flower in the corn? No?"

Tillie laughed. "Wait and see. Madonnas are hard to suit, though. If they like it any place, you can't root them out. But if they don't, they just disappear. I think they'd like it here, though."

"I do, anyway. And I'll send Newt out tomorrow; you mark out your fence." He kissed her and picked up his brush. "I've got time to finish this side before I go in for Loretta. Ask her what she thinks about us trying to spend the winter out here. You'll be all alone, you know, so much. But it could be kept warm. Lots of room for a little pipeless furnace under the dining-room."

The same severity of decorative treatment prevailed inside the house as out. Narrow vertical boards, in lieu of plaster, lined the rooms. George had looked with distaste at the dirty, heavily varnished brown wood. "We'll have to take this stuff off, won't we, and plaster it properly, and put some paper over it?"

But Tillie could not think of insipid flowered paper for her house. And she felt no response for the all-purpose oatmeal paper that held dust in every flake, and was found in every house.

"This is a good warm construction, though. It would be a pity to pull it apart, surely?"

"Think the house would come down with it?"

So the walls were well scrubbed with ammonia-water and painted white. Tillie had given the decoration of her walls loving and long consideration, and George left her to decide. "You'll spend more time here than I will. Have it the way you like it." And she was left with the problem like an eager child with a fresh, new slate and a handful of coloured chalks. But in the end, none of the coloured chalks seemed to be completely satisfactory, and she reluctantly put them back in their box and used the white all through, downstairs.

"Won't they get dirty awful soon?" the painters inquired, uneasy at doing an unusual job. But Tillie would not be convinced. "They won't get dirty any faster. It will just show more. We'll keep them clean."

The dirty pine floor got the ammonia treatment too, and replaced boards, and then deep oxblood-red paint. The rich beautiful colour satisfied some urge of Tillie's for the chalk-box colours, and when heavy clear varnish brought it up to a hard, invulnerable finish, George approved strongly of the floors. Tillie hesitated long over the bolt of white linen she had found in the bottom of the trunk. She fingered the supple stuff, appreciating the excellent quality of it. To the makers of the cloth it was enough that it should be strong, durable, and of even weave. She could see that it was beautiful too, with endless potentiality for taking colour and design. It came to her with a pang that she had had to leave her people to understand the worth of their achievement. She knew it now, in many ways, better than they did themselves, and she could never tell them. This linen that she held in her hand was a symbol of it. In the end she had sent it to the city to be dyed a deep soft blue. It hung now on the windows, fashioned into full curtains. The combination of strong rich colour and broad plain spaces was utterly pleasing to her. It was a chaste, almost monastic effect. She was standing at the door to enjoy it once again when she head Loretta's voice behind her. Loretta handed her a sack.

"Here's some peony roots. George said you were going to put some in."

Tillie's eyes lit up. "Oh, thank you, Loretta. Do you happen to know if they're pink or red?"

"I knew you'd ask that, so I made a jackass of myself and sat out there tying ribbons on them, before I let Newt cut them out. The ones with red thread are the rose peonies, right there by the back porch, with the perfume, you remember—the pale pink ones have pink thread, and the others are the white ones, as near as I could tell."

"I'll set them out right after supper."

"You're sure this is the right time to plant them, are you, Tillie? I can't remember when those old bushes of ours went in."

"September is right for peonies. I think I'll make a bed of the pink ones, just all pink, down by where the gate will be." She chewed her lip in concentration, seeing the rotting stump gone and a blaze of pink mop-heads in its place. "And the red and white ones together, up there, by the dining-room door."

"Anything else I can bring you, let me know."

"Thank you. In the spring there'll be some things I'll be in after. I'd like a piece of the mock-orange, if you could spare one. I wish there were something I could give you, but—" She looked over the raw earth and laughed. "Well, sometime perhaps there will be. Come in and see how we're getting on."

"You got the curtains up this week, I see." She gave the windows a sharp critical scrutiny. "Not a bad job of them, anyway. Is that all you're going to do with them? No lace curtains at all?"

"No," said Tillie firmly. "I like to see out."

"Umhum. Well, I don't know that I'd call it fancy, myself. But perhaps it's the kind of thing you ought to have. When you get used to it, it looks not too bad."

She turned her bright eyes on the recently completed fireplace which George had insisted upon, although to Tillie it merely recalled butchering day, and the reek of boiling flesh. But this skimpy little thing would admit of no cauldron boiling in it, let alone two."

"Going to spend the winter here?"

"Tillie wants to. What do you think?"

"I don't know why not, if she wants to. Though to tell

you the truth I'd been kind of hoping you'd find it con-
venient to spend a little time with me, this winter. This
girl I have from Rossing is no great shakes, yet. There's
plenty for Tillie to do, anytime, George. If she gets tired
of you, I'll take her back." She laughed her hoarse laugh.

"If you do decide to spend the rest of your life here,
I'll send the piano out to you, Tillie. I wouldn't want it to
be here without any fire all winter, but if you decide to
stay, you can have it."

Tillie would have no help in the planting. She knelt in
the newly ploughed earth and pressed the soil firmly about
the transplanted roots with the strong heels of her hands.
Loretta and George sat out on the new pine boards of the
veranda and watched the sun stretch long shadows over
the lake.

"Well, you got yourself a real wife, George. She's making
a lovely place, out here."

George nodded. "She's unique, Loretta, absolutely
unique. I ought to know."

Loretta's eyes lingered on the opal clouds and the green-
black trees. "I can't get over those white walls, though.
Last thing I'd put on my walls. Pretty cold-looking, to my
eye."

"I'm not so crazy about them, either, but she likes it
that way, and what she says goes."

"Well, you can't change people, not really change them.
It's what you're used to, in the end. All the walls in the
house at home were whitewashed, I suppose."

George thought of his glimpse into the dining-room in the
farmhouse.

"I believe they were," he said, "now I come to remember."

"Umhum. Does she hear from her folks at all?"

George shook his head. "Not a word."

"It doesn't seem to bother her, though?"

"Well, not as far as I know, Loretta." He laughed a

little ruefully. "I don't know that I'd be just absolutely sure that I *would* know."

"I know what you mean. She could always keep her thoughts to herself. But as for the Shantzes—never thought much of the females of that family, but Levi himself I'm a little surprised at. Doesn't the Bible have something to say about the stiff-necked sinner?"

"She's the sinner, though. That's the catch there. Wonderful conception, isn't it? Of all the millions of people in the world, only the little people with the black hats are chosen of God."

"What's the news of Simon Goudie?"

George shook his pipe out on the post. "There's no change. And there won't be. It's a damn shame." He laughed a little bitterly. "They hold her directly responsible, you know. I can't quite figure out why."

Flushed and fulfilled with her garden-making, Tillie joined them on the porch. George got a chair for her, sat on the edge of the floor with his back against a newly squared pillar, and filled his pipe. There was stillness and peace in all the world.

It seemed to George and Tillie, as they sat there that evening, that no wind would ever again ruffle that water, or bend those trees, or send clouds scudding over that dark velvet sky; and that no impatient alien hand could twist the smooth and pleasant fabric of their lives.

30

ARLY IN February Tillie felt life. She had put down
her book, and was standing in the bay of the
dining-room, now blooming with daffodils and hya-
cinths, to watch the scarlet cardinals gather in the cedars
on the slope, when she felt the first flutter. She caught
her breath and stood utterly still for a moment, listening
with her whole being for another, surer manifestation.
Outside the window the setting sun threw blue shadow-
cones on the white snow, for the cedars and the spruce and
hemlock were bowed down with weight of snow. The little
barn in its new red paint matched the cardinals for gaiety.
From here she could not see the desolation of the boarded
summer cottages, abandoned to winter, but only the snow-
heavy hills to the south. Soon now the light cutter would
splash another scarlet accent on the green and white and
blue picture. She glanced at the clock. In another half
hour there would be bells in the air. Her spirit lifted, as
it always did, at the thought that George would be back
with her. She still, at times, found it hard to realize that
this rich life was hers to last forever.

She walked delicately away from the window, as if a
too rough movement might disturb the little creature within
her, who had made his first sign. As she filled the kettle
and lifted the stove lid to put the water over the flame, and
pulled up the dumb-waiter to find butter and fruit; as she
threw a polished damask cloth over the table and set it
formally, for two, her face was set in a distant, listening,
secret smile. She had scarcely dared to believe that she was
pregnant. With her old capacity for dividing her mind
into compartments, she had deliberately closed off the
section which assured her, rationally, that she was with

child. In these first few months she would not permit herself to acknowledge that it was really true. She was so radiantly well that she was not physically reminded of it, and for days together she did not think of the child, except to draw a deep rapturous breath, when, unbidden, the realization flashed across her consciousness. There was within her a strong and curious reluctance to admit the actuality, to allow herself to cultivate this happiness. She might almost have been fearful lest, in the admission of it, it somehow would leave her control, or come to the notice of some jealous gods who could not bear to see mortal so happy. There was danger in dwelling upon it, until much nearer her time. She scarcely allowed herself to compute the time when she might be expected to give birth. There would be so much delight in the act of discovering the date, that she was saving this pleasure for a later day, unwilling, too, to box the fulfilment into too narrow a space. Sometime in July, perhaps.

July shone like a golden gift away at the other end of the winter road, beyond the spring flowers, after the full leafing out of the trees. Tillie stretched her arms up above her head, and brought them back in full circle, closing over her breast, and drew a deep exultant breath. There was the sound of distant bells, and the baby leapt again.

George stamped in, shining with cold, and kissed her before he took his coat off, rubbing the cold rough sleeve teasingly over her face.

"Best looking woman I've seen today. I like that dress. Been warm enough?"

"The house has been comfortable, all day."

"Good." He gave her shoulder a little squeeze and let her go. "I'll go down and stoke up before supper."

Tillie heard him whistling in the cellar, and the heavy logs crash into the furnace. In a minute the house was full of the smell of fresh fire, and hot air puffed into the rooms above from the fragrant burning. He ran up the stairs with an armful of split fat pine roots and threw them with a bundle of newspaper into his fireplace in the small parlour beyond the dining-room. He put a match to it and the roots kindled and blazed.

"We're not going to be cold, are we?" Tillie teased.

George looked with infinite satisfaction upon her, at the well laid table, the low pot of purple crocus which centred it, the leaping fire on his own hearth. He grinned at her, and then spoke slowly and seriously.

"No," he said, soberly, "we're not going to be cold. Or hungry, or poverty stricken, or sad. Not if I can help it. And I think I can."

"Did Maida go all right today?"

"She hasn't got a thing the matter with her, as far as I can see. I believe the little wretch just wanted to have a baby, and faked that knee."

He smiled across the table at her. "Just like any other woman. Couldn't wait."

"I wonder if she knows, really?"

"Sure she knows. Told me all about it, on the way home."

Tillie laughed. "Does Tiger know too?"

"Not yet. Maida thinks she won't tell him, for a while. Bound to be upsetting. Saw Loretta today, for just a minute. She's complaining that she never gets a glimpse of you, any more."

"I know. As a matter of fact, I thought I might go back with you tonight." Tillie knew herself to be so utterly contented within the walls of her own home that she felt little urge to leave it. She looked about her now, appreciating the flick of firelight on the dark red floor, the lighting up of the square piano, so much too big for the little room, but such a joy to Tillie. She cleared the table quickly; George liked to be back in the store by seven.

"Can we leave the fire like that?"

"In a few minutes it will be all right. Those roots burn fiercely, but they don't last long." Tillie slowly pulled on her green broadcloth coat, feeling the fur lining heavy about her knees. Her big beaver hat matched the coat almost exactly. She pulled pensive, deliberate fingers through the black ostrich plume.

She went into the cold whiteness of the little spare bedroom off the dining-room, which was not permitted to take heat from the rest of the house except when someone came to stay the night. Tonight the sudden cool air seemed pleasant to her hot cheeks. In the half darkness she pulled out a hand-made cedar chest from under the bed, and took from it the cool loveliness of an Alaska sable caperine and muff which George had given her for Christmas. Under the light from the dining-room lamp, in the mirror over the sideboard, she hooked the strong steel clasp. She noted with almost detached approval the successful balance of black hair, feather, fur, with the blocks of vivid green.

Waiting for the bells in the firelight she saw that the apple boughs, forcing in the crock by the archway, as Loretta always did them, were beginning to show pink. The titles of the books in the new little case glimmered with gold. It was perfect now, as it was. Perhaps any other being coming in, even their own child, would alter the perfection. She picked up the book which was to go back to the library, and closed the door on the warmth and colour and the fragrance of the flowers, a little reluctantly.

George drew up at the corner of Church and Main street.

"Shall I take you straight down to Loretta's?"

"No, I have to go to the library first. And Maitland's, now that I'm here."

"All right. Don't carry the stuff, though. Have Harry Maitland bring it round to the store. He can just slide it in the back door."

"Yes. I'll ask him to send it over."

She hesitated a moment before she said, "I'm going to buy some wool, and things, at the milliner's. I should be starting on something for the baby, now."

"Should you? Already?"

"George—he moved, today. I felt him move."

George looked down at the bright still face under the big green hat. She looked at him with the faint, ineffable smile which made his heart leap, always. In the clear cold air her cheeks were red and peach-like.

"No? Are you sure?"

"Quite sure. Twice."

"I didn't think they started so soon, did you?"

"I didn't know."

"It seems to bring it close, though, doesn't it?"

Tillie nodded, dumb. George rubbed the back of his driving-glove softly over the cheek near him. "Funny thing," he said, "I never thought about having children. God knows I thought about everything else I was going to do. But now that he's really coming, I can hardly wait. Isn't it the damndest?"

Tillie put the gloved hand to her mouth, and for a second rested her cheek in the palm of his hand. George pulled his hand away in mock alarm.

"Get out, Mrs. Bingham, and stop making love to me in public. I can't kiss you here!" Tillie flicked her muff in his face and stepped from the cutter.

"I'll walk down, when I'm through. And if she isn't home I'll come to the store."

"Fine. I'll close up sharp on time, if I can, and be down for you about half past."

George watched her tall figure disappear into the store, and heard the bell clang behind her. He felt a flush of deepening affection for her, and for this good new life which was, a little miraculously, his. And for the coming child he knew an unexpected surge of curiosity. But it was a long time yet, and he had work to do. He lifted the reins.

"Get along, pony."

Cutters lined both sides of Main Street, bright blankets

flung over the horses' backs. The desultory music of their bells enlivened the air as George put the horse away and hurried to his store.

Tillie came out into the cheerful Saturday-night street with her arms full of the best Canton flannel and a pound of the finest wool yarn that the milliner stocked. Mrs. Wilmer's old eyes were bright with knowing curiosity, but Tillie gave no explanation. She was torn between an inarticulate urge to tell everyone she met of this wonderful thing, and a deeper necessity to keep the knowledge to herself. She hugged the secret to her heart.

Now she looked at babies and children as if she had never seen them before. She considered the sleepy flushed faces of the little children pulling on their mothers' skirts, in the aisle of the grocery store, and then, almost with wonder, at the calm, unspeaking faces of their mothers. They too, those stout women in the heavy rough coats, some of them jigging a baby in their arms as well as keeping tight hold on the little fellow travelling on his own feet, those women had all known this fulfilment and this peace. She felt a new, warm kinship with them.

The village was full of sound tonight. As Tillie left the library, the band in the little zinc-topped rink struck up emphatically with "Come Back to Erin." She smiled to hear the big drum beat out the time, and to think of all the people in the rink there, swinging in unison to the bright loud music. It seemed to Tillie that she had reached the summit of human happiness. There was nothing that she needed, nothing she could even think of, which was beyond her grasp. And now, walking alone through the snowy street, searching in spite of herself for a cutter that might, perhaps, belong to someone she knew, or used to know, she felt a tremor pass through her. She stopped, her hands clasped hard in the muff. But the double cutter that looked so much like her father's was not, when she came to see it more closely. Occasionally, now, since she had known that she was to have a baby, it seemed to her that she must see her father. Her mother, too, at this period she seemed to know as she had not before, and value. But she had shut herself out from all that, and thought only once in a long time of her old life. She had so successfully made a new one.

All the hitching-posts in front of the drug store were in use, she noticed. Should she run across and peek in at George? She caught sight of his white coat through the wicket of the dispensary, and smiled. He was busy, in there, certainly. The new clerk was leaning over the counter, evidently talking in a low voice to a man from the country, and Billy Davis was loading up his school sack with parcels.

George was having a good Saturday night. She noted the display in the window, and passed slowly on, looking back in case he might just happen to glance out and see her. She wanted to see the cheerful grin and wave of his hand which he would give, if he did. But his back was turned; he did not know she was there.

She turned to cross the street again, wrapping her coat tight against her to avoid the runners of another double cutter. A bulky shape in the back seat moved towards her as she passed. She saw that it was a bearded man, wearing a black fur hat with the ear-lugs pulled down. He raised himself, threw off the black robe that had been around his shoulders, and struggled to get himself out of the blankets. Tillie half withdrew her hand from her muff, to offer help. Then the face was turned directly towards her, and under the black brows she saw the red-black glint of the eyes. The mouth was working furiously now, but no words that she could understand issued from that frenzy.

"Simon!" She whispered the name, staring in unwilling recognition of the struggling creature. She looked at him with fear and horror, then ran without looking back, too terror-stricken to pause, across the road and down Lock

Street. The starchy snow squeaked under her feet, and she could hear heavy breathing, closer, closer now, until surely he must be upon her. She had not known she could run so fast; never had she imagined this fearful urgency. Why, why had she come this way? Why had she run so far, instead of doubling back and into the store? Was that his shadow, gaining on her now, that heavy blue lengthening streak? Oh, what if Loretta were not in? If there were no light at Loretta's, would she have the strength to run back to the store? He would be able to catch her, though, long before that. She was tiring already, slowing down. But the shadow slowed too. There was a light. Thank God, there was a light! She ran up the steps, fumbled for a minute at the door, and flung herself in.

Loretta, her reading-glasses still on her face, peered over them at the gasping girl.

"Are you going some place?"

Tillie pointed over her shoulder to the road.

"Simon's out there. He chased me. Simon!"

"Sit down, you're all tuckered out." Loretta strode to the door.

"Don't open it, oh, don't open it!"

"Eh? You go on back into the dining-room." Loretta cautiously opened the door to an empty street. She stepped outside, to see if any figure could be lurking in the shade of the veranda. There was nothing. The side entrance had been blocked up all winter. There were no footprints there.

"There's no sign of anybody, Tillie. You couldn't have been imagining things, could you?"

Tillie shook her head, her whole body trembling.

Loretta looked sharply at her and bent down to the sideboard cupboard. She poured a swallow of brandy into a ruby glass.

"Drink this, make you feel better. Do you think I'd better give George a call?"

"No. Oh, no. He's going to call for me here. I'm all

right now. I am sure he was right behind me. He must have gone back." But she crept to the window and looked doubtfully out to the empty snow.

"What have you got ready for the baby, Tillie?"

Tillie relaxed her tense muscles and opened her bundle. Loretta inspected it closely.

"Pretty good. Not bad, anyway. I've got some beautiful nun's veiling you ought to take, though, for good dresses. Cream. Just off white. Lovely stuff. And you'll want a few sacks, I suppose. Delaine. Come on through to the workroom and I'll show you."

The women stayed in the workroom till George came, Loretta seeing to it that Tillie was occupied and interested in materials and patterns. But when the bell rang Tillie's face whitened and she almost ran back into the dining-room.

Loretta met George at the door. "She's had a shock," she whispered, indicating the dining-room with a sharp movement of her head. "Thought Simon Goudie was chasing her here." They came into the room to find Tillie white and rigid in her basket chair, nervously clutching the arms of it until her knuckles stood out. She relaxed at the sight of George's concerned face, and leaned back. Loretta went to the kitchen to put the kettle on and arrange the tray.

George looked almost sternly at his wife. "Tillie, Simon Goudie was in town tonight, all right. I saw him in the rig outside the store. But he never got out of it."

"But—but he saw me, and I heard him running, George. I could hear how he was breathing, right behind me, though!"

George shook his head. "No. No. I saw them drive away. He was with them, all the time. Just sheer imagination, Tillie." He adopted a professional manner which was more effective than anything else he could have done. "It's your condition, honey. A pregnant woman can imagine anything."

Tillie smiled, uncertainly. "Anyway, I'm glad you're here, now."

George shook his head disapprovingly. He brought in the tray and Loretta handed them cups of scalding tea. Colour came back to Tillie's cheeks and she seemed to have forgotten her fears.

"Still determined to stick it out there all winter, are you?"

George glanced at Tillie. "Are we?"

"Oh, yes."

"Don't mind being alone there, Tillie?"

"No, I don't seem to. There's always plenty to do. And now—"

"Well," Loretta sighed, "sewing all alone is pretty nervous work, I think. Do you do the fires, too? I suppose you do, if you aren't going to freeze, all day."

"I don't mind the fires."

George looked thoughtful. "All the same, Tillie, I don't like to think of you heaving that furnace stuff around, much longer."

"It'll soon be spring."

"Soon? We'll have the furnace going three months more, anyway."

"Well."

"She's as stubborn as they come, Loretta. And she's not going to leave her own house for anybody, I guess." .

Loretta caught George's attention, as they were leaving. "She ought to have somebody with her, though, if she won't leave. She was badly scared tonight. I wouldn't want her to be like that out there, alone."

George's firm jaw was set. He nodded his head. "We'll have to get somebody."

They slipped home through the dark roads of the moonless night, snug under the taut buffalo robe. The farmhouses they passed were nearly all black now, but an occasional one lit the night with a pair of unshaded windows. Tillie was silent, in the grasp of a terrible dread.

297

The fearful thought had come to her that her baby might be in some way marked, because of the fright which she had had, in seeing Simon Goudie. She felt her whole being turn to jelly, at the remembrance of that face, the livid flesh and the burning lost eyes beneath the black fur hat. What terrible mark could it leave, on the baby? Old stories flashed back to her consciousness. She recalled half-heard remarks passed from an aunt to her mother, ceasing when they had noticed that she was there. Mrs. Jake Bawtinheimer, down the second, what was it they said about her baby, the one that nobody ever saw, except the mother and the doctor and Jake? It only lived a few days, that one. That was God's mercy, people said. And afterwards Jake only shook his head and wouldn't talk about it. Then, of course, there were other children, and they were all right. But in the back of Tillie's mind there was always a horrified curiosity, about that one baby. And Mrs. Abe Sherk, after the fire in the barn, and the little boy that had the birthmark, just like a flame, up the side of his cheek, into the hair, almost. From the one side he was all right; but when he turned his head! Sometimes, too, the Devil himself had a hand in it. There could be a kitten, born from a woman. Would it be a real kitten, like the black one now nearly a cat, with soft fat paws, and sudden gold coin spots of eyes, coming out of the darkness there behind the stove? Or would it be part baby, and part kitten? Tillie caught her breath.

She looked up at George, his face a pale blur in the darkness. Should she ask him if he believed it could be true? True that such a thing could happen to her? But she knew, instinctively, that he would pooh-pooh it. She had a high regard for George's knowledge, and his opinions on nearly everything she took as she once took the gospel. All the knowledge he had of his business, and the strange information about what went into those bottles, and the mixing, all this was beyond appraisal, from her position.

298

But there were little practical matters, so simple and so much a part of her daily acceptance from birth that she knew them without realizing that she did, of which George was amusingly ignorant. He would say, of course, that such things did not occur. But could he be really sure? What about the woman—? It was in matters like this that she had poignant need of her father. Whatever he said, she could have wholly believed.

Now that she was a woman, she had found so many things that it would have been useful to talk about with her father. He could not discuss them with her when she was a little girl, but now that she was grown, perhaps he could have helped her to know truth and values in the new path of her life. She felt in an obscure way that both she and George had flung their childhood behind them too soon. They were in the front rank of obligation and responsibility before they were quite ready for it. So many times, in spite of her fine feeling of independence and confidence in her own capabilities, it would have steadied them both to have experienced support behind them. In all honesty she realized that much of what they did, and thought, and hoped to do, was outside the pale of Levi's interest and acceptance. But in things of the spirit, and in the question at hand, which was a torment to her, she could have believed Levi, and rested in his assurance.

"We'll have to have some help for you, in the house." The words came firmly from George's cold stiff lips.

"If you really think so."

"Have you anybody you think of?"

Tillie considered. If she had to have somebody, it would have to be a person who would not break in by force of personality to the happy established rhythm of the house. A stranger would be hard to have. To have to accommodate themselves to a new face and voice in the house would be unpleasant in any case. It was, Tillie realized sadly, the beginning of the end. "I don't know of anybody, except Bertha, that I'd not mind having around all the time."

George sighed. "All right. We'll have Bertha."

Tillie was gone again in her reverie. It could not surely be a kitten, not a real kitten. Of course it wouldn't be; it would be partly devil, that way.

31

THE SUN shone on Dominion Day. In the blue pearl morning air, windless and soft, there was promise of the heat to come. All of the village of Kinsail was geared to the great summer holiday. Flags flew from the Mansion House windows, and nearly every house in the village broke out at least one Union Jack. Merchants, clothed in their best, passed their closed shops a little self-consciously, as if those drawn blinds, those flags in the doorway, that front that now seemed to need a little paint, could have nothing to do with them. There was a perceptible air of excitement abroad, and people in their Sunday clothes sought the main street and the entrance to the ball park, hours before two o'clock when the game was to start. And after the game there would be the racing.

With the opening up of Lake Marie to the south for the increasing number of visitors, Kinsail began to fancy itself as a summer resort of some importance. The little building boom at the lake continued, and Kinsail dreamed of rivalling Port Rossing, and maybe showing it a trick or two. For the first racing ever to be done, officially, in the village, they had laid out a half-mile track surrounding the ball park, the little diamond in the middle seeming now lost in the immensity of the track. Merchants brought out their calendars showing the large picture of Dan Patch and displayed them prominently in their shops. George had gone to the length of having his put in a heavy oak frame, and displayed in the show window surmounted by crossed flags. Kinsail, for the first of July, took on a definitely horsey flavour. Up and down the concessions the young men with the fast horses regarded them anxiously, and polished their leather.

The men of the Committee were more than a little nervous this morning. They scanned the blameless sky as if it might at any moment be filled with black thunder. They met at the ball park and anxiously inspected the track. They were proud of their track, and, they felt, justifiably proud. Luck had been with them all the way. There had been pretty nearly a showdown, in the Council, over voting the money to build it. "Too many Methodists trying to run this town," Doctor Percy, a Methodist himself, said, with grim amusement. But they had got it through, and one of the cottagers turned up with a visiting uncle from New York, an old man now, who had spent sixty years building tracks for harness racing. He looked at the vast expanse of unbroken field with the light of a forgotten enthusiasm in his eye, and gave advice in the selection of elevations for the turns. It would have cost the Council hundreds, if they had had to pay for it. They trued off the sandy hummocks, levelled the ground to the standard requirement of half of one per cent, and laid six inches of clayey loam over the stretches and turns. They built a triumph of a ribboned fence, with a new feature called "rub-boards." They were all the rage at the big meetings, the old man said. They kept the hubs of the high-wheeled sulkies from hitting the posts themselves. A safety measure, really. There was nothing like that in Port Rossing. The low spot behind the grandstand had been filled with cinders, and then load after load of clay dumped in and rolled down.

The old man said there wouldn't be any shallow duck-ponds on their track if they built it as he said. And it looked as if he had been right. They were proud of it. The convener of the Committee put his practised hand on the gates and the newly erected judges' stand, and pronounced them good.

"Just as long as they don't try to put twenty men in here, instead of the four or five we've bargained for," he said, testily. "They can see just as well, and better, from the grandstand. Or anywhere along the fence. But there's always half a dozen have to be right where the bell rings." All the men of the Committee pushed against the steep little building, one by one, and thought it was solid enough.

Little boys ran around the diamond, following in the trail of Newt Kribbs and his pail of lime. They pegged fresh oilcloth sacks down at the bases, and four boys scratched industriously at the pitcher's mound with their heels. A sudden series of blasts from the bandstand indicated that the band had gathered for the final practice; and now, with a loud preliminary tooting, they broke brassily into a wavering "Rule Britannia." They stopped, and started again, gathered together by the stern face of the bandmaster and a little sample phrase he played for them, strong and confident. This was only shirt-sleeve practice; their uniforms, navy blue with silver buttons and a braided cap, would not be seen until this afternoon. But the people in the village smiled with quickened pleasure in their holiday, to hear them play.

It looked as if they would get the crowd. By eleven o'clock the sheds in the Mansion House were filled, and the Methodist church sheds, hospitably close to the ball park, could house no more. Country families with flushed faces walked a little diffidently along the streets, enjoying the sight of strange people and the flags and flowers. Stout farm women with greedy eyes for gardens paused before the bank manager's house to see the round beds proud in their loudest summer colours, the mounting plants culminat-

302

ing in a flaunt of broad slippery leaves and the flame of the scarlet canna from the circling blue of lobelias and harlequin foliage. By noon the shade lay deep under the heavy maples along the street, and the cement between them burned white hot to the feet of the visitors.

The Women's Committee met in Mrs. Doc Percy's latticed summer-house beside her lilac hedge, and made a blanket of flowers for the winner. Mrs. Percy had seen one of these blankets at a big race meeting down in Carolina.

"I didn't see it close, girls, but it just looked wonderful, from where I was. And I thought, if they can have a blanket of flowers for their horses down there, so can we."

"Nobody ever thought of it up at Port Rossing, either."

They considered the construction, and finally made the blanket from green burlap, lined with a flannelette sheet, doubled, to give it body. When they had sewn weights in the corners, they spread it out on the rustic table and arranged their flowers on it. With laughter and brisk comment they covered the burlap with shasta daisies and petunias, and a few blousy cabbage-roses like medallions in a Persian carpet.

"It's the loveliest thing I ever saw in my life," the lawyer's wife said.

"All those flowers!"

"In a way it seems a pity!"

"Oh, I don't know, they die so soon anyway. Maybe it's better to have a short life and a merry one, if you know what I mean."

"Well, I hope one of our own horses wins it. I'd hate to have gone to all this trouble and see it go up to Port Rossing."

Mrs. Percy laughed comfortably. "Young Jack says he could beat anything entered yet, with Effie, if George Bingham would leave that yellow streak of his at home."

"Will George be racing today, though?"

"I expect he will; why not?"

"Oh, I thought—well, we heard—"

"You mean because she's expecting?"

Miss Barclay-Thomas lowered her eyes. There was a time for everything, and everything had its place, but this was not a thing to be discussed in public. Although quite possibly it was thought of differently, in a doctor's house. She selected a purple petunia and whipped the stem to the burlap, arranging the head among the petals of its neighbours.

"Well, yes, then."

"George isn't having the baby, is he?" asked Loretta, crudely.

"Of course not. But I don't think, when she—Anyway, if it were my husband, I wouldn't like to think of him—"

Miss Barclay-Thomas flushed. Mrs. Percy looked at her with a faint smile. "It's too bad she can't run the horse herself. She's a wonderful driver."

"She'll be sorry to miss it all."

"Maybe she'll come in though, and see the decorations and things."

"Not likely. She's too far gone."

"So kind of romantic, wasn't it? The way she left her home, and all her people, and got married to a man who was such a stranger to her, in a way."

"Quite a change for her, all right."

"Don't you think she's got a little bold? Drives the car all alone."

"The old people have given her up, altogether, I understand."

"Oh, yes. Nothing at all to do with her any more."

"I always think it's kind of hard, though. A time like this, especially, a girl needs her mother."

They sewed broad white tabs on the ends of the blanket, to tie under the horse's belly, then admired their work, and laid it in the dark cool fruit-cellar in Doctor Percy's basement, to keep the flowers fresh until the last minute. They drank a drop of dandelion wine from Mrs. Percy's beautiful olive-and-dart wine glasses, which she had inherited from her grandmother, and broke wafers of lemon biscuits in their hands. Then they went slowly and reluctantly out in the sun again, to join the stream of light-coloured dresses and white flannels which flowed down Church Street to the ball park.

The pasture field when George picked Tiger out of it was deep-drifted yellow and white and orange with daisies and buttercups and devil's paint brush.

"Come on, boy, here's your chance to show that you're worth your feed. Clayt's going to get you all licked up and we'll go to town."

Tillie walked slowly down to the gate to see them off. Tiger shone in the sun like dull gold. The white of his stockings and the cream of his mane and tail were immaculate. George fitted him with a shadow-roll which by chance was just the colour of his mane, and gave him the quaint air of having a little extra natural equipment.

"Do you think he'll be better with that?" Tillie smiled at the horse and his driver.

"I hope it will keep his mind on his business a little. Better, of course, if we could put something in his ears, so he wouldn't be side-tracked with noise. It's harder on him than seeing things."

"He's going to be a good boy, though, aren't you, Tiger?"

Tiger bent his long ears comically towards her, trying to see where the voice was coming from, and pawed the ground impatiently.

"I wish you could come along, honey. See how you feel, after your rest, and jump in the car and come over for a few minutes, if you want to see your horse win!" George looked regretfully towards the field where Maida stood alone.

"I will, if Bertha will let me."

Tillie glanced back, laughing, to the house where Bertha stood in her black dress and little white coif, keeping close watch with her bright eyes.

"Bring her along!"

Their eyes met in appreciation of the absurdity of that idea. Bertha's interest in the sulky and driver was one of horrified fascination, like that of an audience watching a daring tight-rope walker; George was circling hell itself, setting out to race horses. Bertha sucked in her breath. Tillie regarded her with affection and amusement.

"I'm glad to have her, though!"

"Oh yes, sure. Been an absolute godsend this winter. We couldn't have managed without her. And she'll be even more useful later. Unless Clayt marries her off!" They turned to see the hired man rattle his buggy down the lane and out.

"No danger of that!"

"I guess not."

"But I won't be long now. I begin to feel it will be soon."

"Thank God for that. But you've been marvellous, Tillie. No nonsense about fancies, and fears, and all that sort of thing, have you?"

Tillie shook her head. "Not a thing any more, for months now. Not since that night in Kinsail. Wasn't it silly of me? I couldn't feel better than I do. Only a little tired carrying him around."

"You're a damn good girl. Tiger and I both think so, don't we, Tiger?"

Tillie laughed and gave the horse a solid soothing stroke of her hand along his neck.

"Some of the boys will likely want to come out, after the show is over. Do you think you could be bothered with a few people tonight?"

"Be nice. I'd be glad to see them. Bertha baked all day yesterday, and cleaned house all this morning. We should be able to have company."

"Fine. You can always hike off to bed, if you get tired, or we can send them home. Don't crank the car yourself. Get Bertha to do it."

306

"She's frightened to death of it."

"Nonsense. She'll have to get over that. Bertha!"

Bertha ran down the path.

"Do you think you could crank the car for Mrs. Bingham?"

"Oh, Mr. Bingham. I'm scared of that thing. I'm scared it might start to go right off and run me down! I'm scared it would run me down, though!"

"Oh, come on, Bertha, you're a good sport. Why, I'll bet you could drive it yourself."

Bertha parted her lips in a wild grin.

"I don't think we should let Mrs. Bingham do it, Bertha. So you try, eh? She'll show you how. You will, won't you?" George smiled at her.

Bertha rested her brown eyes on Tillie. "Well, I guess I could try. Yes. I guess I could."

"Good girl. I knew you would."

He reached down for Tillie's chin, cupped it in his hand, and kissed her tenderly. He raised his hand in farewell and the sulky flew down among the cedars and was lost.

Down in the ball park feeling ran high as boys in the brown-and-white sweaters of Kinsail handed the ball game to the boys in the crimson jerseys of Port Rossing. The crowd yelled and cheered and jeered on the grandstand and the field as strike after strike was called on the local team. Occasionally one of the old men bowling on the green beyond the bandstand raised his head and shook it as the salty language came to his ears. Mrs. Jimmie Baker, a gentle woman at any other time, the wife of the harness maker, stood in her long white dress and ruffled hat, as close as she dared behind first base, and uttered imprecations in her hoarse voice until she had no voice. She shook her white parasol at the Port Rossing pitcher and advised him in cracked tones that he had a glass arm. But the ball continued to whip across the plate, and if a Kinsail boy hit it, it flew like a homing pigeon to the glove of Port Rossing. Old Mr. Silvester, who weighed nearly three hundred pounds and did not like to trust himself to the grandstand, sat as he always did, in his special Windsor chair, out in the field between second and third base, his white boots straight out in front of him, weighing chances for the team and finding them poor. One more scoreless inning. The game was over, and in spite of defeat the band played "O Canada" with spirit. The race was called, and old Mr. Silvester turned his chair to face the horses.

Late in the afternoon Tillie drove in to Kinsail. The crowds were lined along the railing, and the horses scoring down for the final heat, when she slipped the blunt-nosed car into a slot between a buggy and the watering-cart. She stood up in the car to look over the heads of the crowd, and saw the horses' heads flash down and turn and come up again; three times they went away, and three times the man in the long white duster rang his bell and brought them back. There was a quiet on the field. Then she heard the "Go!" and they were off.

"One up and one down for your horse, Mrs. Bingham," somebody unknown to Tillie shouted to her. "Broke when the band started in the first heat, but come in good the last time."

She nodded, waved her thanks and felt her throat tighten. So Tiger had done it! At least once he had done it!

As she stood there in the sun, feeling the excitement of the crowd around her, and the strong play of colours— green grass and yellow track, the elm trees beyond framing the whole, the white and blue of the old men bowling on their perfect little green, oblivious to ball and horse alike— she caught a sudden clear little picture of herself, as she used to be. This was a little like that day in the Methodist church, when she had first felt this overwhelming exultance in colour and gaiety and fragrance, and felt that she must be one with it. She had gone a long way, since that day. To remember was like looking at a very small snapshot, almost unrecognizable, of herself, taken in a summer long ago, by a stranger.

She pressed herself against the windshield, her duster hot and dry to her bare arms, forgetting everything now but the yellow horse.

It was a contest for two. Tiger was on the outside, still behind the quarter pole; young Jack Percy's beautiful grey mare was careening for the turn, when the band stood up and struck the first note of "Britannia." They were all together, this time, and the blast acted on Tiger like a whip spur up the tail. He leapt like a rocket, he seemed to jump twice his length. His wheels blurred. He flew past the mare.

"My God," said the old man in the Windsor chair, reverently. "Passed her as if she was tied." -

George pressed into the sulky rail, the loops tight over his arms, holding him by reins that seemed suddenly like bars of iron in his hands.

"Don't break, oh darling, don't break!" he heard himself almost sobbing, in entreaty. "Hold it, boy, steady, hold it!"

Tillie climbed unsteadily to the seat of the car, her hand to her throat, to watch the dizzy turn. Tiger seemed to be tilted from the solid track at an angle of forty-five degrees. The Percy mare lengthened her stride, put all her heart into it, and gained ground. She flashed her strong legs until she seemed to be weaving a solid pattern of grey, but she was demoralized, and Tiger was gone. He came down the home stretch alone nearly all the way.

The crowd melted from the grandstand and the rail on to the track. The band played on.

Tillie's heart seemed to be fluid in her breast, and tears streamed down her face. She sank down behind the wheel, sobbing, exhausted, carried away. The blood was pounding in her veins, and she could find nothing but a big red bandana of George's in the pocket of her duster to wipe away the gush of tears. The band finished the wavering triumph of its tune, and there was clapping and laughter through the crowd. The Committee were trying to get the people off the field, and the village's one policeman, with his real policeman's hat, although not yet a uniform, pushed them back behind the rail again. Tillie from her car could see only a mass of people and a nest of nodding horses' heads. She dared not get down into that press. Then the crowd divided and she saw that it was Tiger and George they were trying to make room for. Walking slowly now, and with his old petulant gait, the pale gold horse picked his way through the milling crowd. He wore the blanket of flowers. George looked anxiously about for Tillie, and when he found the brass muzzle of the car, waved, and brought the winner up to stand before her. He gave a comical little gesture of triumph, with head and shoulders, and turned away again, bending to speak to a friend at the rail before he drove off the field. The man, whom Tillie did not remember ever seeing before, came over to the car and said, "If you want to go now, George said I should crank the car for you. He will be along a little later. Shall I?"

Tillie smiled at him without seeming to know what he had said, her whole being transformed for the moment into a vessel containing only a distillation of sunshine and music and summer flowers, and the beauty and loveliness of the speed of horses. But she came out of her dream, and found he was speaking to her again.

"Yes, yes, thank you. I am going home now."

The man bent over the crank and the car quivered.

"It's very kind of you, thank you." The man touched his cap and departed. Tillie backed the car slowly out of her slot in the line of buggies and cars and turned it into the crowd that reluctantly strolled back along Church Street, their strength and enthusiasm a little dissipated by the excitements of the long afternoon.

The Ladies' Committee under pink striped parasols with long ivory handles passed languidly under the maple trees, their cheeks flushed with the heat of the day and the triumph of their celebration. Loretta alone scorned a parasol, letting her small stiff sailor serve to keep the sun from her head. Tillie drew up beside them and squeezed the bulb of the horn. They turned smiling faces on her, except Miss Barclay-Thomas who flushed a deeper rose and looked away. Loretta and Mrs. Percy stopped and leaned on the car.

"Well, Tillie, your nag deserved it. I never saw a horse travel so fast!" Mrs. Percy put a thick hand on Tillie's arm. "Good for you, to come in and see your husband race. You deserve a blanket of flowers all to yourself." She nodded, and went on.

"Come out with me, Loretta?"

"I was hoping you'd ask me," said Loretta, hoarsely. "I've lost all the voice I ever had, between those maniacs in the striped sweaters losing flies all afternoon, and then these last three heats. Glad to get back to the quiet life. But I enjoyed it. Takes you out of yourself. You're looking well."

Tillie was radiant. "I am feeling wonderfully well."

"Do you mind coming home with me for a few minutes? I want to feed Florence, and make sure I'm locked up."

"Certainly. Oh, look at the flags! A lot more at this end of the town."

"Look nice, don't they? Does the old place good to bust out, once in a while. Quite a horse you've got. Anything new in the garden?"

"No, there won't be much more, now, till the zinnias and marigolds come out."

"What about the peonies? I thought I saw buds on them two weeks ago."

"They're going to be good, too."

"Did you get the right colours in the right places?"

"I think so. You can't be quite sure, from the buds. I'm not going to let them flower this year, of course."

Loretta stared at her. "How did you ever have the courage? If I saw a bud, on anything, I couldn't possibly pull it."

Tillie smiled. "Oh, but it's better for them, in the end. They shouldn't have to put their strength in flowers till they get strong roots, and a good start with their foliage."

"Well, it takes you! Come in and we'll have a cool drink before we start out, eh?"

"I'll have to leave the engine running, then. Let's not be long. George doesn't want me to crank it."

Tillie drove into the side of the road and a little doubtfully left the engine idling. Loretta took off her boater and pushed the curly hair up from her hot neck.

"Oh, turn it off. I'll bet I could wind it up for you. Or somebody will. Let's have a little rest."

Tillie walked heavily up the well remembered wooden slats.

"Here you are, sit in your old chair."

Tillie lowered herself gratefully into the chair, reaching for a cushion from the hammock for the small of her back.

"It's nice to be here like this again. Like old times." She smiled to recollect Loretta's kindness and the haven she had found in this house.

"Glad to have you. Got used to somebody round the house, when you were here. Kind of spoiled me for living alone."

"The Davis girl wouldn't stay?"

"Don't want her. I like to pick my company. Have a ginger snap."

Tillie stretched herself into comfort in the basket chair, and fanned her hot face with a round palm fan. She was utterly content.

"Next year at this time your young fella'll be ready to get to his feet, likely. Tempus fugit."

Tillie smiled. "I don't realize it myself. I can't believe even yet, that it's true." She could think of a little baby, flat in its cradle, but the thought of a little boy running about the rooms of their house was strange, and disturbing. When she thought of it she had a picture in her mind of a strange little boy. He had no connection with this baby she was carrying.

"You're lucky to have been so well, I should think. D'you mind the heat more? I always thought it'd be awful hot, carrying that weight around. Not that I'm not sorry I never had the chance." Loretta bent her thin frame into a hairpin curve and set out a dish of salmon for Florence, behind one of the posts on the porch.

"There. If she comes home at a decent time, there's her dish. If she doesn't, a skunk'll get it, likely, and serve her right. Just as long as they don't both want it at the same time."

Tillie sighed a little, to see the straight body twist and bend with such ease.

"I'll be glad to be thin again."

They drank tall glasses of raspberry shrub and sat silent in the shade, then Loretta successfully cranked the car and they drove out to the lake. There were already three buggies and a car in the barnyard. Tiger, bereft of his coat of many colours and fragrances, nibbled contentedly at the flowers in his field.

"You must be having quite a party!"

"George said there'd likely be people out for supper."

"Can you feed all these spongers?"

Tillie smiled gaily. "We're used to it."

There were fireworks in the park, during the evening; the cottagers could see the frail spray of stars from the dying rockets. Over Lake Marie itself the silver-penny sounds from the pavilion mingled with the songs from the Binghams' gramophone, and the rich full waltzes that Tillie played for the dancing on her veranda.

The golden globe of summer moon which stood over the red barn when Tillie first sat at her piano to play for the revellers had travelled the sky and dropped behind the low hills across the lake before the party was over. It was just dawn when George wakened the sleeping telephone operator to call Dr. Percy and ask him to come at once; the baby was on his way.

32

ERTHA, HER eyes red with crying, and the skin of her twisted face blotched and drawn, answered the hesitating knock at the back door. Old Jake Nighswander stood blinking before her, a handful of dog-eared order slips in one hand and a little sample suitcase in the other. He carried a bundle of bright purple and red mottoes under his arm.

"*Wie gehts?* Is there anything here you might like to see? I got—"

"No, we don't want nothing."

Old Jake smiled deprecatingly. "But I can come in and show you, though? Last time, the lady wanted—"

"We're in trouble in this house."

Jake looked his interest and regret. "Jah, trouble, how trouble?"

Bertha's uncouth face crumpled horribly. "The baby's dead. Go on now, we can't buy nothing. The baby's dead!" She pulled up her apron and cried loudly into it. Old Jake's eyes watered in sympathy. He could feel the sting in his nostril that meant that in a minute he would be crying too. He snuffled and kept back the tears. But the universal human necessity to recognize and name was upon him.

"Ain't you Levi Shantz's hired girl, though?"

Bertha assented, muffling her incoherent answer even more effectively through the apron. "I been here since March."

"You ain't up with Levi, then, no more?"

"'No. When Tillie needed me, I came. I always said if she needed me, I'd come way down here."

Slowly the intelligence worked into Jake's dull mind. This must be the place that Levi's daughter came to when she married the man and Simon Goudie got in with the boar. There was something about that, he remembered now. Kettie told him, there at the time, but now he didn't remember, though, like he could when Martha was alive. Why then, that Mrs. Bingham, that one that ordered all the little pear trees, when he was round here last' fall, why that was Levi's girl, then. The company sent them direct, the fruit trees. Anything over four dollars' worth. It must have been Levi's girl, bought all those little pears. He glanced down at the little suitcase in his hand, full of spices and shoe polish, packages of coloured flavouring and cans of pudding powder. The girl bought a good lot of those, last time he came, too. But maybe she wouldn't want to be bothered with things like that now. Not now that her baby was dead.

"Well," he said, awkwardly, "then I'll be getting along. You tell the lady I come to see how the pear trees was doing. And to see if there was anything else. I'm awful sorry, about the baby, you tell her."

"I'll tell her. Good-bye."

Jake stood for a moment on the back porch, pondering on all this circumstance. The lady in there, only it was really Levi Shantz's daughter, she'd be feeling bad, all right, about the baby. Where, he wondered, did she plant them little trees? Somewhere on the north side of a hill, likely, on account of the frost not so likely to heave them. He went out behind the little barn and climbed the slope to see if he could see the plantation of pears. There they were, just about where he thought she would have put them. He skirted the barnyard and made his way to the young orchard. He bent over and felt the smooth bark, noting with warm approval that she had had them pruned, open top, properly. "She's got a good stand of pear, here," he thought, with satisfaction, and made his way to his chunky old white horse tied by the trough. Somebody was just driving in. He'd have to wait for the buggy to pass.

The young man who got out of the buggy just nodded to Jake. The peddler looked closely at him. Yes, it looked like the druggist. Why, then, that was why he walked slow, like that. He had sorrow. Jake remembered how it was first there, when Martha died. Now he was a little used to it, but he kept on the road as much as he could. Sometimes, even, he did not take the horse home for two or three weeks. When he was taking orders for the spring, like this, he could stay with a brother ten days, maybe, and drive out from his place. Soon now he would be finished, around here. Then, perhaps, would be the time to start up near Lemonville, or up to Peaches. Aways he was welcome at the Shantzes', too. They made a good home, there. Levi, though, Levi would be feeling bad, about the baby. The young man was leading the yellow horse into the barn. Maybe he should speak to him.

He trotted after George, into the dark stable. The horse's feet made ringing noises, on the cement floor. George turned a bleak face on the little man and said in a toneless voice, "Well, Jake, how's business?"

Jake smiled gratefully. "Oh, well now, it's all right. Jah. All right."

"That's good." George reached for the measure and dipped it into the oats.

"I heard about your baby. I'm awful sorry to hear that."

George stretched out his hand, and took the thin-skinned old fingers in his. "Thank you, Jake. It's good of you." The shadow of a smile crossed his face.

"Levi, Levi will be sorry. I didn't quite know, yet, that it was his girl, here." The smile left George's face as empty as it was before.

"I guess Levi won't care," he said, coldly. "He doesn't know anything about it." He laid his hand on the old man's shoulder. "Come in again, when you're round, Jake."

The old horse jogged comfortably down the sandy road. Jake puzzled his brain over the last communication. Levi didn't know about the baby? But why was that? Maybe it was just today, though. Well, when he got up there to Peaches, he would tell Levi. Levi would want to know that.

For two weeks after her baby was born Tillie lay in her bed, not more than half conscious of the life about her. But there came then a morning when she woke free from the clouds, the dreams and the hallucinations that had bedevilled her since for one stricken moment she had taken in the knowledge that she would never see the baby she had been so desirous for. "Oh, George, not once to have seen his face!"

George tried to tell her how tranquil the doll-like face had been, but she could get no picture of it, and her grief mounted again. It seemed to be beyond her bearing. Dr. Percy shrugged his shoulders in perplexity when her temperature would not stay down, and the periods of delirium occurred again and again.

"I wouldn't have said she would take it this way, George. She's a strong, well-nourished woman. And she didn't have a too stormy time."

He looked questioningly at George. "Is there anything that would be bothering her, do you know? Anything that she doesn't talk about, that you know of? Sometimes, not often, I have known it to happen that a secret resentment seems to affect their physical condition."

George shook his head. "Always seemed as happy as a grig, Doctor. Pleased as punch, at the thought of a youngster. I knew she'd be terribly upset, but not like this."

"What about her people, the break she made. Was she bothered about that, do you think?"

"She never mentions them, at all. Not to me, anyway."

"Cut herself right off, didn't she?"

George nodded agreement, his head a little on one side, listening for some call from upstairs.

"Yes, she did." He shrugged his shoulders, ruefully. "They didn't give us a chance to do anything different. We have the hired girl, you know, that was with her family. There for years, I understand. But I don't think, even with her, that there's any talk about them."

"Likely not. Better perhaps if she did bring it out in the open, if there's anything there. But I wouldn't worry too much. She's young, and she's healthy. Hard to beat that combination."

The doctor looked about the pleasant little house, noted the strain on George's face, and pursed his mouth.

"An almost perfect confinement, till just at the last. Tell her that. Make her see that there isn't a chance in ten thousand it would ever happen again."

"She doesn't listen to me."

"She will. Women get to brooding, thinking it's some fault of theirs, that these things happen. Something they've done, or haven't done. Nothing of the sort. Nothing anybody could have done would have made any difference. Physically there isn't a thing the matter, that I can see. We'll just have to give nature a chance. I'll look in again."

Very early one morning in the third week in July Tillie woke, after a disturbed and shadow-ridden night, to an hour of pure lucidity. The light off-shore breeze flicked the blinds at her windows and brought her to her feet. She softly stole to her cupboard, her bare feet soundless

318

on the rag carpet, and took her warm wrapper to slip over her nightgown. Walking with caution, supporting herself shakily by the banisters, she crept downstairs and outside. She let herself into the hammock, holding her wrap tightly about her, and looked out with grave eyes on the morning. Mist hung over the lake, half in shadow and half in the rising sun, like a torn gauze curtain, or the fumes from some gigantic witches' brew, unable to rise like honest steam.

The new little white houses on the sunny side assumed a kind of pearly appearance, as if they were bent on exhibiting the very spirit of cleanliness. No creature moved about the cottages, yellow and green and brown, and scrubbed, it seemed, by the morning light into a new glitter of paint. Over on the dark side, Tillie's end of the lake, she watched the broad band of deep green shade surrender to the golden banding of the sun. Then the blue mists dissolved, wisp by wisp, and all the lake came out of its shadows to shine in the sun.

For a long time she stayed there, gently swinging in the hammock and looking steadfastly, and with courage, over the quiet lake. Her mind was clearing its shadows, like the lake; and then she rose, as if to take the brimming cup of bitterness before her and drain it to the last drop. She fell on her knees, bowing her head almost to the boards in an abject plea for an easing of the pain she knew. Someone stirred, within the house. She got to her feet and slipped quietly through the door. She went to the downstairs bedroom closet to find the blue lustre dress. Almost feverishly she pulled off her rings and put them in the little gilded china box on the dresser. She hesitated longest before the black boots with the bulbous toes, but in the end she put them on too, although she no longer had any black stockings to wear with them, and the sturdy black leather was clumsy and harsh in contrast with the thin silk stockings. Breathing fast, with excitement and unwonted exertion, she rested for a little on the bed before she put her hair back in long tight braids to make the old coronet about her head. Her hand poised a moment over the box of rice powder, but she remembered in time and withdrew it as though it had been in danger of burning.

George came down to find her sitting in the little rocker in the parlour, rocking furiously, the light wooden toes of the chair and her heavy heels making an agitated tattoo through the house. She smiled over to him, stopped her rocking, and held up her hand as one who has made a great discovery, and must tell it to another, will do. But when she saw his dark face, the bewilderment and question in his eyes, she dropped the eager hand, and the light went out of her face.

George ignored the metamorphosis in her appearance.

"Up early, aren't you, honey?"

"I felt so much better, when I woke up, today. I can't spend all my me in bed, can I?" Her voice had the pleading quality of a little girl's.

"Well, that isn't the way we'd figured it, certainly, dear." He looked at her and sighed deeply. "But then, so many things aren't just the way we'd like them, these days."

Tillie's mouth trembled. George took in the black boots and the dark severe dress with a curt gesture. "You're not going back to all that stuff, are you?"

Tillie's shoulders sagged and she looked imploringly at George. There was no use, anyway, trying to explain to him; there was nothing in his background which could make him understand what she had done. He would not believe what she knew to be true, that the loss of the baby was her punishment. The memory of the weeks and months before the child was born passed her mind's eye with an unbelievable vividness, and brought astonishment and misery. It was not possible that she had sung and played

and danced, in this wicked abandon, and supposed that
there would not be retribution. She remembered evenings
in the city, theatres and strong drink. She was filled with
amazement to remember the road-brushing, George with
Maida, she herself behind Tiger, wheel to wheel on the
Sunday roads. "Revenge is mine," saith the Lord.

George stood looking sternly upon her, and waited for
his answer. Twice she tried to speak, and then whispered,
"I have to, George, I have to."

He went out to the stable without another word. In
a few minutes she heard the car back out and he was
gone. Bertha put a scared face in the doorway, rapidly
tying on her apron.

"Goin' to get his breakfast down to the Mansion House,
he said." She looked with swift curiosity at Tillie. "Give
me another few minutes and I'd 'a' got him his breakfast.
He don't have to go to the Mansion House."

In the fervour of her resolve Tillie scarcely heard the
words, or realized their implication. She was not strong
enough, yet, to cope with all the problems which sprang
up about her. But this first she must do. She must make
all retribution, so that they need not be punished further.

On Sunday she would go, in all humility and penitence,
back to the cold drab church in Kinsail, and under the eye
of the whole congregation, under Keturah's accusing, and
now triumphant face, she would confess her sins, empty
herself of all earthly resolve, from now and henceforward,
forever. In God's house she had renounced His way of
life, and in His house she would ask again to be received.
At home here, in this house in which she had been so
happy, with a wicked, sweet, stolen happiness, she could
not reach through to Him. All about her there were too
many evidences of godless living. What would come afterwards she had no clear idea. But this she must do. God
who was so swift and powerful that He spared not the life
of a little baby, that He might make His words obeyed,

had shown Himself too strong for her feeble will to with-
stand. "For I the Lord thy God am a jealous God, visiting
the iniquities of the fathers upon the children unto the third
and fourth generation—" She was defeated now. He had
won. She dared no longer live except as He had ordained.
She was going back. She could scarcely wait for Sunday.

33

A S THEY drove back from the lake, Loretta met
George's eyes with a bleak expression. She shook
her head in a bewildered fashion. "I'm right out
of my depth, George. Wish I'd never opened my mouth.
Damned delicate business, anyway, meddling with this kind
of thing, for anybody, I should think. Certainly too tricky
for me."

"You haven't got any idea, then, what we ought to do?"

"I don't know. Of course I don't know. But I think—
I think, if I were you, I'd not try too hard, just now. Let
her have her head, as much as you can. I can't believe she
won't come round."

George's mouth set in new discouragement. He fanned
out his fingers in a gesture of hopelessness.

"Kind of a tough proposition, Loretta." He smiled
faintly, in apology. "I'm being all kinds of a weak-minded
fool, I know. But we seemed to have the world by the
tail. Just such a little while ago, too. I can't realize that
we're in the shape we are." The light went out from
his eyes, leaving his whole face utterly desolate. "I can't
believe it. And yet here we are, and the worst of it is

there doesn't seem to be one damn thing I can do to help it."

Loretta nodded. "I know."

"There's no use talking to a woman who knows before you start that she isn't going to believe what you say!"

"I felt a little the same way, this afternoon. I couldn't get near her, either. But I'll come out on Monday night, again, if you'd like me to. She ought to have some company, if it's only me."

"Be grateful, if you would."

"Maybe if we just ignore this new phase, and treat her as if she were herself, gradually she'll come back."

"Perhaps," said George dubiously.

When she got out of the car Loretta laid her hand on George's arm. He jumped as though he had been stung.

"Oh Lord, Loretta, excuse me. I'm as nervous as a cat, these days." He grinned feebly. "Gone right to pieces, eh?"

"Get out of that contraption and come in and talk to me, for a while. Tillie'll be asleep by now. I'll get you a drink."

Loretta looked at him with compassion. This ordeal seemed to intensify his youth, she thought, rather than age him, as she might have supposed it would. But sitting there in the cool dusky dining-room, where the shades had been drawn since morning, against the heat, he might have been a lad not long from school, grieving over some youthful disappointment. Her almost maternal concern for Tillie extended now to George. "Sure sign of age coming on," she told herself, "when married men and women begin to seem like children to you."

"You're having a tough spell of weather, George, but it won't last. She's off balance for a little, and no wonder. Both you and I have put her over some stiff hurdles this last year, you know."

George looked inquiringly at her. "You mean you think she's suffering some kind of reaction, from too much sudden change?"

"Something like that."

323

"Did she ever say anything to you that would make you think she regretted any of it?"

"Never a word. And I don't think she does. But she's been subject to more strain than either of us realized, all the same."

"I don't know. I thought she was as happy as any one could be."

"She was, too, and she will be again. She's a very strong woman, George. Full of gentle ways, but an iron core. She takes things harder, both ways, perhaps."

"Yes, I think she does, but I don't know that that makes it any more likely that she'll come back. Just as much proof that she'll go the other way, and stay there." He sighed deeply, and drained his glass.

"I've got every damn thing I want but the one thing I have to have to make any of the rest of it worth having, Loretta."

Loretta took off her hat and sailed it across the room to the couch.

"Won't have you at any price, eh?"

"Won't have any of it. You saw how she is. Gone back to her old clothes, says she's going to the old church, Sunday. On her knees, I gather."

"So she told me. I don't like to see her do that till she's stronger, physically. Couldn't you persuade her to wait?"

George shook his head. "I can't persuade her at all, any more."

"She's in no state to stand all that hallelujah stuff."

"I know she isn't."

"Oh, George, she'll jump out of this."

George shrugged his dejected shoulders. "Well, I certainly hope you're right. But I haven't seen any sign of it; the place is like a morgue."

They sat silent, for a moment, Loretta searching for any thought that might brighten George's outlook. Perhaps it would do him good, just to talk about it.

"I didn't know she was quite so set on having a baby, though."

"I don't think it's just that, Loretta. In fact I know it isn't. She's convinced that she lost it because she's a sinner, or something. God did it on purpose."

"Not anything to do with the scare she had down here in the winter, is it? She doesn't connect that, in any way?"

"Oh no, I'm sure it's nothing to do with that, at all. She got over that, right away; laughed at herself, in a day or two. But I think the sight of that poor wretch affected her pretty severely. Although she never speaks of it."

"Umhum. Certain to, of course. Feel better if she would talk, though. I tried to get her to feel that once you let yourself in for this kind of thing you're up against the common hazards of birth and death. It's all part of the fabric of good rich living. Would to God I'd had a chance at it myself. Even this way, you're more rewarded than to miss it altogether. Got to be vulnerable before you can expect the rewards. No way to shut yourself out of it altogether, and the more vulnerable, the greater the possibilities, both ways. Talking like a preacher, but I feel it strongly."

George looked at her with almost his old whimsical smile.

"Somebody missed a good bet, Loretta."

Loretta laughed hoarsely. "I think they did myself. When I see a lot of married women slopping around down town I think I could have done better than that!"

George got up from his chair, reluctantly. "I'd better go back, Loretta. Too restless to stay long in one place, these days."

Loretta followed him out to the car. In the darkening air it was easier to speak. "One more thing, George. Just a little old-maid wisdom—wait for it, I know it's true. The most important thing for anybody is that he should be in love, really in love, with someone else. If someone else loves back, that's fine. But it isn't the most important thing, not by a long shot. You love this girl, I know that.

325

You're so lucky, you could make a living at it. You go
steady, boy, and remember that. It's what will balance
it all up, in the end. You are among the most fortunate
people on earth, you two. Because she loves you too. You
wait, now. That stuff doesn't dissolve through misfortune.
Keep your shirt on."

"Yes? I used to think so too, Loretta; now, well, I
wouldn't be so sure." Loretta heard his voice harden. "I
can't live with a woman who smiles at me as if I were
a hundred miles away, and meant no more to her than a
stray cat."

He cranked the car and stepped in. "Well, thanks for
letting me blow off." His voice dropped. "Thanks a lot,
Loretta." The car roared down the road.

34

IN THE LONG line of black buggies filling the sheds of
the Mennonite church, George Bingham's new scarlet-
wheeled turnout was as conspicuous as an oriental
poppy in a bed of mignonette. Its soft tires and flashy
wire wheels and light build seemed elegantly fragile beside
the heavy useful democrats, and Tiger in his yellow hide
and silver-mounted bridle was as misplaced as his rig.
George felt acutely self-conscious as he left him there. But
there seemed no choice. Tillie had not wanted to travel
in the car. She did not explain why, but George suspected
it had to do with some notion that the car was a wicked
thing. So Tiger stamped among the heavy horses, and
George wandered aimless up and down Main Street, keep-

ing in sight of the church. He had offered to go in with her, but she had not wanted that.

"You wouldn't like it, George," she had said, stating simple truth. Heaven knew he wanted no part of this business. No part at all. With great reluctance he watched her go. Bertha stayed close to her, giving her strong arm in support. George saw her pass from the sunny porch to the shadowed vestibule and felt stir in his heart the grave presentiment that she had gone from him forever. This thin pale-faced woman under the black bonnet that now seemed to have been built for someone else, a bigger person altogether, had lost significance for him.

The days of the week had been almost intolerable. It was like living in the house of a stranger, instead of his own. He worked long hours in the store, and came home only when he could no longer keep on his feet. Business was wonderful, though. His little idea about the ice-cream parlour had paid off beyond any modest hope he had had for it. He had set up a kind of order department, too, for the cottagers, sending in collective orders once a week for special things they could not get in Kinsail. But in Kinsail they could get a great deal more than they ever could before George Bingham came and livened the town up. There was always more he could do. The town was full of people. It was easy to find reasons for staying in town, when there was no comfortable reason to come home.

He sat in the sun on the stoop of the long vacant building which had been one of the village's four hotels in the roaring eighties, and lit his pipe. He could see the church door from here, and wondered what she was finding beyond it.

She had been bent on going. There was no stopping her. She was the prey of an intolerable urgency. She had turned to give him a little sad smile just before the inner door closed behind her. She might have been saying good-bye to the beautiful world and its wickedness, and turning her head to the peace and reward of righteousness in the house of the Lord. He had raised his hand in resignation and farewell. He could not look after her now; she had passed beyond his ken.

Bertha had her orders. "She has a long way to go yet, before she's really well. She thinks she has much more strength than she has. I doubt if she'll be able to sit the service out. Keep your eye on her, and if she looks too tired, persuade her to come out. I won't be far, just around here, somewhere."

Tillie pulled herself up the steep steps leading into the body of the church, holding to the heavy railing for aid. She gently disengaged her arm from Bertha's grasp and entered the room alone, looking about her as a stranger might have done, to get her bearings. She indicated a pew near the back, for Bertha to enter, and slowly followed her the short stretch down the aisle in the attitude of a woman listening with her whole body for a message which would come, she knew not from what point, to tell her that she was at home again.

The church was only half full when they arrived, almost the last to come. It was so quiet that the tick of the old bishop's watch sounded through his black broadcloth like a clock, in Tillie's ear. He knelt on the low unpainted platform at the front before a metal-braced kitchen chair which served the preacher for pulpit chair as the small varnished table served him for pulpit. Now his moment of silent prayer was over, and he stood up, feeling the weight of old bones. He had asked for God's help, this morning; for words to be put in his mouth which would guide and strengthen and make whole these seekers after His truth. He felt that his prayer had been answered, and power entered into him. He raised his arms, exultant, and asked the people to join with him in singing, on this God's day, in this God's house, praise to Him who is the giver of all good things. Mrs. Burkholder shifted her baby from one arm to the other and gave out the note. The congregation rustled their hymn books, and hearty and whole, they sang.

> "Come, Thou Fount of every blessing!
> Tune my heart to sing Thy praise;
> Streams of mercy never ceasing
> Call for songs of loudest praise.
>
> Teach me some melodious sonnet
> Sung by flaming tongues above;
> Praise the Mount, I'm fixed upon it,
> Mount of Thy redeeming love."

Tillie felt her heart lift like the sudden flight of a strong bird at the sound of the voices. She could not trust her own throat, but closed her eyes and gave herself to the strong rhythm and sweetness of the old tune.

> "Here I raise my Ebenezer,
> Hither by Thine help I'm come;
> And I hope by Thy good pleasure,
> Safely to arrive at home."

Tillie found voice to enter into the broad harmonious "Amen." All around her the voices murmured, "Yes Lord, safely to arrive at home." Her heart joined with them. They found their seats again and waited for the sermon.

It seemed to her as her eyes ranged over the awkwardly proportioned little structure that it must surely have been altered since she saw it last. Could it always have been as low as this? Were the dimensions as narrow then as they seemed now? Of course there could have been no change, and yet it seemed all changed. The windows which had seemed to her when first she came to Kinsail to be so long and large, in contrast with the church windows at home, she now saw as only smallish openings in the grey plaster walls. They were not as big as the ones she had put in the dining-room bay, at home. Surely once this aisle between the men's side and the women's had been wider than now? Her recollection was of a broad aisle, leading with dignity to a taller, more spacious dais than this. Was it here she was to find the power and the glory, the rapture and the grace which would snatch her from the burning and bring her back into the ways of truth and righteousness?

Under the black bonnets she saw the fat and simple faces, pure and devout, untroubled ever by doubts or dangerous thinking. They had no concern, and would never have any, for anything beyond the bounds of their well-kept houses, the generous furnishing of their tables, the keeping of their children clean. What then had she, what other concern? What had filled her mind, since she had left these people, which had been so satisfying to her? The words which came to her would be meaningless in their ears. How could she talk of the books she had read, books which split horizons for her, to people who had never read even one book? How tell of the deepening and widening of her interests and enthusiasms, the unparalleled delight which had come to her in the new consideration of colour and shape, the uniquely satisfying tingle of creation in her hands? The gaiety of the life in the rebuilt house, the coming and going of the groups of skating, dancing, snow-shoeing youngsters who had formed the society of her winter by the lake, would be incomprehensible to these who were her people.

The stranger who saw with her eyes observed the rough red necks of the men, the gnarled, work-worn fingers, and compassion filled her for the toil that these men accomplished daily. But no amount of compassion would make them her brothers, again. The shock-headed boys, the girls with fat arms bulging beneath their tight Sunday sleeves, the women whose clothes were heavy and ill-made, these were people with whom she could never again be one.

She identified the string-taut back of Aunt Keturah, a few seats ahead, and the bunchy little shoulders of Elmina. Keturah turned once and looked directly at Tillie. Tillie, unbelieving, returned her stony gaze. Where had the stature, the authority, the unassailability, gone? It was impossible to believe that she had ever been even a little frightened by Keturah. She was a tight grey old rope of a woman, of no possible consequence, the fire in her eyes dead long ago. Tillie realized that she herself had grown, mysteriously and painfully, out of proportion with these people, this building, and these walls. She swallowed as if her throat hurt, and put her hand to her mouth.

Bertha watched her with concern. When the hymn started she leaned towards her and urged her to come home now. But Tillie shook her head. There was communion, this morning, and the washing of feet. Perhaps, even yet, her heart would be touched, and she would feel the old warm rejoicing. She would not leave the church till the end.

With cold dry eyes she watched the old familiar division, the clearing of the front seats, the putting of the little movable railing which made a kind of pen or paddock, for those who would join in the humble ritual. The bishop stepped down from the platform and began to read.

"After that he poureth water into a bason, and began to wash the disciples' feet, and to wipe them with the towel wherewith he was girded. Then cometh he to Simon Peter: and Peter saith unto him, Lord, dost thou wash my feet? Jesus answered and said unto him, What I do thou knowest not now; but thou shalt know hereafter. Peter saith unto him, Thou shalt never wash my feet. Jesus answered him, If I wash thee not, thou hast no part with me . . . . So after he had washed their feet, and had taken his garments, and was set down again, he said unto them, Know ye what I have done to you? Ye call me Master and Lord: and ye say well; for so I am. If I then, your Lord and Master, have washed your feet; ye also ought to wash one another's feet . . . . If ye know these things, happy are ye if ye do them. Amen."

The bishop turned back his cuffs and poured water from a white crockery jug into an enamel wash-basin. He bent over old Abe Morningside, and asked if he might wash his feet. The old man hobbled over to the men's paddock, and took off one shoe.

The bishop's wife rose from her seat near the front, and looked over the women's side. Her dim old eyes caught sight of Tillie, sitting in reticence and humility and strangeness near the back. She came gently down the aisle, the sound of her footsteps lost in the ceaseless wail of song. She came remorselessly on, and Tillie saw what she was about to do. She stopped beside her, and laid her kindly fat hand on Tillie's shoulder. Her lips moved in a gentle, forgiving smile, entreaty in every line of her good face. "Sister?"

Tillie felt the weight of that hand on her shoulder like a burden. She felt her mouth tremble. But slowly, decisively, she shook her head. The woman asked again. "Yes? He has commanded it." The words came softly, prayerfully. Tillie shook her head again, and the woman closed her eyes, moved her lips now in a silent prayer, and passed on, giving Tillie's shoulder a little loving sad pressure as she went. "I'll pray for you."

Tillie's shoulder shook. She covered her face with her fingers, and bitter tears slid through them to her lap. Bertha, close beside her, regarded her with apprehension. She put her arm about her. "Don't cry, Tillie. Oh, Tillie, don't cry!" Her own crooked face was wet with tears. She whispered urgently, "Come home now, let's go home."

Tillie felt in the cloud of tears for her handkerchief, and rose unsteadily. As she stumbled out of the church the full untroubled voices followed her, surely and confidently singing.

"I have a peace, it is calm as a river,
A peace that the friends of this world never knew.
My Saviour alone is its Author and Giver—
And Oh, could I know it was given to you."

The three in the gay equipage drove silently home. George searched Tillie's face to see what he could find there, either of strength renewed or of hope for the re-establishment, on some sure foundation, of the broken structure of their marriage.

He all but lifted her out of the buggy, at the new garden gate, and held her despairing figure to him until she reached her chair.

"You'd better go to bed, darling. I didn't think you were ready for junketing around, yet." He was frightened at the hollow dark temples and the dull, withdrawn expression in her eyes.

She shook her head, and tried to smile at him. "No, I'll be all right, dear." She put out a long hand to touch his coat sleeve, but it dropped half way, as if there, too, there could be no more comfort. She had left herself no solace, anywhere in the world. Neither in this world nor the next was there any more a haven for her. She was drooping with weariness. "Perhaps I had better rest, just for a while. Help me upstairs, Bertha."

George looked hopelessly after them, and went out to the stable.

"I'll just lie down for a while. Get Mr. Bingham a real good dinner. Is there anything green in the garden? He likes green things. Maybe there'd be some little beets about big enough, now. And cook the greens, separately."

Bertha lifted the blue lustre over Tillie's head, and Tillie looked at the dark heap on the chair where Bertha threw it. "If that dress is any good to you, take it. I won't be wearing it again." She searched in her cupboard for the cashmere dressing-gown which she had made for herself. It wrapped round her thin body like a blanket.

"You ain't going to lay down with that on, are you? You'll be terrible hot. It's hot, up here, anyway."

Tillie lifted her shoulders in a shudder. "I don't feel warm, Bertha."

The hired girl pulled back the white counterpane, and Tillie gratefully sought the smooth high bed. "Just put the afghan over my feet, will you, and then go down. Mr. Bingham will be ready for his meal."

"What about you, will you want some of them greens, too?"

"No, I just want to rest. I'm not hungry. See if there are any more raspberries ready."

"I got two quarts raspberries, down cellar, and I'll give him a plate of butter tarts with them, and there's cold meat, and coleslaw and—"

Tillie smiled and closed her eyes. "All right, Bertha, just so he has a good dinner."

In the evening she came down again, and George drew in his breath to see her. She had put on the old cream shantung she had made with Loretta, and brushed her hair up from her thin face in the soft high pompadour which she knew he liked best of all the ways he had ever seen it dressed. Around her neck she wore the slender pear-drop pendant he had bought her to go with her opal engagement ring. She went out among her flowerbeds, for the first time in weeks, holding tightly to George's arm, and found a clump of spicy pinks to her liking, for a bunch to put in her belt. She broke off long stiff zinnias, carefully choosing them in only the pale pink and off-white tones, for the crock in the small parlour. George felt his heart leap as she carefully arranged the uncompromising stems in the mottled blue crock, for he saw that she was wearing her rings again. He put out his hand instinctively towards her, to tell her that he was so glad, that it would be all right again, now. But there was still a little shadow in her face that caused him to draw it back. Perhaps it would be best to leave her alone, a little while yet. In her own

334

way, and in her own time, she would come back to him. He could be content at this moment, surely, with this certain indication that all the nonsense about going back to the brotherhood was over. George sighed deeply, with great relief. God knew he had had about all he could take of that.

Bertha brought them their supper on a low trestle, on the veranda. George carried out the heavy morris chair and adjusted the back to Tillie's absolute comfort. She smiled at him and he thought he could see in the flush of her cheeks and the eager movement of her hands the beginning of a return to herself. His heart sang. He had done well to let her be, to let her go through all that foolishness. In a few weeks, now, she would have got over the idea that the death of the baby was sent as a judgement. Then, when she was quite well again, they could start another baby. He smiled to see her there, with promise of life in her face. After all, she couldn't grieve forever over a baby who had scarcely lived at all. His own heart had been wrung, when he saw the little thing. Like wax, almost, it was. But for him, after all, he knew there would be only a small grief for this lost one, later. She must be made to see it like that, too. And she would, when she was stronger. Even now, perhaps, she was beginning to be reconciled. Maybe it was a good thing she went to the church, this morning.

"You're looking better, honey."

She brought her eyes back from the distant hills to his face and smiled with her lips. "I get better every day now."

"You must drink up your nice milk," he said banteringly, "and you'll get to be a big strong girl."

She obediently picked up the big goblet.

"That's the girl."

George finished his tea and felt in his pocket for his pipe. Perhaps now they could begin to get back to the relaxed and satisfying evenings they used to have. He might be able to keep the pipe going, again. But the little tamped-down heap of tobacco was not content to glow. He threw away five matches, and tapped it out. Tillie used to watch this performance with amused detachment, but now she did not notice. He got up. "Sit here, will you, till I come back? Maida's making up her mind to have her foal, I think. I'll just take a look at her, and be right back with you." He hesitated, then bent down and kissed her forehead. "It's great to have my girl back, Tillie."

She watched him trot down the garden, jump the gate and hurry along the driveway to the stable door. Bertha came out and carried away the dishes, not able to think of what she could say to this quiet woman lying back in her mattressed chair, looking out across the lake in the tender evening to the slow setting sun and finding no comfort in the bright colours of her flowers, or the pink clouds beyond the black trees, or the soothing voice of her husband as he spoke to the anxious mare.

She felt as a woman might feel who found herself laid aside on a plateau, or the table-top of a high hill. On either side there were roads and pleasant villages in which other, happy people lived and walked, but these paths and these habitations were not for her. There was no road for her to travel down among these happy places. She tried again and again, with all the force of her necessity, to distil from the memory of the meeting at the Kinsail church one drop of comfort, or hope for comfort, that she could take to herself. For her the strength of the simple hymns they sang was lost now in the meaningless allegory. She could not now find solace in the strong sweet words which she could not fully accept. The preacher spoke a language so familiar to her as to need no smallest effort at interpretation, but to her newly awakened intelligence it brought no food.

She had looked about her at the congregation, feeling their quickly averted but bright curious eyes upon her, with indifference. She saw them again, these sweet-faced, un-questioning people, almost as a stranger might have done. And she knew that it was no use her asking to be admitted to their community again. Not because they would not have received her, but that she herself could no longer be one of them. In their forgiving, God-willing way they would let her come, she knew. But there would be no use in her going. Perhaps that was always how it was.

Everything had an entity of its own, and everything changed, and went on changing. She herself had changed so that there was now no place for her in the old world which she had discarded, with the thought in the back of her mind that she could enter it again, at any time. Now she knew that that door was irrevocably closed to her. But the closing of the door had not taken away the fear; it had intensified it. If she could not enter God's house again, and become one of his children, where could she go, what could she do, to be safe from Him? She had left herself without a refuge, and without hope.

The look of her, lying back there, her face closed to all influence, worried Bertha. Again and again she came out to the front, to see that she was safe, though what the danger was she could not have said. Finally she could bear the silence no longer.

"Long time since we've had any music round here," she said, in a complaining tone. "Don't you think we ought to have a little music, round here?"

George came back from the stable to find the veranda empty, and slow sounds of the piano coming through the open window to the outside. He tiptoed along the boards until he could look through and see her. Tillie sat, white-faced and rigid, playing soft, searching, broken music. Bertha sat crouched in anxiety on the little armless rocker by the fireplace, looking at her with fearstruck eyes.

"Tillie! Tillie!" George spoke urgently, in a loud

whisper, as if he were afraid to startle her too suddenly. "Bertha. Can you stop her? For God's sake stop her!"

But she was deaf to words; she did not know that they were here, but played on for her own comfort, and found none.

35

IT WAS VERY early on an August morning when Levi Shantz set out in his double-hitched democrat, all alone, to leave his flat and fertile fields behind him, to climb into the sand-hills, and down again to the rich rolling country about the little lakes and the village of Kinsail. At noon he rested his hot horses under the pine trees in a school yard, and sat down on the unpainted platform of the empty school to eat his sausage and bread. A long faded red threshing outfit steamed slowly past the corner, rattling its joints like a giant grasshopper. The men on the blower turned to look curiously at the big man with the big hat, and the driver of the buggy following the machine waved his hand in greeting; but Levi saw none of them. He drowsed uneasily on the shady side of the building, looking at his watch from time to time. He would give the horses an hour, then push on again.

The corn was in tassel, man high, and higher, in the fields out from Kinsail. Transparent apples hung yellow and ripe in the orchards that he passed. The Astrachans were reddening, and the Duchess and Wealthies were handfuls of mellowing flesh. The hot summer had brought out the grain heads early, and many fields already were cut, and shocked for the harvesters. On every hand, in every field, there was rich manifestation of the fruitfulness of the earth, under the Lord's hand. But of all this Levi saw nothing. He sat rigidly in his seat in the democrat and kept his eyes on the quiet road, his mind and his heart busy with the work he had before him. The horses carried him slowly through the length of the village, pausing hopefully of their own accord in front of Keturah's house. But Levi put them back into the road. He had other business to transact today. He lifted his eyes to Jake Nighswander's house. The place already had an unkept, straggly look. A man cannot have his heart in two places at once. Poor little Jake. Well, Betsey would see that he was looked after for a while, now.

He paused at the top of the hill, where once Tillie had stood to see the frozen lake across the snowy mile of unknown country. Levi could see it today, a green-blue light just discernible in a line beyond green hills.

"Perhaps I've come out of my way," he thought, as he dropped down the sloping road and lost sight, immediately, of the water. "At the other end of town, where I came in there, perhaps that would have been the way. Shorter, that way, maybe." But he could doubtless get to it from here, and he drove on down into the narrow swamp road, always cool from the tall cedars and the little spring creek that ran unquenchably along the ditch.

Now that he must be getting very near, Levi's heart swelled in his breast. The horses were tired, and walked a little disconsolately along this strange road to which they knew no end. Occasionally a light buggy, driven by a brilliantly garbed young man with a fast horse, forced the democrat to the very edge of the ditch. Levi looked on these travellers with neither reproach nor interest, waited until they had gone by, and started on again. Once an automobile with a blaring horn sent him over a narrow culvert. The horses made some pretence of shying, but they were too tired to be really frightened.

Little hand-lettered signs began to appear on trees here and there. Levi looked curiously at these messages, thinking they might give direction, but they meant nothing to him— Dewdropin; Bide-a-wee; Kumonin. He did not know what these words meant. They could have nothing to do with his concern. The road ran close to the water, now, and Levi's searching eyes saw that there were cottages built along here, and a few little shed-like buildings right out into the water, it seemed. He craned his neck to read the sign on one of these strange structures, still seeking for a word which would tell him where to go, now that he was here, so close, perhaps. Perhaps in only a few minutes, now, he would be there. A great sigh that was nearly a sob shook his big frame. He straightened his sagging shoulders and worked at another word. These letters made no sense either, although they were painted in bright red on the fresh boards—Driazel. Along the side of the tiny building a narrow wharf supported a red canoe, with the same cryptic word. Levi mouthed it over, but could make nothing of it.

Down in the water in front of the cottages, groups of children screamed and splashed. Little boys in bathing trunks and girls in white braided sailor-type costumes paddled waist high in the brown water. Here and there on the bright expanse a frilled cap like a giant water lily floated near the centre of the lake. This curious phenomenon stirred Levi's lethargy to look and look again. Then one of the blossoms turned towards the shore and was discovered to have a human face beneath its petals. The woman climbed up on a little wharf, revealing long black-stockinged legs, skirtless from the knee. Levi averted his eyes. A curve in the road brought the water straight ahead of him again.

Right out there in the middle of the lake was one of these little red shells. Still afternoon it was, too, the best part of the day, and a big, able-bodied man sat in one end of it, doing nothing but dip a shining board in and out of the water, so that the boat could move along. In the other end of the boat must be a woman, who had nothing to do either. Just sit out there in the sun, with a pink ruffled umbrella over her head, and let herself be floated over the water in the heat of the day. Levi looked on these things and sighed. This curious little world in which he found himself such a stranger seemed full of people who had nothing to do. As he passed the pavilion he saw two young women whirling wildly round and round, their hands on each other's waists and shoulders. A determined thumping music came out of the piano, although the girl sitting at the instrument did not seem to be touching it with her hands.

Levi lifted his handkerchief out of his pocket and raised his broad hat, to wipe the sweat from his forehead. "It is the heat. I am feeling the sun, once," he said to himself.

Some little way past this building was the old gate to the Armstrong farm. Now it could not be far away. He moistened his lips and turned the corner, then stopped the horses, to reconnoitre. It was many years since he had been in this part of the country. He did not quite know what it was he was looking for. But he thought he could remember the old house, though. They were living in the old house, Jake said. He should have been there, by now. Perhaps, after all, he had taken the wrong road? When a man has a task before him, such as he had, he should be able to do it in the morning, when he is fresh, not at the close of the day, when he is tired and hot and discouraged. There was no old house here. He should have asked someone before, but he hated to ask. So many people knew him, here, it would not quite do to ask someone where his daughter lived. No. It was funny, they would have thought, that he should have to ask. Jah, and it was funny, too.

But now he would have to find out from somebody, because he saw nothing here, nothing that he remembered to have seen before. The young people who passed him on the road, with gay striped sweaters and cameras, he could not bring himself to stop. It was inconceivable that they should know, their faces were so young, so hurried and eager. But there was a little red barn, all neat, up there on the left, with a new white ribbon fence all around the house, and a little field behind. In a place like that there might be somebody who would know.

Tillie was resting in the lacy tamarack grove down by the road. She lay back against the gaudy canvas, her long fingers trailing listlessly on the ground, her eyes closed. To rest was to gain strength and purpose, the doctor had said. But she was not sure that she wanted to be strong again. What now had she to go on to? She opened her eyes to look on the nut-brown house with the apathy that was all that remained to her. It was a shell, a thing which no longer could have any real significance for her, except as so much wood, so much stone, a shelter from the grey rains and the wind and snow. But of her old pride in its creation, of her joy in the garden blazing now under the August sun, there was nothing left.

She was still so weak that the little gulf between sleeping and waking was soon crossed, and she slept lightly, under the hot sun. She thought she was dreaming still, when she felt a shadow fall between her and sun, and opened her eyes to imagine she saw her father standing there, tears raining down his cheeks. The dream figure knelt down beside her and took her hands in hands which were too hard and familiar to be phantom flesh.

"Oh, Tillie, I heard you lost your little baby!"

Her mouth trembled, and she nodded her head, unable to speak. Levi leaned towards her and took her shaking thin figure in his arms.

"Well now, well now, don't cry. Don't cry." He stroked her shoulder as if she had been still his little girl, suffering some childish loss. "There now, there now. You mustn't do like that! The little baby is maybe better, up there, with God, than down here in this world, you know. God

has his plan, for us all, and we do not always know."
She rested her head on his shoulder, comforted a little,
in spite of herself, by the familiar, rumbling voice. "And
you are so young, yet, Tillie. There will be lots more babies,
likely. You must not grieve so hard, though, for this first
one."

Tillie straightened herself up. She must not allow herself
the luxury of this haven. "No, Father," she said slowly,
"there will be no more babies. No. I—I—couldn't go
through this again."

"Oh, Tillie, Tillie, there will then!"

But she shook her head, and spoke her heart, as she
had not been able to speak to George. Levi sat a long
time quiet, looking at her, his face a face of consummate
sadness. When she had finished, he took her hands again
and bent over her with some of his old fire.

"No, Tillie. No, it is not like that, with God. It is
we, mortal men, who are revengeful, and punish those
we love, and who love us, when they do not do what we
think they should do." He looked earnestly into her face.
"Oh, I know, Tillie, I know! It is not God who took your
baby for your sins! No, no! God is our father. He is a
God of love, remember. When I heard that you had lost
your baby, why, I had to come, because I knew you would
be feeling bad, and needed maybe to see your father. But
your Heavenly Father would not punish you, this way.
Never, never, would He! Oh, I am sure of that, now!
Praise His name!"

Tillie smiled weakly at him. "I am glad you came,
Father." But the burden was still there, in her heart. She
looked at him a little fearfully, to see if his stature had
diminished, as had the others, and was comforted to find
that it had not. She saw now a nobility and comprehension
in his broad face, where before she had seen only simple
humour and kindliness. But there was change, there, too;
a new deep line from the nose to the mouth, and a netting
about the eyes that had not been there before. His hair,

which had been nearly black, or so she remembered it, was now more white than black. She felt a hand on her heart, to find it so. But the lively dark eyes remained the same, perplexed now, at the sight of her unlighted face.

"There is more than the baby, Father. Even if I could think—" Her heart leapt, at the thought that she might have been putting the wrong interpretation on it. The pure grief of losing the baby, she could bear. She remembered Doctor Percy's words, and the continued asseverations of George, tender at first, and then emphatic, and ceasing only because of the uselessness of speaking to her. Perhaps after a while, when she had told her father everything, she could come back to this hopeful thought. But not yet.

"What happened to Simon would not have been, but for me, though."

Levi sighed. He slowly shook his head. "It is a dreadful thing. Jah. Such sorrow for Abraham. But the more I grow older, Tillie, the more I see that what happens to anybody is because you are like you are. It is never somebody else who makes you do this, or that. It is yourself, and your own strength or weakness—unless you make sure that you have God, with you."

Tillie stirred, and spoke in a dull voice. "I feel it is all so long ago, Father, I can't believe it is only a year, last spring."

Levi gazed at her. "Jah, so it is, only a year!" He swallowed heavily, and his eyes grew troubled. "He came to see me first, you know. He was beside himself. Jah, he did not know what he said. He could not stand it, that you had left him."

"I could not help it, Father." There was no urgency in her voice; all emotion had been drawn out of her.

"No. No, I see that now. I see some things now, every day, that I never saw before. Sometimes I think maybe I was blind, all my life, Tillie!"

Tillie's eyes lifted quickly to his.

"Jah, if I had to do over again, maybe I would do a

little different, too. Maybe we shut ourselves up too much, and don't look to see if another man, maybe he is quite a lot different, but he has a good way to live, too. And God is with him, although he is not like us. Perhaps, there, I could have seen that what was enough for your mother, and for me, just the quiet old ways, would not satisfy you. And—"

"But you did, Father. You let me go away from home."

"Jah, but I did not want you to go away from our ways, though. Because we think, always, that our way is best. For us, it is best, too. But now, perhaps, not quite for you." He looked sadly at her, and then over to the gay little barn and the bright garden. "Perhaps not, though, for you."

Tillie drew her hands across her eyes as if a web, which she could not quite find, hung over her face. Levi looked closely at her.

"Why are you out here, though? Are you sick, Tillie?"

"No, Father, just—" She spread her hands out helplessly.

"Now you must get up, and go about your business here. This is your place now, and it will not be a good place for your man, if you lie here and cry, just. You are strong enough?"

"Yes, oh yes."

"Come on, then, get up. When does he come home? I must see him too."

"Soon, now. If he comes."

"If he comes?"

"He stays at the hotel sometimes."

"Jah?" He looked doubtfully at her. "But your mamma will not like it, when I say Tillie's man can't get to eat at home, he goes to the hotel!"

Tillie smiled, wanly. "He gets enough to eat here. Bertha feeds him!"

"Why, I forgot, of course, she is here! I will see her, too. We miss her, back there, but she knew better than I did, when you needed her." Levi's face clouded. "Jah, the poor foolish thing, she knew better than we did. God forgive me."

Tillie slipped her hand lovingly through her father's arm. He reached for it and held it firmly in his. They walked tranquilly together towards the house. Tillie paused to consider the peonies, for the first time since her illness. They had pulled vigour from the earth and grew sturdily by the gate, throwing out thick stocky branches. Another spring, they would be full of flowers.

There was the sound of a motor, and the car emerged noisily from the cedars. George raised his hand in greeting, and drove past them into the shed.

"That is him, now, Tillie?"

"Yes. Open night, isn't it? He won't stay home long."

"You go on in then, and fix things."

"You'll stay for supper, Father?"

Levi smiled down at her, and pushed the hair from her forehead with his rough hand. "Jah, sure, I can stay for supper."

Out in the driveway George laid his hand on Levi's shoulder.

"I can't tell you, sir, how I appreciate your coming, like this."

Levi grasped his other hand, and the two men stood there, for a moment, looking at each other as if it were for the first time, taking the measure, and finding it good.

"I came to see Tillie, jah, but I came more to see you. I came to ask you to forgive me. God has forgiven me. I feel that He has. When Tillie left—when she was gone—" Levi's voice dissolved in his throat. He could find only a thick whisper, to continue. He was full of tears. "When she was gone, it was more than I could bear. The Lord hardened my heart, and I shut myself out from the stream of mercy. I did not think, then, as I know now, that it would have been wicked for her to go, with Simon Goudie, out there to Africa, when the call was not really come to her, and she found that she did not feel right about him. But I was slow. Slow, and so sure that it was only ourselves that could be right. I could not see any other way."

George withdrew his hand, gently. "No, I'm sure you couldn't sir, but—"

"When she tried to tell her father, I would not listen." He looked at George with astonished, tear-filled eyes, as if he could scarcely credit his own words. He rubbed at his face with his handkerchief.

"And when you came, so nice, all the way up to our place, there, I would not hear you, then, but sent you away, too." He smoothed his long beard with both hands, down to the very end, again and again, and said in a voice of unutterable sadness, "Jah, that's how it was."

George looked at him in acute embarrassment.

"Well, never mind, sir. We were pretty much in a hurry, too, I guess. Didn't give you much time to get used to the idea, either. If there's anything I can say, consider that I've said it. Fresh start, eh?"

"Thank you. Thank you." He smiled at the young man, a beautiful, heart-warming smile. "Well then, from now on we will be different, jah? Praise the Lord!"

"Until this last business," said George, speaking in the tone of a man who talks with a close friend, "we have been so happy. Now I don't know what to do. She can't get over losing the child."

"In a little time, now, she will. I talked to her."

"More than I've been able to do," said George, grimly.

"Maybe I helped her understand, a little. She will be better; she will be well, soon now."

"You think so, do you? You think she will be, ever, like she was before?"

"No, not just like. A woman who has had a child, and lost it, she will never be just quite the same. But it has not spoiled her, though. You must have just more patience. I know you have, too, plenty of that. She told me. Jah, down there in the chair, when I first came, this afternoon, she told me."

"Did she?" George brightened. "Good girl."

They walked together slowly, into the house. George took Levi's big black hat, flicked a speck of dust from it and hung it carefully on the stand.

"Will you go on in and have a chair? I have to wash up, be down in a minute."

Tillie came out from the kitchen, flushed and eager.

"Come out and see Bertha, Papa?" Tillie watched his face intently to see what he might be thinking of her house. He walked through into the kitchen where Bertha chopped wilted lettuce into a bowl of sour cream.

"Well, Bertha! So you like it better here, now, than up at home with us!"

Bertha blushed red and held her hand over her open mouth to hide her laughter. Levi pointed to the shallow gold-rimmed dish. "So you eat Dutch some, then?" Tillie smiled and disappeared down the cellar-way.

"Jah, some things we do. Mr. Bingham, he likes the bartzelbaamkuchen, too."

"Does he, once!"

Levi inspected the big cast-iron frying pan full of puffy brown crusted cake. A golden syrup flowed in rivulets over the top of it, significant of rich preserved peaches underneath.

"Just like we have at home, too. Can Tillie make like that?"

"Jah! Sure she can! She can make anything!"

Tillie came up from the cellar with three glowing jars in her arms.

"You did down fruit too? You have fruit here?"

"No, we bought the fruit. Soon though we will have some."

Levi clucked disapprovingly. "To have to buy fruit, though! To put down! That is such a dear way!"

"Soon be time to start again!" Tillie looked at the cake, set down her jars, and tested it with a light tap of her finger.

"Another time not quite so much flour, Bertha. And the smaller pan. Just make about half, for just ourselves." She turned to her father. "It's hard to make just enough for so few people."

"Jah, I guess it is, when you're used to so many, there."

Bertha set the table, unable to keep the laughter from her face. "I never thought Levi'd come way down here, but he come, all right. Yes. He come!" She studied Levi's face, furtively, from the dining-room. "Things going to be better, round here, now, maybe. Maybe things'll be better, round here, now." She lingered over the placing of the last dishes on the stiff shining cloth, to hear what they were saying, in there.

"You must come, now, and stay at our place, a little."

George looked questioningly at Tillie. Did she want to go back there?

She was smiling. "We could come out, some time. It isn't so far, with the car."

Levi swallowed stiffly. "No. No, not so far with the car, once. The little fellas there, they need to know their sister more, and her man, too, they need to know." He sighed deeply, as one who learns with difficulty.

After supper Levi sat for a while in the little parlour with them, noting with interest and approval the shining cleanliness of floor and furnishing, the immaculateness of wall and woodwork. "You got it pretty nice, here."

"All Tillie's doing!"

"Jah? That's good." He nodded his head towards the piano.

"You play some, yet, Tillie? Being a married woman, with all this to look after, you have time to play?" His gesture included furniture and pictures and books and plants.

349

George smiled proudly. "Sure she plays, Mr. Shantz. Keeps the lake ringing with it, don't you, Tillie?"

"Jah, does she though? Maybe, later on, she can show me."

He looked a little wistfully at George. There was so much he had to learn of him, and so much they both must know, before they could be like one family, together. He spoke a little shyly.

"I always liked the music, too, you know. My mother, Tillie's grandmother, here, she could play too. Not with lessons, of course, like her."

"You used to play yourself, Father."

Levi laughed a little self-consciously, like a small boy praised before guests. "Oh, just a little, not much ever. But I like to hear it, though, in the house."

He leaned towards the piano from the chair, easily reaching the keyboard with his big hands, and picked out the air from the glory song, with a comical air of triumph. "That's it, eh?"

"Good for you!" George laughed. "I see that Tillie comes naturally by it, then!"

The big man smiled lovingly upon them. George stood up with a sigh.

"I'll have to be getting back, soon, I'm afraid. Let's go out and see the colt first, shall we?"

Levi rose from the deep morris chair and straightened his back gratefully.

"Not used to being so easy," he said, apologetically. "You go on, you two. After a while I'll come too, but she won't want too many, all at once." He walked through the house and looked out on the garden and planting to the east of it. "I'll take a little walk and see your place."

The sound of the opening door caused Maida to lift her slender ears nervously. She got to her feet and turned to their voices. The foal staggered up, seeming to untangle unnecessary extra lengths of legs between the joints, and stood splayed like a rocking-horse, the star that was his father's mark blurred between his great soft eyes. Tillie turned to George and laughed. She leaned impulsively over the half door and put her hand under the black velvet of his muzzle. But Maida insinuated her slender face between Tillie and the colt.

"Oh, go on with you, she won't hurt your baby, darling! Want him all to yourself, do you?" George reached out a hand for the mare's neck, but she bared her teeth and manoeuvred the foal into a corner of her box-stall, holding her body as shield.

"We'd better leave them alone, George. She doesn't want anybody else around, just now."

They closed the stable door softly, and set the young cat down outside. Tiger, lonely by himself in his small field, came whickering down to the gate. They walked over to keep him company. Tillie looked with vast love, and a little amusement, at her father's broad back. He was inspecting a planting of potatoes, in the little level area beyond the pear orchard.

"He can't understand how we expect to get any crop out of there."

"We don't, do we?"

"No. But it's the best way to start, for the croquet lawn."

"Do you know everything, sweetheart?"

Tillie smiled up at him and his heart swelled. "Certainly. Nearly everything, anyway."

George's voice was rough. "You take the long view, don't you? Are we going to be here long enough for the lawn to grow, and the pears to bear, and Maida's colt to win the King's Plate?"

"Of course we are!"

George took her in his arms. "Oh, Lord, Tillie, you don't know how I've missed my wife!"

Levi's voice reached them faintly, carried by the rising off-shore breeze towards the setting sun.

"For I know whom I have believed
And am persuaded, that He is able,
To keep that which I've committed
Unto Him, against that Day."

He was singing as he walked among the little pear trees.

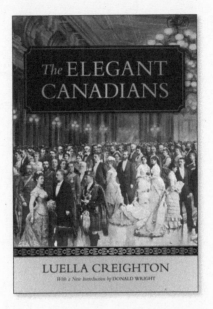

The Elegant Canadians
Reissue

The late LUELLA CREIGHTON
Introduction by DONALD WRIGHT

First published in 1967, exactly one hundred years after Confederation, Luella Creighton's *The Elegant Canadians* shows a Canada in the best of all possible worlds. Gone is pioneer poverty and environmental hardship, replaced now by thriving sophistication. At the same time, this is a world that still retains some respect for social hierarchy, decent manners, and old-fashioned inherited wisdom—the unspoken corollary here is that the Canada of 1967 has grown sloppy, noisy, and vulgar. Lovingly researched and assembled with sixty images, this depiction of Canada in the 1860s reveals much about our own history and myth-making.

Paperback | 544 pages | 6 x 9" | 9780199008520

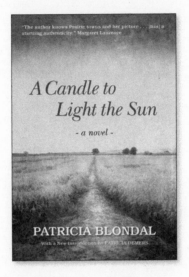

A Candle to Light the Sun
Reissue

The late PATRICIA BLONDAL
Introduction by PATRICIA DEMERS

"The author knows prairie towns and her picture . . . [has] a startling authenticity."
—Margaret Laurence

"Dazzlingly brilliant." —*Books in Canada*

World history rumbles ominously in the background of Patricia Blondal's beautiful, compelling novel set in the Canadian Prairies of the 1930s. In this novelistic world of sharply drawn contrasts, human life on a diminutive scale wavers before a wide open, unprotecting Prairie. The young David Newman comes of age in a harsh world fuelled by class and ethnic tensions; in this apparent desolation, however, David uncovers kindness, warmth, and creativity. The novel, written as the author was dying of cancer, shows and admiration for resilience and survival against the apocalyptic silence of empty space.

Paperback | 320 pages | 6 x 9" | 9780199008964

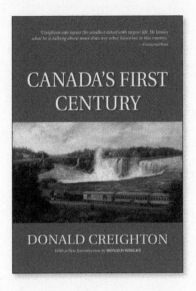

Canada's First Century
Reissue

The late DONALD CREIGHTON
Introduction by DONALD WRIGHT

"Creighton can invest the smallest detail with urgent life. He knows what he is talking about more than any other historian in this country."—*Financial Post*

Canada's First Century paints a large and complex canvas of historical rise and fall: a great transcontinental nation is built, but it is eventually undone as Canada turns its back on the British Empire and embraces a continental role alongside the United States. A courageous and contentious book for its day—Creighton is intensely anti-American and highly critical of Quebec nationalism—it was met with criticism, but, as Donald Wright points out, *Canada's First Century* initially outsold *Everything You Always Wanted to Know About Sex* and, for a time, even the Bible.

Paperback | 416 pages | 6 x 9" | 9780195449228

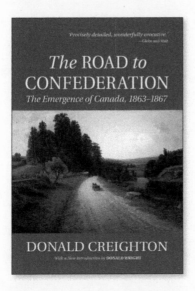

The Road to Confederation
The Emergence of Canada, 1863–1867
Reissue

The late DONALD CREIGHTON
Introduction by DONALD WRIGHT

"A happy, nostalgic celebration of the people and the process that had made Canadian federal union; precisely detailed, wonderfully evocative."—*Globe and Mail*

Donald Creighton was for many years one of Canada's foremost historians, a firm believer that history was closer to art than it was to science. Marked by beautiful, carefully crafted prose, *The Road to Confederation* reflects a style that perhaps no contemporary historian would dare: romantic, suspenseful, fearlessly narrative, and full of unapologetic opinions. It is a fascinating exploration of the personalities, the political logjams, even the debt problems that marked the period leading to Confederation.

Paperback | 544 pages | 6 x 9" | 9780195449211